The Bride Wore Black Leather

"Green's superlative twelfth Nightside novel . . . ratchets up the stakes for series protagonist John Taylor in an intricate and action-filled plot that seamlessly blends crime and the supernatural . . . The pace never flags, and the sardonic Chandler-esque narration is perfectly suited to the Nightside's fantastical mean streets." —*Publishers Weekly*

"There is still the classic Green breakneck pacing, the quirky character twists, the joys of name-drop references (to his other books and pop-culture icons alike), but they're accompanied by a wonderful narrative sense of melancholy, as if Green hates parting with John as much as we do." —*Tulsa Book Review*

"Simon R. Green walks us through his most thoroughly developed setting and its vast assortment of strange, devious, and downright weird characters . . . The Nightside may be shuttered for now, but Green never forsakes his darlings for long; readers may expect to see John Taylor, Shotgun Suzie, or other denizens of the Nightside infiltrate his other works in the future. At the very least, they've been given a proper send-off. Recommended." —*SFRevu*

"The outstanding twelfth installment in the always-entertaining Nightside series . . . This reviewer highly recommends this terrific book and very much looks forward to a return visit to the Nightside." —*Bitten by Books*

"A hugely satisfying windup for one of fantasy's most memorable constructs." —*Kirkus Reviews*

continued . . .

"*The Bride Wore Black Leather* has everything I expect from a Nightside book. Taylor is the Sam Spade for the twenty-first century, willing to stare down an angel, a demon, or a god. Nightside has the meanest of the mean streets, and John Taylor is right at home there. Sunnyside? Not bloody likely."

—*Fantasy Literature*

"[The] great drama and the mystery killer scenarios were impressive . . . I cannot wait to get my hands on any future books by Mr. Green. This is a wonderful read."

—*Night Owl Reviews*

A Hard Day's Knight

"A super-refreshing Nightside entry . . . Fast-paced and loaded with action."

—*Alternative Worlds*

"Readers who prefer their gore with huge melodramatic flourishes and a side of slyly amusing repartee will find John Taylor at least the equal of Jim Butcher's Chicago wizard PI Harry Dresden."

—*Kirkus Reviews*

The Good, the Bad, and the Uncanny

"The latest Nightside fantasy provides the readers with a fresh glimpse into the frightening community . . . The story line is fast-paced and filled with action, but it is the cast, especially Taylor and his three clients, who make for an entertaining walk (make that a sprint) on the Darkside."

—*Alternative Worlds*

"The gripping, suspenseful, and wry tenth tale in the Nightside supernatural detective series proves every bit the equal of Jim Butcher's better-known Harry Dresden books . . . Longtime fans and first-timers alike will applaud Green's blend of fantasy, mystery, and humor."

—*Publishers Weekly*

Just Another Judgement Day

"Simon R. Green delivers up yet another roller-coaster ride through the dark fantasy nightscape of the Nightside, throwing an opponent at John Taylor who is truly out of his weight class . . . Certain to please Green's legions of fans, offering a strong new tale . . . Recommended."

—*SFRevu*

The Unnatural Inquirer

"Sam Spade meets Sirius Black . . . Inventively gruesome."

—*Entertainment Weekly*

Hell to Pay

"If you're looking for fast-paced, no-holds-barred dark urban fantasy, you need look no further: the Nightside is the place for you." —*SFRevu*

Sharper Than a Serpent's Tooth

"This is Green's tour de force culmination of the Nightside books. Anyone who's enjoyed the series to date absolutely must read this installment. Highly recommended." —*SFRevu*

Paths Not Taken

"A fantastic fantasy . . . Action packed."

—*Midwest Book Review*

Hex and the City

"Urban fantasy with a splatterpunk attitude, a noir sensibility, a pulp sense of style, and a horror undercoating."

—*The Green Man Review*

Nightingale's Lament

"Filled with supernatural creatures of various sorts, the action leavened by occasional bits of dry humor." —*Chronicle*

Agents of Light and Darkness

"I really enjoyed Green's first John Taylor novel, and the second one is even better. The usual private eye stuff—with a bizarre kick." —*Chronicle*

Something from the Nightside

"The book is a fast, fun little roller coaster of a story!"

—Jim Butcher

THE BRIDE WORE
BLACK LEATHER

SIMON R. GREEN

ACE BOOKS, NEW YORK

THE BERKLEY PUBLISHING GROUP
Published by the Penguin Group
Penguin Group (USA) Inc.
375 Hudson Street, New York, New York 10014, USA

Penguin Group (Canada), 90 Eglinton Avenue East, Suite 700, Toronto, Ontario M4P 2Y3, Canada
(a division of Pearson Penguin Canada Inc.) • Penguin Books Ltd., 80 Strand, London WC2R 0RL,
England • Penguin Group Ireland, 25 St. Stephen's Green, Dublin 2, Ireland (a division of Penguin
Books Ltd.) • Penguin Group (Australia), 250 Camberwell Road, Camberwell, Victoria 3124, Australia
(a division of Pearson Australia Group Pty. Ltd.) • Penguin Books India Pvt. Ltd., 11 Community
Centre, Panchsheel Park, New Delhi—110 017, India • Penguin Group (NZ), 67 Apollo Drive,
Rosedale, Auckland 0632, New Zealand (a division of Pearson New Zealand Ltd.) • Penguin Books
(South Africa) (Pty.) Ltd., 24 Sturdee Avenue, Rosebank, Johannesburg 2196, South Africa

Penguin Books Ltd., Registered Offices: 80 Strand, London WC2R 0RL, England

This is a work of fiction. Names, characters, places, and incidents either are the product of the author's
imagination or are used fictitiously, and any resemblance to actual persons, living or dead, business
establishments, events, or locales is entirely coincidental. The publisher does not have any control over
and does not assume any responsibility for author or third-party websites or their content.

THE BRIDE WORE BLACK LEATHER

An Ace Book / published by arrangement with the author

PUBLISHING HISTORY
Ace hardcover edition / January 2012
Ace mass-market edition / January 2013

Copyright © 2012 by Simon R. Green.
Excerpt from *Ghost of a Chance* by Simon R. Green copyright © 2010 by Simon R. Green.
Cover art by Jonathan Barkat.
Cover design by Judith Lagerman.

ISBN: 978-0-425-25644-2

ACE
Ace Books are published by The Berkley Publishing Group,
a division of Penguin Group (USA) Inc.,
375 Hudson Street, New York, New York 10014.
ACE and the "A" design are trademarks of Penguin Group (USA) Inc.

PRINTED IN THE UNITED STATES OF AMERICA

10 9 8 7 6 5 4 3 2 1

ALWAYS LEARNING   PEARSON

There is a night that never ends. Hidden deep in the dark and dangerous heart of London lies the Nightside; an empire on which the sun has never set and never will. A business empire of sin and corruption, wonders and marvels, and every kind of dream come true, all of them at very reasonable prices. The thrills and chills of the hidden world, laid out before you in all their sleazy glory . . . but none of it for the faint of heart or those of a nervous disposition. In the Nightside, where it's always three o'clock in the morning, the hour that tries men's souls and finds them wanting, the dawn never comes . . . You can find the baddest clubs and the maddest music, parties that will never end as long as someone's got cash in their pocket or credit on their cards, and the fun goes on forever. Put on the red shoes, of your own free will, and dance till you bleed. And don't ever complain that no-one warned you.

In the night that never ends you can find heroes and villains, gods and monsters, angels and demons . . . and you can be sure that somewhere, someone is always singing the blues. Hot neon burns like warning signs in Hell, while men and women with bad pasts and uncertain futures swarm up and down the rain-slick streets, in pursuit of pleasures that might not have a name, but most certainly have a price. Temptation winks from every street-corner, and there's always a quiet back room where you can sell your soul. Yours, or someone else's. Dance in the streets, run wild in the night, bet your soul on a roll of the dice . . . and then grin at the dealer and ask if you can go double or quits. You can chase every dream you ever had in the Nightside if it doesn't end up chasing you.

There is a night that never ends. Or at least, that's the smart way to bet.

ONE

One Last Case

I went walking up and down the packed streets of the Night-side, making my way through all the desperate conversations and dodgy deals, through all the damned and the disgraced, and all the lost souls searching for something they could buy, then call love; and everywhere I went, people nodded quickly and politely to me, out of respect. I still wasn't used to that. John Taylor has always been a name to conjure with in these dark streets, a name to inspire fear and hope and disapproval, but the kind of reputation I'd built, through years of taking on the kinds of cases no-one else would touch, was more designed to keep people at arm's length. My rep has always been about striking terror into the hearts of the ungodly and keeping everyone else at a secure distance, for their own safety. I wasn't used to people actually sticking around long enough to smile and nod respectfully. I kept wanting to glance over my shoulder, to see who they were really looking at.

I strode purposefully down the crowded streets, and people

moved quickly to get the hell out of my way. At least I could still rely on that. The streets . . . looked as they always did. Hot neon signs to every side, gaudy as Hell's candy, and just as bad for you; multi-coloured come-ons for every sucker who thought the Nightside was only another playground for those with more money than sense. Oh, you could find all the usual tourist traps here; but our traps have teeth and an endless appetite for fools. I strode past questionable enterprises and houses full of sin, all of it shop-soiled and marked down but still bright and shiny as any tinsel. Past dark alleyways where darker figures made the kinds of deals that cannot be made in the light. Past women wailing for their demon lovers, and men crying their hearts out over the ones who got away; past golden boys and golden girls with heavily mascaraed eyes and cold, cold smiles on their lips. Love for sale; love, or something like it.

The street traders were out in force, lined up along the curb, selling their cheap and cheerful wares from flimsy stalls or open suitcases propped up on stools. I slowed down enough for a glance here and there, despite my better instincts. Most of it was the usual tourist trash. Brightly hand-painted Toby jugs with knowing smiles, which would shout a warning if someone poisoned the drinks they were holding. Joan the Wad figures, to guarantee good weather. Bottles of Lourdes Cola, the Real Deal! All the latest sex films, from celebrities on their way up. Or down. On DVD, Blu-Ray, 3D, and 4D. Some so hot their jewel-case covers were sweating. And any number of steaming stalls offering food so fast it could give you indigestion while you were still eating it.

Pigs in blankets! Toad in the hole! Jugged bears! Eel pretzels with just a squeeze of lemming! Something wriggling on a stick!

All the usual cries. I once saw a pie jump off its stall and walk away on its own. I'll never eat from a food stall again.

The street traders dealt in all the lesser flotsam and jet-sam that turns up in the Nightside, through Timeslips and dimensional doors, or from tourists forced to empty their pockets and sell everything they own, in return for a ticket home. High-tech artefacts and baffling personal items, treasures and curiosities, from out of the Past or any number of possible futures. From all the worlds that ever were, and some that might never be. Rarely with anything remotely like an instruction manual, or any kind of provenance, or guarantee. Or a refund. Buyer beware, and please don't open that until you're a safe distance away.

The night was hot and sultry, the air more than normally close. Out of open doorways of a dozen different ethnic restaurants drifted savoury smells strong enough to bring tears to your eyes and a spark to your step. All kinds of music from the kinds of clubs that never close; from hot saxophone breaks to heavy bass lines that shuddered in your bones. Trouble on the air, danger in the night, sex and violence tugging at everyone's elbows. Business as usual, in the Nightside.

The traffic roared up and down the road, never slowing, never stopping. There are no traffic lights in the Nightside; vehicles that defy the laws of physics every day have no time at all for the rules of the road. Anything and everything travels through the Nightside, from places best not considered to destinations beyond our comprehension. From horse-drawn carriages to deep-freeze super-tankers, to black taxi-cabs that dart back and forth, duelling with swivel-mounted machine-guns over disputed territories . . . Super-streamlined cars from alternate futures, ambulances that run on distilled suffering, and articulated transports carrying unknown loads on unknowable journeys. While overhead, something the size of a dozen planes sweeps slowly by, its grotesque shape blocking out the stars in the sky, with not even a murmur of flapping wings.

So if you want to cross from one side of the road to the other, you either have to do something quite appalling to a chicken . . . or do what everyone else does, and use the underpass. Walk down a flight of steps, travel through the simple concrete tunnel that passes beneath all the havoc and horrors of the traffic above. You're a hell of a lot safer in the underpass than you ever are up on the street because all the underpass tunnels are monitored and protected by the Authorities, in the general interest. Can't have the tourists coming to any harm before our many and voracious businesses have squeezed every last penny out of them.

I strolled through the brightly lit corridor, and unlike on the street above, everyone was calm and polite and not in any way violent, and gave everyone else lots of room. Because each and every underpass is patrolled by unseen trained poltergeists. Courtesy of the Authorities. You'll never see them coming, but if you make any kind of trouble, they'll turn you inside out in a moment. And leave you that way. It's surprising how long you can live in such a condition though that's not necessarily a good thing. And that's the standard punishment. Really piss off a poltergeist, and it will demonstrate that not only has it got a really nasty sense of humour, but also absolutely no restraints when it comes to experimenting with the human form in appalling ways.

But they can't be bothered to do anything about the graffiti artists. Apparently they consider them beneath their dignity. So the walls are covered with overlapping scrawls of names and boasts and urgent messages from the subconscious of the Nightside. *Meet the new Walker, same as the old Walker. Razor Eddie does it with surgical precision. Supersexuals of the world unite, you have nothing to lose but your inhibitions. Where have all the elves gone and who do we go to to say thanks?* And, a bit intriguingly, *Let the sunshine in.*

And, of course, the inevitable buskers. I think the poltergeists let them hang around to brighten up their endless job. But only as long as the musicians maintain a professional standard. The untalented and overambitious can often be seen hobbling out of the underpass with their instruments stuffed where the moon doesn't shine. I dropped the odd coin in every other cap or outstretched hand I passed, on the grounds that the wheel turns for all of us, and karma can be a real bitch. The only difference between any of us and the homeless is one really bad day.

The usual buskers lined the way, giving it their all, such as it was. A trio of Greek Muses were singing a ska version of the "Ballad of Eskimo Nell," in close-part harmonies. Complete with gestures. A ventriloquist with a vampire dummy had the dummy singing "Love You till the Sun Comes Up Again," while drinking a pint of blood. An old-fashioned ghost with its head stuck underneath its arm was singing "I Got You, Babe," in a duet with itself. And a punk barber-shop quartet were making a real mess of that old punk favourite, "She Fucked Me with a Chain-saw and It felt Like a Kiss." A little style can be a dangerous thing.

I came up out of the Underground on the other side of the street and headed out of the naked jungle and into the expensively suited jungle of the business section. People started giving me even more room than before, often actually stepping aside to let me pass. Of course, they weren't stepping aside for John Taylor, PI, but for the new Walker, representative of the Authorities. Those powerful but shadowy grey eminences who ran the Nightside, inasmuch as anyone did, or could. Some people faded back into dark doorways, or disappeared down even darker alleyways, and a few actually turned around abruptly and headed back the way they'd come. Part of me thought I could get used to this.

I stopped for a moment, to consider my reflection in a shop-window to see if my new authority had changed me in any way. But the same shabby face looked back at me, a little more battered and hard-used as I headed towards the end of my thirties. The same long white trench coat, traditional armour for a tarnished knight-errant. Tall, dark, and handsome enough from a distance, that's me, with cold eyes and a colder smile. And perhaps only I could see the beaten-in tiredness, from carrying so many burdens. I made a face, to keep me from getting above myself, and continued on my way.

It does help that I have a special gift for finding things, and people. Whether they want to be found or not.

There was a time when the burdened and the disenfranchised, the desperate and the hag-ridden, would have approached me in the street and hailed me as a King in waiting. The rightful ruler of the Nightside. But I declined that dubious honour; and for my pains ended up as the new Walker, both more and less than a King. I had become the Man; the very thing I spent most of my life fighting against. I suppose we all grow up to become our parents, in the end.

I headed deeper into the business sector, thinking of many things. I was going to my office, a thing I rarely do, if only because it intimidates the hell out of me. I could have used the Portable Timeslip contained inside my gold pocket-watch; one last gift from the previous Walker, before I killed him. It would have teleported me right to my office door, but . . . I felt the need to walk, to tread the familiar streets, and feel the Nightside turn slowly beneath me.

My office was located in a pretty up-market, almost respectable area, where no-one would even think of fleecing the tourists. They dealt in high finance and stole millions from the defenceless every day, without a second thought. The buildings were all much of a muchness, official soulless affairs with little style and no character. You could always tell when you'd reached the business area because the tourists and the punters and the seekers after forbidden knowledge seemed to disappear, replaced by smart-suited functionaries with enchanted briefcases, snapping orders into their mobile phones, to let everyone else know how important they were. Hurrying to their next meetings, to screw someone over before they got screwed. And then there were the rent-a-cops, professional security men and bully-boys, in their private and very gaudy uniforms, carrying all kinds of weapons. They were there to enforce . . . well, if not the law, at least the vested interests of their employers. A business man might steal millions with a straight face but wouldn't stand for having his pocket picked on the way to work or his office burgled while he was out.

All the rent-a-cops knew who I was, but none of them so much as stepped forward to challenge me. They hadn't had the guts to face me down while I was just a private investigator, and now that I was Walker, all it took was the occasional cold glance to put them in their place. Some of them actually saluted me as I passed, though none of them could bring themselves to smile. I had history with most of the companies that supplied rent-a-cops to the suits, and it was the kind of history where the cops tended to shoot first and ask questions afterwards, through a medium. They hated me, and I despised them. They were only standing their ground now because Suzie wasn't with me. If Shotgun Suzie had been striding along at my side, they'd have run away and hidden until we were gone. Though to be fair, most people do that when they see Suzie heading their way. If they've got any sense.

Up above, the gargoyles leaned a little further out from their perches on top of the older buildings, to get a better look at me. I made a point of sticking to the far side of the pavement. Gargoyles have very basic humorous urges and a complete lack of restraint when it comes to making use of their bodily wastes. Statues shuffled a little further back into their niches as I passed, their stone eye-balls moving slowly to follow me, with the faintest of grinding sounds. Doors quietly closed and locked themselves, and windows turned suddenly opaque. Good to be the Walker . . .

And then I had to stop suddenly, as the B9 Presence appeared out of nowhere, right in front of me. The B9 is a shimmering white shape of roughly human proportions and obscure scientific origin. Someone did try to explain it to me once, but I fell asleep the moment they used the word *quantum*, in self-defence. Suffice it to say that the B9 Presence is a thing of twisted energies and appalling power, driven by a conscience not easily understood by mortal men. It roams the Nightside freely, because no-one's worked out how to stop it, appearing to this one and to that one, dispensing words of wisdom and warning, and irritating the hell out of everyone. It moves in mysterious ways its wonders to perform, such as they are, and gets on everyone's tits big-time. Somehow he or she or it had become unstuck in time, and apparently now saw Past, Present, and Future as simply different directions to look in, and now it seemed to feel a duty to apprise certain people of upcoming significant events. In the most obscure, meaningless, and upsetting ways possible. People only put up with the B9 Presence because, well . . . any edge is better than none. The shimmering, almost human shape bobbed and sparkled before me, its voice a rasping whisper.

"What is the one experience left, for the man who has everything? Why, losing it all, of course. Beware the Ides of the March Hare. The Past is never over; it lies in wait, to ambush us. And even the longest night must someday give way to the dawn . . ."

It was gone before I could come up with an appropriate response, so I shrugged, and continued on.

My office was located on the third floor of a tall, ultramodern high-tech building: all gleaming steel and one-way mirrored windows, turning a cold blank face to the rest of the world. The number of floors in the building tended to vary, depending on how successful the various businesses inside were, on any given occasion, and how much sub-letting was going on. Certainly my building was every bit as tall as those surrounding it. Just looking up at the top of the thing gave me a kind of reverse vertigo, as though my feet might suddenly lose their grip on the pavement, leaving me to fly up into the night sky, flailing helplessly. I pulled my gaze away with an effort, shook my head firmly a few times, and strode up to the closed front door.

The only entrance to the building was a large and very solid-looking door of old oak, polished and waxed to within an inch of its life and looking distinctly out of place in such a modern setting. But the best security measures are always based in magic as much as science, and for the best results, it's always best to go old school. There was no bell, no knocker, not even a door-handle, so I hammered on the gleaming wooden surface hard enough to hurt my hand, then stepped smartly back. The sound of my knocking was somehow dull and soft around the edges, as though the wood was swallowing up the sound. A face appeared before me, rising out of the wood, like a swimmer emerging from the depths to break the surface of the water. The face formed itself out of the door, taking its shape and features from the old wood—not a human face, as such, but full of human emotions, the better to deal with human visitors. It yawned slowly and a bit sullenly, as though awakened from deep slumber, then the face fixed me with its blank eyes, and scowled harshly as it recognised me.

"Oh bloody hell, it's you again. No need to announce yourself, John Taylor. Everyone here knows you, whether they want to or not. What do you want? I was having a really nice dream about wood nymphs, and it wasn't only my sap that was rising."

"Open up," I said ruthlessly. "I've got a lot to do today, and arguing with snotty simulacra is not on my list."

"You can't come in unless you know the password," said the door, cunningly. "What's today's password?"

"There is no password! There's never been a password, and you know it! Now tell Cathy I'm here, or I'll rub your surface down with a wire brush!"

The face in the door pouted. "Go on. Abuse me! It's what I'm here for. No-one ever wants to chat, or pass the time. I miss being a tree. I'd throw my nuts at you if I only knew where they were. I'm supposed to be a security measure, you know. Hah! Hah, I say! Half the people who come here try to stuff letters in my mouth."

"Get a move on," I said, unfeelingly. "I've got a lot to get through before my wedding tomorrow."

"Ooh! Ooh! A wedding!" said the face excitedly, rising and falling in the wood. "I love weddings! Can I come? Please say I can come! I'll be very quiet and not get in the way. You could lean me against a wall at the back of the church. I promise I'll be very good and not bother anyone."

"We'll see," I said, wondering how I got into these kinds of conversations. "Now tell Cathy I'm here and want in."

"Oh Cathy!" said the face. "The big boss is here again! Are you ready to receive him, or do you need time to get all those naked people out of the office first?"

The reply must have been of an affirmative nature because the face disappeared back into the solid wood, and the door swung open before me. I strode quickly through, before it could change what passed for its mind. The building's lobby stretched away before me: expensively comfortable, brightly lit, but not overpoweringly so, and so deeply carpeted it felt like walking on water. Which was probably the effect they were hoping for. The usual Pre-Raphaelite prints on the walls. That John Waterhouse does get about. Doesn't anyone like Turner any more? The tastefully uniformed security man sitting behind his high-security reception desk took one look at me, blanched, and looked very much as though he wanted to sink down underneath his desk and not be noticed. But he gathered all his courage and made himself sit upright and nod to me respectfully. I ignored him, heading for the elevators at the far end of the lobby. There was a time I would have made him wet himself, on general principles, for the snob and bully that he usually was and because his main function was usually to keep people like me out . . . but I must have been mellowing. Besides, I didn't have the time.

One of the elevators opened its doors for me as I approached. I stepped inside and told it to take me to the third floor. I preferred when elevators had human operators. You could bribe them to keep quiet. They also ensured that the elevator wouldn't try and eat you. Predators come in all shapes and sizes in the Nightside. But the doors closed easily, and the elevator moved smoothly upwards. It then immediately got on my bad side by playing Muzak versions of 1970s prog rock: ELO, ELP, PFM. There really ought to be an off switch for elevator Muzak. And then, as if this wasn't annoying enough, the elevator started trying to sell me things, in a very posh voice.

"Have you ever considered the advantages offered by really up-to-date life-insurance?"

"I've never really seen the point in someone else having a vested interest in my being dead," I said. "Don't encourage people, that's what I say."

"I could get you a really good premium . . ."

"I'm John Taylor."

There was a pause. "Ah, yes. I see. Right; forget it. Would you like to change your provider for your mobile-phone service? And no, I don't know where the satellites are, so don't ask. Oh do say yes; I get a really nice bonus for every person I get to sign up."

"What use is a bonus to an elevator?" I said. "What use do you have for money?"

"I'm saving up to have my conscious downloaded into something a little more upwardly mobile. Socially speaking . . . Preferably something with legs and hands. You can do a lot if you've got legs and hands. Could I perhaps interest you in taking out a new credit card, from those wonderfully friendly people, EnGulf & DeVour?"

"Do you have an off switch?"

"Do you?"

"Look," I said, "it's up to you . . . Either you stop trying to sell me things, or I'll push all your buttons before I get out and send you up and down the building for ages."

"Beast!" muttered the elevator. "It's not my fault. Never wanted to be an elevator anyway."

"If you are about to tell me that you really wanted to be a lumberjack, you and I are about to have a serious falling out."

Perhaps fortunately, just then the elevator stopped at the third floor and opened its doors. I stepped out, and the doors slammed shut behind me so quickly they nearly trapped the tail of my trench coat.

"Have a good day!" it shouted after me, defiantly.

Chance would be a fine thing, I thought wistfully, and strode down the long corridor before me. My office was exactly where I remembered it. The door was a huge slab of solid silver, deeply scored with protective signs and sigils, and an extremely rude curse in Enochian. Once again, there was no bell or knocker or voicebox, so I announced myself loudly. The door swung slowly open, smoothly and silently, despite its obvious great weight, and I walked in like I owned the place. Which, for once, I actually did.

My secretary Cathy rose up out of her chair like a jack-in-the-box, vaulted over the huge mahogany desk, and raced across the office to throw herself at me. I braced myself for the impact and suffered myself to be greeted with great enthusiasm. Cathy was a tall, blonde, and very healthy young woman, a long way from the ratty-haired teenager I'd first encountered all those years ago. I hugged her back even though I'm not normally a touchy-feely type, and we stood close together for a long moment. She finally let go of me, stepped back, and grinned happily.

Cathy; big eyes, bigger smile, and a pretty face so heavily made-up it was practically a mask, under a heavy bob of expensively styled hair. She was wearing a long white dress of the kind made famous by Marilyn Monroe, and filled it out nicely. She also wore very high stilettos, on the grounds they made for handy weapons in close combat during bar fights. Cathy was bright and crafty and very smart, and ran my office and my business far more efficiently than I ever could. Bangles clattered noisily around her wrists with every movement, and she wore a long set of beads with artless charm. Heavy diamond pendants hung from her ears. She did try to tell me about her other more intimate piercings once, but I declined with all the politeness at my command. Cathy was my secretary, my side-kick, and my good friend; but I have never let it go any further than that. I do have some principles. Cathy's been my secretary ever since she first came to the Nightside as a teenage runaway, and I rescued her from a house that tried to eat her.

I took a look around my office. It had been a while since I'd seen the place. It boasted all the very latest conveniences and luxuries, including several things I was pretty sure were heavily frowned on even in the Nightside. I carefully averted my eyes from them and studied the brightly coloured walls, the deep plush carpeting of a plum-wine colour, spread across a room big enough to swing an elephant in, provided you had a good wind-up.

Oversized cuddly toys with disturbingly large eyes and unnerving smiles peered at me from every gap in the jumble of odd items and even odder office equipment, like animals watching from a strangely civilised jungle. Polka-dot bookshelves took up all of one wall, packed with reference books. A large poster showed off the generous charms of a Finnish all-girl rock group, INDICA. Various pieces of discarded high tech lay piled up in one corner, presumably replaced by more recent versions. Nothing gets made redundant faster in the Nightside than the Very Latest Thing in high tech.

I did notice a few changes from the last time I'd had

reason to visit my office, starting with a tall potted plant that shifted and swayed furtively in one corner, muttering to itself in a breathy voice. A filing cabinet that showed clear signs of the bigger on the inside than the outside spell, without which most buildings in the Nightside couldn't cope. And the massively overstuffed, leather-bound chair behind the desk, from which Cathy had launched herself; which on closer inspection proved to have its own built-in drinks cabinet, Game Boy, and massage function. I've lived in places less comfortable than that chair. Cathy caught my gaze and shrugged charmingly.

"I'm the one who has to work here. You haven't dropped by in . . . ages! I was beginning to think you'd forgotten where this was, again, and I'd have to send you another map. And a compass. Why are you here, boss?"

I persuaded her to sit back down behind the desk again while I sank into the surprisingly comfortable visitor's chair. I looked at her thoughtfully.

"Oh bloody hell," she said immediately. "It always means trouble when you look at me like that. What's gone wrong now?"

"Now that I'm to be the new Walker for the Nightside," I said carefully, "I can't be a private investigator any more."

"Ah," said Cathy, nodding wisely. "Conflict of interest."

"More like I won't have the time," I said. "There's a lot to do when you're Walker."

"John Taylor, the last honest man in the Nightside, is now the Man," said Cathy. "Can't say I saw that one coming."

"Same here," I said. "Or I'd have run extremely fast in the opposite direction. But, better me than someone else who couldn't be trusted or depended on in a crisis; so I have to do it. If I'd have known my conscience was going to cause me so much trouble, I'd have had it surgically removed long ago. But my time as a PI is definitely over, so I won't need this office any more. You're going to have to close it down, Cathy."

"Oh, is that all? I've known that was on the cards ever since I heard you were going to be the next Walker! Don't worry, boss; I've got it all under control." She stopped and looked at me thoughtfully. "I suppose you'll have a new office, as Walker?"

"The position does come with a lot of support," I said carefully. "Most of which I can't talk about."

"Not even to me?"

"What you don't know, someone else can't make you tell them," I said. "It's that sort of job."

"I suppose it must be a lonely sort of job, being Walker," said Cathy. "You can't trust anyone."

I made myself smile easily. "Situation entirely normal, for the Nightside."

Cathy fixed me with an almost accusing look. "Is Suzie really pregnant?"

"Yes," I said.

"How the hell did that happen?"

"Well, if you don't know by now, Cathy . . ."

"But I thought . . . she couldn't bear to be touched, by anyone!"

"That used to be true," I said. "But miracles do happen, sometimes, in the Nightside."

"Damn, boss," said Cathy. "You really can do anything."

"No," I said. "She did it all herself. She's always been a lot stronger than most people realise. And I . . . have always been so very proud of her."

"But . . . do you really feel the need to get married, boss? In this day and age? You don't have to get married just because she's up the stick."

"It seems like the right thing to do," I said. "And doing the right thing seems more important now than ever. Given who and what I've become. But I'm not marrying her just because . . . That gave me the impetus to do what I always wanted to do. I love her. She loves me. Nothing else matters."

"You soft and soppy sentimental old thing, you," said Cathy.

"How do you feel about our getting married?" I said.

"Oh, I love weddings!" Cathy said cheerfully. "I cry buckets."

"Alex usually cries, too," I said. "In memory of his own."

Cathy looked at me. "You knew his ex-wife. What was she like?"

"She lacked patience. And a sense of humour. And she slept with everything that breathed and a few that didn't."

"Did she every try it on with you?" said Cathy.

"Fortunately, I'd left the Nightside by then," I said.

"After Suzie shot you in the back."

"She was only trying to get my attention."

"I'm going to be doing a lot of baby-sitting, aren't I?" said Cathy. "Auntie Cathy! I love it! And Uncle Alex! Oh, he's going to absolutely hate that!"

I looked around the office. "What are you going to do with all this . . . stuff?"

"I've already made arrangements, boss. The really good stuff goes with me, and what I can't sell I'll chuck in the nearest Timeslip, so it can be someone else's problem."

"Okay," I said. "Down to business. Cathy, I want you to find me one last case, as a private investigator. Nothing too big or too complicated because I want it all over and done with before I get married tomorrow. But something really good, to go out on."

And then I stopped, as a thought occurred to me. I looked around the office. "How much am I paying for all this?"

"You never wanted to know before," said Cathy, which I couldn't help noticing wasn't really an answer.

"I wasn't getting married before," I said. "Everyone's been telling me that can be very expensive."

"Relax, boss. Let's say that thanks to the expert way I have been managing your finances and investments all these years, you can afford it."

"I'm solvent?" I said. "When did that happen?"

"You never did have a head for figures," said Cathy, shaking her head sadly.

"Am I rich?"

"Well, by the Nightside's standards, you are comfortably well off."

"Damn," I said. "I really must run out and buy something expensive, on principle. It's been years since I indulged myself."

"Not what I heard . . ."

"What?"

"Nothing, boss!"

Cathy fired up the various computers and monitor screens built into the surface of her desk and made a point of studying them carefully. She gestured meaningfully at the piled-up paper in the trays, marked In, Out, Urgent, and Pay Now. I grabbed a few handfuls and sorted through them while Cathy called up all the most recent e-mails. People still write a lot of letters in the Nightside, sent by personal messenger, because paper can't be hacked. My office has also been known to receive communications from any number of alternate futures. Usually marked Not To Be Opened Till . . . I sorted those out and placed them carefully to one side. Never trust messages from the Future; they always have their own agenda.

"That's nothing," said Cathy, noting my interest. "Sometimes things appear here in the office, arriving out of nowhere by supernatural methods. I only ever open those wearing my special protective mittens. And there's always the ravens, of course."

I looked at the handful of ravens, gathered together on a wooden perch at the far end of the office, patiently waiting their turn to deliver their magically imposed messages.

"I don't know how they get in, boss," said Cathy. "Especially considering this office doesn't have a window. I never ask them what their messages are because then they'd disappear back to whoever sent them. And I'm not doing anything for anyone who'd treat living creatures that cruelly. So I let them hang around here until their messages are safely out-of-date, then I find them good homes."

"You soft and soppy sentimental thing, you," I said.

"And the ones I can't find homes for I make into pies."

I said nothing. Often, I find that's the safest course. I concentrated on sorting through my papers while Cathy worked her way through the e-mails.

"I have programs in the computer to weed out the time-wasters along with the spam," Cathy said finally. "But sometimes messages by-pass the system completely and drop onto my desk out of nowhere, punching their way right through the office's protections and defences. I always treat those messages very respectfully because anyone with that kind of power wouldn't be bothering us unless it was something really urgent."

"Hold everything," I said. "I just noticed that you're using a whole new computer system. Whatever happened to that silver sphere thing, holding rogue AIs from the Future?"

"Oh them . . . They went home again, a few months back," said Cathy. "They were basically data junkies. At first they were as happy as pigs in shit because they thought they'd never run out of fresh new data to investigate and correlate, but eventually even they had enough. They announced one day that the Nightside was too weird, even for them, and it made their heads hurt. And since they didn't have heads, they were going home. And off they went. To wherever or whenever they came from. The computers built into my desk now are state-of-the-art thinking things that fell off the back of a Timeslip. And no, you really don't want to know how much I paid for them. Before they were fitted into my desk, they looked like Robby the Robot's head, if its designer had been having a very bad day while out of his head on really dodgy blotter acid. Sometimes it thinks so fast it gives me the answer before I've even worked out the question. It's called Oliver. Don't upset it."

I decided I needed a break. I got up out of my chair and marched over to the futuristic coffee-pot standing on its special stand. A gleaming metal Moebius monstrosity that somehow never needed refilling and produced steaming-hot black coffee on demand. As long as you were very polite while demanding it. Far too many things in the Nightside have minds of their own. They'll be forming unions next . . . As I waited for my mug to fill, I couldn't help noticing a line of empty champagne bottles stacked up on the floor behind Cathy's chair. Good vintages, too. I didn't ask. I didn't want to know. The mug finally filled, steaming thickly. I took a good sip, and then spat it half-way across the office. I swear the coffee machine sniggered. I glared at Cathy.

"What the hell has happened to the coffee? It tastes like battery acid that someone's pissed in!"

"I wouldn't know," said Cathy innocently. "I haven't touched that stuff since the machine had its nervous breakdown. Personally, I think it's a cry for help. It's only for clients and visitors, these days. I drink vintage bubbly, and the occasional bottle of Stoli. Here . . ."

She fumbled beneath her desk as I put the coffee mug carefully to one side and settled myself in the visitor's chair again. Cathy emerged again, offering a pale blue bottle.

"If you want, you can clear your mouth out with this. Viennese Creme Violette. A desperate and downright threatening thick liquor whose taste could punch through steel plate. This is industrial-strength palate cleanser. An old client of yours sends us a new case every Easter, to say thank you."

"What for?" I said, looking closely at the bottle, then shaking my head firmly.

Cathy grinned as she made the bottle disappear again.

"There's never any name. But . . . free booze is free booze! If there's any left over at the end of each year, I go out and hand it over to the homeless. They're always very grateful. I think they use it to thin out paint-stripper before they drink it. Or to start a fire when it's cold."

"I have also just noticed," I said, "that your state-of-the-art sound system has been replaced by what appears to be an old-fashioned wind-up gramophone, complete with metal horn."

"Oh that!" said Cathy, wriggling excitedly in her chair. "It's the latest thing! You can put on any record you like, adjust the dimensional tracking system, and it will play any variation of the record from any number of alternate time-tracks! It's super cool!"

"Sometimes you make me feel very old," I said. "What's wrong with CDs?"

"Vinyl rocks!" said Cathy.

I returned determinedly to my stack of papers, trying to find something that appealed to me . . . and then looked up again, to consider Cathy thoughtfully.

"It's that look again," she said resignedly. "What is it this time, boss?"

"I did wonder," I said carefully, "whether you might want to take on the office, and the business, after I'm gone. Be a private investigator in your own right."

"Oh hell no," Cathy said immediately. "Not my thing. I only stayed on here because it seemed to me you needed a secretary and a helper."

I had to smile. "And I let you stay on here because I thought you needed something to do, and keep you occupied, while you found your feet in the Nightside."

We both laughed quietly together.

"I have enjoyed being your secretary," said Cathy. "Going out drinking and dancing in all the best clubs and bars, to keep up with the latest gossip and useful information. And getting paid for it. Best job ever! I might keep that part going . . ."

"Are you still in contact with your mother?" I asked.

"We have regular little chats, on the phone," said Cathy. "We get on much better, now there's a distance between us."

"Any chance of your going back, to visit her?"

"Best not," said Cathy, very firmly. She flashed me a bright smile. "So it's definite, then. No more John Taylor, PI. No more faithful girl secretary. The end of an era."

"What are you going to do once this place is shut down?" I said.

"Oh, that's already been decided, boss. I'm going to help Alex run Strangefellows. I love organising things. And people."

"Will you be sad, to see the back of this place, after so long?"

"Nostalgia is for old folks, boss. I always look forward, never back."

I sat up a little straighter in my chair, so I wouldn't look like old folks, and concentrated on the papers before me while she ran through the e-mails. And soon enough, we both started coming up with interesting cases. Luckily, none that involved looking for that notorious black bird, the Maltese Falcon. Which is a very real object, in case you were wondering. Not that I'd touch it with an enchanted barge-pole.

"I've got an intriguing little e-mail here, from last week," said Cathy. "Katherine Karnstein wants you to find her lost innocence."

I sniffed loudly. "I don't think so. I know the lady in question, and she didn't lose her innocence; she threw it away with both hands, first chance she got."

"All right; how about this one? A Mr. William Everett wants you to find lost Atlantis."

"It isn't lost," I said. "It's hidden. There's a difference. Move on."

"The SAS are offering a seriously large amount, for you to find the Holy Grail for them."

"The Salvation Army Sisterhood should have known better than to ask," I said. "They're probably trying to get me in trouble again. They've never approved of me. I had enough problems tracking down the Unholy Grail. What else have you got?"

"A Reverend Lionel wants you to find the last of the Merovingian line."

"Forget it," I said. "That line's been broken so many times down the centuries that properly speaking it isn't a line, any more. Far too many pretenders to the throne, so to speak."

"All right then, Mr. Fussy Pants, what have you got?"

I looked dubiously at the paper before me. "Someone who prefers to remain anonymous wants me to find out why the Moon in the Nightside sky is so much bigger than it should be. Which is actually a fair question. And I am tempted; I always wanted to know the answer to that one. I think it implies that the Nightside isn't actually when we think it is . . . But no. This would be a long-term case, with lots of footwork and asking questions, and I don't have the time."

"Hmmm. Odd little e-mail here, boss. Says, Let the sun shine in."

I looked up at that. I'd seen that same sentiment graffitied on a wall in the underpass. It felt like it meant . . . something. I shrugged mentally. No doubt I'd find out, eventually. And then I sat up sharply as I discovered something genuinely interesting. A letter from someone signing himself, An Anonymous Gentleman, on good-quality paper, in that old-fashioned copperplate hand writing that no-one teaches any more. I put the other papers aside. I held the sheet of paper up to the light and made out a watermark from the Londinium Club. That revered and very private club for the real movers and shakers of the Nightside. I tossed it across the desk to Cathy.

"By any chance, is this one of those missives that appeared on your desk out of nowhere?"

"Got it in one, boss. It was here when I turned up this morning. It does look like the real thing, doesn't it?"

She tossed it back to me, and I read the communication out loud. It seemed the Anonymous Gentleman wanted me to find the secret of immortality. And not just for him, but for everyone. Apparently, a serum existed that could make anyone who took it live forever. He created it, and brought it to the Nightside, looking for someone to mass-produce and distribute it; and, of course, someone stole it. The main suspects were the existing immortal beings of the Nightside, who didn't want any more competition. The Gentleman claimed that the thief would be presenting the serum to the annual meeting of the Nightside Immortals, at the Ball of Forever. Where they would ceremoniously destroy it. The Gentleman wanted me to attend the Ball, find the thief, and recover the serum, for the good of all.

"It does sound like a good case to go out on," I said.

"Can you use your gift to find the Ball of Forever?" said Cathy.

I looked at her. "I don't need to, child," I said patiently. "I know where the Ball of Forever is held. Everyone does. They hold it in the same place every year. It gets major coverage in the society pages of the *Night Times*."

"Will you be taking Suzie with you?" Cathy said artlessly.

"Not this time," I said. "She's far too busy arranging everything for tomorrow's ceremony, and I'm not going to be the one to interrupt her. In fact, one of the reasons I came here looking for one last case was to get out of her way."

"Whipped," said Cathy. "Utterly whipped. I'm going to be

her maid of honour, you know! Even though technically speaking, I'm not qualified. And haven't been for a long time . . ."

"Too much information," I said firmly. I looked at Cathy for a moment. "Would you like to join me, on this case? Be my companion, one last time?"

"No," said Cathy. "It's time to cut the cord and cut it clean. You run off and have fun, and I'll make all the necessary arrangements to shut this place down." She looked at the filing cabinets. "What do you want me to do with all the old case records? There are a lot of secrets in there that a lot of people would probably rather prefer remained secret."

"Burn it all, then put the ashes through the shredder," I said. "And then scatter the ashes in the cellars under Strangefellows. That should do it."

Cathy looked me square in the eye. "Any idea of who this Anonymous Gentleman might be?"

"I've got a few ideas," I said. "But it doesn't really matter. The case is the thing."

"Sure. Right. Do you really believe there's a serum that can make us all immortal?"

"Well, this is the Nightside . . . but no, I doubt it. What matters is whether other people believe it, and what they might be prepared to do, to get their hands on it."

"Including kill each other?"

"Of course. This is the Nightside . . ."

Cathy frowned thoughtfully. "How do you kill an immortal?"

I grinned. "Very thoroughly."

"Get out of here," said Cathy. "Some of us have got work to do."

"Oh," I said. "I sort of promised this building's front door that it could come to the wedding. Make the necessary arrangements, would you?"

"Soft, soppy, sentimental," said Cathy. "Tell me you didn't invite that bloody elevator as well . . ."

"If that bloody thing comes anywhere near the church, you have my permission to shoot it," I said. "Will you be at Suzie's hen night, tonight?"

"Of course!" said Cathy. "I've already booked the male strippers!"

"Just get her to the church on time," I said.

TWO

You're Only Immortal as Long as You Don't Die

Is there anything more fun than deliberately crashing a party where you know you're not welcome, you're not supposed to be there, and you can be absolutely sure that everyone is going to throw a major hissy fit over your very appearance? It's little victories like this, against the rich and the mighty, that keep me going.

The Portable Timeslip inside my gold pocket-watch dropped me off at the entrance to the top (and most select and most expensive) floor of the MEC, the Mammon Emporium Centre. A meeting place and upscale watering hole for the Major Players of the Nightside, or at the very least those rich enough to act like they are. The MEC provides whole floors set apart for private gatherings, complete with uniformed staff, excellent food and drink, and heavily armed security staff, all at only mildly extortionate prices. (If you have to ask how much, you can't afford it.)

The Ball of Forever is one of the oldest and most select

get-togethers in the Nightside, which takes some doing. You have to be immortal to get an invitation, you have to be rich enough to pay the entrance fee and powerful enough to be able to defend yourself against the other guests. For hundreds of years the Ball of Forever was held at Strangefellows, the oldest bar in the world; but then Merlin Satanspawn came back from the dead, declared the bar to be his own private territory, and kicked them all out. (And perhaps only I knew he did this because it wasn't only his body that was buried in the cellars under the bar but that of Arthur Pendragon, the once-and-future King, as well.)

The Ball of Forever moved through various venues over the next thousand years or so, before finally settling in what became the MEC. Which these days provides staff in uniforms of your own choosing, all of them guaranteed very discreet about what they might or might not see, along with every luxury you can think of, and some that would shock less-well-travelled souls rigid. The extremely long-lived have a tendency to develop strange and unusual tastes, and a morality that can best be described as flexible. So the MEC is always careful to provide staff with combat training, diplomatic skills, and a hell of a lot of danger money. In advance.

I stood outside the closed door to the top-floor ball-room, and looked it over thoughtfully. A large sign to one side proudly proclaimed THE MEC WELCOMES ALL IMMORTALS TO THE BALL OF FOREVER. AGAIN. A sign on the other side of the door presented coming attractions: THE JEKYLL & HYDE REUNION DINNER (for all those touched and affected by the Good Doctor's special elixir) and THE GRAND ORDER OF GHOULS MANGES TOUTES EVENING. (No living staff will be provided.)

The personal ads at the back of the *Unnatural Inquirer*, the Nightside's very own scabrous tabloid, are jam-packed with *would like to meet similar* messages.

I turned my attention to the tall and muscular butler standing to attention before the door, staring deliberately through me as though I weren't there. He was wearing the full formal outfit—a tight powder blue frock coat, white tights, and a powdered wig, from the Court of Versailles of Louis XIV . . . and carrying it off with professional dignity. Presumably some of the immortals were feeling nostalgic. I moved to stand directly before the butler and gave him my best cheerful smile. In return, he gave me the butler's professionally cool up and down, managing to imply (without speaking a single word) that not only was I not welcome, not invited, and not in any way the right sort, but also that I was improperly dressed and my flies were open. All in one glance. You had to admire the professionalism. I smiled a little more, and he sighed deeply, before reluctantly deigning to meet my impertinent gaze with his own.

"This is a private gathering, sir. May I see your invitation?"

"You know I haven't got one," I said. "I don't need one. I'm Walker."

"Not quite, sir," said the butler. "Your title has yet to be officially validated, and thus your authority is still . . . in question. Also, you do not possess the Voice. Sir."

"No," I said. "But I've got other things. Want me to demonstrate them, in a sudden, violent, and utterly distressing way? Do you need me to remind you that the last butler who annoyed me got dragged down to Hell?"

"Please go right in, sir. Walk all over me. It's what I'm here for."

He stood to one side and opened the door. I started to walk past him, and then had to ask, "Do they pay you extra, to wear that outfit?"

"It's traditional, sir. It is also ill-fitting, uncomfortable, and chafes in places I don't even care to mention. Damn right they pay me extra. Would sir like me to take his coat? We could store it in the private cloak-room. We could also have it dry-cleaned and perhaps fumigated."

"I don't think I'll leave the coat on its own," I said. "I haven't fed it recently. You may announce me, though."

"Of course, sir. I live to grovel."

The butler pushed the door all the way open and stepped inside. I strolled in past him, smiling easily in all directions, and the butler raised his voice to cut across the babble of many conversations, and the somewhat overbearing piped music.

"My lords, ladies, and others, may I present to you Mr. John Taylor, newly appointed Walker to the Nightside. The horror, the horror . . ."

"You get no tip," I said as I walked forward into the Ball of Forever.

The ball-room stretched away before me, larger than a football pitch, and packed from wall to wall with all the most noted immortal beings still walking this Earth. So, of course, I ignored the lot of them and fixed my attention on the huge running buffet lining most of one wall. I strolled along the trestle tables, nodding to the various waitresses, all of them dressed in vaguely fetish French maid outfits. There were no waiters. Presumably because they wouldn't look as good in the outfits. Knowledge of my presence spread quickly through the tightly packed immortals. Out of the corner of my eye, I watched them watching me as they gathered in little groups to discuss what the hell to do, look blankly at each other, hide behind each other, and stare openly at me from what they hoped was a safe distance. They all knew I was gate-crashing, but none of them felt confident enough to raise a fuss. They all knew I had killed an immortal in my time, or at the very least arranged for his death—the legendary Griffin. And made his children mortal again. Perhaps the worst threat of all.

I looked for something to take the edge off my thirst. There were any number of interesting vintages, including an open jug of a wine so deep red it looked like blood. In fact, given the predilections of some of those immortals present, it might very well be blood.

So I picked up a glass of complimentary champagne I wasn't entitled to, leaned back against the buffet table, and looked around me under the cover of taking a long drink. For all the expensive and elegant setting, the rich and the mighty in all their finery, and the piped music playing Elizabethan airs with a lot of lute action (I suppose everyone has a special taste for the music of their youth), there was still a strange feeling to the gathering. Of a whole bunch of people from all kinds of backgrounds, who would normally have nothing to say to each other, brought together by the only thing they had in common. Not having died yet. After all, you're only an immortal until someone manages to kill you. After that, you were just long-lived.

The huge ballroom was full of gods, superhumans, inhumans, posthumans, and a few things that wouldn't pass for human during a complete black-out. All the products of super-science and the supernatural, come together in one place to talk about the things that only immortals could really understand and appreciate. To prove to everyone that they were still around, to swap useful survival tips, to show off new achievements and new fashions, to reminisce about the good old days . . . and whinge and moan about how no-one appreciates the important things any more. And, of course, to show off for the media. Immortals are, first and foremost, celebrities.

Reporters have always been allowed to attend the Ball of Forever, under sufferance, to write their glowing accounts of the most important ball of the season, but this year, for the first time, they'd allowed in a small camera crew from the Nightside Television Centre. Immortals do move with the times, but only slowly and very reluctantly. I recognised the reporter from the *Night Times*, a tall and bulky oriental fellow in a smart tuxedo. Brilliant Chang was an investigative reporter (not a recipe for long life in the Nightside), but fortunately he was also sharp and tricky and knew no fear. Plus, he could run like an Olympic sprinter when the occasion demanded it. He knew me, too, and nodded briefly in my direction. We'd worked some of the same cases, from different directions. On one side of his face, he still carried the dragon tattoo that marked him as a combat sorcerer. An old Dragon Clan enforcer, in fact, before he saw the error of his ways and abandoned gangsterism for the slightly more reputable trade of journalism. He made a point of casually wandering in my direction.

"Hello, Chang," I said. "What are you doing here, covering this jumped-up bun-fight? I thought Julien Advent reserved you for the really important stories these days. Like hot celebrity action, and who's having whom . . . When are you going to get a proper job?"

"When are you?" said Chang.

Honours even, we relaxed a bit.

"I'm surprised the immortals' security people aren't trying to throw you out," said Chang.

"What security?" I said. "People who've lived as long as these scumbags take a pride in being able to look after themselves. Standing tall and laughing defiantly in the face of danger as a matter of principle, that sort of thing. Even if they're not allowed to bring personal weapons to a supposedly civilised gathering like this. I'm here mainly because they can't be bothered to exert themselves."

"And because they're scared of you," said Brilliant Chang.

"That, too," I said. "Really, what is an experienced crime and corruption writer like you doing here?"

"Julien Advent was very insistent that someone experienced should cover the Ball this year," said Chang. "And he wanted it to be someone who wouldn't be easily impressed or intimidated. I didn't run for the door fast enough, so I got the job."

I had to frown at that. "Why would he do that? What does he think is going to happen, this year?"

"Beats me. Normally, this whole do is nothing more than fodder for the society pages and the life-style supplements. Pick up a bit of gossip, get the prettier ones to pose for a few photos, then stuff your face with the free food. Maybe it's something to do with the television people being allowed in for the first time."

"No," I said. "Julien knows something . . ."

"So do you," said Chang. "Or you wouldn't be here. Are you going to kill someone?"

I had to smile. "The night's barely started . . ."

The *Night Times* photographer saw us both smiling together and stepped forward to take a photo. I gave him a cold look, and he quickly changed his mind and retreated.

"Don't mind him," said Chang. "He's new. Somebody's nephew, I think. I do hope he isn't mine."

The other journalist seized her chance to move in for a quick chat. I knew her, too—Bettie Divine, demon girl reporter for the *Unnatural Inquirer*. She slammed to a halt right in front of me and struck her best confrontational pose: tall and rangy and drop-dead gorgeous. Long jet-black hair fell down around her high-boned face as she fixed me with dark green eyes and a pouting scarlet mouth. Two cute little horns poked up through the dark bangs hanging across her forehead. Demon girl reporter, oh yes. Her last big assignment had been to follow me around the Nightside on one of my cases. She then spent a lot of time afterwards loudly claiming she was suffering from post-traumatic stress disorder. We hadn't exactly parted on the best of terms, but I gave her my best I'll-be-nice-if-you-will smile.

"Don't you smile at me, John Taylor," said Bettie. "I'm not

here for you. Didn't even know you'd be here. I'm only here in case Elvis turns up. What are you doing here?"

"I already asked," said Brilliant Chang. "But our new Walker is being very tight-lipped. Perhaps you have more . . . personal ways of persuading him to talk? I am right in believing that there is history between you two?"

"In his dreams," said Bettie, tossing her long hair dramatically.

"Really? Because a little bird told me . . ."

"Oh fuck off, Chang darling; Bettie's working."

Chang laughed, not in the least affronted, and moved off into the crowd. I looked Bettie over carefully. She was wearing an ankle-length, off-the-shoulder jade-green gown, to match her eyes. It was split right up to the thigh and plunging at the front. Or, at least, that's what she looked like to me. Bettie was half succubus, and her appearance changed constantly, according to whoever was looking at her. For all I knew, I'd never seen her real face, never mind her real outfit.

"What are you really wearing?" I asked, as a reasonably safe opening gambit.

She laughed briefly. "Like I'd ever tell you, darling. What are you doing here, that's what my panting readers will want to know. I mean, you're not immortal. Or has that changed? Have I missed a scoop? Say it isn't so . . ."

"No," I said. "I'm not immortal. I'm Walker."

"Oh, I know all about *that*, darling. That's old news. And, might I say, I saw it coming months ago. So who are you here for? What have they done?"

I grinned. "Like I'd ever tell you."

"Oh poo." She batted her fantastically long lashes at me. "Not even for old times' sake? You can tell me, darling. We're friends, aren't we?"

"I don't know," I said. "Are we? The last thing you said to me was, 'I never want to see you again.'"

"That was personal. This is business." She looked at me

thoughtfully. "A little bird told me you're getting married tomorrow. My invitation must have got lost in the post."

"Sorry," I said. "But we're being very strict on *no reporters*. On the grounds that Suzie has this unfortunate tendency to shoot them on sight. So an ex of mine who's also a reporter? They'd be fishing pieces of you out of the guttering for weeks."

Bettie smiled. "I'm an ex? Did something happen that I didn't notice?"

"Not for want of trying on your part," I said.

"Not the way I remember it, darling," said Bettie. "Some people simply don't know how to flirt. Oh come on, sweetie, please . . . you have to give me something I can use or the editor won't sign off on my expenses. Is there going to be trouble?"

"Of course," I said. "I'm here."

Bettie stuck her cute little nose in the air and stalked off. The moment she was safely away, the television news crew moved in, scenting blood in the water. The Nightside has its very own television station, covering all the stories the outside world never gets to hear about. It broadcasts across the Nightside and reaches out to a whole bunch of other worlds, dimensions, and special-interest groups. Subscription only. Lots of people like to keep up with what's happening in the Nightside—if only so they can have advance warning of which way to duck.

The female news reporter shoving a microphone right into my face was not unknown to me. I'd seen her stuck behind the news desk, on occasion, reporting the lighter stories with an unrelenting professional smile, but we'd never met. Charlotte ap Owen was short, blonde, and busty, currently kitted out in a skin-tight leopard-skin outfit, for that important streetwise slutty look. (It said so in a woman's magazine I happened to be reading in my dentist's waiting room.) She had a face so surgically perfect, it was almost characterless, and she pointed her mike at me like it was a weapon. To my knowledge, this was her first assignment outside the studio, and Charlotte was positively bursting with practised charm and barely restrained nervous energy.

"No, Elvis will not be making an appearance here, as far as I know," I said solemnly, before she could get a word in. "Also, yes, I am the new Walker, and no, I'm not going to tell you what happened to the old one. If you're expecting any scandal or excitement at the Ball of Forever, I'm afraid you're going to be very disappointed. Nothing of any real interest will happen here because nothing ever does. Immortals are very private people and wouldn't dream of doing anything that mattered where outsiders might see it. The real meetings, wheeler-dealings and love affairs will be conducted somewhere else, behind firmly closed doors, as always. Immortals do have their feuds and disagreements, their business deals and vendettas; but those tend to play out over centuries, one move at a time, because these people have all the time in the world to get even."

"But something is bound to happen," said Charlotte in her best hot and smoky voice. "You're here! That has to mean something! Why would the freshly appointed Walker of the Nightside come to the Ball of Forever unless there were bad guys to pursue, villains to put down, and injustices to be avenged! I've followed your career for years, and I know what it means when you turn up somewhere unexpectedly. Blood and guts and entrails hanging from the chandelier! You're news!"

"Not if I can help it," I said.

"You must have a reason for being here," Charlotte insisted, taking a deep breath to better show off her cleavage. "Can't you even give me a hint?"

I leaned forward slightly, lowering my voice so she had to lean in close. She looked eagerly at me, her face straining to show some emotion through the Botox.

"If it all does kick off," I said solemnly, "be first out the door. Avoid the rush. Those cameras are expensive."

The man with the camera sniggered loudly. He was so anonymous behind his shoulder-mounted apparatus, I'd almost forgotten he was there. Charlotte glared at him, and he shut up immediately.

"Be sure to get my good side," I said to the camera-man.

"You find it, chief, and I'll get it," he said.

Charlotte ap Owen made a point of turning her back on me and striding away. The camera-man lingered for a moment. "I'm Dave. Don't mind her. She's desperate to get out from behind a desk. She'd defenestrate her own granny for a good story. Bit desperate in other ways, too, if you catch my drift, chief. Never let her back you into a corner unless you like it rough and sudden. I'm not really a camera-man, you know."

I looked at him. "Oh yes?"

"I'm an actor, really. I'm pointing this camera at things till something better comes along. Filling in between acting jobs, you know how it is. Sometimes I pretend I'm actually in some reality show, where I'm pretending to be a camera-man."

"Does it help?" I said.

"Not really. Hello; she's coming back. Little Miss Up Herself. Brace yourself; she's got the light of battle in her contact lenses. She looks like she knows something. Would anyone here have an interest in dropping you right in it, chief?"

"Oh yes," I said. "Really. You have no idea how many."

Charlotte ap Owen gestured airily for Dave to start filming, then stuck her microphone in my face again. "This is Charlotte ap Owen, reporting from the legendary Ball of Forever at the MEC. I'm here talking with the very recently appointed Walker, the infamous John Taylor. Mr. Taylor, I've been hearing some very interesting things about your connection with one of the most far-reaching disasters to hit the Nightside in recent times, namely, the destruction of the independent power plant, Prometheus Inc. Its sudden and unexpected loss plunged much of the Nightside into chaos and cost many lives. Would you care to comment on your involvement in this catastrophic event?"

I thought for a moment. "No," I said.

"But you do know something, Mr. Taylor. I have my sources . . ."

"No, you don't," I said. "I can say that with complete confidence because I know for a fact there aren't any sources remaining as to exactly what happened at Prometheus Inc., except me. I've no doubt someone here has been telling tales out of school and passing round the gossip, but they don't know. Only I know. I could tell you what happened, but then I'd have to kill you, too."

Charlotte opened her perfectly sculpted mouth to ask another question, caught the look in my eye, and thought better of it. She jerked her head at Dave the camera-man, and he stopped filming and trailed after her as she stalked off into the crowd, presumably in search of some less obviously dangerous exclusive. She might try to use the footage she'd already got to embarrass me, but her editor would only spike it. He knew better than to annoy Walker. Or worse still, my Suzie. Who once sent an over-enthusiastic gossip-columnist back to his editor in thirty-seven separate parcels. Gift-wrapped. Owing postage.

I watched Charlotte ap Owen, Bettie Divine, and Brilliant Chang as they made their rounds through the packed crowd of immortals, many of whom were happy to stand and smile for the cameras, but walked away if anyone tried to question them. That wasn't what they were there for. Some immortals would always primp and preen for the media, and some simply wouldn't. It was always surprising which dangerous and even infamous names could behave like real drama queens when someone recognised them. I moved off in the opposite direction, doing my best to mingle with the immortals. Most of them avoided my gaze, refusing to be interrupted in their conversations, or actually turned their backs on me. They stopped doing that after I goosed a few of them. It's always amusing to see who'll squeal like a little girl when you do that. I smiled and nodded in every direction, and a few familiar faces nodded coolly back. Some were friends, some were enemies, and some were both. It's like that, in the Nightside.

I found Razor Eddie, Punk God of the Straight Razor, standing alone in a corner, observing the merry-making with a detached gaze. A tall, thin presence in a grubby grey coat, mostly held together by grime and filth. The light seemed a little bit darker where he stood, and the smell was really bad. Living on the streets and sleeping in shop doorways will do that to you. His face was hollowed and haunted, and he studied the immortals at their play with dark, dark eyes. He was holding a bottle of designer water but hadn't bothered to open it. Flies buzzed around him, dropping dead out of the air when they ventured too close. Don't ask me how they got in. He attracts them, that's all.

"Hello, Eddie," I said. "What's a disturbing presence like you doing at a party like this? Are you immortal?"

"I'm a god," said Razor Eddie in his thin, ghostly voice. "That's even better."

"Do you have business here?" I said. "Is there someone here who needs killing?"

"Undoubtedly," said Eddie. "But nothing urgent. I was down on the Street of the Gods, visiting with an old friend. He told me he'd had a glimpse of the Future. Not uncommon, in those parts. Having so many gods, powers, and presences crammed together in one place does something very disturbing to linear Time. Anyway, Dagon told me he'd Seen something really dangerous coming to the Nightside."

I waited, but that was all he had to say. "Well," I said, "nothing too scary about that. It's pretty much business as usual, in the Nightside."

"Not this time. Dagon said that whatever it is that's coming, it's a threat to the Nightside itself. A final end to the longest night in the world." Eddie looked at me unblinkingly, his lips twitching in what might have been a smile. "He also said he Saw you and me, going head to head, fighting to the death. That's . . . interesting, isn't it?"

I shuddered briefly, as though someone had danced on my grave. "There are many different potential futures," I said carefully. "Nothing Seen is ever inevitable."

"Yes," said Razor Eddie. "I know. But it is interesting. I thought you ought to know. Haven't you ever wondered whether I could take you in a fight?"

"I try very hard not to think about things like that," I said. "Did your friend happen to mention the outcome of this fight he Saw?"

"No. See you later, John."

I took the hint and moved away, leaving him to enjoy his corner. Eddie was a friend, sort of. That's why he warned me. We'd been through a lot together, good and bad. But the Punk God of the Straight Razor went his own way, following his own unknowable purposes. Would he kill me if he thought he had cause? Yes. Razor Eddie was many things, but sentimental wasn't one of them.

I went back to the buffet tables. I felt very much in need of a little light refreshment. Every immortal makes it a matter of pride to bring a bottle of something special to the Ball of Forever, and some of them have cellars that go back centuries. Vintages laid down when that was still a new thing to do. In fact, I think you have to be immortal to withstand what some of those wines can do to your taste buds. I found Dead Boy trying to get a glass of champagne from one of the French maid waitresses, only to have his dead hand slapped repeatedly away on the grounds that she wasn't wasting a really impressive vintage on someone who didn't even have taste buds any more. Dead Boy was good-natured about it.

"Hello, Dead Boy," I said. "How are you?"

"Still dead," he said cheerfully. "Don't worry, I'm not going to make a fuss. I wouldn't waste good booze on me either. I have no palate. Or if I have, it's probably riddled with holes."

I don't know if even Dead Boy knows exactly how long he's been dead. He was seventeen when he was mugged and murdered in the Nightside, long ago, for the spare change in his pockets. He made a deal he still won't talk about to come back from the dead, to avenge his murder; only to discover afterwards that he should have read the small print. He was trapped in his dead body, possessing himself, unable to let go and move on. He's more or less philosophical about it these days and does his best to live the good life despite being quite definitely deceased.

Dead Boy gave up on the champagne and gave his full attention to the assorted snacks and nibbles laid out before him. He crammed his mouth full of delicate culinary creations and filled his coat pockets, for later. Tall and forever adolescent thin, Dead Boy wore a long, deep, purple greatcoat, over black leather trousers and calf-skin boots. He sported a black rose on his coat lapel, and every now and again his coat would hang open to reveal the bare white torso beneath, marked with cuts, scars, bullet-holes and his Y-shaped autopsy scar. Dead Boy never could resist getting into trouble, and as a result was held together with heavy stitches, staples, and the odd length of black duct tape. His long, pale face had a weary, debauched Pre-Raphaelite look, with burning fever-bright eyes and a sulky mouth with no colour in it. He wore a large, battered, dark floppy hat, crammed down hard over a mess of thick, curly hair. Dead Boy did take a pride in his appearance, but it wasn't a pride the living could understand.

"How did you get in?" I asked, honestly interested. "You're not an immortal. You're dead."

"I got in the same way you did, by intimidating the staff. I come here every year; even after they put a fatwa on me. I don't give a damn for these immortal arseholes; I'm here for the food and drink. The MEC really puts itself out for the Ball of Forever—nothing but the best for people who'll come back for centuries. I mean, we are talking delicacies and specialities from all across history! A lot of it supplied by Rick's Cafe Imaginaire; you know, the place that supplies meals made from extinct and legendary animals. I used to go there a lot, before I was banned. How was I to know it was a dog? It didn't look like a dog. Anyway, they have all kinds of tasty treats here, including some so appallingly off-centre that most people wouldn't try them even if you put a gun to their head. Look, larks' tongues in peanut butter on Ritz crackers. Coneys—baby rabbits ripped from their mother's breast and skewered. Stuffed baby Morlock . . ."

"Stuffed with what?" I asked, despite myself.

"Baby Eloi, probably. Those things over there are moebius mice; they stuff themselves. Crunchy . . . but they don't half repeat on you. Hmmm . . . *T. rex* truffles and velociraptor pâté . . . really fast food. And Man's final revenge on the dinosaurs, I suppose. Hello; what's this?"

"Eléphant, sir," said the French maid.

We both looked at the richly steaming meat laid out across a very long plate. "Is that the trunk?" I said finally. "Please tell me that's the trunk."

"Not even close, sir. That is the elephant's penis. Soaked in a dozen different herbs and spices, tenderised with meat hammers, and then char-grilled to bring out the flavour. Would sir like me to cut him a slice off the end?"

"Oh I couldn't," I said. "I'd wince with every bite."

Dead Boy laughed in my face and had a really big slice, beaming happily. "One of the more annoying problems with being dead is that I can only experience the most extreme sensations. I'm only able to enjoy food and drink at all because of these marvellous little pills I have made for me, by this amazing little Obeah woman I know. You can't beat grave-yard voodoo when it comes to getting you things you're not supposed to have. She's called Mother Macabre; though whether that's her name or her title, I've never been sure. Certainly there's been a Mother Macabre in the Nightside Necropolis for more centuries than I can cope with." He looked around the Ball. "She can't be immortal or she'd be here . . . God, this is grand stuff . . . bit chewy, mind. I wonder if they do the balls, as well . . ."

"You ask," I said. "I wouldn't dare."

"You on a case here?" he said easily. "I don't mind helping out. I could use some pocket money. In fact, I could use quite a lot of it."

"Never knew you when you couldn't," I said. "I'll let you know."

He shrugged, and went back to stuffing his face with ele-phant. I wandered off into the crowd again.

Where I met Mistress Mayhem, a tall, lithe, blue-skinned beauty, with a massive frizz of black hair that fell all the way down her back to her very slender waist. Descended, at a great many removes, from the Indian death goddess Kali, she was currently wearing an outfit from the film *Avatar*, cut to show off as much dark blue flesh as possible. She offered me some glowing green snuff from a chased silver snuff-box, and when I politely declined, she filled both her nostrils with enough of the stuff to blow a normal person's head right off. She sneezed briefly, in a very ladylike way, and tucked the snuff-box back into her cleavage.

We'd worked a few cases together, and she'd tried to have me killed a few times. Business as usual, in the Nightside.

"Weren't you going out with Jimmy Thunder, last time I saw you?" I said to make conversation.

"Oh, him! The Norse God for Hire," said Mayhem. "We are currently not speaking. And anyway, he's banned from the Ball of Forever for excessive smiting last year. Just as well;

he can lower the tone of any gathering simply by being a part of it."

My next encounter was with Hadleigh Oblivion. He appeared before me, emerging from the crowd with casual grace, smiling easily, as though he knew something I didn't. Which, given who and what he was, was probably true. Hadleigh knew a great many things other people didn't know and wouldn't want to. He was perhaps the most powerful, and certainly the most influential, of the legendary Oblivion brothers. Tommy Oblivion was the Existential Detective, specialising in cases that may or may not have actually happened. Larry Oblivion was the Dead Detective, the Post-Mortem Private Eye. And Hadleigh . . . was a product of the Deep School, and the current Detective Inspectre, only called in on cases where reality itself was under threat. He was wearing his usual long, black leather coat, dark as a scrap of the night, all the better to show off his stark white face and his mane of jet-black hair. He also had sinister dark eyes and a downright unnerving smile. Hadleigh always gave the impression that wherever he was, that was where he was supposed to be.

I made a point of nodding easily to him, conspicuously unimpressed. You can't let people like that know they've got to you, or they'll walk all over you.

"Something's going to happen here," Hadleigh announced, quite casually. "I can feel it in the air, like a thunder-storm drawing closer. I take it you feel it, too?"

"Oh yes," I said. "Something like that." I didn't feel like mentioning the Anonymous Gentleman's warning note. It's important to keep up appearances. "But what could be so important, as to bring you, me, Dead Boy, and Razor Eddie to the same place? Can't be a coincidence."

"Coincidences are the universe's way of arranging things neatly," said Hadleigh.

"Are you immortal?" I said bluntly.

"Bit early to tell yet," said Hadleigh. "Whatever this thing is, it had better get a move on. I can't stop long; I've been called in to consult on a case with the London Knights. They actually requested my presence, which is unusual enough that I've agreed to go out into London Proper to give them a helping hand." He fixed me with a cool, considering look. "You know the London Knights. Is it true that King Arthur has returned to them?"

"Yes," I said.

"Is he everything the legends say?"

"That and more."

"Interesting," said Hadleigh. "I wonder what he wants with me . . . But consider this; if Arthur Pendragon is back, can Merlin Satanspawn be far behind?"

"Oh God, I hope not," I said.

"Leave Her out of this," Hadleigh said firmly. I can never tell when he's joking.

"You're Hadleigh Oblivion, aren't you?" said Charlotte ap Owen excitedly, waving for her camera-man to catch up with her.

Hadleigh smiled, produced a pale blue rose from out of nowhere, and held it up before Charlotte. He then brought the rose up to his mouth and inhaled steadily. The colour faded out of the petals, and we all watched speechlessly as Hadleigh breathed in the life essence of the flower. One by one, the colourless petals cracked and fell apart, falling in grey sprinkles to the floor. Hadleigh smiled and let the dead stem fall from his hand.

"That's nothing," said Dead Boy, passing by. "You should see what I can do with a fart."

Hadleigh smiled easily at Charlotte, who looked like she wanted to be sick. She backed away into the crowd, taking Dave the camera-man with her. I gave Hadleigh a hard look.

"Studying at the Deep School ruined you."

"No, it didn't."

"Well, something did."

I went back to mingling. I listened in on a great many conversations because the immortals were too proud to stop talking even though I was there, but I didn't learn anything important. Most of it was about who was having whom, and what someone else would do when they found out. Typical party chatter. No-one even mentioned the immortality serum I was supposed to be looking for. Short of grabbing people by their lapels and slamming them up against a wall, I didn't see how I was going to persuade anyone to talk about it. And I don't do things like that. Not any more.

I bumped into the Lord Orlando, fresh from changing sex again. He'd come dressed in a chequered black-and-white Harlequin outfit, complete with a cute little domino mask and heavy stubble showing through his white face make-up. He was still boring for England, talking loudly and relentlessly at anyone who'd stand still long enough, and name-dropping all the famous people he claimed to have slept with, in one sex or another, down the ages. And still going on about how traumatised he was, from being kidnapped and briefly replaced by the Charnel Chimera, a few years back. I got the impression he was mostly upset that no-one could tell the difference between the bloodthirsty monster and the real thing. I could have said many things there, but didn't. I must be mellowing.

I pointed him in Bettie Divine's direction, thus annoying two birds with one stone, and headed towards a couple of people I was actually looking forward to meeting; the Bride, and her current paramour, the latest incarnation of Springheel Jack. The Bride towered over both of us, a good seven feet tall and well fleshed. The Baron Frankenstein had made all his early creations oversized, so he had enough room to fit all the bits in. The Bride's face was pale and taut, as though stretched by too much plastic surgery, but she'd always looked that way. The Baron might be a creative genius when it came to Life and Death, but his sewing skills left a lot to be desired.

The Bride had huge dark eyes that didn't blink often enough, a prominent nose, and lips red as sin itself. She would never be described as beautiful, but she was most definitely attractive, in a spooky, scary kind of way. She wore her long black hair piled up in an Amy Winehouse beehive, and she wasn't bothering to dye out the white streaks any more. Or using make-up to cover the heavy stitching at her neck and wrists. She wore a flouncy white blouse, cut to show off her magnificent cleavage, midnight blue slacks, and knee-length riding boots with silver spurs. Up close, she smelled of attar of roses with a hint of formaldehyde.

She crushed my hand in a powerful grip and smiled broadly. We'd never actually met before, but with reputations like ours, we knew of each other. The Bride had a lot of personality and didn't mind spreading it around.

"I'm here representing the Spawn of Frankenstein," she said loudly. "All those dead but definitely not departed creations of the old Baron, bad cess to his soul. I did hear you'd killed him a while back, and I was going to send you a thank-you note; but it turned out to be another other-dimensional duplicate. I hate those. Still, thanks for the effort. It's the thought that counts."

"Happy to do it," I said, flexing my numbed fingers surreptitiously. The Bride was a big girl and didn't know her own strength. "One less god of the living scalpel has to be a good thing."

"Do you know my new boy-friend?" said the Bride, draping a more than usually long arm across her companion's shoulders. "He's the current inheritor of the Springheel Jack inheritance; but don't hold that against him."

We shook hands briefly. I couldn't help but remember the time when a more than usually virulent Springheel Jack meme had invaded the Nightside through a Timeslip, overwriting everyone it touched and turning them into Springheel Jacks with nothing but bloodshed and slaughter on their minds. Suzie and I had no choice but to go out into the streets, hunt down everyone afflicted, and kill them all. If this Jack knew, he had the grace not to mention it, so I didn't either.

He was tall and slim, cool and calm, with a dignified bearing. He was handsome enough, in a sinister sort of way. He wore the traditional long black cape, which swept about him like bat-wings, and an old-fashioned top hat. The look came with the incarnation. He wore it well enough. He had a pale face and ice-cold blue eyes, that were a lot older than they should have been. It was the burden of every Springheel Jack to carry all the experiences of his predecessors.

"What brings the new Walker to the Ball of Forever?" he said, in a slightly detached voice. "Are we to take it that you're immortal?"

"Hardly," I said. "My title isn't like yours; I'm just the latest to hold the position. I'm here following a lead in a case, to see where it goes." I looked thoughtfully at Jack, then at the Bride. "Are either of you immortal, technically speaking?"

"I am both dead and alive!" the Bride said grandly. "Which means I outrank everyone here. Besides, I'd like to see anyone try to throw us out . . ."

"While I am an idea that manifests itself through possessing people," said Springheel Jack. "So I suppose I am immortal, in a serial sort of way."

And then everybody at the Ball of Forever stopped talking, and turned their heads to look as news of the latest arrival spread rapidly through the room. I looked around, too, impressed. Even I hadn't made that much of an impression. A silence fell across the ballroom as King of Skin stood in the doorway, large as life and twice as nasty, swaying on his feet and sniggering to himself, wrapped in all his usual sleazy glory. King of Skin was the only immortal in the

Authorities, that quiet background group who run the Nightside, inasmuch as any does or cares to. The group I supposedly now served and took my authority from. King of Skin was potent and powerful, a King in glory when he took his aspect upon him. He could disturb people he hadn't even met yet. Rumour had it he'd spat on Heaven and Hell because he wouldn't be bound by anything, even a philosophy. He had the power to undo possibilities and rewrite them in his favour. He could pick out your worst and most private nightmare, simply by looking at you, and make it real. King of Skin was a major-league scumbag, even by Nightside standards; but he could do things for you that no-one else could, or would. So people made a lot of allowances. Lot of that going on, in the Nightside.

Don't ask what he really looked like; everyone saw what he wanted them to see. Mostly he projected a sleazy glamour of constantly shifting details, real enough to make you extremely uncomfortable on a very basic level. Everyone was always very polite, wherever he turned up, if they knew what was good for them, and gave him plenty of room. I'd known him for years, usually from a distance, and I still had no idea what he was about or what he wanted. Just another lost soul, more powerful than most, walking the dark streets in search of something even he probably couldn't name. He was hard to kill though many had tried, and none of us knew the beginning of his story. Because he liked it that way.

He started forward into the ballroom, swaying and sniggering, grinning nastily in all directions, enjoying the effect he was having on the gathering. Even the most powerful immortals fell back, to give him plenty of room to move in. King of Skin reached out to touch the people he passed, in brusque and brutal inappropriate ways, trailing his fingertips across bare flesh, caressing a face here and a breast there, and no-one said or did anything. I had to wonder what he was doing at the Ball. Was he representing the Authorities? Had he heard about the serum? Or was he here to cause trouble because he could? There were gods here who would turn their gazes aside rather than upset King of Skin because even gods have nightmares, and King of Skin wouldn't hesitate to use them as weapons.

He knew I was there but ignored me completely, working the crowd in his own nasty way. He would stop here and there, for a moment, to indulge in a few neatly tailored insults, dropping quick references to things no-one else was supposed to know about. He mocked and abused people and laughed in their faces; and they stood there and let him do it because they had no choice. Because the alternatives were worse. People cursed and swore under their breath after he'd moved on, and some even wept bitter tears of rage or affront. Because King of Skin knew things . . . and the best you could hope for was that he wouldn't tell anyone else.

No-one ever disputed his right to do these things because he was King of Skin.

To my surprise, he actually sought out Razor Eddie in his corner. A lot of people started backing away. I mean, you don't upset the Punk God of the Straight Razor. Not if you like having your organs on the inside. I've seen gods and powers come running out of the Street of the Gods, crying their eyes out, because Razor Eddie was on the rampage. But no; King of Skin walked right up to the thin grey presence and sniggered in his face.

"So, Eddie," said King of Skin, "when are you going to tell everyone where you really got your pearl-handled straight razor?"

Razor Eddie looked at him, and the silence lengthened uncomfortably. King of Skin snarled and growled under his breath, and turned abruptly away. And I stopped holding a breath I hadn't even realised was caught in my throat. It was as though two great racing cars had played chicken, and one had turned aside at the last moment. King of Skin strode up to Dead Boy, who was still making serious inroads on the buffet and sucking his dead fingers noisily. He straightened up as he sensed King of Skin approaching and turned unhurriedly round to face him.

"So, Dead Boy; how's your girl-friend these days? Still changeable?"

"Fuck off, Skinny," Dead Boy said flatly. "You can't frighten me. I'm dead."

"Even the dead have nightmares," said King of Skin, the air rippling and puckering around his hands as he played with probabilities.

Dead Boy smiled suddenly, and it was a most unpleasant smile. "I made a deal with my worst nightmare. You invoke that, and it'll rip the soul right out of you."

And again, King of Skin turned suddenly away, faced with something even worse than he was. He snarled with frustration and turned on Mistress Mayhem, who started to back away, then made herself hold her ground. It was always worse if you made him chase after you.

"Love the blue skin," said King of Skin. "Hope you don't run out of dye. And you didn't want the baby anyway. Don't worry; I won't tell the Thunder god what you did."

A single tear ran down Mayhem's blue cheek, but she wouldn't give him the satisfaction of saying anything. King of Skin sniggered loudly and turned his hot gaze on Lord Orlando before dismissing him as easy prey. The Lord Orlando almost fainted with relief. King of Skin looked around him, laughing breathily every time someone flinched, and finally advanced on the Bride. She glared down her nose at him and didn't budge an inch. Springheel Jack stepped forward and stood between King of Skin and his prey.

"Wait your turn, boy," said King of Skin. "I'll get to you."

"Leave the lady alone," said Springheel Jack. "Or else."

"Or else? You think you can threaten me, boy? I know all about you. Who you were before, what you really are now. Does the Bride know . . ."

"One more word, and I'll open you up and let your lights see the light," said Springheel Jack.

"You think you can hurt me, boy? I have made myself into a thing that cannot be harmed by mortal weapons!"

"My razors are no mortal weapons," said Springheel Jack. "And there's nothing left you can scare me with. Because I've already been through it."

King of Skin looked at him, his hot gaze meeting cold, cold eyes; and again, he looked away. No-one could believe it.

"Come away, Jack," said the Bride. "He's not worth it."

She led her beau away, one huge hand on his arm, and King of Skin whirled around, watching everyone watching him, and rage and frustrated malice filled his face. And while he stood there, undecided, Hadleigh Oblivion strolled out of the crowd to stand before him. He smiled easily at King of Skin, whose eyes narrowed as he drew himself up to his full height. The whole ballroom was utterly still, utterly silent, as everyone watched, fascinated, to see what would happen.

"When are people going to realise that your power is nothing more than skin-deep?" said Hadleigh.

King of Skin flinched as though he'd been hit. I didn't know what Hadleigh meant, but his opponent clearly did.

"When are you going to tell your brothers about the price you paid to be allowed entrance to the Deep School?" said King of Skin.

"King . . . of what, exactly?" said Hadleigh, still smiling. "And . . . of Skin? Who's skin, or skins? How deep does beauty go with you?"

And to everyone's surprise, even shock, King of Skin broke first. He seemed to shrink in on himself as though some vital part of his confidence had been broken. He turned his back on Hadleigh, marched over to the buffet table, and made a big show of being interested in the delicacies on offer. Hadleigh looked after him, clearly considering whether he should continue the confrontation; but he smiled briefly and wandered off in the opposite direction. Quite clearly the winner. Of something. Many hands came out, to clap him on the back or the shoulder, though no-one actually said anything. King of Skin might have picked the wrong victims for one day . . . but no-one doubted there would be other days and other victims.

A slow buzz of confused, mystified conversation rose among the gathered immortals as they tried to work out what had just happened. After all, no-one defied King of Skin. Everyone present was very interested in working out the details, if only so they could use it themselves, in the future.

I went back to working the crowd, but even after what had just occurred, no-one was prepared to talk to me. A scary reputation only works when you aren't surrounded by people even scarier than you. I passed by the Merlin Memorial Chair, standing on its own in a corner; much like Razor Eddie. The chair was a duplicate of Merlin's old throne, made from dark ironwood and wrapped in fresh mistletoe. The immortals always give it a place of honour at their Ball because most of them are convinced he's coming back. I was pretty sure he wasn't, but I've been wrong about that before, so I didn't say anything.

I sat down on the throne, casually crossing my legs, to make a point, and looked out over the crowd. I'd never seen so many immortals in one place, acting more or less politely. And then . . . a teenage boy caught my eye. A long, sulky streak of lukewarm water, wearing distressed jeans and battered knock-off sneakers, and a grubby T-shirt under a hooded grey jacket. He stood alone, scowling at everyone, his hands stuffed deep in his jacket pockets, the archetypal teenage hoodie. I couldn't make out what the hell he was doing at the Ball of Forever, among people who were probably ancient before his great-grandparents were born. I didn't recognise him as anyone special, or important. No-one had actually challenged his right to be there, yet, but he was getting a number of glances, none of them good. So I got up off Merlin's throne and went over to find out who he was. Because if there was going to be trouble at the Ball, I wanted to start it.

I walked right up to him and planted myself in front of him, so he couldn't ignore me. "Hello!" I said cheerfully. "Isn't the ambience awful? You probably know who I am; but who are you?"

He looked me straight in the eye, and like that he didn't look like a teenager any more. His eyes were old, very old, and his slow smile had generations of experience behind it.

"Call me Rogue," he said, and his voice was rich with contempt and soaked in pride. "I'm one of the few real immortals here, from the Family of Immortals."

Everyone around us stopped talking, to stare at Rogue. We'd all heard of the Family of Immortals; the half-legendary, very long-lived family supposed to run the world from behind the scenes, for a thousand years and more . . . but no-one had ever met one, before now. Everyone at the Ball was an immortal of one kind or another, but none of them had families. They were all unique, unable to pass on what made them immortal. But the Family of Immortals had bred slow, but true, for hundreds of years.

Everyone here had heard the story, that the Family of Immortals had very recently been wiped out, slaughtered, by the equally as legendary Drood family, those very secret agents for the Good. I wasn't the only one startled to discover that one of the few survivors of that massacre was this sulky-looking teenager.

"I did hear that the Family of Immortals is no more," I said carefully. "The Droods are, after all, usually very thorough when it comes to wiping out threats to Humanity."

"Some of us got away," said Rogue. "Even Droods can't be

everywhere at once. A few of us grabbed some useful items from the Family Vaults, then escaped through the emergency teleport gates. Now those of us left are spread across the world, hiding behind new identities and keeping our heads down. And I came here because the Nightside is one of the few places in the world where Droods are forbidden to set foot, by ancient compact. One of the few places in this world or off it where I thought I could be safe.

"Of course, I hadn't been here long before I heard that the Drood family had also been destroyed, repaid in their turn. The universe has a warped sense of humour."

"Are you sure about this?" I said, hearing a new buzz of conversation start up behind me. "I'd heard stories, but no details . . ."

"Oh yes, I'm sure," said Rogue, and again there was a very old, very adult unpleasantness in his voice. "I took a quick look, through a scrying glass. Drood Hall has been destroyed, blown up and burned down. They're all dead. Such a marvellous sight: half-melted golden figures strewn across the rubble, like broken dolls. I wish I could have seen it happen . . . but you can't have everything."

"They're all dead?" I said. "Every single Drood?"

"One got away," said Rogue. "Because he wasn't there when it happened. Only one left, out of all those self-righteous, murdering bullies. Eddie, the last Drood. I really must get around to killing him when I have a moment. There'd be no fun in doing it now, you understand, while he's still grieving. Better to wait till he's recovered and started rebuilding his life . . . and then there I'll be, to put an end to the last Drood."

"Who the hell could be powerful enough to wipe out the entire Drood family?" I said, because I felt someone should say it.

Rogue smiled and shrugged easily. "Haven't a clue. Don't know anyone who does. But I will find out, eventually, if only so I can shake him by the hand."

"Okay," I said. "So far, you're everything your family was supposed to be. Where are the rest of you?"

"Oh, here and there," said Rogue, deliberately vague. "All over the world, hidden in plain sight, making their plans for the return of the family."

He grinned suddenly, the first youthful thing I'd seen him do.

"And we will be back. You can count on it. We are the real immortals, and we have ruled this world for longer than anyone in this room has been alive." He looked disparagingly around him. "Call yourselves immortals? My family has walked this Earth for fifteen centuries!"

"So how old are you?" I said.

He scowled suddenly, sticking out his lower lip in a proper teenage pout. "I was cheated out of my inheritance by the Droods. I've had barely eighty years of playing with Humanity! I should have had centuries as part of the most important and powerful family there's ever been, to walk up and down in the world and change the course of human history as the whim took me. I should have had a life of wealth and influence, dispensing Life and Death, success or failure, at my pleasure! But I'd barely got started . . . It isn't fair!"

He broke off, startled, as I stuck my face right in close to his. I'd had enough. "That was then, Rogue, this is now. As far as I'm concerned, you're only another refugee, on the run in the Nightside. My Nightside. So behave yourself here. You try to play with the lives of people under my protection, and I'll drag you down to the Street of the Gods and feed you to something unknowable."

"Of course, Walker," said Rogue, his voice suddenly entirely reasonable. "I'm a guest in this wonderfully gaudy, tawdry city. I wouldn't dream of making any trouble."

"You're overdoing it," I said.

He smiled distantly, backed carefully away, not taking his

eyes off me, and moved on. A lot of people were quite keen to talk to him, to make themselves known to a living legend.

I stood alone, thinking. I'd seen and heard a great many interesting things at the Ball of Forever, but none of it to do with what I was here for. No-one had so much as mentioned an immortality serum; either to discuss its possibilities, its price, or whether it should be destroyed. And somebody would have by now. Perhaps its owner was holding court in some hidden back room, unknown to any but the most select immortals. But I hadn't seen anybody drifting away, or disappearing and reappearing . . . and it's really hard to hide secret doors and rooms from me. I was beginning to wonder if the serum actually existed. A drug that could make everyone immortal would set off all kinds of alarms. The universe itself resents the existence of immortals, which is why there are so few of them. They mess things up, disrupt the natural order . . . and the universe has been known to react when it feels there are too many, in quite brutal and efficient ways. Trust me; you don't want to know how.

I was still considering the implications of that when a great cry went up, followed by a number of screams. People were shouting, backing away, and pressing forward. I pushed my way through the crowd, following the screams, and there on the floor by the buffet, very quiet and very still and quite definitely dead, was King of Skin.

THREE

Time, See What's Become of Me

I moved in quickly to kneel down beside the motionless body, to check for signs of life; but there was no pulse at wrist or neck. The skin under my fingertips felt cold and clammy, and strangely slack . . . It moved too easily and too freely under my touch, as though it wasn't properly attached. I checked that King of Skin wasn't breathing, then stood up and looked coldly around me. The immortals stood huddled together in little groups, for comfort and support, staring at me silently with wide, fascinated eyes, like traumatised children. None of them were strangers to death, even sudden and violent death; but a murder, of one of their own kind, in a place where they should have been safe . . . that was something else. No personal weapons were allowed for anyone at the Ball of Forever, supposedly to prevent things like this.

I caught Hadleigh Oblivion's eye and beckoned him forward. He slipped easily through the crowd and moved forward to join me. He looked at the body, then looked at me expectantly.

"You're the Detective Inspectre," I said. "Do you want to take over the case?"

"You're Walker," said Hadleigh. "This is your jurisdiction."

"Then do me a favour. Go stand by the door, laugh in anyone's face if they try to leave. No-one gets in or out until I've finished my investigation."

"I'll stand guard," said Hadleigh. "It should be . . . amusing."

He shot me a quick smile and strode through the crowd to the far door, without always waiting for everyone to get out of his way. The immortals were finding their voices now, the clatter of questions and demands becoming louder by the moment. I was going to have to make a stand—be Walker, and take charge of the situation. Or none of them would talk to me. I raised my voice and addressed the gathered immortals, and they reluctantly quietened down and looked at me.

"All right!" I said. "Pay attention! King of Skin has been murdered. That makes this ball-room a crime scene, and you're all suspects. So none of you are going anywhere soon. Get used to it. Now, I'm going to need your help and cooperation to find the killer. He's still here, hiding; and the sooner I find him, the sooner you can all feel safe again. I'm going to have to ask all of you some questions. None of you should take it personally . . ."

"We don't answer to you!" snapped a man wrapped in a purple Roman toga, to which he might or might not have been entitled. "Jumped-up functionary! We are leaving; all of us! Before the murderer strikes again!"

"No you're not," I said, fixing him with my best hard glare. "No-one leaves until I've found the killer."

Jasmine de Loir stepped forward, cocking her oversized head back, the better to sneer down her aristocratic nose at me. She was dressed as Elizabeth I, complete with red hair and a very high forehead. "You can't keep us here! You're only a mortal. You have no authority over us!"

"He isn't even really a Walker!" said another voice from somewhere safe in the back of the crowd. "He doesn't have the Voice!"

"I'm John Taylor!" I said loudly, and the crowd fell quiet again. I smiled nastily around me, and a few actually shivered. "You've all heard of me. The man with a gift for finding things. Now be quiet, and behave yourselves, or . . ."

"Or what?" said Jasmine.

"Or I'll find your missing husband," I said.

Jasmine hesitated and was lost. She slipped back into the crowd. I looked unhurriedly around me, nodding to faces I recognised.

"You there, I could find where the missing funds from your company went. Or you. I could find where you buried the bodies. And as for you, sweetie, I could find your old nose and put it back where it used to be."

They were all very quiet now, looking at each for support and not finding it. They all had secrets, and none of them wanted me looking at them too closely. Of course, I was mostly bluffing, throwing out a few educated guesses based on the latest gossip; but they didn't know that. I turned my back on them all and knelt beside what was left of King of Skin.

He was lying face-down, half-curled into a ball. There was a single bloody wound in the small of his back and more blood soaking his tattered coat. He'd died quickly, bleeding out in seconds. With his glamour gone, without his usual spooky aspect, he looked much smaller and very ordinary. I turned the head carefully, so I could see the face. His real face, at last. Not particularly handsome, or ugly; nothing more than another face in the crowd. His clothes were old and comfortable, and not in the least stylish. Very worn, very lived-in. And then, as I looked at the face, it suddenly shrivelled up into a mass of wrinkles. As though all the years of his considerable age had caught up with him at once. The wrinkles kept appearing, criss-crossing each other, sinking deep into the flesh, until I was looking at the face of a man who'd lived at least a hundred years, and most of them hard ones. The few immortals who'd edged in for a closer look let out horrified gasps and hurriedly retreated. Time's catching up was an immortal's greatest fear.

I checked the rest of the body thoroughly. Just as old, but no more wounds. The stab wound in his back was wide and deep, and it had been made with something with a jagged edge. Not a knife, or any other bladed weapon. Whatever it was, it had irregular, serrated edges . . . I went through King of Skin's pockets and found nothing. Not even a wallet or a handkerchief or a ring of keys. The killer couldn't have had time to rob his victim; which suggested King of Skin had arrived with empty pockets. Perhaps because he relied on his glamour to get him what he needed. Didn't rule out robbery as a motive, though . . .

I stood up, straightened my aching back, took out my mobile phone and put in a call to the Nightside CSI. Alistair Hoob; nice guy, multiple personalities, a whole department in one head. Crowded, but efficient. He took a long time to answer his phone.

"Yes? What is it? (I'm busy!) Oh, hello, John. (You call him Walker now.) I know! (He knows, he knows.) Someday I swear I'm going to buy a spirit gun and shoot all you other voices in my head."

"I've got a murder at the Ball of Forever," I said loudly. "Nasty business, with nasty implications. How soon can you get here?"

"Ah well," he said. "That's the problem. I'm already working another murder, at the Old Haymarket Theatre. That's right on the other side of the city. (Bad business. Actors. Very touchy people.) (Who knew the old fellow had so much poison in him?) I'll get to you as soon as I can (blood), but it'll take me a while. (I want a pony.)"

"Do your best," I said. "Got a feeling I'm going to need all the help I can get on this one."

"Do you want me to alert the Authorities? (Who's been messing with my DNA kit again?)"

"Tell them," I said. "And then tell them to stay out of it. It happened on my watch, right in front of me, so it's my murder, my case. Tell them I'll be in touch when I've found the killer; and not before."

"Your funeral, Walker. (Ooh, can I come? I love funerals!) See you in a while."

I put my phone away and looked down at the body again. A stab wound in the back meant he never saw it coming. The assassin had struck from behind . . . but who would King of Skin turn his back on, in a place like this? He would have known better. So, had the murderer sneaked up on him? Without being noticed, in a crowded room? I glared at the watching immortals.

"Who found the body? Come on; somebody screamed."

A tall, gangly fellow dressed in Puritan blacks raised a hesitant hand. "I was startled, that's all. You don't expect something as vulgar as common murder in a select gathering like this. I saw him lying there, and the blood, and I let out . . . an involuntary noise, that's all."

"You saw the body lying on the floor?" I said. "You didn't see the actual murder?"

"No! No! Just the body. Isn't that enough?"

"Don't go anywhere," I said because you have to say things like that. And I went back to looking at King of Skin.

The three reporters finally fought their way through the tightly packed crowd and stared at the dead body with fascinated, eager eyes. Brilliant Chang seemed as calm and serene as ever. He'd seen his share of bodies before, in his time as an enforcer. Bettie Divine's face was flushed, and she was breathing heavily at the prospect of covering a real story. She didn't get many of those, working for the *Unnatural Inquirer*. And Charlotte ap Owen's face was an open book, for all her many nips and tucks. This story was her passport to the big time, and she was damned if anything was going to get in her way. She snarled for Dave the camera-man to get good coverage of the crime scene, and I let her. I could always commandeer the coverage later if I needed it. I nodded for Brilliant Chang to step forward. I could use a cool head to talk with.

"Am I not a suspect, then?" he said amiably.

"You're a combat sorcerer," I said. "If you'd wanted him dead, you could have killed him in a dozen ways and never left a mark."

"True."

"Why are you standing around, Taylor?" snapped Charlotte. "Why don't you use your gift and find the killer!"

"Because it doesn't work that way," I said. "I have to ask my gift a specific question to get a specific answer."

"A question occurs to me," said Chang. "King of Skin was not a well-liked man. He knew things, and wasn't loath to let people know it. So, which of his many secrets was a step too far? Which one was important enough to be worth killing over, to keep it secret?"

"Good point," I said. "But he's been hoarding secrets for years. He always knew how far he could push things . . . Wait. Hold everything. Something's happening to the body."

Chang and I both knelt beside King of Skin, while Charlotte shrieked for Dave to get a close-up. King of Skin's deeply wrinkled face was twitching, rising and falling, as though something was moving underneath it. And then, as we all watched, his entire face peeled off and dropped away, revealing another face beneath it. A second, completely different set of features. And then it aged, too, shrivelling into a mess of wrinkles, before dropping off to reveal yet another face beneath. The process went on and on, face giving way to face, skin to skin, aging and slipping away to reveal another, like those Russian dolls that nest inside one another. As each face fell to the floor, it rotted quickly, decaying and falling to dust in a matter of seconds. Skin under skin, face under face, until the process finally stopped, with a face I recognised. I'd seen it once before, on the future King of Skin, who'd been a member of my Enemies, in the terrible possible future I'd visited. And then that face aged, too, and fell in upon itself, a mask of far too many years.

"It's stopped," said Chang. "Do you suppose that last one was his real face? His original face?"

"I think so," I said. "Remember what Hadleigh said to him? He said King of Skin's power was skin deep. He knew about this."

"You think you can get Hadleigh to talk?" said Chang.

"Probably not," I said. "It's his job to know things like this, but he never talks about his job. Hell, I'm not even sure exactly what his job is. Stick to the point. Is this how King of Skin became immortal, by wrapping himself in other people's skin? Stealing their skins, their lives, their life energies, to bolster and prolong his own?"

"I have heard of such measures," said Chang. "But I never knew . . . His name! King of Skin! He was taunting us all with his name. His own greatest secret, right there in the open for everyone to see."

He carried on talking, but I wasn't listening. A thought had struck me. A very personal, very selfish thought. With King of Skin dead, the group of Enemies I'd seen in that potential future couldn't happen. Which meant . . . that future couldn't happen. Did this mean that, finally, the Nightside was safe from the terrible destiny I'd seen? The end of the world that I was supposed to bring about? Oh please God, let it be so. I could do with one less burden to carry. I realised Chang had stopped talking and was looking at me quizzically.

"Sorry," I said. "King of Skin's death has many repercussions, and I'm only starting to see some of them."

"I was wondering . . . what's become of the murder weapon?" said Brilliant Chang. "It isn't in the victim, or anywhere near the body."

I got down on my hands and knees and looked back and forth underneath the buffet tables. Dust bunnies, dropped food, and what looked very like rat turds, but nothing that could have killed King of Skin. I got back to my feet, brushing dust from my knees.

"The murderer must still have it on him," I said.

"Do you have the authority to search everyone here?" said Chang.

"I could try," I said. "But I think that might be a step too far for most of them. They'd see it as an affront to their dignity. Some of them would rather fight a duel or defy the Authorities than be physically man-handled in front of their peers. And anyway, the murderer's had plenty of time to dispose of the weapon by now. It could be anywhere."

"Anywhere inside this room," said Charlotte ap Owen, chipping in to remind us she was still there and not being left out of anything.

"Excuse me! Hello, excuse me! I've got an idea!"

I looked round to see Bettie Divine bouncing on her feet and waving her hand in the air excitedly, like a child in class who knows the answer.

"What have you got, Bettie?" I said patiently.

"We all saw the different faces King of Skin was hiding behind. If they are the faces of people he killed, to take their life energies for his own. well, mightn't they have friends or family who'd want to avenge their deaths? If someone had found out King of Skin was a serial killer, that could be your motive right there!"

"Good point," I said. "Well done. Unfortunately, all the faces have rotted away to dust. I'll see if the CSI guy can dig out some evidence from what's left, when he finally gets here; but I'm not hopeful."

"I got all the faces on camera," said Dave. "Close-ups of each, before they rotted."

"Good man," I said. "We can study the coverage later."

"For a price," Charlotte said quickly.

"Don't push it," I said. I looked round at the crowd of assembled immortals, and sighed deeply. No easy fixes here. I was going to have to do this the old-fashioned way, by asking a lot of people a lot of questions they didn't want to answer and trying to sort the truth from a pack of lies.

I said as much, and Bettie grinned. "You mean, establishing alibis! Where were you when the lights went out, and all that sort of thing! Can we watch?"

"No. Chang, you keep an eye on the body and make sure no-one interferes with it. Bettie, Charlotte, Dave . . . You can interview anyone you can get to talk to you but don't get in my way, or I'll have you arrested for something I may or may not make up on the spur of the moment."

"You're going to make a fine Walker," Chang said solemnly.

"Now you're just being nasty," I said.

I went off to have a private word with Razor Eddie. He was still standing in his corner, quietly observing the drama. He nodded briefly to me.

"You're right. I'm a suspect. No secret that King of Skin and I were enemies. But he was never powerful enough to take me on, or annoying enough to be worth my time."

"He knew something about you," I said. "What did he mean when he asked where you got your straight razor?"

Razor Eddie looked at me for a long moment with his cold

cold eyes. "He knew things. But not enough to be worth killing over. My secrets . . . remain my secrets. You know too much about me as it is, John."

"Then how can I be sure you didn't kill him?"

Razor Eddie smiled slowly, showing ruined grey teeth. "Because if I had killed him, I'd have been a lot more thorough. You'd have found pieces of him all over the room."

I had to nod. I'd seen the Punk God of the Straight Razor's handiwork before, and it was always messy. He didn't simply kill people; he made a statement.

"Don't go anywhere," I said. "Please."

"Ah well," said Razor Eddie. "As long as you're saying please . . ."

I left him, and went over to join Dead Boy, who was still hovering at the other end of the buffet table and still eating. He looked at me a little guiltily, put down the plate of mushroom vol-au-vents, and wiped his fingers on the front of his greatcoat.

"Sorry. Bad timing, I know. Should show respect for the dead, and all that. But I'm already dead, and I get no respect. I want to enjoy as much of this as I can before the pills wear off."

"Where does all the food . . . No, I don't want to know."

"Very wise," said Dead Boy. "Why aren't you questioning the butler? It's always the butler who did it, on occasions like these. You saw him when we came in, very shifty-looking fellow."

"It's not him," I said patiently. "On the grounds that he was on the other side of the door when the murder occurred."

"Ah," Dead Boy said wisely. "But that's how they do it! It's always the least likely suspect!"

"No," I said.

He sulked. "It was the butler last time. With the Griffin."

"We are changing the subject," I said firmly. "What did

King of Skin know about you? He said something about your girl-friend."

Dead Boy scowled. "It's not easy having a sex life when you're dead. Most of the kinds of girls who do come looking aren't the sort you want to encourage. So when I do find someone special, someone who can . . . reach me, she's going to be very special. So I'm not going to talk about her. But, if I had wanted King of Skin dead, which I didn't, because basically he was only an annoying little tit . . . If I had wanted to kill him, I've got more sense than to do it in front of a roomful of witnesses, and you. I'm dead, not stupid."

"True," I said.

Dead Boy looked at me thoughtfully, choosing his words carefully. "You do know it's almost certainly Hadleigh Oblivion who did it?"

"What?"

"It's common sense. Think about it. Who else here is powerful enough to kill King of Skin, in front of all these people, and not be noticed?"

"But . . . why would he want to?" I said. "He's the Detective Inspectre; why would he lower himself to common murder?"

"Because King of Skin knew something about him. And he knew more about King of Skin than any of us. Maybe . . . King finally stumbled on a secret he should have kept quiet about." Dead Boy looked over to the door, where Hadleigh was standing guard. "If it is him, can you arrest him?"

"Of course," I said. "I'm Walker. I can do anything. In fact, I'm pretty sure that's part of the job description."

"Well, yes," said Dead Boy. "Obviously. But this is Hadleigh Oblivion we're talking about. The Detective Inspectre, whatever the hell that is."

"I'll have a word with him," I said. "But for now, he's just another suspect."

"Along with me and Razor Eddie?" said Dead Boy.

"Very definitely including both of you," I said.

"Ah," said Dead Boy. "But what if it was both of us, working together? What would you do then?"

"Improvise," I said. "And phone Suzie Shooter for backup."

"The horror, the horror," said Dead Boy. And went back to his vol-au-vents.

I was heading for Mistress Mayhem when I was interrupted by Bettie Divine. She planted herself right in front of me, hands on hips, and glared at me.

"You don't really see me as a suspect, do you, sweetie? After all we nearly meant to each other? I'm not guilty of anything!"

"No?" I said. "What about the Schalcken affair?"

"A clear case of mistaken identity," Bettie said briskly.

"The Lovett pie-shop fiasco?"

"I was misinformed. Anyone can make a mistake."

"Big John . . ."

"They never proved anything! Look, the point I'm making is I'm not the kind to go around killing people! I'm not capable of it!"

"Anyone is capable of anything," I said. "Given sufficient motivation. Now, if you want to make yourself useful, try turning that devastating charm on the assembled immortals and see if you can get someone to admit to something. If anyone can, you can. I have work to do."

I passed her by and nodded politely to Mistress Mayhem. She was hugging herself tightly, as though against some chill, and she looked a lot younger than she had before. Almost like a teenager playing dress-up at her first adult party. She fixed me with a defiant gaze.

"I didn't kill him. Didn't even know the man. I never even met him before tonight."

"He still knew things about you," I said. "He knew you touched up your skin with dye to maintain that dreaded

Kali connection. And he knew about the baby you would have had."

She was shaking her head all through this, but the truth showed in her face. When I said the word *baby*, all the strength seemed to go right out of her. When she finally spoke, her voice was little more than a whisper.

"I never told anyone. How did he know? I was never even going to tell Jimmy. It would have upset him too much. But I am a descendent of Kali! I am! I could have killed that slimy bastard with a touch! If I'd wanted. Withered him like a flower, like Hadleigh did . . . They're saying someone stuck a knife in him. Is that right?"

"He was stabbed in the back," I said carefully.

"Well, I haven't got a knife! Look at me! Where would I hide one in this outfit?"

She had a point.

"I'm talking to everyone," I said. "Don't take it personally. Did you come here with anyone?"

"No."

"Then go talk with Dead Boy. He's appalling company, and his conversation rarely ventures far from the inappropriate, but he's got a good heart. He'll look after you and make sure no-one bothers you."

I steered her in Dead Boy's direction, then stopped abruptly as a Neanderthal man came rolling through the crowd towards me. He was barely five feet tall, hunched right over but powerfully built. His heavy face was all bone and gristle, with massive lowering eye-brow ridges and hardly any chin. His knees splayed out, and his knuckles barely cleared the floor. He was wearing a shining white seventies disco outfit, complete with a big gold medallion on a chain hanging over his extremely hairy chest. He nodded amiably to me.

"Greetings, Walker. I am Tomias Squarefoot."

"I know," I said. "We met once before. Long ago."

He shrugged calmly. "It is entirely possible. I am the oldest of the immortals. I have met pretty much everyone, at one time or another; but my memory is not what it was. I do not claim to speak for the immortals, but as the oldest here, I think I can represent them. And I think I can speak for all of us when I say it is clear that there is an obvious suspect."

"Is there really?" I said. "News to me. Who did you have in mind?

"The young man who calls himself Rogue, of course," said Squarefoot. "He appears out of nowhere, with no invitation, claiming to be part of the notorious Family of Immortals. A group famed for their duplicity, treachery, and general backstabbing. Either he isn't who he says he is, in which case what is he doing here, in this company? Or he is who he says he is, in which case, what is he doing here? What secret purpose has brought him to a Ball no other member of his family has ever graced with their presence? On top of that, do I really need to point out that we never had a death here, at any of our meetings, until he showed up?"

I turned to look thoughtfully at Rogue, standing on his own, some way off. He had a drink in his hand and looked far-away, lost in his own thoughts.

"All right," I said to the Neanderthal. "You have a point. I'll have a word. But only because you helped save my life, that time."

Squarefoot shrugged his massive shoulders. "It is possible. I meet so many people; you must forgive me if you don't stand out. All you mortals look the same to me."

I nodded and moved away. He was right. It had been almost two thousand years since he helped save me from the Wild Hunt of the old god Herne. But I hadn't forgotten.

Rogue saw me coming and took a long drink from his champagne flute before facing me, apparently completely unconcerned. I slapped the glass out of his hand, grabbed him, and turned him around and slammed him up against the wall. He hit hard enough to knock the breath out of him, but he didn't complain or struggle. He simply stood there, entirely relaxed, as I frisked him from top to bottom, making a thorough job of it. I found all kinds of interesting objects in his pockets, the accumulated flotsam and jetsam of a very long life, but nothing that could have been used as a weapon. I stepped back, and he turned around, adjusting his clothing here and there, with neat fussy movements that were completely at odds with his teenage appearance.

"Typical mortal manners," he murmured. "No respect for your elders. Be careful, young Walker, be very careful, lest I decide to teach you some manners. I could break and cripple you in a dozen awful ways, and there would be nothing you could do to stop me."

"Oh, you'd be surprised what John Taylor can do," said Dead Boy, moving in on one side of me, while Razor Eddie slipped into position on the other. Dead Boy sneered at Rogue. "Walker can look after himself. But he doesn't have to; not while we're around. You behave yourself, young immortal, or I will knock you down and stamp on your head, and Razor Eddie here will make origami out of your insides."

Rogue looked from Dead Boy to Razor Eddie, then back to me. He smiled charmingly.

"It's always good to have friends you can depend on. Rest assured I will do everything in my power to cooperate with the Walker's investigation."

"Thanks for the support, guys," I said. "But I think he might speak more freely without an audience."

Dead Boy and Razor Eddie drifted away, talking quietly together. I would have given a lot to hear what those two very different souls might have in common, but I had a job to do.

"I didn't know King of Skin, except by reputation," said Rogue. "So what possible reason could I have for killing him?"

"I was hoping you might tell me," I said. "Why did you come here tonight, for the first time?"

"Every time is someone's first time," said Rogue. "My family has been destroyed. Murdered. I was looking for something new to belong to. One must make a family where one can, these days. But it is very hard to make new friends when nobody trusts you."

"Lot of that going around," I said. "Don't go anywhere; I may have more questions."

Rogue smiled sweetly. "I come and go as I please."

I gave him a hard look. "Even if you could get past Hadleigh at the door, which you can't, there's nowhere you can go that I couldn't find you."

"Ah yes," murmured Rogue. "Your famous gift. I have a gift too, courtesy of my family."

And right before my eyes, the flesh shifted suddenly on his face, slipping back and forth, until my own face looked back at me, complete in every detail.

"I can be anyone," said Rogue, with my lips but his voice. A really very disturbing effect.

"Ah yes," I said, carefully casual. "Flesh-dancing. I had heard the stories . . . that everyone in your family could change their face or body, to hide in plain sight. That's what made you all such marvellous traitors and back-stabbers."

"Well, quite," said Rogue, changing back to his own face.

I gave him my best sneer and left him to it. Something about Rogue's supercilious manners and quiet contempt got on my nerves, but not enough for me to peg him as a major suspect. He was right; he had no motive. Never been here before, never even met King of Skin, wasn't even here long enough to be insulted by him. But there were no murders until he turned up. Something to think about.

I found the Bride and Springheel Jack arguing quietly

but fiercely with Hadleigh Oblivion. They wanted to leave, and he was having none of it. They all looked round as I approached. Springheel Jack took a step towards me, but the Bride stopped him immediately with a large hand on his arm.

"Sorry," I said. "But the Detective Inspectre is following my orders. Nobody leaves till we've sorted this out. Do you have somewhere you need to be?"

"An unseen murderer, with an unknown weapon, hiding among the immortals?" said Jack. "I want the Bride out of here. It's not safe."

"Your concern is touching, Jack, but if you don't cut this condescending crap right now, I will slap you a good one," said the Bride. "I am old enough to be your great-grandmother, and I know how to look after myself."

"King of Skin almost certainly felt the same," said Springheel Jack. He looked around the crowded ball-room. "Something isn't right here. I can feel it. Like a premonition . . . Someone else is going to die here. There's a wolf hiding among the sheep, and oh his teeth are sharp . . ."

He seemed almost to be in a trance. I looked at the Bride.

"Does he have the Sight?"

"I don't know," said the Bride. "Being Springheel Jack makes him more aware of the horrors of the world, but the state doesn't exactly come with a user's manual. If he says someone's going to die, I'd put money on it . . . Jack. Jack!"

He looked at her blankly for a moment, then shuddered suddenly, as though someone had tripped over his grave.

"We need to get out of here, lover. Something bad is coming."

"Then help me find the killer," I said. "You can start by answering some questions."

"Go ahead," said the Bride.

"King of Skin spoke with you," I said to Springheel Jack. "He said he knew what you really are. He also said he couldn't be harmed by mortal weapons, and you said your razors were more than mortal."

"That's right," said Springheel Jack. "They are. But you don't stab someone with a cut-throat razor. I've seen the wound in his back; you're looking for a large jagged-edged weapon. Doesn't sound like a straight razor, does it?"

"I would quite certainly have smacked him round the head a few times for what he said," said the Bride. "But he wasn't worth it. King of Skin is part of the entertainment at these dos. We all turn up to see what he'll say about other people. We expect him to have a go at us. It's part of the game. You have to be able to take some, to hear some. Look, Jack and I both vouch for each other. We were together, when we heard King of Skin had been murdered. Haven't left each other's side since we got here. So we are each other's alibi."

"Yes," I said. "But as a wise woman once said, 'You would say that, wouldn't you?' "

"I'm cold," said Springheel Jack. "I'm so cold . . . It's close, and it's getting closer."

His eyes had gone fey again. The Bride looked at him worriedly.

"Come with me, dear, and I'll find you a nice large brandy to warm you up."

She led him away, into the crowd. I looked at Hadleigh.

"Could you really have kept them in if they'd wanted out?" I said.

"Oh, I think so," said Hadleigh. "Is it my turn now? I can't vouch for my whereabouts as I have no idea where I was when King of Skin was murdered. I have no alibi. But you must know; I wouldn't need a weapon to kill someone. Or I could have made him disappear. Sent him somewhere awful, to suffer for his many sins, and no-one would ever have known a thing about it."

"Do you do that a lot?" I said, somewhat creeped out.

"When necessary," said Hadleigh Oblivion.

"You're really not helping your case," I said. "What better way to hide your intent than a deliberately clumsy attack?"

"I have no weapons on me," Hadleigh said easily. "I don't feel the need for such things. Search me if you like. You won't find anything. I guarantee it."

But I was still thinking about the rose he had withered by breathing it in. And how King of Skin's faces had withered away . . .

"You knew about King of Skin's other skins," I said. "No-one else did. And he said he knew the price you paid, to gain access to the Deep School. What kind of price was that? What did you do, that you couldn't tell your brothers? Did King of Skin know something that you couldn't afford any-one else to know?"

"He knew nothing," said Hadleigh. "The only people who know anything about the Deep School are those who've been there. And we never talk."

I was getting ready to pursue the point when another great cry went up. A man, crying out in shock and horror. The immortals were already falling back, scattering like panicked birds, from something that had happened on the other side of the room. I forced my way through them, to find Springheel Jack kneeling by the still-and-lifeless body of the Bride. He was holding her in his arms, rocking her back and forth like a sleeping child, his face gaunt with horror and loss. The Bride's eyes were wide open and staring. She looked like a broken doll. I could see a jagged wound in her side, soaked with blood. Jack looked at me.

"Why didn't you listen to me? Why didn't you let us go? None of this would have happened if you'd let us go!"

I looked quickly around. No-one had a knife or any other weapon in hand, and no-one looked particularly guilty. Most of them looked shocked, unable to believe that a second mur-der of an immortal could have happened in a place where they should have felt safe. I could see the same thought start

to appear in several faces—the need to get out of this dangerous place.

"Everyone please move to the back of the ballroom!" I said
loudly. "Back up to the door. Hadleigh is there; the Detective Inspectre. He'll keep you safe. And, no, it couldn't have
been him because I was talking with him when the murder
happened. Now move back, keep an eye on whom you're with,
and leave me to get on with the investigation. Shut up and
move!"

They moved. I turned my back on them, to concentrate
on Springheel Jack and the Bride. He was crying now, great
racking sobs that shook his whole body. The Bride looked
large and ungainly, the way she never had in life, her long
body sprawled across the floor. I knelt beside her and checked
her neck and wrist for a pulse, but there was nothing. I never
thought there would be. I was going through the motions
while my mind worked frantically. I looked at Springheel
Jack.

"I'm sorry. She's gone."

"No," he said, forcing the words out between sobs. "She
can't be gone. She was born from the dead, a triumph of the
Baron's skill. He put her together using the finest parts of a
hundred women, that she should have all their strength. She
was born of the lightning . . ."

He stopped abruptly, and his tears stopped, and his head
came up as a great inspiration filled his face. He pushed the
Bride's body away from him and scrambled to his feet. The
body slammed back against the floor, and he didn't even
notice in his excitement.

"Born of the lightning! Of course! You can't kill the Bride
of Frankenstein just by stabbing her! He made her better
than that!"

He grabbed an ornamental lamp from the buffet table, and
ripped the lamp free from its cable. Sparks sputtered from

the ragged metal ends. Springheel Jack laughed breathlessly, grabbed the cable, and sank down beside the body of his Bride. He pressed the bare wires against her wounded side, and her whole body convulsed. He hit her with the electricity again, and the Bride sat bolt upright, drawing in a great ragged breath of air. Springheel Jack threw the sparking cable aside and held her in his arms, burying his face in her neck. She patted him absently with one oversized hand and looked dazedly around her.

"What the hell happened? And why does my side hurt?"

She looked down at the bloody wound in her side and swore briefly. She checked it out carefully with her fingertips, then sniffed loudly.

"Nasty business. But nothing that won't heal itself. It's already stopped bleeding . . . Jack. Jack, sweetie, it's all right! I'm all right. I'm fine."

They helped each other to their feet. Springheel Jack got hold of himself with an effort but wouldn't let go of her.

"All right," I said. "What happened here?"

Springheel Jack glared at me. "Someone tried to kill her! I warned you! I told you this was coming, but you wouldn't listen!"

"Hush, dear," the Bride said firmly. "No-one ever listens to prophecy; it's the only reason the universe allows it." She looked down at her side. "Someone stabbed me from behind. I never saw anyone. I'd seen that awful Lord Orlando heading towards me, so I moved off the other way. Next thing I know, there's a great stabbing pain in my side, then I'm riding the lightning and I'm back again! Well done, Jack. Quick thinking. Usually I wake up in a morgue somewhere, giving some poor doctor a heart attack." She smiled briefly. "Much as I hate to admit it, the Baron did good work. He made his creations to last."

"You saw the Lord Orlando?" I said.

"Wasn't him," Mistress Mayhem said immediately. "He was right here, boring me rigid, when we both heard the scream."

"Well really," said the Lord Orlando.

Springheel Jack took the Bride away to one side for some mutual support and comfort. The immortals stuck together, on the far side of the room, looking at me with wide, frightened eyes. Expecting me to put everything right. Charlotte ap Owen hauled Dave the camera-man over to interview the Bride and Springheel Jack on their ordeal. Jack gave them one look, and they both ran for their lives. I spotted Bettie Divine over by the doorway, doing her best to vamp Hadleigh Oblivion, presumably to find out what he and I had been talking about. Brilliant Chang was hovering nearby, so I summoned him over with a jerk of the head.

"Any nearer spotting the killer?" he said bluntly.

"No," I said. "I've questioned the most obvious suspects and got nowhere. They all seemed plausible enough . . . Any number of people had any number of motives for killing King of Skin, but I don't have a weapon, and I can't put any-one at the scene of the crime at the right time. No-one here saw anything. How is that possible?"

"Don't look at me," said Chang. "I'm a crime reporter, not Agatha Christie. You're the detective."

"I was never a detective! I was a private investigator, and I relied on my gift far more than most people ever realised. I always said I wouldn't know a clue if I fell over one, and it's starting to look like I was right."

"Giving up?" said Chang.

"No. This is my last case as a private investigator, and I'm damned if I'm going to let it beat me. I need to think . . . Okay, wait a minute. Chang, have you heard anything about an immortality serum? Possibly for sale?"

"No," said Chang. "Hasn't even been a whisper, and it would be hard to keep news of something like that quiet."

I nodded slowly. "Okay. Thanks. Go and rescue Hadleigh from Bettie, would you? I don't want him distracted, in case someone tries to make a break for it."

He laughed and wandered away on his mission of mercy. And I moved off among the packed immortals, hitting them all with the same questions, over and over again. Where were they when the murders happened? Who were they with? What did they see? Most had alibis, or said they did, and no-one had seen anything. Most of them were too shocked and upset even to think of giving me attitude, but a few still refused to talk to me, on principle. I let them get away with it. The more I thought about the killings, the more convinced I became that I was missing something.

I even questioned the waitresses in their French maid outfits, huddled together for security behind the buffet tables. But all they'd had eyes for was Dead Boy making a pig of himself. None of them had seen anyone near King of Skin. None of them had wanted to get anywhere near him. Which was understandable. One of them said she thought she'd seen the Lord Orlando somewhere at the buffet, not far from King of Skin, but couldn't be sure when. That was enough to point me back in his direction. The Bride had said she'd seen him approaching her not long before she was attacked.

I did my best to question the Lord Orlando, and he did his best not to burst into tears at the very indignity of it all. Mistress Mayhem and another immortal called Polly Pariah insisted that he'd been boring their arses off right when Springheel Jack screamed, some distance away. I couldn't see why either of them should lie.

I ended up back at the buffet table, chewing on a barely warm pig in a blanket, and thinking hard. If I had to point a finger at anyone, it would be Rogue, but why would he want to kill King of Skin? He didn't know him; and given that this was the first time Rogue had ever been to the Ball of Forever, the odds were he didn't know anyone. He came to make friends, or so he said. Though his family didn't exactly have a good track record in that regard.

All right. Since I wasn't getting anywhere with the suspects, maybe I could do better with the murder weapon. I couldn't use my gift to find it without discovering something unique about it, something my gift could lock on to . . . But I did have something! With this second attack on the Bride, the weapon was the only thing common to both attacks, which meant I could find it! I raised my gift and concentrated, and immediately my head snapped round, to look down the length of the buffet table. I strode down it, following the tug of my instincts, until my gift brought me to a large open jug of dark red wine. The one I'd suspected was full of blood. It stood there, in the middle of a great many other bottles and jugs and flasks donated by various immortals, apparently innocent, looking no different than any of the others; but my gift was telling me otherwise. I leaned over the jug and studied its contents carefully. There was a definite dark shadow, deep in the dark red contents. I reached in, with a thumb and forefinger, gripped on to something hard and unyielding, and pulled it out.

I held it up before me. It took me a moment to realise what it was—a jagged-edged piece of mirror glass, dripping red wine. Not a knife after all, then, though the edges were certainly sharp enough to do real damage. In fact, the whole shard was so sharp everywhere, I was hard put to see how you could hold on to the thing without lacerating your own hand. And no-one in the room had shown any damaged hands . . . I jumped a little as I realised Bettie Divine was standing beside me, smiling brightly.

"I sensed you using your gift all the way across the room, so I came over to see what was happening. What is happening? What have you found?"

"You sensed . . ."

"Half demon, darling, remember? These horns aren't just for show. Now be a dear and tell me what that is you're holding! Is it important?"

"I'm pretty sure it's the murder weapon," I said.

Bettie squealed excitedly. "Wonderful! I knew you'd solve the case, sweetie! Never doubted you for a moment! Where was it?"

"In that jug of wine. That's why both murders took place next to the buffet table. He smuggled the shard in easily enough, then dropped it surreptitiously into the jug . . . where it waited till he had a need for it. He took it out, stabbed his victim, then dropped it back in again. The wine would even wash the blood away though I think I can see traces of dried blood, trapped in the jagged edges . . ."

Bettie leaned in as close as she could get without actually touching the mirror shard with her nose. "Definitely part of a mirror, darling. But why make a weapon out of it? And what does it have to do with the way King of Skin . . . shrivelled up?"

"Good question," I said. I held the shard up close to my face, so I could see my reflection in it. There was something . . . odd, something off, about the image; but I couldn't put my finger on it.

"There's magic hovering all about that piece of mirror," said Bettie. "Old, bad magic. I can See it, but . . . You've got better Sight than me, sweetie. What do you See?"

I concentrated, raising my gift again, using it to study the reality of the thing before me, opening up my inner eye, my private eye, to See the world as it really is. And then I almost dropped the shard as I realised what it was I was holding.

"What?" Bettie said excitedly. "What did you See?"

"Temporal energies," I said. "This mirror shard is soaked in Time, in Time magic. I can actually see inverted tachyons, shooting up and down the broken edges."

Bettie gave me a hard look, only slightly spoiled by her pouting mouth. "Yes, very nice, darling, very dramatic. But what does that mean?"

"It means, I know what mirror this came from," I said, pulling a handkerchief from my pocket and carefully wrapping up the vicious-edged shard before tucking it very carefully into my coat pocket. "This is a sliver of glass from the infamous Mirror of Dorian Gray. You must have heard of it. It was up for sale at an auction-house here in the Nightside, not so long ago. Think of it: the mirror that reflected a man soaked in temporal magic. If a crazy magical man stares into you long enough, you become crazy and magical, too. This mirror soaked up Time, leaching the life from anyone who looked into it, and stored it. The perfect murder weapon because who'd ever suspect a mirror. The last I heard, the Mirror of Dorian Gray belonged to the Family of Immortals . . ."

We both turned to look at Rogue, standing on his own, glaring at anyone who even glanced in his direction.

"He said . . . he and his fellow surviving immortals grabbed a few things of value from the Family Vaults, before they escaped," I said slowly. "I suppose in the haste of getting away from the Droods, they must have dropped the mirror. All Rogue got away with, was a single shard. Still powerful enough to steal someone's years if you thrust it right into them."

"A weapon that eats Time," said Bettie. "The perfect weapon for killing immortals, darling, if you wanted to steal all their years and keep them for yourself. But why would Rogue need more years? He's already immortal!"

"Good question," I said. "I must be sure to ask him."

"Are you sure it's him?" said Bettie anxiously. "To accuse an immortal, among a gathering of his fellow immortals, you need to be really *sure*."

"Good point," I said. "But now I've got the weapon, I can use it to focus my gift and get it to show me exactly what happened. Make sure no-one interrupts me."

"You got it, sweetie."

I concentrated hard, and my gift manifested again. My head ached, resenting the strain. Time fled backwards before me, right back to the moment of the murder. I could See King of Skin standing before me, a thin and wispy artefact of Time Past, pawing through the snacks with grubby fingers and a disdainful sneer. I Saw the Lord Orlando approach King of Skin, with his usual simpering smile. King of Skin growled at him and deliberately turned his back on Orlando. And that was when the Lord Orlando's face slipped and changed as he became the Rogue Immortal. He took the mirror shard out of the wine jug and stabbed King of Skin in the back. King tried to cry out and couldn't. I could See the temporal energies swirling and spiralling around him as the shard sucked his future right out of him—all the years, all the life he would have had. And then King of Skin collapsed, measuring his length on the floor. Rogue tugged the weapon out of his back, flicked a few drops of blood away, and slipped the shard neatly back into the wine jug. The whole thing had only taken a few moments. Rogue became Orlando again and wandered off.

And no-one noticed his movements because no-one cared where he went. He was the only person the immortals would turn their backs on because no-one ever wanted to talk to him.

I followed him until he turned back into Rogue, unnoticed in the crush of bodies. His face was calm and unconcerned, untouched by what he'd done. No trace of anger or regret. Only the hint of someone who'd performed a distasteful but necessary task—a small smile, typical of a teenager who has got away with something. I shut down my gift and looked at the expectant Bettie Divine, all but dancing with impatience before me.

"Well?" she said squeakily. "Well?"

"Got him," I said. "Rogue killed King of Skin."

"And the Bride?"

"I didn't hang around long enough to See it; but since they were both killed with the same weapon, it had to be him again."

Bettie frowned. "Then why didn't the mirror shard shrivel her up the way it did King of Skin?"

I thought about it. "Because . . . the Bride was made of dead parts, then brought to life. She only has a human lifetime; but when she dies, she can be brought back again, for another life. Thanks to the Baron's handiwork, she's basically . . . rechargeable. Technically immortal, but only one life at a time."

"Gosh, you are clever, John darling," said Bettie.

"Flattery . . . will get you an exclusive interview. Later. For now, do me a favour and round up Dead Boy and Razor Eddie. Have them stand by in case it all goes pear-shaped when I accuse Rogue . . ."

"On it, sweetie."

She blew me a quick kiss and disappeared into the crowd. I moved over to join Rogue, taking my time. I didn't want to spook him. Chases are so undignified. I was almost upon him when he turned suddenly and smiled coldly at me.

"So," he said, "you worked it out. You really are as good as some people say you are."

"Only some ?" I said. "I must be slipping. So you admit to the murders?"

"Admit to them? I'm proud of them!" Rogue laughed softly. "I am of the Family of Immortals, the only true immortal here!"

His voice rose loudly across a growing silence as everyone in the ballroom realised what was happening and shushed each other. By the time he'd stopped speaking, everyone was looking at us, drinking in every word. I kept my gaze fixed on Rogue. I couldn't afford to give him the slightest advantage.

"I killed King of Skin and loved it," said Rogue. "I gloried in it! Spreading a little fear and horror in the night . . . is what my family have always done best. I killed the Bride, too; but unfortunately, she got over it. I'll have to try harder next time." He smiled around him, and hardened immortals actually flinched back from him. "You call yourselves immortals; you're nothing but food to me."

"I know how you did it," I said. "I even have the weapon, which explains what happened to King of Skin's body. Now tell me why you did it. Come on; you know you want to."

"King of Skin was an offspring of my family," said Rogue, apparently entirely at his ease. "A half-caste. Only potentially immortal. He found a way to extend his life by killing people and wrapping himself in their skins, their lives. Harvesting their stolen years. He's been at it for well over a century, to my certain knowledge. You saw all those skins . . . And you had no idea what he really was, did you? No idea at all that you had a serial killer as part of your precious Authorities."

"You knew about him; but you never did anything about him, till now," I said. "Why now?"

"I didn't care what he did. He only killed mortals; and that's what they're for. I only killed him now because I had a use for him. You should be grateful, Walker. I've done you a positive favour. He would have had to come after you eventually, you and all the other Authorities. He couldn't risk your finding out the truth about him. And then . . . he would have been the Authorities and ruled the Nightside. The wolf in charge of the sheep."

"You still haven't said why you killed him."

"I killed him first because he was so full of life. And I wanted it."

"And the Bride?" I said.

Rogue sniffed. "I shouldn't have, but I never could resist

temptation. She wasn't really suitable for what I was after, but . . . she led the Spawn of Frankenstein when they fought alongside the Droods to invade my family estate! The Spawn live there now, in what used to be my home! She wasn't on my list; but when I saw her standing there, I couldn't hold back. She deserved to die for what she did to my family."

"You weren't going to stop with King of Skin," I said. "He was only the first . . . You said you had a list?"

"Of course," said Rogue. "I only came here to make my mark, with these so-called immortals. I came here to identify them all, so I could track them down afterwards and steal their lives. It's not like they were doing anything important with them. I would have used the mirror shard to take their future years, store them, then use them to create a new Family of Immortals! We don't breed true, you see. Never have; or the world would be hip-deep in immortals by now. We breed slow and rarely, and the offspring are only ever long-lived. But with so many stolen years at my disposal, what a family I could have made! We would have moved into all the important places and positions, here in the Nightside, and taken control. And then we would have used the Nightside as a base, from which to re-establish the family's power in the world! Become what we once were, what we were meant to be! Then, let all the peoples of the world tremble and despair!"

"You had it all thought out," I said.

He looked at me sharply, annoyed at having his ranting interrupted. "Thought out in every detail. When you're an immortal, you get used to planning for the long term. King of Skin was just the beginning. I had a reign of terror planned for all the Nightside immortals, and it isn't over yet. But I hadn't expected Hadleigh Oblivion to be here, guarding the door, preventing me from making my escape. He would have seen though any face I took on. He shouldn't have been here. You shouldn't have been here. What were you doing here, tonight of all nights? Well . . . It doesn't matter. I will do what I will do, and none of you can stop me."

He laughed in my face, then turned and plunged into the watching crowd. They shrank back with loud cries of alarm, but he was already in among them, his face changing as he flesh-danced. In the space of a moment, he was someone else, and in all the confusion no-one was able to say who he'd changed into. There was a general rush to the door, to get out of the ballroom. Hadleigh stood his ground, and raised one hand. Bolts of lightning stabbed down out of nowhere, striking again and again inside the ballroom, making a barrier between him and everyone else. The light was blinding, and the air stank of ozone. The rush to the door was over as soon as it had begun. Everyone stood very still, looking nervously around them, trying to spot the danger in their midst; but wherever they looked, only familiar faces looked back. Razor Eddie and Dead Boy forced their way through the crowd to join me. I looked at them both carefully.

"Oh come on," said Dead Boy. "Who'd look like me if they didn't have to?"

"Tell me something only you could know," I said.

"All right," said Dead Boy. "You're a dick."

We both laughed. Razor Eddie looked at me strangely.

"We both loved the X-Men movies," I explained.

Razor Eddie nodded and produced his pearl-handled straight razor. The steel blade shone supernaturally bright, and everyone felt a sudden strong desire to be somewhere else. I nodded, and Eddie put his razor away again. Some things you can't fake. We all looked out over the watching crowd.

"How do you want to do this?" Dead Boy said quietly.

"I use my gift," I said, just as quietly. "He can't hide from that. I'll pick him out, and then you two help me slam him to the floor and stamp on his head until we're sure he can't concentrate enough to shape-change again."

"Sounds like a plan to me," said Razor Eddie.

I raised my gift again. It was getting to be hard work now; the more I used my gift, the more it took out of me. I felt a quick runnel of blood spurt out of one nostril, and a sharp fierce pain filled my forehead. I'd pay for this later; but right now there was work to be done. I forced my way past the pain and concentrated; and immediately a single figure stood out in the crowd. I plunged forward, with Dead Boy and Razor Eddie right behind me, and the crowd scattered before us like startled pigeons. I ignored all the cries of shock and protest, fixed on the figure before me. He didn't try to run. He stood still and regarded me with a single raised eyebrow.

"And what do you think you're doing?" said Hadleigh Oblivion.

"Nice try," I said. "But Hadleigh's still at the door, where I told him to be."

"I was standing at the door," said Hadleigh, "until Bettie Divine came over and said you needed help, so I came forward. Whoever's at the door now, that isn't me."

I didn't even look at the door. "Nice try, Rogue," I said. "But Hadleigh wouldn't leave his position unless I personally put someone there to relieve him. My gift found you here. And my gift is never wrong."

Hadleigh's face slumped suddenly, and his shape changed in a moment. Where Hadleigh had been standing there was now an eight-foot-tall centipede, black as night with a nightmare head, striking out with dozens of clawed legs. It reared up so that its flat head banged against the ceiling, its complex mouth parts clacking loudly. The immortals climbed all over each other, trying to get away. Dead Boy waded in, slamming powerful punches into its heaving thorax, while Razor Eddie darted and whirled around it, severing one clawed leg after another with his straight razor.

The centipede disappeared, replaced by a huge, muscular

man I didn't recognise. A great brute of a man, with a flat, characterless face as though all the detail of his creation had gone into his massive muscles. He lashed out at Dead Boy, and the unstoppable blow picked Dead Boy up and set him flying a dozen feet away. He crashed to the floor hard and didn't move. He couldn't feel pain, but he could still take damage. Razor Eddie cut at the brute again and again, moving so fast now he was only a blur; but no matter how deep his blades cut into the brute's flesh, it healed again immediately. (That was how he could handle the mirror shard without obviously damaging his hand, I thought.) Dead Boy lurched to his feet again and charged the brute, slamming into it from behind. The brute staggered, but didn't go down. Dead Boy hit him hard, while Razor Eddie cut at the brute's throat again and again, trying to keep the wound open long enough to do some damage.

I stood back and watched. I can fight if I have to, but it's never been what I do best. I wiped blood from my face with the back of my hand, and raised my gift one last time. My head was throbbing sickly now, but I have always been in control of my gift and never the other way round. I concentrated, reaching out, and found the switch inside Rogue's head, the one he used every time he decided to make a change. And then it was the easiest thing in the world for me to push the switch all the way back. The brute disappeared, replaced by a very surprised-looking Rogue. He opened his mouth to say something, and I stepped forward and kneed him briskly in the nuts. Rogue folded over, and Dead Boy and Razor Eddie beat him to the ground with great thoroughness. Rogue raised his head and looked up at Razor Eddie with my face as though that might slow him down. Eddie kicked him in my face, and by the time Rogue crashed unconscious to the floor, he looked like himself again.

The watching immortals applauded loudly. Razor Eddie

and Dead Boy checked to make sure that Rogue wasn't faking by kicking him a few times somewhere painful, then looked at me.

"What will you do with him now?" said Dead Boy.

"He goes to Shadow Deep," I said. "Deep down under the Nightside, in the endless dark, nailed into his cell until he dies there. He can change shape all he wants in his cell; it'll be company for him." I looked at Eddie. "At the end there, when he looked like me, do you suppose that's the fight between us that your friend saw?"

"Oh no," said Eddie. "That's still to come."

"You can't send him to Shadow Deep," said Hadleigh Oblivion.

We all looked round sharply. None of us had heard him arrive, but then no-one ever does.

"Why not?" I said politely.

"Because he's a flesh-dancer," said Hadleigh. "He has control over every part of his body. He could probably ooze out of his cell through the cracks around the door. He's far too dangerous to be allowed to run loose in the Nightside."

He leaned over the unconscious immortal, grabbed his shirt front, and pulled Rogue's face close to his own. Hadleigh inhaled deeply, and all the colour went out of Rogue's face. Hadleigh continued to inhale, and the immortal's face cracked and fell apart; and then every part of him collapsed into dust. Hadleigh straightened up, brushing dust from his hands. Several of the watching immortals were noisily sick. Dead Boy whooped loudly.

"You have got to teach me how to do that!"

Razor Eddie sighed. "Can't take him anywhere."

And that was my last case as a private investigator. Not a bad one to go out on. I caught the murderer, stopped a plan to take over the Nightside, and made the front pages of the *Night*

Times and the *Unnatural Inquirer.* I even made the television news. There never was any immortality serum; someone had wanted me to attend the Ball of Forever. Someone . . . who'd known what was in the wind. And I had a pretty good idea who.

FOUR

One Last Night of Freedom

Under pressure, I agreed to hold my stag night at Strange-fellows, on the grounds that whatever mess we made there, it wouldn't show, and also that whenever the trouble inevitably broke out . . . no-one would notice. It's that kind of bar and has been for centuries. The party was already well underway by the time I got there, thanks to my little visit to the Ball of Forever overrunning, and joy and merriment were already unconfined, not to mention pissed out of their skulls. The bar was packed wall to wall with disreputable customers as I clattered down the heavy metal stairway into the great stone pit that makes up the bar proper. I couldn't believe I knew that many people. Or at least, so many people who didn't want to kill me. There were friends, and enemies, and a great many people who'd been one or the other or both at various times in my life. That's the Nightside for you. Everyone seemed to be getting on quite amiably together. Cheap booze and no closing time will do that for you.

People smiled and nodded and even waved as I made my way through the crowd, but no-one actually interrupted their drinking or carousing to talk to me, which was fine by me. I've never been the demonstrative kind, and casual acquaintances hug or air-kiss me at their peril. Besides, I was still feeling distinctly fragile, from overusing my gift. My right nostril stopped bleeding after I shoved half an ice cube up it, but my head still ached fiercely, and my bones creaked and protested with every movement. Sometimes I wonder whose side my gift is on.

I reached the long wooden bar and leaned heavily on it, and the bartender gave me a stern look. Even at my farewell party and pre-nuptial send-off, Alex Morrisey was still dressed all in black, complete with dark glasses and a stylish beret. (Pulled well forward to conceal a receding hair-line. Even though it fooled absolutely nobody.) Alex wasn't going to let a small thing like general celebration and goodwill all round get in the way of his being a full-time gloomy bugger and first-class pain in the arse. Alex could brood for the Olympics and still take a bronze in feeling hard done by. He looked me over and sniffed loudly.

"Buddha on a bike, look at the state of you. People usually wait till the end of their stag do to look that bad. Only you could walk into your last night of freedom looking like something the cat threw up."

"Never mind the words of welcome, Alex," I growled. "I am much in need of an industrial-strength pick-me-up."

"Never knew you when you weren't." Alex produced a dusty bottle from underneath the counter and slammed it on the bar-top a few times, in a vain attempt to get the contents to settle. He then poured a couple of fingers of thick pink liquor into a glass and pushed it towards me. "Try this. I keep it handy for really apocalyptic hangovers. It's called Angel's Breath."

I looked at the drink suspiciously. "Is it really . . ."

"No of course it isn't. Truth in advertising never did catch on in the Nightside. This stuff is only called Angel's Breath because if you knew what really went into it, you wouldn't touch it even if someone put a gun to your head. In fact, that's usually the best way to take it. Now hurry up and knock it back, before it starts scouring out the inside of the glass, and you can have a nice sweetie afterwards to take the taste away."

I knocked it back in one, doing my best to sneak it past my tongue. There was a brief taste of something very like orange, followed by the most vile and awful taste I have ever encountered. And I've been around. My taste buds exploded with fear and loathing, the whole of my mouth shrivelled up in panic, and tears of pure affront leapt from my eye-balls before the lids squeezed shut in self-defence. I grabbed on to the bar with both hands, making loud noises of distress. When I have really bad nightmares, I can still almost remember that taste. When I was finally able to force my eyes open again, Alex was waiting politely before me with a glass of Lourdes Coke. I snatched it from him and drank it thirstily. It helped. When I finally put the glass down, I was surprised to find that I actually felt human again, with no more aches or pains. I wasn't entirely sure that was worth what I'd just been through . . .

"There," said Alex, smugly. "Wasn't that a fuss to make over a nasty taste?"

I thought about it. "No," I said, very firmly. "Half my taste buds are still crying their eyes out, and the other half are threatening to sue for post-traumatic stress disorder."

Alex cackled happily. "Big girl's blouse. Come on; you've got some serious drinking to do if we're to get you into a suitable state for your stag do. This is going to be a night to remember! People will speak of it for years to come, in hushed and respectful whispers, saying *You should be glad you weren't there.*"

I gave him a hard look. "I told you—no strippers."

Alex grinned and leaned forward across the bar. "I can't believe you chose me to be best man at your wedding. I'm going to have to make a speech, aren't I? Oh, the possibilities for embarrassment and revenge . . ."

"Suzie will be sitting right next to you," I pointed out. "And yes, she will most definitely have a gun somewhere about her person."

"Duly noted," said Alex. "I won't mention Deirdre Birchwood then."

"Best not to," I agreed.

I looked down to the end of the bar, where Alex's pet vulture Agatha was no longer crouched brooding on her post. She'd finally laid her egg. It was a great deal bigger than any vulture's egg had a right to be, and it was a deep black in colour. The vulture was sitting on the egg, with a certain amount of support from two side cushions, and was cooing contentedly. Alex sniggered.

"When she finally laid that thing, you could hear the outraged sounds she was making out in London Proper. She was really quite indignant about the whole affair."

"I've never seen a black egg before," I said. "And certainly not an egg as dark as that . . ."

Alex nodded slowly. "If you look close enough, it's full of stars."

"Any idea yet what the father was, that was actually brave enough to have sex with that vulture?" I said.

"I have been giving the matter a great deal of thought," said Alex. "There is a betting pool if you're interested. After some consideration, I would have to say my money is on my own appalling ancestor, Merlin Satanspawn. A lot of the legends have him down as a shape-shifter."

"But . . . he's been dead for centuries!"

"Didn't stop him from sleeping with my ex-wife."

"All these years in the Nightside, and I still can't believe where some of my conversations end up," I said.

Alex regarded me thoughtfully, pulling down his stylish shades so he could peer at me over the top of them. "Seriously though, John. Why me? Why choose me to be best man?"

"You're my oldest friend," I said. "And, on occasion, my oldest enemy. And everything in between. Who else has suffered all the things we've been through? Who else has seen the things we've seen? We have heard the chimes at midnight, and laughed in the face of gods and monsters. Nobody knows the trouble we've known . . . And isn't that what being best man is all about? Plus, I was best man at your wedding."

"And look how well that turned out," said Alex. "I'd sue you if I had a sue. But you're right; it does fall to me as your oldest friend and foe and occasional legal advisor to guide you through the horrors to come as you embark on the stormy seas of matrimony."

"You are so good to me, Alex."

"Did you get a pre-nup? Tell me you got a pre-nup!"

I had to smile. "We did have some good times together in this place, didn't we, Alex?"

He glared at me. "If you start getting maudlin this early in the party, I will slap you a good one, and it will hurt."

"You're quite right," I said. "Don't know what came over me."

I put my back against the wooden bar and looked out over the crowded room. Up on the small elevated stage, the band was really getting into it. Leo Morn and his band were providing live music (or at least something very like it). I'd agreed to let them play for sentimental reasons, and was already regretting it. Leo prowled back and forth across the stage, striking a series of rock poses as he belted out the lyrics. A skinny wild-eyed presence in purple jeans, with a very hairy torso, he was currently singing Warren Zevon's "Werewolves of London." Down in front of the stage, Betty and

Lucy Coltrane, Alex's body-building lady bouncers, were tangoing wildly, giving it lots of erotic action and passing the rose stem back and forth between their teeth. An Ann-Margret channeller from *Divas! Las Vegas*, looking very glamorous, was dancing up a storm on a table-top, along with Ms. Fate, the Nightside's very own transvestite costumed adventurer. They danced well together, arms waving and legs slamming in unison, while their stiletto heels made a real mess of the wooden table-top.

Leo Morn crashed to the end of his song, his musicians stopped playing at pretty much the same time, and there was actually some perfunctory applause. Or perhaps they were showing how pleased they were that it had stopped. Leo showed his teeth in a few defiant snarls, jumped down from the stage, and slouched over to join me at the bar. He'd been sweating up a cloud on stage, and carried with him the smell of a large dog that has recently been exercised. Alex had a vodka and mistletoe waiting for him, and Leo drank it thirstily.

"All right," I said. "I'll bite. What are you calling the band this week?"

"Odin's Other Eye," he said proudly. "We've gone prog rock. Sort of."

"Only because all the other genres wouldn't have you," said Alex.

"We're doing a lot better!" said Leo. "I don't have to change the band's name nearly as often now to make sure they'll book us again. We opened for the ClanDestined just the other week, and they said they'd almost certainly want us back. Sometime." He rapped his empty glass on the bar, to indicate he was ready for a refill, and grinned easily at me. "So! The knight in a tarnished trench coat is now the Man! Didn't see that one coming. Am I going to have to change my wicked ways, or at the very least be very careful about what I admit to in front of you?"

"I've always been more concerned with justice than the law," I said.

"That's what they all say," said Leo. "All I know is, if I ever see you heading my way while wearing a suit and a bowler hat and carrying an umbrella, I will leg it for the nearest horizon at a speed that will amaze you."

"Never happen," I said. "I might be Walker now, but I'll never be that Walker."

"That's what they all say," said Leo, heading back to his band. One of them had made the mistake of asking for requests, and the packed room was obliging him with some very basic answers. The crowd at Strangefellows has never been strong on witty repartee.

"I did try to get Rossignol for the music," I said to Alex. "She's the leading torch singer in France these days, and I was hoping she might say yes, for old times' sake. But it seem she has a regular spot at the Crazy Horse Salon in Paris, and she couldn't get away. Probably for the best. She was never actually an ex of mine, technically speaking, but . . ."

"Yes, but," said Alex. "Suzie's never been one for letting technicalities get in the way of venting her emotions. Preferably with a large gun."

"Rossignol did send me a card, with a view of Paris," I said. "Which was nice of her. Would have been nicer if she'd remembered to sign it, but . . ."

"Change the subject," Alex said wisely.

"All right. How is it you're tending the bar on your own, on what promises to be a very busy night? I thought you'd be hiring extra staff, to help you cope with the madness and mayhem to come?"

"Mostly, I'm letting people help themselves," said Alex. "I've hired a tame poltergeist to keep a check on the stock, take care of trouble-makers, and clean up afterwards. The bar bill for tonight will be my wedding gift, to you and Suzie. Oh, and Cathy's bought you a foot spa. Don't ask me why."

I looked at the dusty and deceptively innocent-looking bottles crowded together at the back of the bar. "I thought you had some pretty dangerous stuff back there."

Alex smiled. "Oh, I do, I do. It's all carefully marked OFF LIMITS, along with a sign saying TRESPASSERS WILL BE TRANS-MOGRIFIED. If anyone's dumb enough to ignore the warning signs, they deserve everything that happens to them. I was sort of hoping Cathy would be free to help out, but it seems she's organising Suzie's hen do. Probably involving obscenely named cocktails and unsafe humping and grinding with improperly dressed Chippendales. The poor bastards. And no, before you ask, I don't know where it's being held, and we're almost certainly better off not knowing. We can listen for the sound of excessive gunfire and explosions."

He moved away, to put out small bowls of bar snacks that no-one in their right mind would touch, and I went back to looking over the crowded room. Dead Boy and Razor Eddie had turned up. Dead Boy was loudly talking up the murder case at the Ball of Forever and greatly exaggerating his own part in it. He already had his arms around two female ghouls dressed in rotting Playboy Bunny outfits. Razor Eddie stood a little to one side, sipping his designer water and nodding in agreement, now and again. The girl ghouls eyed him uncertainly, and manoeuvred Dead Boy to make sure they maintained a respectful distance. Because there are some smells even ghouls have trouble with.

Dead Boy swaggered over to the bar to order two Really Bloody Marys for his new ghoul-friends, and nodded easily to me. He reached inside his long greatcoat to scratch fitfully at his autopsy scar, his usual sign that he had something embarrassing he needed to discuss.

"There are rumours going around," he said carefully. "Foul and vicious exaggerations, no doubt, that there's a fight brewing between you and Razor Eddie. He won't talk to me about it, but then he rarely talks to me about anything. Never was much of a one for the talking, our Razor Eddie. Tell me it's not true, John. Tell me you have enough sense not to pick a fight with the legendarily dangerous Punk God of the Straight Razor."

"It's some prophecy," I said. "A glimpse of a future that might or might not happen. Certainly I've no intention of letting things get that far."

"You do know," said Dead Boy, not quite looking in my direction, "if it does all kick off, you can always rely on me."

I looked at him thoughtfully. "You'd take on the dreaded and justly feared Razor Eddie, for me?"

"Well," he said. "Not necessarily for you, John, or at least, not just for you. But, come on; you must have wondered at some time or another whether you could take Razor Eddie. I know I have."

"Testosterone is a terrible thing," observed Alex.

Razor Eddie turned his head suddenly to look at us as he settled into his private booth at the back of the bar, with his usual calm and unconcerned face—as though he knew we were talking about him. Even though there was no way he could have heard us through the general bedlam of raised voices. Except . . . he was Razor Eddie. We all nodded to each other, as though our gazes had happened to meet, in a friendly enough way; and then he went back to staring at nothing, and Dead Boy and I looked at each other.

"He really is a spooky bugger," said Dead Boy, nodding to Alex as he collected his two Really Bloody Marys with real blood, and a Valhalla Venom for himself. He gave me a sideways look. "I've never known what you see in him."

"Lot of people say the same to me about you," I said.

"Really?" said Dead Boy. "Can't think why. Life and soul of the party, that's me, even though I'm dead. You'll have to excuse me now; my new ghoul-friends are waiting, and I don't know how long they'll last."

He took his drinks away, and, after a moment's thought, I

made my way through the tightly packed crowd to join Razor Eddie in his private booth. I sat down opposite him, and he nodded to me gravely. There was plenty of room at the table; no-one else was going to sit with him. And not only because of the smell. I leaned forward and made a point of meeting his cold, cold gaze.

"It seems a lot of people have heard about this prophecy of yours, Eddie," I said. " How accurate is it likely to be?"

"You said it yourself, John," murmured Razor Eddie. "There are any number of possible futures. And people will always talk."

"They're not only talking; they're laying bets!"

"Well, of course they are." The ghost of a smile passed briefly across his pale lips. "Do you want to know the latest odds?"

I sat back in my chair and looked at him thoughtfully. "Would you really kill me, after everything we've been through together?"

"Oh, I think so," said Razor Eddie. "Perhaps because of all the things we've been through together. I will say this—it would have to be for a very good reason." He considered me for a long moment. "You always were too soft-hearted for your own good. They should have made me Walker. I would have brought real justice to the Nightside."

"Well, yes, possibly," I said. "But I have to wonder how many would still be left alive after you'd finished. Besides, you've seen where that kind of single-minded self-righteousness leads. You remember the Walking Man."

"Yes," said Razor Eddie. "I remember the Walking Man. The Wrath of God in the world of Men, he said. And you faced him down when I couldn't. I haven't forgotten that, John."

"Do you want to end up like him?" I said steadily.

Razor Eddie actually took some time to think about that

one. "I admired his arrogance," he said finally. "His cold certainty. But he turned out to be soft, too, in the end. I suppose I am . . . fond of you, John, in my way. But it would be a relief to know you wouldn't be around any more. To get in my way, to stop me doing things that need doing. So be careful, John. Never give me a reason to go up against you. You know it makes sense, Walker."

"Well," I said, getting to my feet, "I'm glad we had this little chat. We really should do this less."

On my way back to the bar, I nodded to Springheel Jack and the Bride. Even being dead, again, wasn't enough to keep the Bride from a party. Jack was sitting on the Bride's lap as they fed each other pieces of bread soaked in gooey stringy cheese, using the fondue set that had arrived as an early wedding present. From someone who didn't really know Suzie and me all that well. I'd donated it to the party, in the hope someone would break it or steal it. Back at the bar, Alex had a large wormwood brandy waiting for me.

"Who did give you that fondue set, anyway?"

"Julien Advent," I said. "He never really got over the seventies. I suppose we should be grateful he didn't give us a Soda Stream."

Alex winced. "Can you still get those things?"

"This is the Nightside," I said. "You can get all kinds of abominations in the Nightside."

"I haven't seen the Lord of Thorns yet," said Alex. "Imagine my relief."

"I did ask him," I said. "Because you sort of have to when he's performing your wedding; but luckily, he's busy preparing for the ceremony at St. Jude's. Just as well. He didn't strike me as a party animal."

"I'll tell you who is here, large as life and twice as stuck-up," said Alex, not even bothering to lower his voice. "Two-thirds of everyone's favourite disturbing brothers: Tommy and Larry

Oblivion. At least Hadleigh isn't with them. I don't know if this place could stand being pushed that far up-market."

I looked where he indicated. I'd sent invitations to all the Oblivion Brothers but never actually expected them to turn up. Larry was sitting perfectly upright at his table, a tall pale sight with flat yellow hair, dressed in the very best Armani. Larry was dead and looked it, but he had made a concession to the party atmosphere by loosening the knot on his tie. He wasn't drinking or eating anything, (because he was very firm about being dead, and having no illusions about the state), but he did seem to be picking up something of a contact high from his surroundings.

Tommy Oblivion slumped bonelessly in his seat, grinning happily in all directions, a tall and terribly effete person in brightly coloured New Romantics silks. Unlike most of us, the existential private eye had enjoyed a pretty good eighties. No doubt being so utterly existential helped. I could hear him loudly boasting to one and all that he was so existential he couldn't even be sure of exactly what he was drinking. It might be sparkling water from the River Ganges, and therefore good for his karma. Or it might be still water from the Reichenbach Falls. Or possibly even shimmering water from Chernobyl, the only isotonic energy drink that glowed in the dark. And if you drank enough of it, so would you. Already people around him could be heard asking if he couldn't tune his existentialism down a bloody bit, so they could be sure where they'd left their tables?

I was rather more interested in Old Father Time, who'd come in specially from Shadows Fall (that quiet backwater town where legends go to die when the world stops believing in them, an elephants' graveyard for the supernatural). He was holding court at one of the larger tables and being avuncular to one and all. A wiry but imposing figure with a sharp-featured face and a great mane of pure white hair, he dressed to the very height of Victorian fashion. He stood straight-backed at the head of his table, both hands clutching firmly at his lapels, dispensing wisdom for all those with the wit to hear. There wasn't anything he didn't know about Time, so I wandered over to have a quiet word with him. He nodded happily at me and moved away from his table to grasp my hand in both of his.

"John Taylor, my dear boy! Come, talk with me. I've been expecting you. And congratulations, on becoming Walker! About time you settled down and stopped making trouble for everyone, eh? Eh?"

"I'm not retiring," I said. "I'm . . . changing direction."

"Quite so, dear boy, quite so."

"Who's running the Time Tower, while you're enjoying yourself here?" I said.

"Oh, I'm there, too," said Old Father Time. "And I'm back at Shadows Fall, in the Gallery of Bone. Being in more than one place at the same time is one of the first things you learn in the Time business." He let go of his lapels long enough to beckon me in close, lowering his voice as much as he could and still be heard. "There's something I haven't been meaning to tell you, until you were ready, and now I fear I may have left it too late. Now what was it, what was it? Hmm? My memory isn't what it used to be, if it ever was. Ah yes! We, that is to say all of us here in the Nightside, we are approaching . . . a moment of decision. You know the sort of thing, one of those focal moments in Time, where everything depends on the decision one vital person will make. Which may or may not be you. The moment is very near. Oh yes. And whatever it is that's about to happen . . . it could see the sun finally rise over the Nightside, an end to the longest night the world has ever known; and then nothing would ever be the same again."

"And it had to happen the night before my wedding," I said heavily.

"Well," said Old Father Time, "that's Time."

He went back to his table, his eyes far away, looking at the things only he could see.

"Don't mind him," said Time's usual companion, the young woman called Mad. "You should never take him too seriously. I don't."

Mad was a punk, and proud of it. All leathers and chains and uncomfortable-looking piercings, with the word HATE tattooed on both sets of knuckles. I was pretty sure I hadn't noticed her at Time's table, but then Mad had a gift for turning up where she wasn't wanted. (There were those who said Mad was short for Madeleine; but I've never been convinced.) She looked at me with her angry, fey eyes.

"He's been going on about the End of All Things for as long as I've known him," she said carelessly. "And we're all still here. Hey, want to see a really upsetting party trick I can do with two flick-knives and an unwilling volunteer?"

"Not right now," I said.

Harry Fabulous was on the prowl and on the prod, moving easily from one group to another, smiling his professional smile and working his professional charm, happy and eager to supply everyone with anything that was bad for them, at very reasonable prices. I hadn't actually invited him, but trying to keep Harry Fabulous out of a convivial gathering was like trying to keep ants out of a picnic. Always sharply dressed, always smiling a smile that never reached his eyes, Harry used to be the best go-to man in the Nightside. He could get you absolutely anything if you could meet his price. But then something happened, in the back room of some very private members-only club, and he was never the same afterwards. These days he does his best to Do Good Things, while he can, to save his soul from certain damnation. He seemed cheerful enough, but I noticed he never liked anyone to get behind him, and he had a tendency to jump at his own shadow. Or anyone else's. I strolled over to join him. He saw me coming, thought about running, thought better of it, and greeted me with his best smile.

"Mr. Taylor! Hello! How's it going?"

"Hello, Harry," I said. "Are you being a good boy?"

"Always, Mr. Taylor; you know that!" His smile switched on and off as though he couldn't quite see the point in working the thing when the person before him was never going to believe it anyway. "I'm here to see that everyone has what they need, to have a good time on your stag night. In a good way, of course. Is there anything I might have on me that would tempt you, Mr. Taylor? Got some very nice black centipede meat, very spicy. Or how about a little snuff, made from the crushed and ground-up bodies of Egyptian mummies? Black Lotus Smoothie?"

"And this is you, being good?" I said.

"Good?" said Harry Fabulous. "At these prices I'm practically martyring myself!"

I left him to it. William and Eleanor Griffin, no longer immortal and looking much happier for it (especially after the Devil himself turned up in person to drag their father down to Hell), were bellying up to the bar and ordering the very best champagne Alex had to offer. Which would make him very happy. No-one ever notices they're being overcharged when ordering the very best champagne. William and Eleanor nodded benignly to everyone and did their best to fit in before blowing it completely by asking if anyone could recommend a truly trustworthy butler?

Percival Smyth-Herriot had also turned up, all the way from the Museum of Unnatural History, with a miniature *T. rex* on a leash. A tall spindly figure in a shiny suit, with breakfast stains on his waistcoat that might have been fresh, or might not. He was a lot happier now the Collector was dead, and no longer blackmailing him. I had persuaded the Authorities to donate all of the late Collector's public assets to

the Museum of Unnatural History, for public display, and
now Percival couldn't do enough for the Authorities in general, and me personally. It's always good to have a tame expert
you can rely on, for when you need to know something really
important in a hurry. Percival was currently on his second
G&T and feeling very daring. He waggled his fingers at me,
and I nodded back. Percival didn't get out much. Dead Boy
collared Percival and dragged him over to meet one of the
female ghouls. I decided not to get involved.

Chandra Singh and Augusta Moon had also turned up,
surprisingly arm in arm, two great monster hunters representing the Adventurers Club. They were sharing their table
with a great hulking yeti (with any number of cute pink rib-
bons in its shaggy grey fur), a talking mongoose called Cliff,
and Klatu the Thing from Dimension X. I would have given
a lot to listen in on that conversation, but I was distracted by
a polite but imperious cough from the next table.

The Rogue Vicar Tamsin MacReady sat elegantly upright
in her chair, drinking beer from a straight glass with her little finger extended. A tiny little thing, the vicar was barely
five feet tall and slender with it. She had kind eyes and a winning
smile, and a backbone of tempered steel. She wore a simple
grey suit with a vicar's white collar. She didn't look like a fire-
breathing zealot, but then the real ones seldom do. Sitting
beside her was her close companion, Sharon Pilkington-Smythe.
A healthy-looking young lady, wearing a baggy grey jumper
over thoroughly worn-in riding britches. She had shaggy red
hair and fierce green eyes, and a smile that took no prisoners.
She was drinking snakebite from a brandy glass, and fooling
no-one. I sighed inwardly and sat down with them. A vicar
will always catch you, no matter how fast you run.

"I have to say, sweetie, that I am a bit put-out that you
didn't want my Tamsin to officiate at your wedding," said
Sharon immediately.

"Oh hush, dear," said the rogue vicar. "I'm not one to put myself forward, you know that."

"Of course not, sweetie; that's what I'm here for."

"The Lord of Thorns will be performing the ceremony," I said. "At the Church of St. Jude's."

"There, you see?" said the vicar, waggling a finger in remonstration at Sharon. "Definitely outclassed. I just represent God in the Nightside; the Lord of Thorns has personal chats with Him on a regular basis."

"Well, yes, but you do real heart-to-heart stuff at your weddings," Sharon said stubbornly. "Really makes a person feel *married*."

But Tamsin MacReady was already looking thoughtfully at Razor Eddie, in his private booth at the back. She said something very un-vicar-like, under her breath, and looked sharply at me.

"I have heard talk . . . that Razor Eddie might be getting above himself. You're Walker now; you don't have to deal personally with every threat that comes your way. If you wish, I could set Sharon on him."

"Does everyone here know about the prophecy?" I said, a bit miffed.

"Pretty much," said the rogue vicar. "Any news about Razor Eddie tends to do the rounds fairly quickly, if only so the rest of us know which way to jump when the trouble starts."

"Grubby little upstart," said Sharon. "I could take him." She studied Razor Eddie with her hungry eyes, and I remembered the brief glimpse I'd once got of her true, hidden nature, a brief vision of huge teeth and ragged claws, of something indescribably vile and vicious.

"Sharon, sweetie, I could take him," Tamsin MacReady said firmly. "He's only another god from the Street of the Gods. I serve the true God, and His strength is mine."

"No-one's taking anyone," I said, just as firmly. "Let us all play nicely together, if only for one night. Thanks for the offer, though, Vicar. But I solve my own problems. That's how you get to be Walker."

"We like what you've done with Suzie Shooter," said Sharon. "We're all very impressed with how you've calmed her down. We were worried we might have to do something about her."

I had to smile. "I haven't calmed her down in the least. I've helped her channel her anger more productively."

"Love conquers all," said Tamsin, smiling fondly at Sharon. "That's what it's for."

I moved on again. It was my party, my stag night, but I couldn't seem to settle. As though I were looking for the one person who wasn't there, but should have been. I went back to the bar.

"It's early yet," said Alex. "People will be arriving for ages yet whether we want them to or not. Oh, don't tell me you invited the Authorities?"

"I sort of had to," I said. "But it was kind of understood on both sides that I was being polite. Julien Advent's okay; but most of the others could stop a party at twenty paces. And anyway, right now they've got more pressing worries. You have heard of King of Skin's murder . . . of course you have. Anyway, they've got to choose a worthy replacement, and quickly, or risk looking weak and indecisive."

"I don't mind Julien Advent," said Alex. "He only drinks the good stuff, pays his bar bill on time, and hardly ever starts a fight. But I've never been too sure how you and he get on. I wouldn't have thought you'd have anything in common. Some days you're the best of partners in crime, and the next he's offering a reward for your arrest and writing nasty editorials about you in the *Night Times*."

"We're friends, sort of," I said. "But he's never approved of the way I get things done. He's got principles. He's always been a hero, the real deal, whereas I have always taken a more pragmatic approach to things. We get along. Most of the time. We know where we stand with each other."

"Oh, hell," sad Alex. "Speak of the devil, and up he pops."

I looked around, and sure enough there he was. Julien Advent the Great Victorian Adventurer, standing at the bottom of the stairs and looking around the bar as though he couldn't decide whom to disapprove of first. A very moral and upright person, Julien Advent, despite having lived in the Nightside all these years. He still looked like the English Gentleman and Hero of the Empire he used to be before being pushed through a Timeslip and ending up here in the 1960s. He hadn't aged or changed a bit in all that time and still dressed in the grand old style, complete with red-lined black opera cape; and standing quietly there, entirely at his ease, he looked every inch the hero and adventurer he still was.

The whole room was going quiet. People had noticed he'd arrived. Some people were pleased to see him, some averted their eyes, and some hid under their tables, hoping he hadn't noticed them. Even the band stopped playing though the mike was picking up a low, angry growl from Leo Morn. Julien nodded politely to the assembled company, with his usual impeccable manners, then he turned his head and looked straight at me. I sighed inwardly. I knew what that meant. It meant he was determined to talk to me in private, about a matter of some importance, and that I really wasn't going to like anything he had to tell me.

I led him to one of the few empty booths, at the rear of the bar, and we sat down facing each other. Well, I sat down; he took a few moments to remove his cape and fold it carefully before sitting down. He didn't look at me once while doing this, which meant he wasn't at all comfortable about what he had to say and was putting it off. We've known each other a long time, and we can always read each other's tells. He eventually sat down, leaned forward, laced his hands together, and leaned them on the table-top before finally fixing me with a calm, resolute gaze.

Oh hell, I thought. *This is going to be really bad.*

"I need you to take on a very important, very urgent case. Right now," said Julien Advent. "And before you ask, yes, it really is that urgent, no it can't wait until after your wedding tomorrow, and I am not prepared to take No, Absolutely Not, or even Go to Hell as an answer. You've had your last case as a private investigator; this will be your first official case as the new Walker. And yes, John, I know all about what happened with King of Skin. I know every detail. I am editor of the *Night Times* as well as a member of the Authorities. I know everything."

"You didn't know that King of Skin was an immortal serial killer," I said. "Or that he was planning to murder you all, wrap himself in your skins, and rule the Nightside as his own private kingdom."

"I'm only human," said Julien. "I don't care what the rumours say." He sighed, separated his hands to make a point, started to say something, then broke off, and finally settled for drumming his fingers on the table before looking me square in the eyes again. "If you will agree to take on this case, immediately, I have been authorised by the remaining Authorities to offer you an . . . inducement. We will cover all the expenses for security at your wedding. We guarantee to keep all your many enemies at bay and ensure that everything goes smoothly and quietly at the ceremony. The fact that I am willing to go along with such a blatant attempt at bribery should give you some indication of how seriously I take this case."

I thought about it. Covering the expenses would be a weight off my shoulders. I'd already had to hire Hell's Neanderthals to set up a defence barrier for half a mile around St. Jude's; and those cloned barbarians don't come cheap.

"What's so important about this case?" I said resignedly.

"Someone is determined to put an end to the long night," said Julien Advent. "To raise the sun at long last and bring the dawn to the Nightside. To bring an end to the longest night this world has ever known and destroy the Nightside forever."

I nodded slowly. After all the hints and warnings I'd had this evening, I wasn't surprised. I never thought I'd hear such a thing for real again in my lifetime. After all the wars I'd been through, defending the Nightside, I thought we'd earned some time off for bad behaviour. And I couldn't help flashing back to the warning phrase I'd already encountered twice this evening; *Let the sun shine in.*

"Who the hell's got enough power to do that?" I said.

And to my surprise Julien looked away, avoiding the question. As though he knew the answer, knew the name, even, but didn't want to say it. And that wasn't like Julien Advent at all.

"You have to take this case, John," he said finally. "The other members of the Authorities are divided as to whether to keep you on as Walker after this unfortunate business with King of Skin. He died on your watch, right in front of you. Yes, you caught his killer, but you didn't keep him from being killed. Some of them are worried as to whether you deliberately allowed him to die, so that the Authorities could never become your future Enemies. And yes, of course we knew."

"If the Authorities are debating my future as Walker, why aren't you there defending me?" I said.

"Because I've already cast my vote, in your favour. This is more important. I have to ask, though. Did you let him die, John?"

"No," I said steadily. "I'm not that subtle."

"That's true," he said. "But I felt a responsibility to ask. Now, answer the question. Will you take the case?"

"Of course," I said. "I take my responsibilities as Walker seriously. Where do we start?"

"With a crime scene. The Hawk's Wind Bar & Grille is gone. Vanished."

I looked at him for a long moment. This was turning out to be one hell of an evening for surprises. "What do you mean—gone? How can the ghost of a building be gone? You mean—stolen? Destroyed? Kidnapped? Exorcised?"

"Unknown," said Julien. "There's a bloody big hole in the ground where it used to be and not a trace of the Bar & Grille anywhere. Or, for that matter, any of the important and significant people who were inside it at the time . . ."

"Ah," I said. "Tricky . . . But how does the Bar & Grille's disappearance tie in with this threat to bring the dawn to the Nightside?"

"Come with me and find out," said Julien Advent, rising to his feet and pulling on his cape. "We'll be working this case together."

I took my own sweet time in getting to my feet, to show I wasn't going to be hurried. "This was supposed to be my stag do. My last night of freedom."

"If we don't put a stop to what's coming our way, this could be everyone's last night of freedom," said Julien.

"Why do you always have to have the last word?" I said.

"Because I'm an editor," said Julien.

"Let's go," I said.

Everyone else couldn't believe I was actually leaving my own stag party, to go to work. But secretly, I was pleased to be leaving early, before it inevitably degenerated into "surprise" strippers, karaoke, demolition drinking games, and general puking. But could I really solve a case this important, in one night, and still make it to my wedding on time tomorrow? I'd better, or Suzie would kill me. I did consider calling her in, but I already had the Great Victorian Adventurer at my side, and besides . . . it was probably best not to disturb her. I looked at Julien, as we headed for the stairs.

"Whatever happens, if you value your life, get me to the church on time."

FIVE

Walking Among Ghosts

I took Julien Advent through the back door and out into the rear alley. The clamour of my continuing stag do shut off abruptly as I closed the door firmly behind us. Julien's nostrils flared sharply as the unique ambience of the rear alley assaulted his senses. He looked around him and, without saying a word, made it very clear that he was not impressed. He had a point. The dimly lit alleyway stretched away before us, half-full of garbage and the things that feed on it. Something had left a thick, slimy trail across the cobbled ground and half-way up the adjoining wall. And a small pile of severed shrunken heads, draped with ivy and mistletoe, suggested the Little Sisters of the Immaculate Chain-saw were celebrating Christmas early again this year. There was nothing in the alley that you'd want to see, and even less that you'd want to see you. Julien gave me a very cold look.

"What, exactly, are we doing out here, John? I have known

Victorian slum-dwellers who would have looked down their noses at a location like this."

"Sorry," I said. "I'd call in the exterminators, but we still haven't found out what happened to the last crew they sent. We're here because I can't use my Portable Timeslip inside Strangefellows. Alex paid out a lot of money for state-of-the-art protective shields, specially to prevent anyone from dropping in when they felt like it. At one stage, it got to the point where he was opening fire on anyone who teleported in without warning, or even at people he hadn't noticed before. So Alex has his shields, and I try to be polite about such things, when I can."

"Alex has shields strong enough to keep you out?" said Julien. "I didn't think that was possible any more."

"It isn't," I said. "This pocket-watch could punch through Alex's shields like a bullet through a paper bag. But I don't want him knowing that. Partly because I don't want him upset, and partly because I might need to make a sudden and strategic and surprise entrance into his bar someday."

"Typical Walker," said Julien, smiling. "You'll fit into the job nicely." And then he froze and made a brief moue of distress. "Something large and furry has just scurried across my shoes, and I'm really hoping it was a much larger than usual rat."

"Don't look down," I advised him.

"Is there a reason we're still standing here?" said Julien.

"You're the one who started making conversation," I said.

And then we both looked round sharply as a figure paused at the end of the alleyway and looked in at us. Something in a frock struck an evocative pose and smiled professionally.

"Evening, gents. Fancy a horrible time?"

"Not now, George," I said. "We're working."

"Well, pardon me, I'm sure. Catch you on the flip side, darlings."

"I really think we should be leaving now," Julien said firmly.

I opened the gold pocket-watch, and the darkness within jumped out to swallow us up. I had a brief glimpse of things in the alleyway shrinking back from the living dark and even disappearing into concealed doorways; and then there was only falling and falling in the endless dark, surrounded by voices thundering in no human language. Spend too long in that terrible dark, and you start to understand what the voices are saying, and that's even worse. My feet slammed suddenly against hard and unyielding ground, there was a flash of light, and the world returned. Julien and I were standing in a street familiar to both of us, bathed in the warm glow of amber street-lights and flaring neon signs. And right before us, where the legendary Hawk's Wind Bar & Grille should have stood, was a great hole in the ground, dug out between two lowering buildings like the empty space left by a pulled tooth. Julien Advent shuddered and glared at me.

"That . . . was a most unpleasant experience. Is it always like that when you travel through the watch?"

"Mostly," I said. "I keep hoping I'll get used to it. Walker did."

"Either that, or he was an excellent actor," said Julien.

We were only saying things so we wouldn't have to talk about what was really bothering us. Rather than look at the hole in the ground, I took a good look at the watching crowd. Quite a large gathering had turned out to see what was going on. Disasters and catastrophes count as free entertainment, in the Nightside. A slow buzz of conversation and comment moved through the crowd as they recognised Julien Advent and me. A few started to drift casually away. I couldn't help but notice that most of the onlookers seemed far more interested in Julien than in me.

"It's not fair," I said. "You always get more respect than me."

"Well, you get more fear," Julien said generously. "And now you're Walker, I'm sure the respect will come. In time."

"All the hard work I put into building a reputation that

makes grown men weep and grow weak at the knees; and all you have to do is show up and no-one even notices I'm here." I sniffed loudly. "I could have a neon sign over my head, listing all the people I've brought to justice, and they'd still look at you first."

"I have been around a lot longer than you," said Julien. "And I do have more . . . classically handsome features."

"Never mind that," I said. "Answer me this. What are all these naked people doing here?"

I indicated the dozen or so entirely naked men and women cordoning off the great hole in the ground and discouraging anyone else from getting too close, apparently simply by looking at them.

"Ah, yes," said Julien Advent. "I phoned ahead, to have them close off and protect the area till we could take a look. These very impressive individuals are the Tantric Troops. The very latest addition to the Authorities' private army of security personnel and useful people."

"Oh, them," I said. "You mean the Fuck Buddies."

Julien winced. "Please, John. Don't call them that in public. We want people to take them seriously. I know there are those who refer to the Troops by that . . . vulgar description, but I think we should insist on the correct name in front of the children. They're so impressionable. The Troops are a puissant force in their own right. Every man and woman here can use tantric or sexual energies to power their magic; and no, I don't want to go into the technicalities."

"I'd love to be around when they recharge their batteries," I said.

"Let us not go anywhere near there. The point is, no-one is going to intrude on the crime scene while the Troops are around."

"What do they do?" I said, honestly curious. "Threaten to bukkake people to death if they get too close?"

"For you, taste is something other people talk about, isn't

it?" said Julien. "I am told that if anyone does threaten the crime scene's integrity, the Troops are quite capable of sending the perpetrator's sex drive into reverse. I don't know exactly what that entails, but it doesn't sound like anything I'd want to experience."

Some of the people at the front of the crowd heard all this and showed a distinct interest in getting to the back of the crowd. I was careful to avoid the gaze of any of the naked people. Glancing in their general direction was enough to give me a pleasant but subtly disturbing buzz.

"The previous Walker had a similar set of enforcers: the Holy Trio," said Julien. "You broke them, didn't you?"

"You know damn well I did," I said. "You wrote a whole editorial about what I did to them. Walker set them on me because I'd defied the previous Authorities. The Holy Trio derived their very unpleasant magics from energies stored up by a lifetime of celibacy and denial. I . . . defused them."

"You had them jumping each other in the street!" said Julien.

"I made them happy," I said, with dignity. "Which is more than the Authorities ever did. I'm told it took the medics three weeks to get the smiles off their faces."

"You always did fight dirty, John," said Julien. "Anyway, the Tantric Troops work directly for the Authorities, not you. One less thing for you to bother yourself with."

"You're so good to me," I said. "You mean one more thing you can hold over me if I go off the rails or off the reservation. Let us be clear here, Julien; I am my own kind of Walker, and as long as I'm on the scene, I have authority. Not you, not the Authorities, and not this bunch of supernatural flashers."

"Of course," said Julien. "Of course."

I gave him my best disdainful look, then, because we'd said all we could and couldn't put it off any longer, we strode forward to look down into the hole. The naked people immediately fell back to give us room, for which I was quietly grateful. Walking between them sent my heart racing uncomfortably. They weren't naked in a Strippers or Chippendales way, they were more like sky-clad witches, men and women of primal power, unbound by everyday restraints. They burned with dangerous attitude, drawing the eyes to them like moths to a naked flame. I stared straight ahead till I was comfortably past them, then stopped to stand right at the very edge of the great hole, looking down into it. There was nothing much to see. Only broken ground, dark earth, and bare stone; not even a single piece of rubble to mark the Hawk Wind's passing. Julien stood beside me. If the Troops had bothered him, he kept it to himself.

"The fire that burned down the Hawk's Wind Bar & Grille was before my time," I said. "But you were here, in 1970. Does this look anything like what was left behind then?"

"There's not a lot of difference, that I can see," said Julien. "The blaze was . . . sudden, and extensive. The whole building went up in moments, with flames so fierce no-one could get close or even look at them directly for too long. Not a trace of the Bar remained; even the cellar was gone, leaving a hole exactly like this. Some said arson; some said a magical attack against one or other of the significant individuals who often visited. A few romantic souls said it was self-immolation, as a protest against the splitting up of the Beatles. No-one ever found out for sure.

"The Bar's owners were suspiciously eager to draw a line under the proceedings and replace the Bar with an entirely new building, something more modern and up-to-date. They'd made no secret they were tired of the whole sixties look, and that only public affection (and high profits) had kept them from making changes. This was their chance to go up-market, and attract a better (and better-paying) class of clientele.

"And then the Hawk's Wind Bar & Grille came back. Twenty-four hours after it burned down, there it was again. The ghost of a building, a haunting so strong you could walk around inside it, just like the original. Time passed, but not inside the Hawk's Wind. The sixties lived on, as the decades passed, preserving all kinds of drinks and food and music you couldn't find anywhere else. And to the fury of the owners, the Bar became more popular than ever, with visitors dropping in from Past, Present, and any number of possible futures.

"The owners went ballistic. Took it as a personal affront. They tried everything to get rid of the ghost Bar. They called in heavy-duty exorcists; had Bishop Beastly curse it with bell, book, and candle; even got the old rogue vicar Pew in to give it a good scolding . . . I'm even told they quietly and quite illegally imported some barely trained poltergeists to go in there and tear the place down. Only to watch the poltergeists come running out, screaming. I believe a few of them are still at large in the Nightside, running their own security business. But the Hawk's Wind Bar & Grille stood its ground.

"You have to understand, John; none of us had ever seen anything like this before, even in the Nightside. The ghost of a building, so real and solid it was almost undistinguishable from the original. I always thought it came back simply because so many people loved and missed it . . . Anyway. Eventually the Bar's owners shrugged, threw up their hands, and said *Have it your own way*, and went off to sulk in private. And count their profits, of course."

I frowned. "Could the owners have finally found a way to dismiss the haunting, and reclaim their property, after all these years?"

"Unknown," said Julien. "But unlikely. If they had, they'd be here now, dancing and celebrating and boasting how they'd finally won. And they were never more than a pair of minor business men. To do something like this . . . would take real power."

"Hold that thought," I said. "I spy a pair of well-dressed city types heading in our direction, who look a lot like owners to me."

Julien looked round, nodded sourly, and gestured for the
Troops to let them pass. The two men strode up to us and
glared right into our faces, which was brave of them. They
both looked prosperous enough, in an obvious sort of way.
Two old men, well into their seventies, in good suits, coats,
and gloves. Men with hard faces and harder eyes, and flat,
determined mouths. The kind of business men who hadn't
been talked back to in far too long. The taller of the two men
produced his business card with a snap of the hand, like a
conjuring trick, and thrust it at me. I refused to even glance
at it, on general principles, so he pushed it right into my face.
So I took the card, tore it into little pieces, and scattered them
over him like confetti. Start as you mean to go on, that's what
I always say.

The tall man's face went pale, then flushed a dangerous
shade of purple. "We are Tattersol and Vane!" he said angrily.
"We own this most valuable property, and we have a legal
right to be here! I am Tattersol, this is Vane. Show him the
documents, Mr. Vane!"

While Vane hurriedly fumbled important-looking papers
out of his briefcase, I took the opportunity to look the two
men over carefully. Tattersol was well dressed in a casual sort
of way, while Vane was well dressed in a careless sort of way.
Tattersol had thin black hair with pronounced white streaks,
while Vane was almost entirely bald. Tattersol had a hulking,
powerful presence, while Vane had a shifty, detached presence. I was irresistibly reminded of Badger and Mole from
The Wind in the Willows, but kept the thought to myself. I was
Walker now. Dignity at all times. I was prepared to be tact-
ful and polite, right up to the point where someone got on
my tits, and I said *To hell with it*, and booted someone somewhere painful. I beamed on Tattersol and Vane in my most
avuncular fashion.

"So what can the Authorities and their newly appointed
front man do for Misters Tattersol and Vane?"

Vane finally fished out a handful of legal documents and shook them at me meaningfully. I ignored them, so he thrust them at Julien, who looked at him in a disturbingly thoughtful manner until Vane lowered his papers and looked away. Tattersol glared at Vane, then at us.

"We have a legal right to this land! Isn't that right, Mr. Vane?"

"Of course we do, Mr. Tattersol! I have all the necessary documentation right here!"

"Quite so, Mr. Vane. We are here to demand access to this location, our property. We also insist that you do *absolutely nothing* that might assist the ghost of the Hawk's Wind Bar & Grille to return. It is gone, and we want nothing more to do with it. Do we, Mr. Vane?"

"Nothing at all, Mr. Tattersol! We wash our hands of it, at long last. The law is on our side in this matter!"

"We are the law, inasmuch as there is law," said Julien, entirely unmoved by the two old men shouting at him. "This is a crime scene, and the crime is under investigation. If only to ensure that other buildings don't start disappearing, too."

"None of the other buildings are ghosts or phantasms!" snapped Tattersol. "We demand access to our property so we can . . . protect it! Isn't that right, Mr. Vane?"

"Indeed it is, Mr. Tattersol! We have documents! Signed contracts! The law stands four-square behind us!"

"When has the law ever mattered, in the Nightside?" I said, honestly curious.

"Ah, but this is business law!" said Tattersol, with the air of someone closing a trap. "Contracts must be honoured! Or no-one could make a profit here!"

"He may be obnoxious, and far too loud for his own good, but he has a point," said Julien.

"Exactly!" said Vane. "What?"

"I was saying you had a point," said Julien.

"Oh! Yes!" Vane glared at me. "You had better watch your

step, Mr. So-called Walker! Or I will have you hauled up before the Better Unnatural Business Committee!"

"You made that up!" I said. I looked at Julien. "Tell me he made that up."

"Unfortunately not," said Julien.

"And the Authorities have a duty to enforce business contracts!" said Tattersol, with the air of someone slamming down an ace.

"He's right," said Julien. "We do. There are very old agreements to that effect."

"But I am Walker," I said. "And I don't have to agree to anything. In fact, I think that's part of the job description. Mr. Tattersol and Mr. Vane, while I accept that your legal position is undoubtedly correct, I also find you both guilty of obstructing an on-going investigation and getting on my nerves in a built-up area. I have work to do, and you are getting in the way. So be good little business men and go away, and we'll let you know whatever we feel like letting you know. In special legal writing. Won't that be nice? Wave bye-bye, or I'll run you both in for disturbing my peace of mind."

"The abuse of authority comes naturally to you," murmured Julien. "You're going to make a fine Walker."

Tattersol's face was going through a series of dark colours that really didn't speak well for his blood pressure, while Vane had gone white with shock. And then they both began to splutter loudly.

"I will have your heads for this!" yelled Tattersol, his impeccably gloved hands clenched into fists. "I will have you dragged through the streets by horses! I will ruin you, and your family, and everyone you know and care about!"

"We'll take everything you own!" said Vane, just as loudly. "Do you have a house? We'll seize it! Do you have a wife? We'll throw her out on the streets to starve!"

"Oh no," Julien said quietly.

"A wife!" said Tattersol, thinking he saw a weak spot.

"We'll sell her to a sporting-house, to sell her body for other men's pleasures! We'll . . ."

I used an old magical trick then, one I mostly use to take the bullets out of threatening guns, and ripped every filling, crown, implant, and piece of bridgework right out of their mouths. They all disappeared in a moment and fell in a silent rain from my outstretched palms. Tattersol and Vane clapped their hands to their bloody mouths and made loud noises of shock and distress. They looked at me, horrified, and I looked back at them.

"Never threaten his wife," said Julien.

"Get the hell out of here," I said, "before I decide to show you a similar magic trick, involving your lower intestines and a row of plastic buckets."

They couldn't leave fast enough. Some of the watching crowd applauded, and some decided they were urgently needed elsewhere. Most of them carried on watching. It takes a lot to impress a Nightside crowd. I looked at Julien, who was shaking his head sadly.

"What?" I said.

"Oh, nothing, John. You've bullied and assaulted two old men who were technically in the right, very successfully. What do you have planned for an encore? Kicking a puppy?"

"Have you got one?"

"John . . ."

"All right; perhaps I did over-react. But remember; they were business men. Which makes them fair game, in the Nightside. It's probably time we started culling them again, to thin back the numbers."

"You see?" said Julien. "That, right there. That is the difference between how you and I operate. I use reason, you favour brute force."

"It worked, didn't it?" I said. "They're gone, aren't they? In fact, if you look down the street, you can still see them going, at some speed."

"But they will be back!" said Julien. "Probably attended by serious bodyguards, and, which is even worse, with lawyers! They do own this land, and they do have a legitimate claim to be involved with what happens here. All right, I agree; I don't like them either, and I don't want them preventing the return of the Hawk's Wind. But it behooves the Authorities, and you as Walker, to walk carefully around vested business interests."

"Statements like that are why I never wanted to be Walker," I said. "I will defend what is right and just, and let the law catch up when it can. That doesn't suit you or any of the other Authorities, get yourselves another Walker."

"You can be a real pain in the arse sometimes, John," said Julien. "Especially when you're right." He sighed. "They will be back."

"They'll have to visit a dentist first," I said. "That should buy us some time."

"I don't know why I even bother to talk to you, sometimes," said Julien.

"Because you have such a beautiful speaking voice," I said.

Julien ignored me, giving all his attention to the great hole in the ground. "I knew the Hawk's Wind Bar & Grille when it was still real," he said finally. "It was a marvellous place, in its prime. In the sixties. Everyone who mattered made the scene at the Hawk's Wind. It was neutral ground, you see; much like Strangefellows today. So on any given night, you could expect to encounter good guys and bad, famous heroes and infamous villains, and everyone in between. Where the Underworld could meet the elite, gods could sit down with monsters, and every night a whole new gaggle of worshipped celebrities and the briefly fashionable showed up. Some nights you could hardly breathe for all the charisma hanging on the air. The Hawk's Wind was a celebration of the place and the time . . . And it was such an exciting time to be alive . . .

"I came here many times, with my original assistant and

companion. A lovely young lady of great charm and enormous energies, what was known back then as a dolly bird. Her name was Juliet; she was an exotic dancer. My first friend and advisor, when I was still coming to terms with having left Victorian England for the Technicolor sixties. Juliet . . . kept me sane, in the face of so many changes, and a whole new world that often made no sense to me. A brave new world that had so many wonders and nightmares in it. Ah yes; all the adventures we had together . . . Solving mysteries, tracking down evildoers, exposing corruption and brutality and then doing something about it. There was a lot of that going on, in the sixties."

"So what happened to her?" I said. "To Juliet?" I was fascinated; Julien doesn't talk much about his early days in the Nightside.

"She left me," he said, not looking at me. "When I gave up free-lance adventuring to work for the *Night Times*. It seemed the most obvious thing to do, to me, the next obvious step; I thought I could do more good that way. To put pressure on the Powers That Be, to bring about real and lasting change. But she didn't see it that way."

"You gave it all up to become the Man," I said. " Like me."

"Because somebody has to do it," said Julien. "And better us than someone else."

"Exactly."

He did look at me then. "Adventuring is when you do it for yourself. Crusading is when you do it for other people."

"So what happened to Juliet after she left you?"

"Oh, she runs a night-club now, the Adamant. Very fashionable, I'm told. Very selective. I stay away. Because she's got older, and I haven't. It wouldn't be fair, to keep reminding her . . . I think it's better that we keep our happy memories."

"Why don't you grow old?" I said, pushing it since he was in a talkative mood. "Is it to do with the serum you created? The Anti-Hyde?"

He looked at me then and smiled briefly. "The Anti-Hyde? I suppose that's as good a description as any. Dr. Jekyll created a serum to bring out all the evil in a man, release the beast within. I never did understand why anyone would want to do that. To wallow in the mud when they could fly with the angels. I created a serum to bring out the best in a man and tested it on myself. I suppose it worked. I can't tell; I'm too close. But I do know I haven't aged a day since I took it."

"Are you immortal?" I said, the subject being much on my mind.

"Too soon to tell. I hope not. Most of the immortals I've encountered have been an utter waste of space." He looked back at the hole in the ground. "I used to visit the Hawk's Wind all the time, back in the sixties. But I rarely went back after it became a ghost. I kept bumping into Time-travellers, from the Past and the Future, and they always wanted to tell me things . . . I wonder if one of them was trying to tell me about this . . ."

"When the Bar disappeared tonight, there were still people inside."

"Of course. A great many of them famous and important people, from the Past and the Present and a whole bunch of different futures. A few got out, but they're still in shock. They don't remember much. The English Assassin died, getting his sister to safety; but he'll get over it. He always does. The point is, we have to get the Hawk's Wind back, so we can rescue the people trapped inside, and return them to their proper places in Time. Because if we don't . . . God alone knows how much damage that might do to the time-stream."

"Do we have any names, for these famous and important people?" I said.

"Some. The Shimmer Twins; very big rock-and-roll stars. Zodiac the Mystical, from the eighties. Possibly a very-high adept, possibly a major con man. Either way, a Major Player in his day. Shame about what happened to him . . . The

Amber Prince, and the Grey Fox. But most importantly . . . I'm in there, John. With Juliet. We Time-travelled here, from the sixties, following a case. I don't remember the details . . ."

"But if you were in there, in your past, you must remember what happened to the Hawk's Wind!" I said. "Where you were taken, how you were rescued!"

"No," said Julien Advent. "It was all too traumatic. All I had was a gap in my memory. I didn't remember any of this until the Bar disappeared today; then some of it started to come back. Most of it's still gone. Temporal fugue."

"I hate Time travel," I said, feelingly.

"Well," said Julien, "you do have more reason than most."

"Why did you bring me here?" I said flatly. "What does the Bar's disappearance have to do with the current major threat to the Nightside? Is the same person behind both events?"

"Yes," said Julien. "He's called the Sun King. And he has come a very long way, to reach this time, this place, this moment. He wants to bring the sun here, in a long-delayed dawn, and put an end to the longest night in the world. He wants to turn the Nightside into Sunnyside. No more shadows, no more shades of grey. He wants to bathe the Nightside in the harsh and unrelenting light of truth and justice. No more hiding places for old gods and lost monsters, for heroes and villains and those in between."

"You've never approved of the way things are, in the Nightside," I said carefully.

"No," he said. "But I want to help and save the people here, not destroy them. The Nightside has it uses; it serves a purpose. It must be preserved."

"Who is this Sun King?" I said. "I never heard of him."

"Before your time," said Julien Advent. "But he really was big, once upon a time. He was the real happening of the sixties. He was born out of the famous Summer of Love, in 1967. The herald of Man's true evolution, and the mind's true liberation. He believed we could all become more than human, become living gods and walk in glory forever. And he actually managed it. He stepped up and out of the human condition, and became the Sun King. Now he wants to bring back the Big Dream of the sixties, and put us all on the right path again. He believes we've lost our way, betrayed the Dream and ourselves. He's come back to change the world, and he intends to make a start with the Nightside. No more night, no more shadows; *Let the sun shine in . . .*"

I looked at him sharply. "You know him; don't you?"

"Oh, we all knew the Sun King, back in the Summer of Love," said Julien Advent. "But yes, I knew him personally, back in the day. I knew him as just a man, before he burst out of his cocoon and became the Sun King. I left the Nightside to go travel the world and see how much it had changed, since my day, when Victoria was still on the Throne and the British Empire was the greatest the world had ever seen . . . So much had changed, and so much hadn't, and the more I saw, the less I understood. In the summer of 1967, I went to San Francisco to wear some flowers in my hair. It made as much sense as anything else. These days, the word *hippy* has become an insult, but back then they were the bravest of the brave, determined to overthrow an unjust society without using violence. That was a revelation to me. My generation changed the world through brute force, with armies and opium and gunboat diplomacy. But these were a new kind of young people, gentle people with strong convictions, dedicated to non-violent action. Sticking flowers in the barrels of soldiers' guns, knowing that some of those soldiers were quite prepared to shoot them. Standing up to be counted even though they knew someone would club them down. And the Sun King . . . was the very best of them.

"His real name was Harry Webb. No-one knew much about who or what he was before he came to America and made his way to San Francisco. Another young Englishman, walking across the USA, to see what there was to see. He found his way to Haight-Ashbury, and the counter-culture, and following the path of so many of the questing souls of those glorious days, he turned on, tuned in, and dropped out. We met when we crashed together in the same cheap boarding-house. I liked being among people who'd never heard of me, and we all sat and talked for hours about everything under the sun.

"So far, only another story of times past. But then one day, right at the height of the Summer of Love, Harry Webb went to the park and took what Timothy Leary would call an heroic dose of LSD. His mind expanded and exploded, and in that transcendental state . . . he made mental contact with Entities from Beyond.

"Now, a good many people said they did, while under the influence of the many and various mind-expanding chemicals of the day; but Harry really did. The Entities talked to him of many things, and he listened, and when he finally came down again, he wasn't Harry Webb any more. He wasn't human any more. He was transformed, he was transmogrified, he was the Sun King. The living god of LSD, the true Acid Sorcerer, the Miracle Man. Psychedelic rock and roll played around him wherever he went, manifesting out of nowhere—a glorious music that we could never remember or reproduce afterwards. He and his music led us through the streets of San Francisco, like a psychedelic pied piper. Hundreds, thousands strong, our minds blown and expanded by his very presence. We would have followed him anywhere, done anything for him. Lived for him, died for him. Oh yes, I was there, swept up in it all. He was our leader, our prophet, our guru. And all he ever wanted of us was that we should become like him, shine like him. He wanted to raise us all up, into all we'd ever wanted or hoped we could be. A world of turned-on, non-violent superhumans.

"The gentle knights, the lords and ladies of a new Camelot.

"He walked through Haight-Ashbury, and we followed after him, hundreds of thousands strong, singing Hallelujah. He healed the sick with a look, raised up the broken-spirited with just a word, turned on the straights and blasted everyone's minds into something better. A living god, he walked in sunlight wherever he went, and miracles and wild happenings burst out all around him.

"The local authorities totally freaked out. The cops arrived first, with their uniforms and guns and night-sticks; and the Sun King stopped them in their tracks and stunned them with the truth. Of who they really were, as opposed to who they'd wanted to be. And some of them joined us, and some of them ran away to hide in the shadows, and some of them drew their guns and opened fire. But the Sun King smiled, and their bullets turned into flowers and fell out of the air.

"So they called in reinforcements, and they met us with armoured vans, and bigger guns, and water cannon; but none of them made any difference. The Sun King had no weapons; he was benevolence personified, and the natural world itself rose up to protect him. He . . . made you want to be better, to do better, by example. And through his presence, his example, we were."

Julien stopped talking, his eyes far-away, lost in the past. I'd never heard him say so much, or speak so eloquently. Or talk about someone else the way most people talked about him. The Great Victorian Adventurer; the crusading editor of the *Night Times*; the man even his enemies admired.

"What happened?" I said. "What went wrong?"

"He went back to the park," said Julien Advent. "And he raised up a huge and wonderful White Tower, with nothing more than a wave of his hand. It appeared before us, huge and magical, all complete in a moment, a Tower with no doors or windows. He walked through the wall and disappeared inside the Tower, shutting himself off from the clamour of the world, and his followers, so that he could meditate on what to do next, and commune with the Entities from Beyond. All the people came from far around, in their psychedelic clothes and pretty painted faces, with flowers in their hair and in their hands, and they sat around the Tower in endless ranks, closely packed circles spreading out for as far as the eye could see. All the beautiful people, the flower people, the good and groovy people. And there they sat, talking and singing, waiting patiently. Until the light went out of the day, and night fell over the park, and the White Tower blazed like a beacon. And still they stayed, eating and drinking, laughing and loving, dancing and singing in celebration of what they'd seen and the hope of new wonders to come. For twenty-four hours they waited for the Sun King to come out and lead them to glory.

"And exactly twenty-four hours after he disappeared into the White Tower, the Tower with no doors and no windows . . . after they'd all exhausted themselves and there was no more singing or dancing . . . the Tower disappeared. No-one saw it go. No sound or fury, no great explosions of colour; people looked up, and it wasn't there any more. No trace to show it had ever been there. Strangely enough, there weren't any tears or protests, no demands for explanations. Slowly, a few at a time, the people went away. And within a few days, most of them had forgotten about the Sun King, and everyone got on with their lives. The Sun King became another marvellous story from that magical time."

"You were there," I said. "You sat and watched, outside the Tower in the park. Didn't you?"

"Yes. I was there. I knew him, walked with him, saw what he could do. I walked beside him, as he entered the White Tower. It wouldn't let me in. I can still remember how the white wall felt, under my fingertips. Like cold coral, from the bottom of the sea. I waited, because I believed in him and wanted to see what he would do; but when the Tower vanished and took him with it, I knew it was over.

"Hardly anyone talks about the Sun King now. Perhaps because he promised so much and disappointed so many. So that they wanted, needed, to forget him. There are conspiracy sites that dismiss the whole story as CIA black propaganda. Disinformation, to discredit the counter-culture. But he was real. I was there. And they were right; he was dangerous because he was the best drug ever. A transforming presence, a way to break out of the Reality Trip, and lead a better life. He was the revolution. Or, he could have been."

"Do you think . . . the authorities of that time were responsible for his disappearance?" I said.

"I don't know. I always thought he'd be back someday . . . but not like this."

"I never knew you could speak fluent sixties," I said.

He smiled, slightly. "I've been around a long time, John, and lived more lives than most people realise. A man plays many roles in his time, and I've had more time than most . . . You used to be a private investigator; now you're Walker. Who and what will you be, in ten, twenty, thirty years?"

"Dead, probably," I said. "I seem to keep picking life-styles and vocations that contain far more threat and danger than is good for me." I looked at him steadily. "You're sure he's back? The Sun King?"

"Oh yes, John. He's finally returned to us, and he really doesn't like what we've done with the world in his absence. His love and devotion and benevolence are things of the past now, replaced by a righteous rage and fury. Because we, the people, have betrayed the Big Dream of the sixties; sold our hopes and our principles for a mess of pottage. And most of all, we never lived up to the potential he showed us. *We can all shine like the sun,* said the Sun King. We were supposed to become superhumans, living gods, like him. Haul ourselves up by our own spiritual bootstraps; embrace the mind's true liberation and make a Paradise on Earth. Imagine his reaction, when he finally walked out of the White Tower and got a good look at the twenty-first century.

"He knew some time had passed, that he'd been gone a while; but he hadn't realised how long. So he spent some time walking up and down in the world, walking among us as one of us, hiding his light behind a bushel of ordinariness . . . Catching up, looking the new world in the eye and disapproving of most of it. And now his long walk is over; he's returned from the wilderness, and he has decided to put things right. To wake people up from the nightmare they're living in and help them make a better world. He can change things simply by thinking about it, backed by the power of the Entities from Beyond. Whatever they actually are. And he's starting with the Nightside because, as far as he's concerned, it's the most representative of everything that's wrong with the world."

I had to ask. "How do you know all this, Julien?"

"Because he told me. He rang me up, in my editorial offices in the *Night Times*, and I knew his voice at once. I could never forget that voice. We talked for ages, bringing each other up to date, then he told me of his plans. He was very eloquent. And really quite cheerful about it. He wanted me to know, so I could tell everyone else. So I could tell the Nightside he was coming. I was to be his John the Baptist, announcing his return and warning of the great change to come. I think he was actually quite shocked when I refused and put the phone down on him. How could I run all that in the *Night Times*, John? After all the wars and upheavals we've been through? There would have been mass panic, and God alone knows how many cases of over-reaction. The Nightside can't afford another disaster, John. We have to stop him."

"You and me?" I said. "How the hell are we supposed to do that?"

"I still think . . . If I can find him, and speak to him, I can talk him out of this," said Julien. "I can help him remember who he used to be: the gentle man, the living god of non-violence. Not this hate-fuelled avatar of revenge."

"You always did have more faith in people than me," I said. "Do you really think he can do what he says? Raise the sun here, in the Nightside?"

"The man I remember certainly could," said Julien. "And who knows what he's capable of now, after so many years communing with the Entities from Beyond?"

"Whatever they really are," I said. I looked at the great empty hole. "You believe he did this?"

"I know he did this. He told me he was going to. But it wasn't until I remembered that my earlier self was there, that I knew why. I think that he thinks he can keep me from interfering by holding my old self, and Juliet, hostage."

"Is he right?" I said.

"No. He's been gone too long, and he doesn't understand the modern world. All he can see is what's wrong with it and not all the marvellous things we've achieved. I don't entirely disagree with him, that we have lost our way, and that the world could use a good hard kick up its spiritual backside; but he's wrong about the Nightside. It's necessary. It serves a purpose."

"Yes," I said. "It does."

"This is why I insisted on joining you on this case, as your partner," said Julien. "I have to be here because I know the Sun King. He was my friend once, and a good man, as well as a great one. If you can find him, I'm sure I can reach him. And I wanted you on this case so I could prove that you are worthy to be Walker. Show the other Authorities you can stop a threat like the Sun King, and none of them will be able to deny your right to be Walker."

"Every now and again, I forget how devious you can be," I said. "I think some of me must be rubbing off on you."

"What a truly appalling mental image," said Julien.

I had to smile. "Been a long time since we worked together on a case, the two of us. How many years has it been? Not since . . ."

"We agreed never to talk about that," Julien said sternly.

"So we did," I agree. "I still see her around, sometimes . . ."

"Shut up, John."

"Just saying . . ."

"Can you use your gift to find the missing Hawk's Wind Bar & Grille?"

I grinned. "I can try."

I gave silent thanks for Alex's potent pick-me-up and raised my gift. I reached out in all directions at once, feeling for the familiar sights and sounds and smells of the Hawk's Wind, and got nothing. My mind raced round and round the Nightside in ever-expanding circles; and it felt like groping in the dark for something I knew should be there but that I couldn't quite put my hand on. I could feel the Bar's presence, in a faint and distant way, but only right at the edge of my perceptions, in a direction I could sense but not look in. Hidden behind a corner in reality. I let my mind drop back inside my head and looked at Julien.

"I'm sorry. It's gone too far. I can sense the Bar, but I can't reach it. I don't think it's even in our reality any more."

"There must be something you can do!"

"There is," I said. "And don't you raise your voice to me! I'm not your butler!"

"Of course not," said Julien. "She does what she's told."

I gave him a look, then carried on. "I can use my Sight to call up a vision of Time Past, and See what really happened when the Hawk's Wind disappeared. Hopefully, that will give us some facts to work with."

Julien nodded stiffly, so I raised my Sight and looked back into the recent Past; and there was the Hawk's Wind Bar & Grille, back again, right before me. The ghost of a ghost, a vision of a haunting so real you could walk around inside it and order drinks. The Bar now looked to me more ghostly than it ever had before: all shimmering pastel colours and fraying edges. But even in the tinted shapes and shadows of the Past, it was still a magnificent sight. I reached out and placed a hand on Julien's shoulder, making contact, so he could See what I was Seeing. I heard him take a sudden sharp breath as he saw the Past through my eyes.

A perfect monument to the swinging sixties, complete with rococo Day-Glo neon sign and a Hindu-latticed front door, the Hawk's Wind Bar & Grille stood before us; but even as we watched, the whole structure began to shake and shudder, the walls fading in and out as the Bar lost all coherence. It began to fade away, then suddenly there was the English Assassin, standing in the doorway. He collapsed and fell forward onto the ground, and the whole scene vanished, and all that was left was the great hole in the ground.

I let go of Julien's shoulder, and the real world, Time Present, returned for both of us. The hole was still a hole.

"Fascinating," said Julien. "To see the Past unfold, all its secrets laid bare in a moment, living again before us . . . What I would give, to see the Nightside through your eyes, John."

"I have enough ghosts in my life without calling up more," I said. "The Past should stay where it belongs."

"We're not done yet," said Julien. "We need to go further back, deeper into the Past, to see what happened inside the Bar before it disappeared. Can you do that, John?"

"I can try," I said. "But you should brace yourself; there's a reason why we choose to forget the past and leave it behind."

I raised my gift and focused my Sight through it, to find exactly the section of Time Past I needed; and once again, the Hawk's Wind Bar & Grille rose before me, faded and even more indistinct, the ghostly image of a ghost. I felt Julien's hand drop onto my shoulder, the fingers closing tightly as the image filled his eyes again. I walked us towards the

Hindu-latticed door, then right through it, and we walked into the memory of the Hawk's Wind.

It looked as it always had: big Day-Glo Pop-Art posters, with colours so rich and powerful they by-passed your retinas and seared themselves directly onto your brain. Stylised plastic tables and chairs, flaring lights, great swirls of primary colours splashed across the walls and ceiling and floor. But all of it somehow smaller and diminished. Another remainder of Time Past. Like an old photograph of an old friend. A jukebox the size of a Tardis jumped and shuddered happily in a corner, pumping out an endless stream of hits from the sixties. There was no sound in my vision. I could see people talking animatedly at their tables, but not one word of what they were saying came to me. But from far and far-away, it seemed to me that I could hear Jefferson Airplane's "White Rabbit" . . .

In the centre of the great open floor, two gorgeous go-go dancers dressed mostly in bunches of white feathers danced energetically in two huge golden cages. Birds of paradise, indeed. I looked around the packed tables, and a number of familiar faces presented themselves, famous and important people from the Past, Present, and futures. The English Assassin was there, with his beautiful twin sister, Margaret, comparing ornate sonic pistols and arguing cheerfully over a roll of microfilm. Sebastian Stargave, the Fractured Protagonist, was taking tea with a golden-eyed cyborg. Zodiac the Mystical arranged his cloak fussily about him as he gave his order to the mini-skirted, gum-chewing waitress. And Pierrot and Columbine only had eyes for each other. A typical enough gathering for the Hawk's Wind Bar & Grille.

Julien and I walked among them, the faded figures like so many ghosts and phantoms. Or perhaps we were the ghosts, moving unseen and unsuspected. I led the way, being careful not to walk through anything or anyone. The vision was fragile enough as it was, without my doing anything to damage it. And besides, it always pays to be careful when moving through the Past; you never know what might make waves . . .

The English Assassin's head came up suddenly, and he looked suspiciously around him as though disturbed by a presence he couldn't quite put a finger on. He looked right at Julien and me, and even though he couldn't see us, his steady gaze sent chills up my back. He finally shrugged quickly and resumed his conversation with his sister. Which, given who and what he is, was just as well. Julien studied the English Assassin thoughtfully.

"I've known him for so many years," he said quietly. "With this name and that, one face or another. In the service of chaos, and law. And I'm still no nearer understanding him. He was as much an icon and a representative of the sixties as the Sun King; but he always stood for the darker aspects of that time."

"You don't need to lower your voice," I said. "He can't see or hear us. None of them can."

Julien's hand on my shoulder urged me forward, towards the rear of the Bar. We threaded our way between the tables and finally stopped at a little alcove by the window, and there he was . . . his younger self, sitting with his girl companion, Juliet. Julien didn't look much different than he did now, but there was perhaps a more youthful sense to his smile, his gaze, the way he held himself. He certainly smiled a lot more than the man I was used to. And from the quiet sigh that came behind me, if I hadn't known better, I would have thought Julien was looking at someone who'd died.

"Ah, Juliet," he said. "We were so happy together, for a time."

Juliet was a beautiful and vivacious English rose, with a porcelain complexion and long blonde hair, pale pink lips and flashing blue eyes, and a single small flower painted on one cheek. She wore a dress of black-and-white go-go checks, and tall, white, plastic boots with stiletto heels. And she was so alive: gesturing excitedly as she talked, tossing her long hair so it danced around her head, and silently teasing her more stolid and reserved companion.

"Why did I ever let you go, Juliet?" said Julien, in a voice so quiet I could barely hear it. There was something in that voice that would have broken the hearts of the two young people before us if only they could have heard it. "I want to warn them, John, about so many things; but I can't, and I know I won't, because I didn't."

"This is why I hate Time travel," I said. "Nothing good ever comes of it. This is the only truth that ever comes out of the Past—that nothing lasts."

"But sometimes, people make comebacks," said Julien. He moved in beside me, maintaining his grip, and looked thoughtfully at the crowd behind him. "Can any of you hear me? Do you know I'm here? Do you know what's happened, or what's about to happen? Come on, you're all ghosts; if anyone's not fixed in Time, it's you. Help us to help you."

But there was no response. No-one said anything, or even turned a head to look. It was only an echo of the Past, after all.

"Did you really expect anyone to answer?" I said.

Julien shrugged. "It's the Nightside. Normal rules do not apply."

And then we both looked round sharply as the Hawk's Wind Bar & Grille began to shake and shudder. All around us, people jumped to their feet, shouting silently at each other. The young girls stopped dancing and rattled their golden cages, screaming noiselessly to be let out. A great light seemed to burn in from all directions at once, a fierce, consuming light that ate up everything it touched. People started to fade away, to disappear. The walls of the Bar began to break up as thick beams of light punched through them like battering rams.

Let the sun shine in . . .

A few people ran for the door. Most of them didn't make it, fading softly and silently away, often in midstep. A few tried to fight. The younger Julien Advent tried to protect his Juliet, holding up a large golden amulet with an unblinking eye set in it. They still disappeared, clutching each other's hands so they wouldn't be separated. Zodiac the Mystical surrounded himself with a shield of coruscating energies, silently chanting and stabbing his hands in all directions; but the light sneaked up on him when he wasn't looking and snatched him up, and he was gone in a moment. The English Assassin got his sister to the door, fighting his way through the incandescent light beams, and threw her out the door. He stopped in the doorway to glare about him, sonic pistol in hand; but there was nothing he could shoot at. The light blazed up, dazzling, blindingly bright, then it snapped off; and the Hawk's Wind Bar & Grille was gone.

I let go of the Past, and we were back where we'd started, looking down into the hole. It looked much the same. Some of the Tantric Troops started towards us, but Julien stopped them with a look. Showing rather more sang-froid than I would have shown, in the face of so many naked people. Julien beckoned to one naked woman, and she came forward to stand before him. I concentrated on her face.

"Right at the end there," Julien said brusquely. "What did you see?"

"Light burst in from everywhere," said the naked woman. "Forcing back the night. And then it was as though the two of you were there, and not there, at the same time. Strobing back and forth . . . and then the light was gone, and you were back."

"You didn't see the ghost building?" said Julien. "The Hawk's Wind?"

"No," said the naked woman. "Only you and Walker."

"Thank you," said Julien. "I want this whole area sealed

off. No-one in or out until I tell you otherwise, or the Hawk's Wind returns."

"Is that likely?" asked the naked woman.

Julien gave her a hard look. "It's the Nightside. Who knows anything?"

"Good point," said the naked woman, and she hurried back to join the other naked people and started shouting at the watching crowd to back the hell off. And they did. Julien looked sharply at me.

"You felt the strength of that light, didn't you? It could have taken us, along with the Bar. So why didn't it?"

"Perhaps because we weren't really there," I said. "We were walking in the Past, not part of it. So what do we do now?"

"There is a place we could go," Julien said slowly. "Somewhere that might provide answers. Green Henge."

"Of course," I said. "The Nightside's very own Ring of Standing Stones. Where better to look for an old hippy?"

SIX

The Very Righteous Sisters Meet the Sun King

I have seen many impressive walls, in the Nightside. Everything from the Great Wall of Porcelain China, down by the Desolation Docks, to the Moebius Wall of Murder Mile, which surrounds itself. But the huge stone wall that surrounds the Garden of Green Henge is still one hell of an impressive sight in its own right. My gold watch dropped Julien and me off outside the wall, in one of the shabbier areas of the Nightside. Either the trip was getting easier, or Julien and I were getting used to it, because after a few moments of deep breathing, silent cursing, and carefully not looking at each other, we were both back in command of ourselves and ready for business.

The massive stone wall before us rose some forty to fifty feet into the air, constructed from great stone slabs fitted expertly together, without the need for mortar or cement. Each slab was set so tightly in place, you couldn't fit a knife blade between them; and given the major magical protections

I could sense built into the wall, that would probably be a really bad idea anyway. There was no obvious door, and the wall stretched away in each direction for as far as I could see. As though someone had decided long ago, *This far into the Nightside shall ye go, and no further.* Where the wall met the ground, old blood stained the stones in a regular pattern, like a bloody tide-mark soaked deep into the stone so long ago that no shade of red remained in the dark stains.

Julien studied the blood-stains thoughtfully. "Is this what happened to the last people who tried to get in, do you think?"

"No," I said. "This is what's left from human sacrifices. When they were building the wall, men and women were butchered right here, so their blood and deaths would strengthen the magics protecting the wall and so that their ghosts would remain here, bound to the wall, to hold it up against any forces that tried to bring it down. Old Druidic tradition. Very practical and unpleasant people, the Druids."

"You're saying the ghosts are still here?" said Julien.

I looked up and down the wall. "No. No ghosts here. Somebody screwed up."

Julien sighed quietly. "You can be really spooky sometimes, John. You know that?"

"Only sometimes?" I said. "I must try harder."

Julien was giving rather more of his attention to the less than salubrious surroundings we'd arrived in. The buildings were dark and decrepit, with boarded-up windows and gaping doorways, and most of the street-lights had been smashed. Dark shadows everywhere; with ragged people lurking in them. A few of the braver ones were already shuffling out into the uncertain light to get a better look at whoever had been foolish enough to venture into their territory. Other things, that might or might not have been human but gave the impression of being just as hungry, moved in the shadows and alleyways.

"It's times like this make me wish I still carried my old sword-stick," said Julien. "Couldn't you have materialised us inside the Garden?"

"Possibly," I said. "But I didn't want to upset the Righteous Sisters who run the place. There's always the chance they're old school Druids, the kind who would burn you alive in a giant wicker man, or nail your guts to the old oak tree, then chase you round it, as soon as look at you. We're going to need their cooperation, so I'm being polite. I never used to bother much with that, back when I was only a private investigator, but now that I'm Walker . . . it's that much harder to do appalling things to people in public and not get noticed. And anyway . . ."

"The wall has protections?" said Julien, keeping a watchful eye on the local wildlife.

"Like you wouldn't believe," I said. "You can't sacrifice this many people in one place and not get something for your trouble. I'm sensing defensive magic here that could tie your insides into square knots and send your balls back up the way they came down. Over and over again. So I think we're going to be very patient and polite . . . right up to the point where I don't give a toss any more. There's supposed to be an alcove here somewhere, with a bell . . ."

"Can't you use your gift to find it?" said Julien.

I gave him a stern look. "I have a strong feeling the Garden might take that as an affront, or an attempt to break in. Either way, if I upset the wall, you can bet the alcove will disappear itself in a moment."

"What if we can't find a way in?" said Julien. "Some of these shabby gentlemen are getting a bit too close for my liking."

"Follow me," I said. "Keep your head up; they can smell fear. And don't get too close to the wall. It might bite."

We walked casually beside the wall for a while, both of us doing our best to appear confident and dangerous. Julien carried it off rather better than I did, with his great opera cape swirling around him. I'm more used to being sneaky and dangerous. Some of the rougher elements inhabiting the neighbourhood moved along with us, sticking to the shadows and maintaining a safe distance. They moved more like animals than anything human, their eyes gleaming brightly in the varying light. It didn't take me long to find the alcove, built right into the wall, which I now realised had to be five to six feet thick. What did the original builders fear so much that they had to build a wall like this to keep it out? Or what did they need to keep inside their Garden?

The stone of the alcove was grey and dusty, nothing more than a rough enclosure to hold a single silver bell, hanging from a thick silver chain. The bell was delicately made and shone brightly in the gloom, as though it had been placed there only moments before. The surface of the bell had been deeply inscribed with old Celtic lettering that read, roughly, *Ring Me.*

"Oh, that is entirely too twee," said Julien, when I translated it for him. "If a cake turns up that says *Eat Me*, there will be trouble. Never did like that book."

I checked the floor of the alcove carefully, for trap-doors and other booby-traps. You can't be too careful, in the Nightside. I rang the bell sharply, and a clear, crystal sound rang out on the quiet night air, like a single note of grace in a hopeless setting. The local scavengers froze where they were, half out of their protective shadows, their grimy faces full of a strange wonder. The bell rang on and on, an intense but still beautiful sound, and still the scavengers didn't move. They didn't experience much in the way of beauty in what was left of their lives. The sound of the bell continued, long after it should have died away, as though it had to travel some unimaginable distance to reach the proper ears. But it finally fell silent, fading and fading away, and the cold, empty silence of the street returned. Julien and I waited for something to happen. The scavengers began to remember who and what they were and emerged from the shadows in larger and larger groups. Ragged men in ragged clothes, with wild, feral eyes and mouths full of broken, pointed teeth. Their clothing was such a mess I couldn't even tell what it might have been originally. Bare hands and faces were grey with ground-in grime, and they padded on their bare feet as much as walked. These were beyond homeless; denied any of the comforts of civilisation, they had sunk down to brute basic needs and hungers, to the way of the beast.

"They say that in London, you're never more than ten feet from a rat," Julien observed carelessly. "In the Nightside, it would be more true to say that you're never more than ten feet away from murder and sudden mayhem. I really don't like the look of these unruly individuals. If a door doesn't open in this wall very soon, it may become necessary for us to show these unfortunates exactly which of us is in charge here."

"I think they already know that," I said. "Given how many of them there are. Oh, look, they've moved to both sides of the street now, to surround us. How very ingenious of them. I suppose I could use my gift to find a hidden fault in this wall, and make a door . . . but there's no telling how the wall's protections would react to that. We might end up caught between a hard place and a very angry rock. Can't you do something to scare them off? Go on, scold them in your posh voice. Nothing like an aristocratic tone to put the lower orders in their place."

"Sarcasm is the lowest form of wit, John," said Julien. "Oscar told me that, at one of Whistler's parties. I suppose I could tell them all about the overheads of running a daily newspaper. God knows that scares the crap out of me, every quarter. But I really don't see why I should have to do the scary thing. You're John Taylor! And Walker! You scare them off!"

I looked around. The scavengers were getting very close now, on every side, and growing steadily bolder as their numbers increased. Some had knives, some had broken bottles, some had chair legs and other improvised blunt instruments. They wanted our warm clothes and anything of value we had, and after they were finished taking that, they'd kill and eat us. Hopefully in that order. Nothing goes to waste in a place like this. When you fall off the edge in the Nightside, you fall all the way. I thought for a moment, considering my options, and I reached out with my gift and found the nearest over-priced restaurant. (Which you are also never very far from, wherever you go in the Nightside.) I gathered up all the food in the restaurant, made a connection with where I was, and it was the easiest thing in the world to bring all the food to me. (Simply a reverse variation on the magic I use to make things disappear.) (I'd been working on it.) Food rained down out of the night sky, hot and steaming and succulent. It hit the ground with a series of soft slaps, and lay there temptingly, while more and more of it fell from nowhere. For a moment the scavengers just stood where they were, watching with wide and unbelieving eyes. It had been a long time since they'd been anywhere near proper food. And then they rushed forward, forgetting all about Julien and me, and fell on the growing piles of food. They didn't even have to fight over it; there was more than enough for everyone.

Julien looked at me. "All right . . . First, how the hell did you do that? And second, since when did you become altruistic?"

"First," I said, "I am known for my useful little tricks. And second, I have been down and out in my time and know what it is to be hungry. And lost, and desperate. There was a time I looked a lot like them, and you would have walked right past me in the street, carefully not making eye contact. Always put a penny in the blind man's hat, Julien, because the wheel always turns, and it turns for you as for anyone else."

"You never cease to amaze me, John," said Julien. "But this is no time to be getting soft."

"Not going to happen," I said. I turned away from him to study the alcove carefully. "Tell me about the Garden of Green Henge. You know more about the history of this place than I do. You know everything about the Nightside's history."

"No-one knows everything about the Nightside," said Julien. "But Green Henge has always been an interest of mine . . . Yes. Well . . . Of course the Nightside would have its own Stonehenge, its very own Circle of Sacred Standing Stones. The Nightside has pretty much one of everything from all of recorded human history. And a whole lot of things it shouldn't have, that got edited out of history, or written over. Palimpsests cover a multitude of sins. Except this particular item is a fake. A folly. It was constructed back in Victorian times, as part of the fashion. Society was very big on fake but picturesque ruins, back then, expertly designed to look dark and Gothic and battered by the weather, as though they were ready to fall apart or fall down at any moment."

"That doesn't make sense," I said.

"It was a fad," Julien said patiently. "It didn't have to make sense. It was the fashion, to have half a barn or a decrepit old water-wheel in your back garden, or to have an exact copy of some famous house or monument, so you could visit it without having to track half-way across the countryside. And the Nightside has never been a stranger to strange fads and fancies. Remember the craze for Pet Rocks?"

"Ah yes," I said. "Just the things—for people with rocks in their heads."

"How about the pet alien fad, from the eighties? You were nobody then, if you didn't have your very own pet BEM, to parade through the park on a leash and make do tricks . . . to the admiring or at the very least envious gazes of all. I remember a whole bunch of complaints about that, from the various Alien embassies in the Nightside."

"There aren't any Alien embassies in the Nightside," I said.

"Not any more, there aren't. Apparently just because something is small, green, and cute doesn't mean it isn't some race's Most Honoured Ambassador, who got a collar snapped round his neck when he was out taking a stroll. It also turned out that a lot of the little beggars were actually alien sociology students, observing Humanity. They decided the collars and leashes meant we were all serious S&M freaks, and called for their Home Bases to mount an Intervention, on moral-health grounds. The previous Walker put an end to that by taking them to the Pit night-club and showing them what real S&M looks like. Never heard another word from them, after that. They're probably still holed up in their other-dimensional universities, writing very deep psychological papers about us. And don't even get me started on the Great Tamaguchi Rebellion . . ."

"The things you know," I said, admiringly.

"Mind full of trivia," he said, grandly.

We broke off and looked around sharply as loud cracking and groaning noises filled the alcove, and one whole section of it opened inwards, forming a doorway into darkness. We both leaned in close for a better look, but there was no sign of any Garden beyond; only an impenetrable blackness.

"Are you sure you couldn't have found that?" said Julien.

"What?" I said. "And miss out on your fascinating and enlightening briefing? You know you love to lecture people."

"I do, don't I?" said Julien.

A Druidic Sister stepped abruptly out of the darkness to stand before us, resplendent in pristine white robes and wearing a crown of plaited mistletoe. She was a tall, powerfully built woman, with a calm, serene face. She projected a natural grace and spirituality, and smiled benevolently on us.

"I am Sister Dorethea, of the Very Righteous Sisters of the Holy Druids, and I welcome you both to the Garden of Green Henge. Oh bloody hell, it's John Taylor."

She scowled at me balefully while Julien did his best to hide a smile.

"You must get that a lot, John."

"You have no idea," I said. "Yes, Sister; I am John Taylor, the newly appointed Walker. And this is . . ."

"Oh, I know who he is," said Sister Dorethea, losing her scowl to smile at Julien Advent. "The Great Victorian Adventurer is known to all of us here and is always welcome to enter the Garden of Green Henge. But you, Taylor, your reputation precedes you. You only get to come in on sufferance because you're with him. So watch your manners, don't go straying from the path, and *don't touch anything.*"

I nodded. I always let people set their own restrictions, if only so I can have the fun of breaking them.

"Are you real Druids?" I said innocently. "I mean, if the Stones are fake . . ."

She gave me a full-on look of withering scorn. "The Stones are not *fake*. They are all real menhirs, transported from the south-west of England, from the small town of Avebury. Apparently because they had so many, it was felt they could spare some. The Circles may be . . . more recent, but the Stones are in every way real, and we venerate them as such. The Garden is a sacred site. So watch yourself, Taylor."

"Do you do souvenirs?" I asked.

She turned away from me with magnificent disdain and introduced herself to Julien Advent, who was, of course, perfectly charming and polite. I never really got the hang of either of those. I took the opportunity to study Sister Dorethea's face, that being all there was of her that wasn't covered by voluminous robes. She had the look of a lady of a certain age, where all the children have left home but haven't got around to providing grandchildren yet. Leaving the lady in question with a big gap in her life that she had to fill with something. Good causes usually suffice, but out-of-the-way religions and beliefs often come a close second. If there isn't a local swingers' club. And, of course, the Nightside is no stranger to those with too much time on their hands, and is always happy to provide unusual opportunities. Very Righteous Sisters my arse.

Didn't mean they weren't dangerous, though.

Julien soon had Sister Dorethea smiling and cooing, and she led him through the darkness at the rear of the alcove. I hurried after them, not wanting to be left behind or left out of anything. I plunged into the dark and almost immediately stumbled to a halt again as the darkness was replaced by the silver-grey of a late evening in the countryside. I also heard the alcove closing itself very firmly behind me. Though whether to keep the scavengers out, or Julien and me in, remained to be seen. I looked cautiously about me. I was standing on a wide-open moor, in the twilight of the evening. Night had only just begun to fall here, though the full moon shone brightly overhead, fully as oversized as it was everywhere else in the Nightside. I glanced behind me, and of course the great wall was gone. Open and empty, the moorland stretched away unbroken for miles.

We were in a pocket dimension, a small reality enclosed within a greater one, maintained by the magics built into the surrounding wall. There are a great many worlds within worlds, in the Nightside. It's the only way we can fit everything in. The moor stretched away before me, all the way to a far-off horizon. And I had to wonder why they needed so much space, to hold a Circle of Standing Stones. A cold wind blew, in sudden chilly gusts, wuthering in the quiet twilight. Not all that far-away stood a massive hedgerow maze, maybe half a mile across, with the rows a good ten to twelve feet high. I'd heard of this maze. Green Henge was set right at the heart and centre of the maze, hidden from view by the tall green walls. Only the Very Righteous Sisters knew all the secrets of the maze, and so controlled access to the Stones.

Sister Dorethea led us forward at a brisk, imperious pace. The ground was covered with scrubby grass and dry moss, which crunched loudly under our feet. As we drew closer, I could make out more Very Righteous Sisters, moving unhurriedly in and out of the various entrances to the maze, quietly going about their business like so many white-clad bees tending their hive. None of them so much as glanced in our direction. I couldn't help noticing that there were only women present, not a single man to be seen anywhere.

"I couldn't help noticing . . ." I said to Sister Dorethea.

"Yes, yes, I know; we're all women here, whereas the original Druids famously didn't allow women to be priests. According to the few records that survive from that time, mostly written down by the Romans, who didn't approve of the Druids anyway. But that was then, and this is now. Green Henge may have started out as a folly, but years of veneration have made the Standing Stones sacred again, and the Sisterhood is entirely real if not actually entirely authentic. We've been in charge here for ages, because no-one else could be bothered with the time and devotion necessary to ensure the upkeep of the Stones, and Green Henge."

"So if they want to be wrong, let them," murmured Julien.

"I'm sorry," I said. "I was wondering why there aren't any men here."

"Because they get in the way!" snapped Sister Dorethea. "They are a distraction! We have all given up much to become Sisters to the Stones. We are all of us pure and pristine, and we have every intention of remaining that way."

She stuck her nose in the air and headed straight for the maze. So Julien and I quite naturally slowed our pace, to show we weren't going to be hurried.

"Shouldn't a garden have, well, flowers and stuff?" I said. "All I can see is moorland, and not even a trace of heather."

"I can hear you!" said Sister Dorethea, not lowering herself to look back. "The moor was designed to be this way. No distractions, remember? It is we, the Sisterhood, who grow here, through our service to the Stones. This is a Garden of Stone, where we beat ourselves against the hard surfaces every day to purify ourselves, that we might flourish and blossom and bloom. Spiritually speaking."

"Right," I said. "You go, Sister. Spiritually speaking. But I still have to ask, What is Green Henge for? Exactly? What does it do?"

"It weeds out the unworthy," Sister Dorethea said sternly. "And encourages proper growth. You'll see. Only the pure of intent can pass through the maze, to reach the Circle of Standing Stones and the glory of Green Henge."

"That's it?" said Julien, after a while.

"Isn't that enough?" countered the Sister. "Beware the Ring of Stones and bow down to Green Henge. They are powerful, and significant beyond your mere mortal understanding."

I looked at Julien. "This place may have started out as a folly, but it isn't any more. If enough people believe in a thing, it becomes real. Especially in the Nightside. Green Henge might have been created here to someone's fashionable scheme, but it's become the real deal. Still not too clear on the Druid connection, though . . . Do you still practise human sacrifice here, Sister Dorethea?"

"Of course not!" she said though she didn't sound nearly shocked enough for my liking. "We're not that kind of Druid!"

I was still considering pressing the matter, as to exactly what kind of Druid she was, when Dorethea finally brought us to the entrance of the hedgerow maze. No sign, no map, nothing but a dark opening. The heavy green hedge walls towered above us, stretching away on every side. The maze was frankly huge, and gave every indication of being big enough to contain half a dozen Henges. The hedge walls were composed of some unfamiliar dark green vegetation, with flat serrated leaves and heavy bone yellow thorns. The passage between the walls was barely wide enough to allow Julien and me to walk through side by side. The only light was shimmering moonlight, grey and blue-white, and there were far too many deep, dark shadows for my liking. I turned to Sister Dorethea, expecting her to lead us in, but she stepped back and waved for Julien and me to go on in, bestowing on us a decidedly knowing smile. I stood my ground.

"How long is it going to take us to get to the centre, to the Stones? We haven't got all night."

"It takes as long as it takes," said Sister Dorethea. "The way depends on you."

I looked at Julien. "We can't even be sure he's in there."

"Perhaps," said Julien. "But I think we'll learn something interesting in Green Henge, nonetheless."

I looked at the entrance to the maze. "You really want to do this?"

"We have to, John. This is our path to the Sun King."

I glared at him suspiciously. "There's something you're not telling me, isn't there?"

"There's a lot I'm not telling you. But I need you to trust me on this, John."

And all I could do was shrug because he was Julien Advent, the Great Victorian Adventurer, and if I couldn't trust him . . . I couldn't trust anyone.

"Only those of the correct spiritual frame of mind can hope to navigate the maze successfully," said Sister Dorethea. "Only the pure of intent will obtain access to the Stones, and Green Henge."

"Yes, well, you would say that, wouldn't you?" I said. "Come on, Julien. Catch you later, Druid."

I strode forward into the maze, and Julien was immediately

right there at my side. I can't say I've ever felt safer with Julien beside me because he doesn't do safe; but I've always felt more confident. Julien's a good man to have at your side or your back, because you know you can depend on him to fight to the last drop of his blood; or, more usually, his enemy's. I suppose that's why we've so rarely partnered up. Not only because he so loudly disapproves of me, and my methods, but because I've always felt the junior partner. Julien Advent is the kind of man I always wanted to be and knew I never could be. Because he was a genuine hero, and I'm not. I'm just a man who gets things done.

We took a left and a right and a left inside the maze, and, immediately, I was hopelessly lost. Hadn't got a clue where I was, or where I was going, or even where the entrance was. When I looked back, all I could see were hedgerows, exactly like those in front of me. I've never been any good at mazes. Or crossword puzzles. I've never liked games where you can't bend the rules when you're losing. But when I hesitated, Julien immediately took over the lead, making his choices confidently, as though he was following some trail only he could see.

"I worked my way through any number of mazes, back when Victoria was on the Throne," Julien said calmly. "They all follow the same basic pattern. I think they were only fashionable so young ladies could get lost in them and cry pitifully to be rescued by brave young men. Not a good place to canoodle, though; you never knew who might come round a corner. But this . . . is not a usual maze."

And he stopped dead in his tracks, looking from one way to another, unable to choose.

"I can . . . feel the centre of the Maze," he said slowly. "I could point to it. But I can't seem to go any further. The choices don't make sense any more. It's like looking at a map and finding all the symbols have suddenly taken on new and unfamiliar meanings. It's like something else is required of me, other than logic. A very uncomfortable feeling. How does the maze feel to you, John?"

I shrugged uncomfortably. I did feel something, but it wasn't anything I could put my finger on. "It's only a maze. First rule of the Nightside: when you're playing a game, and the rules say you're losing, change the rules."

"You're going to cheat, aren't you?" said Julien resignedly.

"Of course," I said. "It's what I do best."

I raised my gift, enough to add strength and power to my Sight, and immediately I could sense the exact location of Green Henge. And, more importantly, how to get to it. I plunged forward, darting through one row to another with complete confidence. Julien had to hurry to keep up with me. It was invigorating, racing through the hedgerows with defiant ease, while Green Henge called to me like a great voice in the night. It wasn't just a Circle of Stones, it was a place of power, and Destiny. It was a place where things happened, things that mattered. And the moment I realised that, I slammed the brakes on and came to a sudden halt. Julien stopped with me and looked quickly around.

"What is it? Did you hear something? I thought I heard something . . ."

"No," I said. "It's Green Henge. This was never a folly, Julien. The man who brought the Stones here may have thought so, but the Stones were using him. To transport them to a new place, where they could draw on new energies, to become a greater power than they ever were before. And you knew this, didn't you?"

"I suspected it," said Julien. "How do you know all this, John?"

I scowled. "Just being in the maze, I can feel things. But you knew before we ever came in here."

"I told you Green Henge was an interest of mine. I've done research. The Circle of Standing Stones is a meeting place. It draws important and significant people to it, when the time is right. The Sun King will be there, John. Trust me."

"I do," I said. "You know I do, damn you." I looked slowly about me. "Hold everything. Did you say you heard something?"

"Yes," said Julien. "And I'm pretty sure I heard it again."

"We're not alone in here," I said. "Something else is in the maze with us."

"The Sisters?" said Julien, looking around vaguely.

"No," I said, looking quickly this way and that but seeing only more hedgerows and shadows. "Whatever's in here with us, it's not human."

Both our heads snapped round sharply, as a slow rustle of movement ran through the hedge wall on one side of us, then the other. Julien and I moved immediately to stand back-to-back. My hands had already clenched instinctively into fists. We stood, waiting, listening, ready for an attack from any side . . . but it never came. Nothing emerged from any of the hedgerows. The full moon surrounded us with its shimmering blue-white light, and none of the shadows moved. The maze was deathly silent.

"It's still out there," murmured Julien. "I can feel it . . . It's close. Watching us."

"Yes," I said, quietly. "I think . . . it's hunting us. But my gift can't find it, and my Sight can't detect it."

"Can you still find the way to the centre?"

"Yes. The way's so clear it's like a straight path to me."

"Then we should press on," said Julien. "Get to the centre and Green Henge."

"You think we'll be safe there?"

"Probably not. But that's where the answers are. That's where we'll find the Sun King."

"Still not telling me everything, Julien . . ."

I headed forward into the maze again, taking lefts and rights without even thinking about it. Julien strode along beside me, frowning with deep concentration. Thinking about whatever it was that he wasn't ready to tell me yet. I made myself stick to a steady pace. Whatever was after us might attack if it thought we were fleeing. I could hear movement in the adjoining rows, soft, padding footsteps, drawing nearer, then falling away as I constantly changed direction. And there was a feeling on the air, on the clear, quiet air; of something powerful and very patient, following a ritual as old as Time itself. The maze wasn't simply a maze. It was a testing ground, a proving ground . . .

Only the pure of intent will reach Green Henge . . .

I stopped when I saw the first body. It was human once, but that was a long time ago. It hung suspended, half-in and half-out of the hedge wall. So withered and desiccated, every drop of moisture sucked out of it, that I couldn't even tell whether I was looking at a man or a woman. No clothing, no possessions, nothing to identify the body. One mummified hand thrust out of the dark greenery as though begging for help that never came. The face was a dry mask: no eyes, lips drawn all the way back from the dusty teeth. Thorns from the hedge were thrust deep into the body from all sides, holding it in place.

"There's nothing we can do," Julien said quietly.

"They left him here," I said slowly. "The Sisters. The Very Righteous Sisters . . . They had to know he was here, but they left his body in the hedge. As punishment, or an example, or a warning . . . Because if he wasn't worthy, he wasn't worth bothering about. It isn't right!"

"She," said Julien.

"What?"

"This was a woman," said Julien. "Look at the hip-bones. We have to go on, John. We can't do anything for her."

"I know. We have work to do. Doesn't mean I have to like it, though."

Julien surprised me by clapping me on the shoulder approvingly. "You have a good heart, John. I don't care what anyone says."

I made myself smile. "It's usually you saying it, in one of your editorials."

"You sell papers, John, I've never denied it."

"Then how come I never see any royalties?"

I didn't actually feel better but managed to fake it for Julien. We moved on. Heading for Green Henge. Where somebody had better be waiting with some bloody good answers.

We passed more bodies along the way. Always dried-out pitiful things, mummified, hanging half-in and half-out of the hedge walls. It didn't look like a good way to die. The faces were always the worst part, teeth showing clearly in wide-stretched mouths. As though they'd all died screaming. A cold, dangerous anger burned within me. *We don't do sacrifices. We're not that kind of Druid.* I wasn't sure I believed that any more. If I ever had. I might not be able to help these people, but I could still avenge them. I caught Julien looking at me worriedly and realised I was scowling fiercely, my hands still clenched into fists. I made myself relax, a little.

"Is there any chance these bodies are fakes?" I said roughly. "Maybe . . . seeded through the maze; atmosphere for the tourists?"

"No," said Julien. "I would have heard. I think these people died trying to get to the centre of the maze. Or trying to get out of it."

"Because they weren't in the right spiritual frame of mind?" I said. My voice sounded ugly, even to me.

"Perhaps. There is something at work in this maze, John. I can feel it. And not only whatever it is that's still following us." He stopped abruptly, so I had to stop with him. "I keep hearing noises, footsteps, and what might be breathing, but I haven't even caught a glimpse . . . And after all these years of living in the Nightside, I am really hard to sneak up on."

"Same here," I said. "It keeps moving in on us, then falling back. As though . . ."

"As though it wants to get to us, but it can't!" said Julien. "As though something is preventing it, holding it back!"

"Any idea what?" I said. "I'd really like to know. I'd feel ever so much more comfortable."

Julien shook his head. "How far are we, from Green Henge?"

"Almost there," I said.

"Is your gift telling you that? Is it telling you anything else about the maze?"

I frowned, despite myself. "There's a power here, inside the maze. Nowhere near the same level as Green Henge, but still . . . definitely a power. Set here long ago, for a purpose . . . To weed out the unworthy; isn't that what Sister Dorethea said? But whatever it is, it feels vague to me, uncertain. I can't seem to get a handle on it."

"Wonderful," said Julian. "Marvellous. Terrific. I really must make a mental note to load myself down with any number of powerful weapons and devices the next time I agree to accompany you on a case."

"You came looking for me, remember?" I said.

"So I did. I must be getting old."

We pressed on, and only half a dozen turnings later we were suddenly out of the hedgerow maze, or more properly, into the great opening at its centre. A huge open space, bigger even than the size of the maze had suggested. Someone was playing tricks with Space again. But what really took my breath away was the Standing Stones. Not one Circle, but many. Dozens and dozens of rows, of circles of menhirs, spreading out for as far as the eye could see. Great slabs of ancient Stone, twenty or thirty feet high, hundreds of prehistoric menhirs, and all of them covered in a thick layer of living greenery. Not the spiky grey-green vegetation of the hedge walls; this greenery was a brilliant emerald, bursting with life and health, radiating the wild verdant energy of Green Henge.

Julien and I stood close together, feeling very small in the face of such a huge thing. A presence, as well as a power.

"No wonder the Sisters call it a Garden," I said finally. "But why did they allow the Stones to become so overgrown? Or was it always like this, from the beginning?"

"Not that I ever heard," said Julien. "Is it a Druid thing?"

"Not that I ever heard," I said.

"This . . . wasn't simply allowed to happen," Julien said slowly. "This is why the Stones allowed themselves to be transported here. To become . . . Green Henge."

I looked back the way we'd come. The shadowy hedgerows were still and silent; and if anything in there was still watching us, it kept itself to itself. I shrugged quickly and strode forward into the Circles of Standing Stones. Julien moved along with me, staring openly about him like a tourist. I had more pride though the sheer presence of the Stones beat on the still air like a silent endless heartbeat, demanding respect. I gave each Stone plenty of room as I passed, looking carefully straight ahead. The full moon seemed to fill half the sky overhead, shining directly down on the Stones, bathing them in a shimmering blue-white glare. A light so intense, I could feel it tingling on my bare face and hands.

We seemed to walk for ages, through one Circle of Stones to another, but eventually we reached the centre, and stopped. A single long Stone lay on its side, on the ground, in the exact centre of all the Circles. No greenery touched it, its dull grey surface pitted and pock-marked. Half-buried in the dark earth by its own weight. My first thought was *Sacrificial Stone*, but there were none of the dark blood-stains on it that I'd seen on the outer wall. Julien smiled broadly, his face full of a simple awe.

"Can you *feel* that, John?"

Of course I could. There was the maze, and there was

Green Henge, and then . . . there was something else. Something equally as powerful, perhaps even more so, but very young, as opposed to the ancient presence around us. Suddenly the glowing moonlight was gone, blasted aside by a burst of brilliant sunshine, as the Sun King came striding out of the Stones to join us. The whole of Green Henge was bathed in golden sunlight, rich and glorious, perhaps for the first time in centuries. The greenery surrounding the Standing Stones seemed to writhe and twist in ecstasy, expanding under the pressure of the sun's warmth. A great choir of voices rang out, filling the evening air, surrounding the Sun King as he walked towards us, an angelic choir singing Hallelujahs. And the Sun King came to a halt, to stand before Julien and me, his presence beating on the air like an endless roll of thunder . . . prophesying the storm to come.

"Too loud, man!" said Julien. "Turn it down! I can hardly hear myself think!"

At once, the angelic chorus shut off, and the slow silence of the evening returned to Green Henge.

"Hello, Julien," said the Sun King in a warm, pleasant voice. "It's been a while. Miss me?"

"You know I did," said Julien. "What's with the new music? When did you go religious? What happened to the rock and roll?"

"That was then, this is now," said the Sun King. He smiled easily on Julien, and on me; and even I was impressed by the sheer grace and spirituality blazing off this man. Whatever else he was, whatever else he might have become during his long absence, I had no doubt at all that the Sun King was the real deal.

He was dressed in his Coat of Vivid Colours, a long, linen coat blazing with psychedelic colours and patterns. It reminded me irresistibly of the interior of the Hawk's Wind Bar & Grille. Underneath that he wore only a pair of faded blue jeans. His chest was bare, and so were his feet. He had a great mane of jet-black hair, falling half-way down his back, and a broad, square face with a prominent nose and a wide, smiling mouth. He wore tinted John Lennon granny glasses, pushed well down on his nose so he could peer over them with gleaming dark eyes. He opened his arms suddenly to Julien, and the two men stepped forward and embraced each other fiercely, with much back-slapping and loud, happy cries. I stayed back, feeling a bit left out. This was two legends meeting, after too long apart. I felt like a footnote. The two old friends rocked back and forth together, saying each other's name over and over, and finally they stepped back, looked each other over at arm's length, and gazed into each other's face.

"You haven't changed a bit, Julien," said the Sun King. "All these years, and you still look exactly the same as I remembered you."

"I could say the same of you," said Julien, grinning broadly. "I waited for you, you know."

"Of course you did," said the Sun King. "I wouldn't have expected anything else."

Julien slowly stopped smiling. He let go of the Sun King and stepped back. "You look the same; but you've changed. The man I remember never once gave me any cause to fear what he might do."

The Sun King shrugged easily. "I never meant to be away so long. I never meant . . . that you should all have to wait so long. For my return. Time passed differently inside the Tower, while I communed with the Entities. They had so much to teach me . . . But Julien, I have to ask. What the hell happened? To the Dream, to everything we believed in? Why did it all fall apart without me? I was only ever the messenger, not the message! I was expecting all of you to take up where I left off and carry on. To make the new and glorious world we promised ourselves."

"You were the Miracle Man," Julien said steadily. "When you left, you took the miracles with you. There was never anyone else like you. We fought our battles, day by day, inch by inch, and we did achieve many of the things we believed in. If not always in the ways we expected. But day by day, and inch by inch, the world wore us down.

"The miracles were never the point!" snapped the Sun King. He wasn't smiling any more. He didn't even try to hide his anger, but he made himself nod respectfully to Julien. "When I came back, you were the first one I thought of. Took me a while to track you down—in the Nightside, of all places. You always said you'd never come back here after the light you found in San Francisco. But here we both are. I knew you'd want to see me, so I put all this in your head. So you'd come here. And here I am. You are still my oldest and dearest friend, Julien; even if neither of us is who we were when we first met. Even if it appears . . . we no longer care about the same things."

"You've been messing with my mind?" said Julien. His voice would have made anyone else beware.

"I always did," the Sun King said complacently. "I changed the way people thought just by being near them. You saw me do it; but you never gave a damn as long as I was changing minds you disapproved of. You still believe you can talk me out of what I intend to do, don't you? But be honest, Julien. This world you live in, this brave new modern world, this marvellous scientific twenty-first century . . . Is it the future we hoped for, the world we wanted to make? Where have all the beautiful people gone?"

"You were supposed to come back and save the world, not destroy it," said Julien.

"Save, destroy; it's all in the way you look at it," said the Sun King.

"What happened to you?" said Julien, his voice rising despite himself.

"What happened to you?" said the Sun King. "The Great Victorian Adventurer? I was so proud to have you as my friend, back in good old San Fran. The hero of one age, who became the hero of another. Who gave up God and Empire for something better, something finer. We walked in glory through the streets of Haight-Ashbury, Julien. Walk with me now, through the streets of the Nightside. It can be like it used to be, when we were young and had the world at our feet."

"I can't," said Julien Advent. "You're not the man I remember."

"I haven't changed," said the Sun King. "Not really. You only think I have because you've got old, inside. Look at you, Mr. Suit and Tie man. You wear that cloak like you're ashamed of it. I still wear my colours, proudly nailed to my mast."

"You would have loved the New Romantics," I said, to remind them I was still there. And then wished I hadn't as the Sun King turned his tinted glasses and fierce gaze in my direction. Having the Sun King look right at you was like being punched in the head by a spotlight. His presence was overwhelming; you couldn't think of anything or anyone else. So I deliberately looked away and made a big deal of adjusting my white trench coat, so it fell comfortably about me.

"I know you," said the Sun King, smiling. "John Taylor. The good man in a bad world. The cold knight in tarnished armour, doing good in dangerous ways. You should support me and what I intend to do."

I made myself glare right back at him and matched his smile with my best unsettling grin. "Not a hope in hell. This is my home. My people."

"What people?" said the Sun King. "All I see are broken men with shop-soiled souls, and women selling everything they have, just to get by. I see false gods and pathetic monsters, sin and corruption and blood in the gutters. This is where the lost souls come to hide, because no-one else will have them."

"You think I don't know that?" I said. "You think Julien doesn't? We're here because we're needed. Because not all the world's troubles can be solved with simple, unrelenting concepts like Good and Evil, Law and Chaos, Light and Dark. The world needs us to see outside the box."

But the Sun King wasn't listening. He shrugged and looked away. "If you're not part of the solution, John Taylor, you're part of the problem."

I almost collapsed when he looked away, from the relief of not having to fight off his overwhelming presence. The Sun King didn't notice, all his attention focused on Julien.

"You betrayed the Dream, Julien. Gave up being an adventurer to work in an office. Mr. Nine to Five. Like all the other spineless drones."

"I woke up," Julien said steadily. "I stopped indulging myself, playing hero for the applause of the crowds, and changed tactics. So I could achieve more."

"You got old!" said the Sun King. "Work from within, to change the system? That was a specious argument, even in my day. You can't work within the system without supporting the system; and whatever small changes you do achieve will inevitably be cancelled out by everyone else."

"I wanted to change the Nightside in useful ways!" Julien said stubbornly. "Ways that would last!"

"And have you? All these years you've been trying to save and redeem the Nightside, and what have you actually achieved? What's really changed?"

"I am part of the new Authorities," said Julien. "The old order is dead and gone, and their way of doing things. Your way only worked because of you! And you weren't there any more. I had to find a new, practical way. And I did."

"Dreams aren't supposed to be practical," said the Sun King. "All these years you wasted your life, Julien. The Nightside is the way it is because it likes it that way. And because vested interests make a lot of money out of keeping it that way. From squeezing dirty profits out of all the sad, pathetic losers who come here, to do the things they wouldn't be allowed to do anywhere else. How can you defeat that? It's only night here so people can hide what they're doing."

"It's not as simple as that," said Julien.

"Yes, well, you would say that, wouldn't you?" said the Sun King. "I don't see any of the things you say you see here."

"Doesn't mean they aren't there," I said.

I was confused by the Sun King. He was everything Julien had said, and more, and yet . . . there was something off about him. A living god, but with strangely limited perspective. He could only see what he wanted to see, only think in terms of the man he used to be, forty-odd years ago. It was as though he wanted to be a good man . . . if only he could remember how. If only he could concentrate.

I'm not sure he really heard what we were saying. There was something . . . out of focus about him, for all his blazing presence. I have met living gods, and men who were so much more than human; and none of them had ever seemed as dangerous as this man because he gave every impression of being someone who might sweep the whole world away with a gesture, in a moment, on a whim. Because he couldn't think of anything better to do.

"I'm going to bring it all down," the Sun King said to Julien Advent. "And there's nothing you can do to stop me. Let the sun shine in . . ."

So I put up my hand, like a child in class, and that got his attention. "I have a question, oh great and living god. Who are the Entities from Beyond, exactly? What do they call themselves when they're at home? Only, I've had all kinds of contacts with all kinds of other-dimensional entities, and I never heard of them before. Why are you the only one they've contacted? Or should that be abducted? Why didn't they tell you that you'd be spending years communing with them? What were you talking about, all that time? And what, exactly, do they want in return for all the power they've given you?"

The Sun King surprised me then by smiling easily, completely unfazed by my questions. "I approve of you, John Taylor, I really do. Never afraid to ask the awkward questions. Never afraid to put your life on the line to get at the truth. And I approve of your adopted role. The private eye is a respected icon, a modern archetype, protecting those who can't protect themselves. You're living your dream. But like Julien, I have to ask, what have you actually achieved?"

"Are you kidding me?" I said. "I've saved people who needed saving! I've saved the entire Nightside, and the whole damned planet, on more than one occasion! You should have done your homework. I'm not a private investigator any more. I'm the new Walker."

The Sun King shook his head sadly. "Just like Julien. You gave up the Dream, to become the Man. Sold your soul, for power."

"Isn't that what you've done?" I said. "And I notice you still haven't answered any of my questions. What price did you pay to become the Sun King?"

"I can't answer your questions because you couldn't possibly understand what I've been through," said the Sun King. "Your mind is too small, too limited. Too human. Power, prices, answers . . . these are all human obsessions."

"Because they matter," I said.

"If we're human, what are you?" said Julien. "The man I remember was still a man, for all his miracles, and the Dream he pursued was a human Dream."

"What I could do then was nothing compared to what I can do now," said the Sun King. "See what I can do . . ."

He clapped his hands sharply, and the sun blazing overhead grew suddenly in size, half filling the sky. The sky turned a bright blue, so pure a colour it was painful to look at. The sun was fierce and furnace-hot, and my bare face and hands smarted under the impact. What had been a cool and quiet evening in the Nightside was gone, suppressed, replaced by an almost unbearable desert heat. Air shimmered all around us with heat haze. The greenery surrounding the Standing Stones shuddered with new life, as though suddenly woken from long seasons of sleep. The hedgerow maze rocked this way and that, as though under attack. Flowers blossomed all along the hedge walls, bursting out of the dark green. Thick pulpy petals opened everywhere, in flaming colours the same shades as the Sun King's Coat of Vivid Colours. The flowers unfolded over and over again, while the hedgerows writhed and convulsed as though in pain. Great swellings of moss and fungi erupted out of the dry ground, pulsing like living brains. The air was thick with the scent of all kinds of flowers, filling my head with over-ripe perfumes. Dusty pollen swirled on the air; and the whole Garden pulsed with the beat of living things. But even I could tell these were hothouse flowers, forced into shapes and sizes against their will and against nature. The Sun King put his head back and laughed; and I had to wonder where all the grace and spirituality had gone.

Suddenly the Very Righteous Sisters of the Holy Druids appeared, standing silently among the Standing Stones. Hundreds and hundreds of them, stiff and stern in their pristine white robes, surrounding us in all the Circles of Stones, their cold gaze focused on the Sun King. He stopped laughing and looked unhurriedly about him. If the sheer number of Druids opposing him impressed him at all, he did a really good job of hiding it.

"How did you get in, Sun King?" The Sisters spoke in unison, hundreds of voices blended into one authoritative voice. "The only way to approach the Sacred Stones is by proving your worth, through the rigours of the Maze."

"That's how people do it," the Sun King said easily. "But I'm not people any more. Haven't been for a long time. I can be anywhere I need to be. I don't need to pass any stupid tests."

"Tests?" said Julien, glancing back at the Maze. "Did we . . . ?"

"Of course you did," said the Sun King. "You proved yourself worthy long ago." He paused, and looked at me. "Not sure how you made it through, though. Must be more to you than meets the eye."

I had to smile at that. "You have no idea." I looked at the Sisters, and when I spoke, I could hear the anger in my voice. "The bodies we found, along the way. Did the Maze kill them?"

"Yes," said the Sisters, in their single unrelenting voice. "They were not worthy. They came to the Stones with impure thoughts and purposes. They proved themselves a danger to Green Henge, so they were not allowed through. Sun King, you should not be here. You do not venerate the Sacred Stones."

"Of course not," said the Sun King. "They're nothing but stones."

He clapped his hands again, and the hedgerows in the maze buckled and twisted, erupting into new growth, losing all their carefully sculpted meaning. The dark green walls swayed this way and that, as though under the pressure of some unseen storm though there wasn't a breath of movement in the furnace-hot air. And the greenery surrounding the Standing Stones constricted suddenly, crushing and cracking the ancient menhirs within.

"Let new life replace old stone!" said the Sun King, happily. "Let's have a little fun, in this solemn old place! You're not Druids, Sisters. They knew how to party."

The Very Righteous Sisters ignored him, singing in harmony, a great choir replacing the single voice. Hundreds and hundreds of women, singing a song that was old when civilisation was new. Their song rose on the air, filling the Garden of Green Henge; and the Stones remembered. One by one, the Stones reasserted their ancient presence, and the greenery surrounding the menhirs fell still again. The maze grew still again as the hedge walls resumed their shape and significance. The flowers slowly wasted away, thick pulpy petals shrivelling up, then dropping like multi-coloured confetti to the walkways of the maze. Moss and fungi growths ceased to pulsate and sank back into the ground. The Sisters' song rose triumphantly, as sunshine and heat vanished, replaced by cool evening air. The sky was dark, and the oversized moon was back. The Garden of Green Henge was back, as though it had never been away.

The song broke off, and a familiar quiet filling the evening again. The Very Righteous Sisters of the Holy Druids stood still and silent among the Circles of Standing Stones. And the Sun King looked slowly about him, his face cold.

"Do you really think you can stand against me?"

"We serve the Stones," said the Sisters, in their great voice. "It is the Stones who oppose you."

"Shall I tell the Walker and the Adventurer exactly what it is that lives in the Maze and weeds out the unworthy?"

There was a pause . . . and then the Sisters said, "Shall we let it loose upon you?"

"Give it your best shot," said the Sun King.

There was a familiar rustling movement in the hedgerows, and Julien and I looked back at the Maze. The sounds grew closer, and from out of the Maze stalked a dark grey thing, seven or eight feet tall, made of grey-green vegetation and bone-white thorns. Shaped like a man, it walked like a man though there was nothing of Humanity in it. The murders in the maze were carried out by a manifestation of the maze, given shape and purpose, and a warrant to kill anyone the maze judged unworthy. The hedge thing stood still, the wrath of a green world, the protector of the Garden of Green Henge.

"That . . . is what was following us?" said Julien.

"That is what would have killed you if you'd failed the Sisters' entirely arbitrary sense of what is right and proper," said the Sun King. "It would have sucked the life out of you, then impaled what was left on the thorns of the hedge walls. The Very Righteous Sisters may like to think of themselves as a new kind of Druid; but the fruit never falls far from the tree. What you're looking at is the hedge walking. It still wants to kill you. Because you don't venerate the Stones. Can't you feel it? Your basic goodness is all that's kept it at bay, Julien. But the Sisters could still let that thing run loose, to kill anyone they disapprove of."

The hedge thing was looking at Julien and me, and I could tell it didn't like us. But it liked the Sun King even less. It swayed slightly on its thorny feet, as though readying itself for an order to attack. And I was pretty sure if it did, it wouldn't stop with the Sun King.

"Plants should know their place," the Sun King said firmly. He snapped his fingers, and a great blast of sunlight stabbed down out of nowhere, pinning the hedge thing to the spot. The light and heat were so intense that Julien and I had to throw up our arms to shields our eyes, even as we staggered backwards. The sunlight engulfed the hedge thing in a moment, and it burst into vicious flames that consumed it from the inside out. Fire and smoke rose into the evening air. The hedge thing waved its green arms, and the flames danced hungrily. I thought I heard the thing scream, and some cold place in my heart approved. The beam of sunlight snapped off. And when I was finally able to see clearly again, there was nothing left of the hedge thing but a blackened, smoking mess on the ground and a heavy scent, like burning leaves.

And the Sun King was gone.

"He hasn't changed," said Julien. "He still has to have the last word."

"So," I said, trying to keep my voice light. "That . . . was the Sun King. I thought he'd be taller."

"You weren't seeing him at his best," said Julien. "There was something . . . off, about him."

"Yes," I said. "I felt that. What did the Entities from Beyond do to him, during those long years they had him all to themselves, in the White Tower?"

"And why wouldn't he tell us their real name?" said Julien. "Perhaps because . . . we might recognise it?"

"This is what you wouldn't tell me," I said sternly. "That the Sun King had been putting things in your head. Telling you to come here, so he could talk to you. And you didn't want me to know that, because . . ."

"Because it would have given you the wrong impression," said Julien. "I wanted you to see him as he really was."

"I have," I said.

Julien sighed tiredly. "As a demonstration of power, what he did here was pretty impressive."

"Until the Righteous Sisters turned up and kicked his psychedelic arse."

We looked around, but they were gone, too. Green Henge stood silent and alone, as before, and the maze was very still.

"They would have let that thing kill us," I said. "Like it did all the other poor bastards in the maze. I've half a mind to burn the bloody thing down before we leave."

"But you won't," said Julien. "Because that's the kind of thing the Sun King would do."

"Don't mess with my head," I said. "Because that's the kind of thing the Sun King would do."

"Touché."

"Threeché." I raised my voice. "I know you're still listening, Sisters! I want all those bodies removed from the maze! And no more hedge things! Or I will come back and find a way to really mess things up around here."

There was no reply, but I had no doubt they'd heard me. I looked at Julien, and he was smiling again.

"And that . . . is why I wanted you as Walker."

I shrugged. "There's some shit I just won't put up with."

"Exactly." And then Julien frowned, considering. "The Sisters only stopped the Sun King because they had the backing of the Stones. And because he didn't really care. I'm not sure even the Stones could have stood against him if he'd thought they were a real threat. He was having fun, showing off his power. He wiped out the hedge thing with a thought, and he did bring sunlight to the Nightside; for a while. No-one has ever done that before."

"But as a demonstration of getting his own way . . . not so much," I said. "If the Very Righteous Sisters could slap him down, even for a moment, I have to wonder what will happen when he goes head to head with something nasty from the Street of the Gods."

"I saw him work miracles, back in the sixties," said Julien. "I can't believe he's grown weaker since then."

"Not weaker," I said. "Not as such. But didn't he seem to you . . . as though he couldn't quite get his act together?"

"As though he always had something else on his mind! Yes! He never had any doubts, any second thoughts, back in San Francisco."

"Okay," I said. "Where do you think he's gone now?"

"I don't know. He hasn't put anything in my head if that's what you're thinking. Can't you find him, with your gift?"

"No," I said. "I already tried. I can't even look in his direction. It's like staring into the sun. The light blinds me." I felt suddenly tired, so I sat down on the flat stone in the middle of the Circle, taking the weight off my feet. After a moment's hesitation, Julien joined me.

"I don't think the Sisters will approve of this casual disrespect," he said.

"They can blow it out their ears," I said. "Starting with Sister Dorethea. I don't approve of them. Look, you know the Sun King best. Where would he go next, in the Nightside?"

Julien shook his head. "He's beyond me, John. He always

was. I only knew to come here because he told me. And if he could get inside my head that easily, he already knows everything I might plan to do against him."

"You can't be sure of that," I said quickly. "Just because he has access to your thoughts doesn't mean he has access to your mind. Or your soul. Come on, Julien, give it your best guess. Where should we go next?"

"He really wasn't the man I remembered," Julien said slowly. "His wisdom is gone, never mind his common sense, and his old easy confidence has been replaced by arrogance. You must have noticed: he was happy to talk, but he didn't want to listen. That wasn't like the old him at all. He always had time for everyone, back in Haight-Ashbury. He used to preach; now he boasts. He felt . . . wrong, as though he was acting like he thought the Sun King should. Like a bad copy of his previous self. What did the Entities from Beyond do to him, for all those years? Mental contact with them made Harry Webb into a living god. But years of close communion with the Entities . . ."

"Have made him into a real prick," I said.

Julien actually winced. "I do wish you'd avoid such vulgar language, John. You are Walker now."

"Stick to the point," I said, not unkindly. "I think the Entities spent all those years programming him, impressing their true purpose on him. Whatever that might be. So that when they finally released him back into the world . . . he'd follow their Dream instead of his."

"I don't know," said Julien. "Maybe. Perhaps . . ."

"Should we try the Street of the Gods?" I said. "There's got to be a whole bunch of Entities and beings on the Street who could give him a good run for his money."

But Julien was already shaking his head firmly. "The Sun King was always so much more than a living god, even back then. Damned if I know what he is now. Do we really want to start a god war in the Nightside? Particularly when we can't be sure of the outcome?"

"All right," I said. "Should we go to the other real place of god power in the Nightside? St. Jude's?"

"You really want to bring the Lord of Thorns into this? There'd be smiting everywhere and nowhere safe to hide."

"All right, all right! You think of something! Where would the Sun King want to go next, in the Nightside? Who does he know here, apart from you?"

"Ah . . . There was someone," Julien said slowly. "Someone he knew, back in our Haight-Ashbury days. A woman . . ."

"Of course!" I said. "There's always a woman! Who is she?"

"She was the Goldberry to his Tom Bombadil," said Julien. "His first real love and his first true passion, back in the Summer of Love. She was called Princess Starshine then, when she walked alongside the Sun King. She had power, too, briefly, from being so close to him. But when the time came, the Sun King didn't take his Princess Starshine into the White Tower with him. He left her outside, with the others. After the Tower vanished, she waited and waited for it to reappear. She was the last to give up hope and the last to leave."

"And she's here, now, in the Nightside?"

"Has been for years. She's a doctor, at the Hospice of the Blessed Saint Margaret. I know that because the *Night Times* helps raise funds to keep it going. No National Health Service here, unfortunately. If the Sun King knows she's there, I think he'd go there. For old times' sake. If . . . there's anything left of the man I remember."

"If you want to bring a man down, go through the woman he loves," I said, rubbing my hands together happily. "Good thinking, Julien."

"I used to be such a good man, once," he said sadly.

"So did the Sun King," I said. "And look where that got him."

SEVEN

All Kinds of Miracles

When we finally stepped out of the alcove in the Garden wall and back into the Land of Down and Outs, I was surprised to see a long black limousine already there, waiting for us. It looked more than a little out of place in the kind of area where the words *appalling* and *disgusting* take on whole new and very extreme meanings. I took a quiet look around, but the locals had all disappeared, presumably to sleep off their recent feast. Julien Advent was already opening the back door of the limousine. I stayed right where I was and gave him my very best meaningful cough. Julien looked back and gave me his best urbane smile.

"I called for the car. My stomach has had more than enough of travelling by Portable Timeslip, while many of my nerves are currently on strike for better working conditions. You represent the Authorities now, John, and are fully entitled to all the little perks that go with your new position."

"Fair enough," I said. "But this goes on your expense account, not mine."

Julien smiled briefly. "You're learning. Now get in, so I can shut the door. We're letting all the ambience in."

I slid into the back seat, and Julien followed me in quickly. The door shut itself after him, hardly making a sound. I leaned back in the richly padded seat and let loose a great sigh of pleasure as my muscles were finally able to relax. Julien picked up the interior phone and told the driver where to go. A uniformed chauffeur, of course, though I quickly realised that *chauffeuse* was more correct. A tall and elegant young lady in a white leather uniform, complete with a peaked white leather cap, over a platinum blonde buzz cut. She nodded briefly to Julien, without looking back.

"Sure thing, chief. Buckle up; it's going to be a bumpy ride."

A glass partition slid up, separating us from the driver. Presumably because Julien knew there were all sorts of questions I wanted to ask about how she and Julien knew each other. You can never have too much gossip. Julien had already opened up the interior bar, revealing a sparkling area full of crystal decanters. He helped himself to a glass of very good brandy, and I helped myself to a decanter. Julien gave me a reproving look. I grinned at him, and toasted him with the decanter.

"Any snacks in there? Chief?"

"No," said Julien, very firmly, and he shut the bar quickly before I could go rooting around in it. "But the limousine does come equipped with an ejector seat for those passengers who've outstayed their welcome. Don't say you weren't warned."

I drank some really good brandy, straight from the decanter, and Julien winced. I think sometimes I'm a bit too much for his delicate sensibilities. Probably because I don't possess any. He made a point of not looking in my direction as he picked up the interior phone again and contacted the news desk at the *Night Times*, to catch up with what had been happening in his absence. He listened for a while, then frowned and put the phone on speaker, so I could hear what he was hearing. It appeared that Brilliant Chang had already turned in his piece on what had gone down at the Ball of Forever, and I had come out of it surprisingly well. The voice at the other end of the phone read out some of the choicer bits, managing to sound both shocked and scandalised while enjoying himself immensely. Julien nodded.

"I'm going to have to write a special editorial on the passing of King of Skin when I get back. Doing him justice will be a challenge."

"Will you be mentioning in passing that one of the co-founders of the new Authorities was actually a major serial killer, who wrapped himself in the living skins of his victims?" I said innocently.

"The *Night Times* stands for the truth," Julien said stiffly. "Just not all the truth, all the time. In cases like this, it can be better to let the truth come out a bit at a time, so as not to . . . overwhelm people. On the other hand, we can't hold some things back for fear of being scooped. You did say Bettie Divine was there . . . Damn. I'm going to have to try and balance the good with the bad. King of Skin did do admirable things, in his time. He did help found the new Authorities, and you might remember that he fought alongside us during the Lilith War. A lot of innocent people are only alive today because he put his life on the line to protect them."

"Innocent?" I said, raising an eyebrow. "In the Nightside?"

"You know what I mean."

"King of Skin only took on Lilith's armies because they were destroying his own personal playground," I said, letting the empty decanter drop onto the floor at my feet. Somebody should have refilled it; I'd only got a few drinks out of the damned thing. I sighed, feeling suddenly tired. Contemplating the endless ambiguities of the Nightside can take a lot out of you. "Just because the enemy of your enemy is your ally, it doesn't necessarily follow that he's your friend," I said.

The voice at the other end of the speaker-phone asked, rather nervously, if he should continue, and Julien told him to get on with it. Possibly I wasn't the only one who was feeling tired. We listened silently as the voice did its best to hit the high spots of what was happening in the Nightside. Apparently someone had dumped a whole bunch of piranha into a private swimming pool because someone had blackballed their membership bid. No-one had ever seen so many people leave a pool so quickly. They then turned the heating all the way up, broiled the piranha, and ate the lot. There was a metaphor for the Nightside in there somewhere, but I was too tired to work it out. Someone else had opened the wrong kind of book in the H. P. Lovecraft Memorial Library, and now there was a whole new building standing in the same place, the Linda Lovecraft Library of Spiritual Erotica. Explorers in protective suits were currently investigating the new contents. And something really unpleasant had possessed the lady news-reader of the local television station, on air, right in the middle of a broadcast. It had her saying really nasty and untruthful things for some time before anyone noticed. She had to be wrestled out of her seat and dragged off air, all the time speaking in tongues and swivelling her head round and round. Which is a really bad thing to do when you're projectile vomiting something very like pea green soup. I had to smile. You'd think a Nightside television station would have enough sense to keep an exorcist on staff for emergencies like this. Some savings really are false economies.

On the other hand, apparently that particular news show

boasted the highest ratings the station had ever known, and had already been nominated for several awards.

The black limousine moved smoothly out of the bad lands and into the mainstream traffic lanes. The roar of never-ending traffic embraced us immediately though hardly any of it got past the limo's soundproofing. The usual mixture of unusual vehicles passed by on either side. Ambulances that ran on distilled suffering. Huge articulated trucks with no-one visible in the driver's seat, carrying unknown goods to unknowable destinations. One of them had a big sign on the back, saying COMPLAIN ABOUT MY DRIVING. GO ON. I DARE YOU. And all kinds of cars, from a shocking pink souped-up Model T Ford, to an Edsel with tall, shiny fins and a radio-active back burner, to a 2020 Velociraptor Special, with a motor so powerful it rattled the fillings in my teeth as it shot past.

Most of the traffic had enough sense to give the black limousine plenty of room on the grounds that anything so obviously expensive was bound to have top-of-the-line armaments and protections; but something that only looked like a car moved quickly through the adjoining lanes to ease in alongside us. Up close, it quickly became apparent there was something seriously wrong with the car's shape and details. All the windows were pure black, including the windscreen, the wheels didn't turn, and the thing moved in sudden darts and rushes that would have had its passengers ricocheting around the interior. I drew Julien's attention to whatever it was that was coming our way, but he didn't seem particularly worried. The car thing lurched in close beside us, our two sides almost touching. The all-black window nearest us disappeared, and dozens of dark green arms ending in hooked and clawed hands shot out to attack our windows. They slammed to a halt against the glass and skittered angrily over it, unable to break or even scratch it.

"Bullet-proof, shatter-proof, waterproof," said Julien, a bit complacently.

"Make a good watch," I said, deliberately unimpressed.

The claws and hooks clattered in vain against the heavy glass, then all the arms snapped back into the car thing. The black window reappeared. The car thing cut its power and fell back behind us, taking up a position right on our bumper. Long machine-gun barrels protruded from its dully gleaming grill-work, and the car thing opened fire. Luckily, our rear windows were equally bullet-proof. The limousine hardly rocked at all under the impact. The blonde chauffeuse made an adjustment to something on her dash-board, and flame-throwers opened up from the back of the limousine. The car thing shrieked shrilly as terrible flames washed over it. The featureless exterior scorched and bubbled, charring and blackening like roasted flesh under the extreme heat. The car thing burned fiercely, then exploded. Bits of burning car flesh flew through the air, tumbling end over end, bouncing and splattering off the surrounding traffic.

"James Bond, eat your heart out," said Julien Advent.

I couldn't find it in my heart to feel sorry for the car thing. Some predators are too damned nasty for sympathy. The black limousine moved smoothly on through the night traffic, which treated us with a little more respect than before.

It took us a while to reach the Hospice of the Blessed Saint Margaret. The Nightside's one and only hospital is located right on the outskirts, not far from the Necropolis. So that when things go wrong, they don't have far to move the body. It also allows the rest of the Nightside population to feel that little bit more secure in case anything should escape. Or anyone. Julien made a series of important phone calls to the

editorial desk of the *Night Times*, and I passed the time doz-
ing on the back seat with my mouth open. Eventually, the
black limousine eased to a halt, and I opened my eyes to find
we were right in the middle of the Hospice car-park. The
chauffeuse turned to address Julien, and he lowered the intervening glass panel.

"You want me to wait, chief?"

"No thank you, Gloria," said Julien. "Hospital car-parks
charge a fortune. You take some time off. I'll call you if I
need you."

"Suits me, chief. Try not to pick up anything nasty in
there. I'd hate to have to fumigate the car again."

"Again?" I said, but Julien already had the back door open
and was climbing out. I got out after him, and the moment I
was clear, the back door slammed shut, and the limousine
pulled quickly away. I hunched my shoulders inside my
trench coat against the chill of the night air, and stood beside
Julien while we looked the Hospice over from a safe distance.
Despite having lived most of my very dangerous life in the
Nightside, I'd never actually seen the Hospice before. Julien
saw me frowning.

"Something wrong?"

"Don't like hospitals," I said bluntly. "They get on my
nerves. And don't even get me started on dentists. On bad
days, I need a local anæsthetic, even to make an appointment."

"Back in my old days, the hospital was where you went to
die," said Julien, reflectively. "In Victorian times, surgeons
were butchers, survival rates were frankly terrifying, and we
had none of today's wonder drugs. You had to be tough to
survive a Victorian hospital. And don't even get me started
on the Elephant Man."

The Hospice itself was a huge, bright, white-walled building, sweeping up into the night sky. Searchlights blazed from
the roof, to guide in air ambulances, flying carpets and the
occasional winged unicorn. They'd had a dragon drop in on

the roof once, many years ago, and they're still talking about it. Still trying to get the last bits of dragon dung out of the guttering, by all accounts. That was one sick dragon. All the windows were mirrored one-way glass, to ensure privacy and keep passers-by from seeing things that might upset them. The Hospice was named after the original Saint Margaret, who founded the place when she passed through the Nightside, many centuries ago.

"She didn't stay long," said Julien, when I tried to impress him with my limited knowledge. "We don't get many saints in the Nightside, as a rule."

"Gosh," I said. "Imagine my surprise."

"But she did hang around long enough to found a much-needed leper Hospice. She ran it herself, tending the lepers with her own hands, until she could find someone brave enough to take over; and then she couldn't get out of the Nightside fast enough. The lepers didn't bother her, but she felt contaminated by the general *moral ambience*. Which is fair enough. The Hospice evolved, through various fits and starts, into the Hospice you see before you, the most impressive and experienced of its kind. It deals with supernatural and super-science medical problems, and all the extreme and unnatural cases that inevitably occur in a free-thinking community like ours. It was either this, or fire-bombing whole areas of the Nightside on a regular basis. And don't think that wasn't discussed. The Hospice is supported by many good friends and grateful ex-patients, and even more people with a thoughtful eye to the future."

"You still wouldn't catch me dead in there," I said solemnly.

"That joke was old when I was young," Julien said crushingly.

We walked through the car-park and headed for the main front doors. We'd barely got half-way there before a whole bunch of heavily armed security people emerged suddenly from all sides to cover us. Some wore old military outfits, some wore specially adapted battle armour, and every single one of them kept their weapons trained very seriously on Julien and me. I looked casually around, careful to appear conspicuously unimpressed. All the security people had the same cold, focused, dangerous look. I knew who they were immediately. Who they had to be. A lot of them recognised me, and there was a lot of glancing around to find someone ready to make the first move. I could all but see the buck shifting in mid air. After a certain amount of glancing and muttering, they all carefully chose to point their weapons between me and Julien rather than directly at us.

Just so I wouldn't feel too threatened.

They were all of them graduates of the Fortress, that heavily fortified refuge for people who had been abducted by aliens and were determined never to let that happen again. The Fortress contained more big guns, high explosives, and really nasty booby-traps than anywhere else in the Nightside. They have security cameras in every room and corridor, heavy-duty gun emplacements on the roof, and you're never more than ten feet from a panic button. They have a stuffed and mounted Grey on display in their lobby, and you don't even want to think about what they've done to the reptiloid on display.

(No relation to the Royal Family. None at all. Trust me on this.)

Of course, it turned out that Julien knew many of them by name, and they all relaxed a bit as he stopped to chat with them. I had heard the Fortress supplied security for the Hospice, but I hadn't expected there to be quite so many of them. Or that they'd be so well-armed. A lot of them had attended the Hospice as patients—for psychiatric help, removal of implants, and the occasional bit of exploration to make sure no alien had left anything where the sun doesn't shine. They'd been so impressed by the help and sympathy they'd received, they set up a rota for people to volunteer to help. They made very loyal, very dangerous guards. Exactly what the Hospice needed.

Julien asked a few vague questions about how the shift was going, and if they'd seen anything or anyone . . . unusual. He didn't mention the Sun King by name, on the grounds of not wanting to start a panic if he didn't have to. None of them had seen anything out-of-the-ordinary unusual. It was a quiet night, for once. The officer in charge turned up, an ex–sergeant major in the paratroops, with silver-grey hair and a thousand-light-year stare. He wore a battered flak jacket topped off with a bandolier of incendiary grenades. Any alien who tried to take him again was in for a really nasty surprise. He also wore a pair of specially tinted sunglasses, which he assured us allowed him to detect aliens trying to pass as human. I didn't argue the point. This was the Nightside, after all, and he was holding the biggest gun I'd ever seen. In one hand.

"Why are there so many of you here?" I asked, to make it clear I was part of the conversation.

The ex-SM shrugged briefly. "Always some scumbag trying to break in, sir. Looking for drugs, equipment, magical shit. We show them no mercy. The good doctors keep telling us we're allowed to bring them in alive; but we don't believe in taking chances. Besides, the staff here have enough work on their hands without us adding to it with wounded scumbags. So we shoot their legs out from under them, double-tap them in the head, and everybody's happy."

"Keep up the good work," I said, for want of anything else to say.

"Thank you, sir. Would you like an escort to the front doors?"

"We don't want to draw attention," Julien said smoothly.

"Then you shouldn't have brought John bloody Taylor,"

said a voice from the back. There was a certain amount of laughter in the ranks, until the ex-SM glared them all into silence. Julien and I made our way carefully through the security people and headed for the front doors. Some of them bowed to Julien, and some of them nodded to me, and they all kept a careful eye on us right up to the point where we reached the doors, in case we might get lost, on the way. I also heard the name Suzie Shooter mentioned, in quiet mutterings, followed by a lot of nervous looking about. The Fortress had bad memories of Shotgun Suzie's occasional forced entrances into their building, on the trail of some runaway bounty. Nowhere was off limits to Suzie.

I slowed down as we approached the doors, and Julien looked at me questioningly. "I used to know someone who used to work here," I explained. "Sister Morphine . . ."

"Ah yes," said Julien. "I remember her. I wrote a few pieces about her, back in the day. She worked here for several years as a nurse before she had her crisis of faith, and decided it was more important to heal wounded souls than wounded bodies. You knew Sister Morphine, John? I didn't know that."

I nodded slowly. "She was there, in Rats' Alley, when I was there. When I was down and out, just another of the homeless she tried to protect."

"You don't talk much about that part of your life," said Julien.

"Would you?" I said. "Sister Morphine . . . was the kindest woman I ever knew. She looked after us all when we couldn't look after ourselves, when no-one else gave a damn. She never preached, never held the Bible over us; but she was a great one for stories and parables. She lived with us, amongst us, as one of us. Sometimes we had to force her to eat, when what we could salvage from the Dumpsters and the back doors of restaurants wasn't enough to go round. She always thought our needs were more important than hers."

I didn't tell Julien that when I thought of Sister Morphine

now, mostly I thought about her death. A mob killed her, during the Lilith War. I saw it happen. I could have saved her, but I had other people to protect that I thought needed saving more. Because their lives were more important than hers. War does things like that to you. I'm sure she would forgive me, but that didn't matter. I didn't forgive me.

As we entered the Hospice lobby, it quickly became apparent that this was yet another of those places that was bigger on the inside than the outside. It comes as standard in most of the Nightside, these days. The lobby was huge, breathtakingly so, stretching away before us. Julien and I stopped inside the doors to take a good look around. Everyone else ignored us, intent on their own problems.

"I am moved to wonder," said Julien. "Given all the pocket-dimension buildings we have these days, whether there is in fact an upper limit to how much Time and Space can be contained within the Nightside, without something . . . *giving*."

"We'd better hope not," I said. "If all the containment spells were to let go at once, and all the space within the Nightside broke its barriers and rolled out into the standard three dimensions . . . the end result would probably cover most of London Proper. Always assuming, of course, that we're actually contained within present-day London."

"You don't think we are?" said Julien.

"Look at the size of the moon," I said.

"I've got something more immediately worrying for you to think about," said Julien. "Before we can get to see Dr. Benway, we have to get past the receptionist."

"Don't worry," I said. "I have a way with receptionists."

"You can't kill her!" Julien said immediately. "It would make a very bad first impression."

"Oh ye of little faith," I said.

I took a little more time to look around while I considered

the situation. The lobby was white-walled, brightly lit, and spotlessly clean. And actually quite peaceful. Probably the only place in the Nightside that was. Marble pillars broke up the open space, and there were rows of comfortable chairs and couches for patients and visitors to sit on. Food and drink dispensers seemed to be providing food and drink of a kind that people were actually happy to consume, and pleasant classical music issued from concealed speakers. The air smelled of freshly cut grass and the scent of new-mown hay, all the sweet scents of a summer's day. A nice change from most hospitals' use of heavy disinfectant. Though, of course, both sets of smells were only there to cover up the same things: namely, the underlying, ever-present smells of blood and sickness, misery and mortality. Large notice-boards contained a great many overlapping messages, pleas and demands, and stern reminders that anyone who overstayed their welcome in the car-park could end up with several of their more important inner organs clamped.

The rows and rows of chairs were packed with people waiting to be seen. Men and women and children, and here and there some individuals who were none of the above and never would be. All of them troubled with wounds and fevers, exotic STDs and partial transmogrifications. A man with his hand stuck somewhere very embarrassing, a hunchback whose hump had slipped, a cyborg with Tourette's who kept shouting out long strings of binary numbers, and someone whose grip on reality was so weak he kept fading in and out. Half a dozen winged monkeys dressed as cleaners pushed mops and buckets around, labouring to deal with the usual spills of blood, urine, and vomit, and one small but worrying pool of molecular acid.

Typical night, in the Nightside A&E. I even overheard the traditional interplay between a nurse and a patient.

Patient: Nurse, it hurts when I do this.

Nurse: Then don't do that.

Patient: I am going to have to kill you now.

Nurse: I quite understand.

It's good to know some people are still ready to keep up the old traditions.

Right over to one side was a miraculous spring, a large pool of murky water contained within a low stone wall. It was supposed to have amazing curative properties, but only as long as you had faith, real faith, enough to make it work. And real faith has always been hard to come by in the Nightside. One very determined mother was holding her son by the ankle and dunking him in the pool, over and over again. Between a lot of sputtering, the boy could be heard saying; *I feel much better! Honest! Look will you please stop this I think I'm developing gills!*

Interesting and entertaining as all this was, Julien and I finally had no choice but to give our full attention to the receptionist at the desk. It was a really pleasant-looking reception desk, with vases of fresh flowers, neat and tidy in and out trays, and an absolute minimum of clutter . . . but I wasn't fooled. I could See the industrial-strength magical protections hanging on the air, and the built-in weapons systems.

The receptionist herself was a large matronly figure in a spotless white uniform (that reminded me immediately of the Very Righteous Sisters). She had a pleasant face, cold and unsympathetic eyes, and a mouth like a steel trap. You know the sort; mother was a pit bull, father was a velociraptor. Don't ask me what they ever saw in each other; but it can get very foggy on the moors. She waited to the very last moment to look up from her form-filling and stop Julien and me in our tracks with a stern warning gaze. She recognised Julien Advent immediately and favoured him with a brief nod. And then she looked at me, recognised me, and one hand moved quickly to a large red emergency button. She gave me a brief, meaningless smile.

"Tell me where it hurts, don't bleed on the floor, fill in these forms, and take a number."

"You don't understand," said Julien. "Neither of us is in need of medical attention. We are here to speak with Dr. Benway."

"I'm afraid that's not possible," the receptionist said immediately. "Not without an advance appointment. Dr. Benway is very busy, and I won't have her bothered. I can book you in for an appointment, but I should warn you there's a three-week waiting gap. Minimum. If that's not acceptable, take a number and get to the back of the queue, like everyone else."

"I am Julien Advent, representing the Authorities. This is John Taylor, the new Walker. It is vital that we see Dr. Benway immediately!"

The receptionist indulged herself with a harsh sniff, to show how unimpressed she was. "No queue-jumping. We don't care who you are, here."

"But this is urgent!" said Julien. "Vital, I tell you! The safety of the entire Nightside itself is at risk!"

"Save your breath," said the receptionist. "I've heard it all before. Are you actually dying? Bleeding out? Missing a major organ?"

"We're not," I said. "But you could be. You know me; you know what I can do. So stop pissing me off, or I'll send your spleen to Mars."

I gave her my most cheerful smile. The receptionist opened her mouth to say something, looked me in the eye, then thought better of it. Her hand hovered over the red button, then moved away. She sighed, in her best put-upon way, and reached for the phone.

"If you two gentlemen will give me a moment, I'll ask Dr. Benway if she can make time to see you. But I'm not promising anything!"

"Of course not," I said. "Why break the habit of a lifetime?"

"Stop it . . ." murmured Julien. "She'll turn nasty in a moment."

The receptionist got through to Dr. Benway, spoke quietly for a moment, and listened. She nodded, put the phone down, and gave Julien and me a wintry smile.

"Dr. Benway will see you; but she is very busy right now. So you'll have to wait. With everyone else."

Julien grabbed me forcefully by the arm and hauled me away from the reception desk. It took a while to find a couple of seats together, in the very crowded waiting area, and as far away from the more obviously infectious and messy people, but when we finally sank down into the chairs, they really were very comfortable.

"I think we won that encounter on points," I said. "All right, we still have to wait, but we didn't have to take a number."

"Would you really have . . . ?" said Julien.

"Almost certainly," I said. "I have deep-seated problems with authority figures."

"But you are one!"

"I know! I can only assume the universe has a really mean sense of humour."

We sat, and waited. People came and went, many sobbed and whimpered and read out-of-date magazines, but the size of the waiting crowd never seemed to change much. Julien stared patiently off into the distance, tapping one foot in a thoughtful manner. I recognised the signs. He'd already decided exactly how much time he was going to allow Dr. Benway; and then he was going to go and look for her himself. And God help anyone who got in his way. I'd never seen Julien walk right over a receptionist before. I was quite looking forward to it. Reassured at the prospect of loud and nasty unpleasantness in the near future, I killed time by studying the long list of wards, and their particular areas of expertise, laid out on an old-fashioned wooden wall plaque. They were all carefully numbered, but a lot of the descriptions were in Greek and Latin. I nudged Julien in the ribs and drew his attention to the dead languages. He gave me a long-suffering look.

"In my young days, we were all taught Latin and Greek at school."

"Was that before or after they shoved you up chimneys or down the mines?" I said.

Julien sighed, heavily, and translated the various descriptions for me. With rather more hesitations and uncertainty than you'd expect from someone who was supposed to have had a first-class private education. But after a while he got interested and started a running commentary on what each new description implied.

"Here at the Hospice, they deal with all the more unusual medical problems and conditions of the Nightside. Resulting in some very specialised care and services. There are doctors here to take off curses, put souls or identities back where they came from, reverse transformations, and undo teleport pod mishaps. They can restore kirlian fields and retune your chakras. Can't say I really approve of all this New Age stuff, but you can't ignore alternative medicine these days. Fortunately, I don't see anything here about crystals or flower aromatherapy, or I would have to say something very unfortunate. There are wards here for every need and speciality, including every kind of species you can think of. The Hospice doesn't discriminate. And then, of course, there's Ward 12A, though most people don't like to talk about that."

"Why not?" I said immediately. "What goes on in Ward 12A?"

Julien pressed on, deliberately ignoring my question. "There are wards for unicorns who need reshoeing with pure silver hooves, and for werewolves with the mange. I understand Leo Morn's a martyr to it, in the winter months. For vampires who've made themselves ill by drinking the wrong blood group: Rhesus intolerant. And, of course, a ward to treat all the rare and nasty diseases that will keep turning up in the Nightside through Timeslips: from the Past and any number of unfortunate futures. You really don't want to know about the Plague Ward, John."

He carried on, talking with increasing enthusiasm, extolling the many virtues of the Hospice, genuinely proud of all the incredible services its staff could provide. Often only because of his vigorous fund-raising though, of course, he never mentioned that bit. He talked at length of the giant spiders who lived in the basement, spinning bandages, and the ghouls who were bused in every day to eat the medical waste, and the occasional body too toxic to dispose of in a normal manner. Or too tough to burn. A ghoul's digestion can handle anything, up to and including nuclear waste. Though you really don't want to be around them when they fart.

And, sometimes, ghouls would be called in to deal with certain bodies that were too dangerous to be buried. Any villain who ever said *I'll be back!* as he went to his death at the hands of a triumphant hero . . . never met a Nightside ghoul. But I couldn't help noticing that Julien was saying most of this to cover up the fact that he didn't want to talk about Ward 12A. I mused on this while noticing that all of the porters, including those pushing patients around in wheelchairs, were actually very familiar-looking cat-faced robots. I pointed this out to Julien as a matter of urgency, but he just nodded easily.

"I know," he said. "The Authorities bought them at auction, from one of the vaults discovered after the Collector's death. We donated them to the Hospice. Mark always did have a fondness for this particular kind of automaton, brought back from some future iteration of China, I believe. You don't have to worry, John; they've all been very thoroughly reprogrammed to serve and protect the patients."

I decided I was still going to keep a very careful eye on them. These robots, or some very like them, had tried very hard to kill Suzie and me when they worked for the Collector. In fact, I was almost sure some of them were keeping a careful eye on me. I caught a number of cat-featured heads turning away the moment I looked at them. To take my mind off this, Julien pointed out that many of the nurses working in the Hospice were actually probationary nuns, from the Salvation Army Sisterhood. That got my attention. The SAS were the most hard core, extreme Christian Sect in the Nightside. Certainly not anyone you'd want to argue with when they said you needed an enema. Apparently probationary Sisters were sent here to put their faith to the test and to harden them up. Before they could join the Sisterhood proper and go forth to smite the ungodly where it hurt.

And then suddenly the lobby was full of sirens, bells, flashing red lights, screams and shouts and people yelling at each other. Julien was up on his feet immediately, looking quickly round for people to help and evil to fight. I was still struggling to get to my feet, and looking around for anything that might be coming my way. Everyone else was heading for the front doors, with great speed and determination. Including security people, reception staff, nurses, and robots helping patients, and absolutely everyone in the waiting area. Many of them showed a remarkable turn of speed, considering how ill they were supposed to be. I looked at Julien, to ask whether or not we should be leaving, too, but he was busy looking around to see where the fire was. Or possibly the attack. I grabbed a passing nurse by the arm, and she nearly pulled me over before I brought her to a halt. She was a big girl. Her arm muscle bulged dangerously under my hand, but then the probationary nun recognised who I was and settled for jerking her arm out of my grip.

"What's going on?" I yelled at her, over all the sirens and alarums.

"Red Alert!" she yelled back at me. "Major Emergency and Get the Hell Out! Look, it's Ward 12A, you idiot! If you're not going to run, get out of the way of a nun who can!"

In an instant, she was off and running again, not even looking back. I turned to look at Julien, only to find that he was off and running, too, but heading in the opposite direction, deeper into the Hospice. I looked round the deserted lobby, sighed deeply, and went after him. Thinking, *That man will be the death of me, one day.* I knew he was going to Ward 12A to see if he could help anyone and put down whatever trouble had broken out there. Because he was still the Great Victorian Adventurer, and that was what he did. And if he was going, I had to go as well. Because that was the trouble with Julien Advent; he made you be a better person, in spite of yourself, if only because you couldn't stand to let him down.

We pounded through the Hospice corridors, following the signs on the walls that pointed the way to Ward 12A. We passed a hell of a lot of people going the other way, running as though the Devil himself was hot on their heels. Many of them looked at us incredulously and yelled for us to get out while we still had a chance. Julien kept going, so I had to go on, too. And, of course, along the way we ran into Dr. Benway herself, also heading for Ward 12A. I only knew it was her because Julien actually said her name out loud and smiled with something very like relief. Dr. Benway nodded briefly to Julien and kept going, too.

We soon caught up with her. Benway was a short, stick-thin figure in the usual white doctor's coat. She had flat grey hair, cropped short in a functional way, and a hard-set face, lined with all the marks of a long, busy life, filled with more losses than successes. Her eyes were a cool, thoughtful grey, and her mouth was set in a thin, flat line. She looked strong and capable, someone you'd be glad to have around in a crisis. If only she wasn't leading you right into the heart of it.

"Good to see you again, Julien," Benway said brusquely, looking straight ahead as she ran. "We can use all the help we can get." She glanced at me. "Even him."

"You've heard of me," I said reproachfully. "And you know Julien Advent personally. What a surprise."

"I know everyone," said Julien. He wasn't even breathing hard, the bastard. "How else do you think I know everything?"

"I know a lot of people, too," I said.

"Ah yes," said Julien. "But you know people like Dead Boy and Razor Eddie, while I know people who matter."

"Shut up and run," said Benway. "Save your breath and your strength. You're going to need them."

She actually increased her speed, racing along with her arms pumping at her sides, sprinting through the deserted Hospice corridors with a turn of speed that was frankly astonishing in a woman who had to be well into her sixties. She darted in and out of a series of short cuts, ignoring the directions on the walls, and soon I hadn't a clue where I was. The corridors were starting to remind me uncomfortably of the hedgerow maze. But I knew when we were finally getting close to Ward 12A because I started to hear things. From up ahead of us, to every side, and, even more worryingly, behind us, I heard a series of heavy, slamming sounds.

"That's the steel security doors dropping down into place," said Dr. Benway. "Sealing off the corridors. No-one in, no-one out, until this mess is sorted, and the danger is over. If all the security doors are dropped, that means all the patients who can be moved have been; so we're pretty much alone in here, with the problem."

"What about the patients who couldn't be moved?" said Julien. Typical of the man, to be concerned with innocents even as he raced into danger.

"They'll have to take their chances," Benway said curtly. "They're under guard; God bless the Fortress. Concentrate on what's ahead of us, Julien. If we can't bring this under control quickly, we could lose the whole Hospice."

"What is ahead of us?" I said, not unreasonably, I thought. "What the hell has happened in Ward 12 bloody A?"

"Something got loose," said Benway, in a voice like the end of the world.

We rounded a final corner, and there at the end of the corridor before us was a heavily reinforced steel door, marked simply: 12A. Two young men in white doctor's coats were barricading the door with everything they could get their hands on. Furniture, medical trolleys, even a Hot Drinks! Machine that they were man-handling into place. They suddenly realised they weren't alone. Their heads snapped round, and they both let out girlish shrieks of alarm. They started to run, only to stop immediately as Dr. Benway yelled at them.

"Dr. Burke! Dr. Rabette! Stand right where you are!"

And they did. They turned immediately to look at her, ignoring Julien and me, as the three of us finally came to a halt before the door to Ward 12A. I had black spots dancing before my eyes, my ribs ached, and I had to lean against a wall while I concentrated on getting my breath back. Julien breathed deeply a few times, then strolled forward to observe the barricaded door with a keen interest. Dr. Benway put her hands on her hips and rotated her back a few times. I heard bones creak and crack. She glared at the two young doctors standing uneasily before her, then glared at me.

"These two young fools are supposed to be in charge here. On the grounds that I can't do everything myself. Talk to me, Burke, Rabette! What's the situation?"

The two young doctors looked at each other guiltily. The older of the two was barely into his midtwenties, and they both looked shocked as well as scared as they glanced at the barricaded door. Finally, the older one, Burke, swallowed hard.

"The door is locked and sealed. It can't get out. But we can't go in there! It's too dangerous! Who are these two?"

"Julien Advent and John Taylor," said Benway.

"I think I felt safer before they got here," said Rabette in a high, shaky voice. He smiled quickly, to show it was meant to be a joke. "We'll take all the help we can get, but I don't know what you can do. I don't know there's anything anyone can do. All hell's breaking loose in there."

"We should get the hell out of here!" said Burke, actually wringing his hands together.

"Shut up, both of you!" snarled Benway. "Call yourselves doctors . . ." She turned her back on them and marched over to stand before the barricaded door. She started to push the drinks machine out of the way, then found she couldn't. Julien and I had to help her. Burke and Rabette reluctantly shifted everything else they'd piled up against the door, revealing a portholelike window in the top third of the steel door. Benway walked right up to it, listened carefully for a moment, then peered cautiously through the porthole. I looked at Julien and gave him my best hard stare.

"I think this would be a really good time for you to fill me in on what's so important about Ward 12A, don't you? What do they do in there; what kind of patients do they treat?"

"Ward 12A is reserved exclusively for those unfortunate enough to have been damaged by coming in contact with forces or beings from Outside the realms we know," Julien said quietly. "Remind you of anything?"

"The Entities from Beyond," I said.

"Exactly," said Julien.

I looked at the very solid steel door and hoped it was as locked and sealed as the young doctors had said. "You think . . . maybe the Sun King is in there? Could he really have got here ahead of us, that fast?"

"Who knows what he's capable of, now?" said Julien. "But let's not add to our problems until we have to."

"If you two have finished muttering secrets to each other, perhaps you'd like to take a look," Benway said acidly.

Julien and I moved forward to join her. Burke and Rabette seized the opportunity to back away. Benway had her face pressed up close against the porthole, so Julien and I moved in on either side of her, our heads pressed close together. All I could see were flaring bright lights, sharp and intense, so bright I couldn't even be sure what colours they were. The glare didn't simply blaze through the porthole; it outlined the steel door itself. Great, angry, roaring sounds rose and fell on the other side of the door, none of them in any way human. I glanced at Benway.

"What exactly have you got in there? What's wrong with these patients?"

"In Ward 12A, we deal mainly with possessions and abductions. Men and women, and sometimes children, unfortunate enough to have attracted the attention of forces from Outside. We try to treat people who have been taken and changed, physically and mentally, to adapt them to live on other worlds, or in other realities. Places where merely human forms couldn't hope to survive. Of course, after these beings have finished with their experiments, they abandon their victims and dump them back where they found them. They never bother to undo the changes they've made, don't care that the poor bastards have been altered so much they can't cope with Earth conditions any more. Some of them end up at the Fortress, but the most damaged, or dangerous, are brought here. We do what we can for them, but mostly they're contained here, in a secure facility. Ward 12A."

"And the others?" said Julien.

She looked at him, then looked away. "Some things you don't want to know, Julien. Unless it's your job and your responsibility. Doctors deal with death and worse, every day.

It's the part of the job no-one else wants to hear you talk about."

"How dangerous can these patients be?" I said, as a particularly loud roar made the steel door tremble in its frame.

"Some patients have been here for years," said Dr. Benway. "Some of them are more alien than others. Some contain whole worlds, other realities, inside them—living gateways to other places."

"Think of the Trojan horse," Julien said to me.

"We've spent years developing ways to help these people," said Benway. "Of freeing them from the terrible burdens placed upon them. We use surgery to undo physical changes, telepaths to undo mental changes, and now and again we get our hands on some discarded alien tech that we can use to drag alien booby-traps out of human minds and souls. But sometimes the beings behind the changes fight back. Burke, Rabette, what have you . . . Dr. Rabette, you get your cowardly arse right back here, right now! And tell me what, exactly, is going on inside Ward 12A? Which patient is responsible for all this?"

"We don't have a name," muttered Rabette, not even trying to meet her gaze. "He's John Doe X number 47."

"Something inside him, or beyond him, is fighting to break through," said Burke. His face was white with shock and wet with sweat. "Some other reality is using him as a gateway, to get to ours. And I really don't think it's any kind of reality we would want to meet."

I looked sharply at Julien. "A hellgate. They're talking about a hellgate, draining someone's soul energies to create a doorway between one reality and another. Open a door and send through an army. Sneaky."

Rabette broke and ran, and, a moment later, Burke was off and running, too. Julien shouted angrily after them but stopped when Benway put a hand on his arm.

"They're only interns, Julien. Only been on Ward 12A a

few months. This is way above their pay grade. Let them go; they wouldn't be much use anyway."

"Don't you have any experienced security people to deal with situations like this?" I said.

"Of course, ex-Fortress, mostly. But the security doors are down, remember?" said Benway. "Security are trapped on the other side of the Hospice."

"Well, why don't you keep some here, on hand?" I said.

"Budget cuts," said Dr. Benway, not quite looking in Julien's direction.

"All right, the committee were wrong, and yes, you did warn us," said Julien. "I promise I'll bring it up at the next meeting! Can we concentrate on the problem in front of us, please?"

"So," I said, as cheerfully as possible under the circumstances. "It's down to us to save the day. Again. Where do we start?"

Benway looked at Julien. "Is he always this cocky?"

"Usually," said Julien. "One of the reasons I suggested he be made Walker. He really does have a lot of experience in saving the world against impossible odds. But don't stand too close to him while he's doing it. Dr. Benway, question. Do we have any idea who these invading aliens are? Do we have a name, or even a species description? Any idea at all of what they are or where they're from?"

"No," said Benway. She looked through the porthole again, and winced. "The patient couldn't tell us anything, including his own name. Diagnostic equipment revealed his condition but not who or what caused it. If this were a standard possession or alteration, the Ward's own defences and protections would have kicked in; so I can only assume this is something a lot more powerful than we're used to."

Julien frowned, tapping his chin thoughtfully with one knuckle. "The Authorities keep a watchful eye on the various Timeslips as they come and go in the Nightside because they're the most common launching sites for an invasion, but if these aliens have found a new way to open new doors, less obvious than Timeslips . . . we could be in real trouble. We have to stop this invasion here, slap it down hard, and send the aliens a message they won't forget in a hurry."

"Oh, I can do that," I said.

Julien glared at me. "Preferably a message that will still leave the Hospice intact and standing afterwards!"

"All right, I got it!" I said. "Honestly, you blow up one lousy building, and they never let you forget it . . ."

I edged closer to the steel door. Terrible sounds rose and fell on the other side, and awful lights flared through the porthole. Whatever was happening in there was escalating. I reached out one hand to touch the door, and my fingers sank right into the steel. As though the solid metal were nothing more than soft mud. I snatched my hand back. The soft, pulsating mass that had been solid steel started to stretch after me, then fell back again.

"What the hell was that?" said Benway, clearly shaken.

"I've encountered this before," I said, a little freaked-out. I held my hand up before my eyes and shook it back and forth, checking for signs of damage. My fingers tingled unpleasantly, odd and eerie sensations prickling up and down them in sudden runs. "Remember when the Springheel Jack Meme broke through from another dimension, Julien? The starting point was an old door in an abandoned warehouse, down on Damnation Row. By the time I got there, the whole wall was affected, rising and falling like a heartbeat. The physical reality there had been softened, eaten away, weakened from the other side. The far side of our reality, that we can never see. The very solidity of our world undermined from the other side, so they could break through. In that case, what came through was a supernatural meme, a curse or possession that spread like a virus, overwriting everyone it touched.

"We're at Ground Zero, people; this isn't just an invading

army. A whole other reality is trying to break through and overwrite us, replace this world with their own. This door is less real than it should be because something else is becoming more real. The patient inside Ward 12A is being physically and spiritually remade into a doorway. But that takes a lot of power, which means it isn't up to speed yet. We've still got some time."

Dr. Benway looked at Julien. "Do you understand anything he's saying?"

"Unfortunately, yes," said Julien. "Are you sure about this, John?"

"Of course I'm not sure! This is all inspired guess-work! If you've got a better and less worrying idea, I for one would love to hear it!"

"Knew I should have kept you away from the brandy," said Julien.

He leaned in close to study the steel door, almost but not quite pressing his nose against the metal. "The door is becoming permeable, all the strength and purpose being sucked right out of it, to help fuel the forming gateway. Which means we're not locked outside after all."

He pressed both of his hands against the door and pushed hard. His hands sank deep into the soft metal, disappearing up to the wrists. Julien's face convulsed, lips skinning back from his teeth in a pained grimace. He pushed with all his strength, but the door wouldn't budge. Julien gave up and tried to pull his hands back, then found that he couldn't. Benway and I grabbed an arm each and threw our whole weight backwards; and Julien's hands burst back out of the door with horrible, wet, sucking sounds. He staggered backwards, clutching his hands to his chest. Dr. Benway made him stand still while she checked them for damage, but apparently it was really bad pins and needles from returning circulation. The soft door had sucked all the living warmth right out of them.

"How the hell do we get in?" said Julien, through gritted teeth. "Blow a hole in the wall?"

"Amateur," I said, not unkindly.

I raised my gift, focused on the door, and found the door-handle. My gift locked onto it, onto the basic reality of the door-handle itself, and forced it to be real and hard and solid. And then it was the easiest thing in the world for me to reach out, grasp the door-handle, and open the door. The locks and seals were as soft and weak as everything else now, and the door opened easily under my guiding will. The door started to swing inwards, then gave up its remaining ghost and fell apart into thick wisps of grey fog, already dispersing on the starkly lit air. I was left with only the door-handle in my hand. I carelessly let it drop to the floor and strode confidently into Ward 12A.

The whole room was full of flaring bright lights, sharp and incandescent, acutely painful to the human eye. Great clouds of flailing energies boiled this way and that, discharging violently against anything they touched. One whole wall had become wet and sticky, all the shades of red, pulsing like the insides of something alien. The ceiling seemed to be miles overhead, and the floor felt untrustworthy under my feet. Walking into the Ward was like pushing against a fierce wind, an almost solid intervention of some Outside will. I could feel Space itself stretched taut by some unimaginable influence. I stopped, despite myself, struggling to get my bearings. There were too many directions, too many dimensions inside Ward 12A now, too many ways to look, too many options to deal with. Another reality had been added to ours, superimposed on it, making the world heavier and more complex than it was ever supposed to be. The red wall was full of something like maggots, writhing and twisting. There were dark holes in the floor, dropping away forever. And rising over everything, a horrible feeling, a terrible conviction, that *something was coming.*

Far-away, from Outside or beyond our universe, I could hear something screaming, an endless howl of rage and hate. Drawing steadily, remorselessly closer.

And right there before me, hanging in mid air, was patient John Doe X 47, or what was left of him. His Humanity had been ripped away. His body was gone. He had been sub-tracted from the world and made into something else, and now he was a living tear in reality. A human gap, a human shape full of something that hurt my eyes to look at. A way in for whatever wanted in. I forced myself to look away, to check on what had happened to the other patients trapped in Ward 12A. I knew Julien would want to know. I could see all the beds, and the patients in them; but they all seemed far-away, distant, on the other side of the world. Looking across the Ward, across all its hideously stretched Space, was like looking across the universe. Trying to concentrate on the patients was like trying to look in a new direction, one I could sense but not make sense of. They'd been pushed aside by what was happening, forced out of the way to make room for what was pushing in. I was pretty sure the patients were still alive. But I couldn't tell if they were still human any more.

I yelled back to Julien and Dr. Benway at the doorway, telling them what I was seeing, trying to make sense of it. They'd managed to get inside the Ward but couldn't force themselves any further in. They didn't have my gift—to find a way forward, in the face of everything.

I concentrated, focusing my gift on the human-shaped gap in our world. I tried to reach into the gap, to find the link between the patients and the beings from Outside, so I could break it . . . but it only took me a moment to realise that the patient was the link. I couldn't break the link without killing the patient. And I wasn't ready to that. Not until I'd tried everything else I could think of first. I couldn't sacrifice one life to save many. Julien wouldn't approve. He always was a good influence on me, the bastard. So, since I couldn't touch the alien influence, I found the man and grabbed on to him. I could feel him, held half-way between this world and the other. And the more I held on to him with my gift, the more real I found him, until finally it was the easiest thing in this world to haul him all the way back into reality. And suddenly there he was, hanging in mid air, where the gap used to be. One hundred per cent real and solid and human. I let go, and he fell to the floor. And so did the beings from Outside that had been attached to him, that I'd found and dragged into this world with him.

All of Ward 12A snapped back to normal. The light was soft and even, the awful howling was gone, and the room was room-shaped again, with only the three usual dimensions. Patient John Doe X 47 lay curled up in a ball on the floor, breathing harshly, eyes wide and staring. I'd rescued his body, but someone more experienced in these matters would have to bring his mind back after everything the poor bastard had been put through. I looked at the aliens I'd dragged through into our world, and my lip curled. Rewritten and restructured by the laws of our reality, there were floppy bits of meat, each the size of a man's head, with protrusions that made no sense, squirming and oozing across the floor. They whined and squealed with every movement, as if being in our world hurt them. I only had to look at them to know they were suffering and dying, unable to withstand human conditions. One by one, they fell silent and lay still, and within moments they were rotting and falling apart. I looked back at Julien as he came forward to join me.

"That enough of a message for you?"

"That will do nicely," said Julien. "They'll think twice before trying that again. You did well, John."

"It's a shame they died so quickly," said Benway. "I wanted to stamp on them first."

I had to raise an eyebrow. "Hard core, Doc."

She surprised me with a brief, happy smile. "No-one messes with my patients and gets away with it."

She moved over to the patient lying on the floor, knelt beside him, and spoke reassuringly to him as she checked his vital signs. He didn't even know she was there.

"We are but flies to alien entities," Julien said. "They use us for their sport."

"Bastards," Dr. Benway said succinctly, without looking up.

"You're thinking of the Sun King, aren't you?" I said quietly to Julien.

"Aren't you?" said Julien.

Dr. Rabette and Dr. Burke stuck their heads through the open doorway, attracted by the reassuring quiet. Benway saw them as she stood up, beckoned them into Ward 12A, then drove them to check on the other patients with a furious glare and a fusillade of bad language. Most of the other patients seemed more confused than anything. Having been pushed so far-away, they hadn't been affected by the released energies. Most of them were too preoccupied with their own problems anyway. And once I could see them clearly, I didn't blame them.

One bed was full of three people who'd been mashed together in an ungainly tangle of limbs, their pallid flesh stretched taut, while three faces stared from different sides of the same head. I don't know what their staring eyes saw, but I knew it wasn't anything I wanted to see. A man sat stiffly upright on the next bed, strapped bodily to the headboard. Where his head should have been there was only a brightly shining star. Next to him, a woman squatted on her bed, held in a tightly reinforced strait jacket chained to the wall. Her eyes were simply evil. She laughed softly, continuously, waiting for the moment when someone would be stupid enough to release her. Something that might have been a man or a woman, once, lay in a pool of its own blood, bulky pieces of alien tech protruding through its cracked and broken skin.

Many of the patients had extra organs, or added alien attributes, their bodies changed and adapted so they could survive on some other, alien world. Useless here, of course. They hadn't asked for what had been done to them. Abducted, changed, then dumped when the experiment didn't work out. I wanted to get my hands on the creatures that could do such things and make them suffer for their sins. I looked sharply at Julien, filling my voice with anger so he wouldn't hear anything else.

"This isn't right! It would be kinder to let these poor bastards die."

Julien nodded, understanding things I couldn't say out loud, even to him. "The doctors do help people here. Though I have to say, I didn't know things were this bad . . ."

"But you're the man who knows everything," I said.

"It's part of the job to know that places like this exist . . . but even I can't keep up with the details."

"You don't have to," said Dr. Benway, coming over to join us. "There's a limit to the burdens anyone can be expected to carry." She gestured sharply to Burke and Rabette to carry John Doe X 47 back to his bed. "Being sent here isn't a death sentence, Mr. Taylor. We can help a surprising number of the people who come through our doors. But sometimes the best we can offer is to contain them, keep them comfortable, and hope that someone somewhere is working on something new. New things are discovered, or arrive, in the Nightside every day. So no, it wouldn't be kinder to kill them all. Every day we keep them alive in spite of what's been done to them is a victory. You can't give up hope, Mr. Taylor. Hospitals run on hope."

I nodded slowly. "And miracles do happen, even in the Nightside."

"Perhaps especially in the Nightside," said Julien Advent.

A handful of burly-looking nurses came bursting through the doorway; some of them carrying really big guns. They relaxed a little as they saw that the crisis was over, put the guns in the Ward locker, and moved immediately to see to the patients. Benway relaxed a little, too.

"The security doors must have opened. Let's go to my office and talk."

She gestured for Burke and Rabette, and they came back, reluctantly. Benway surprised them with a brief smile.

"Everybody runs, the first time. Not everyone comes back. Now, make sure the patients are settled and don't be stingy with the tranqs. Stay here till everything's back to normal, and I don't want to hear any whining about overtime. The job is the job."

Burke and Rabette nodded quickly and went back to work. Benway looked after them almost fondly.

"They're young. They'll adapt. Or they'll leave the Hospice and move into some less nerve-racking job, like bomb disposal."

Dr. Benway led us back through the corridors of the Hospice, her hands in her coat pockets, looking a lot more human. She smiled at Julien and actually nodded to me. Hospice personnel hurried past us, back to the wards and patients they'd been forced to abandon during the emergency. Patients were wheeled past on trolleys, or in wheel-chairs, or helped along by nurses and the cat-faced robots. They all nodded respectfully to Dr. Benway and ignored Julien and me. Benway sighed, deeply.

"I really wasn't going to talk to you, Julien. I was going to leave you sitting around in the waiting area until you got the message and left of your own accord. But now that you, and especially Mr. Taylor here, have saved the day, the Hospice in general, and the patients of Ward 12A in particular, I can't really say no, can I?" Julien started to say something, but she talked right over him. "We can't talk here. Too many security cameras and far too many eyes and ears. We'll talk in my office."

She stopped abruptly and pushed back one sleeve to reveal a chunky bracelet of some shimmering metal, studded with read-outs and controls. She punched in a quick series of numbers, and next thing I knew we were all standing in a surprisingly comfortable-looking office. Benway gave us another of her quick smiles, sat down behind the desk, and waved for Julien and me to sit down on the visitors' chairs.

"Teleport bracelet," she said briskly. "Fell off the back of a Timeslip, from some future or other. It's the only way I can be everywhere I need to be, in this place. Won't work anywhere near Ward 12A because of the bracelet's built-in protections. Sit! Sit!"

We sat. Her chair looked to be a lot more comfortable than ours. I made a point of looking round her office rather than waiting to be talked at. Let her wait for a bit. The office was all very neat, very business-like. All the usual comforts and luxuries. But not a single framed photo anywhere, of family or friends or loved ones. Not even a framed diploma on the wall behind the desk.

Benway caught my gaze or read my mind. "No memories of the past here, Mr. Taylor. Some of us can't afford to look back. I don't do nostalgia."

"Is that why you aren't ever pleased to see an old friend like me?" said Julien.

"I see you all the time, at Hospice committee meetings."

"And you always choose a chair at the other end of the table, and you never say a word to me that you don't have to."

"You know very well why I stay away from you," Benway said sharply. "Because I got old; and you didn't. Look at me. I'm an old woman. Should have retired by now. Would have, if I could find anyone half-way decent to replace me. And you . . . you don't look a day older than the day I first met you, back in 1967. How do you think that makes me feel?"

"Emily . . ."

"No, Julien. Dr. Benway; as far as you're concerned. Now and always." She paused, looking at him thoughtfully. "I saw Juliet, the other day."

"Did you?" said Julien. "Did she ask after me?"

"No."

Benway gave me her full attention, studying me with a cold, professional gaze. "I know you by reputation, Mr. Taylor. I've read many accounts of your various . . . adventures. I have to say I'm surprised we haven't seen you in here before now."

"Well, keep it to yourself," I said. "But I have some diluted werewolf blood in me. Not nearly enough to trigger the change, but more than enough to give me a seriously souped-up healing factor."

Julien sat up straight in his chair and looked at me accusingly. "You never told me that! Why didn't you tell me?"

"Because I didn't want to see it turning up in the *Night Times*," I said. "The best advantages are the ones your enemies don't know exist."

"You could have trusted me," said Julien, a little put-out.

"Two men can keep a secret," I said. "If one of them is dead. Unless he's Dead Boy, of course, then you're screwed."

"But . . . when did this happen?" said Julien.

"Hell of a party," I said solemnly. "You should have been there."

"Why are you both here?" said Dr. Benway, loudly and forcefully. "Did you know something was going to happen in Ward 12A?"

"No," said Julien. "Good thing we were here, though. Wasn't it?"

"All right, I get it, hold the moral blackmail," said Benway. "I owe you. But why did you need to talk to me so urgently?"

"It's the Sun King," said Julien. "He's back. Here, in the Nightside."

Dr. Benway sat very still in her chair. She looked like she'd been hit. All the colour dropped out of her face. She wasn't even looking at Julien and me any more, her eyes far-away, remembering yesterday.

"Would you like a glass of water?" said Julien.

"No," said Benway. "I'd like a glass of gin."

She leaned over, breathing heavily, and rummaged around in a desk drawer before coming up with a bottle of Gordon's Dry Gin and one glass. She poured herself a healthy measure, knocked it back in several quick sips, and immediately poured herself another. She didn't offer any to us. Colour blazed in her cheeks, and her hands were very steady. She put the bottle and glass to one side though still in easy reach if she decided she wanted some more; and then she glared at Julien, ignoring me.

"You knew he was back; and you didn't even warn me?"

"I've only known for a few hours," Julien said steadily. "And John and I have only just met him, in the Garden of Green Henge. We came straight here."

Benway considered this. "How . . . What was he like?"

"He looked the same," said Julien. "But he was . . . different. Changed. Still immensely powerful, though."

"Why has he come here? To the Nightside?"

"To destroy it," I said flatly, tired of being left out of the conversation. "He thinks he can make the sun rise here and put an end to the night."

Benway smiled briefly. "He always did think big; even when he was still just my Harry."

"So you were Princess Starshine," I said.

She winced. "Not for a long time! That . . . was somebody

else." She looked at the bottle and the empty glass. She started to reach out, then pulled her hand back again. She looked at Julien. "Did he ask after me?"

"No," said Julien.

"But you think he's coming here, to see me?"

"It seems likely," said Julien. "For him, the Summer of Love is still recent history. And who else does he know here who might still remember him fondly? I have to ask, Emily; back when you were Princess Starshine, you had power of your own, briefly. Do you still . . ."

"Of course not! Do you think I'd let my patients suffer if I still had the power to help them? No . . . He took all that with him, when he went away. When he walked into the White Tower and left me behind." She paused. "I can't even remember what it felt like, to be . . . that other person, now. Most of my memories of that time have faded . . . More like a story that someone told to me, long ago. When I was young . . ."

Her phone rang suddenly, and we all jumped. Benway answered it quickly, listened for a while, and swore, briefly and dispassionately. She slammed the phone down, then fired up the computer screen on her desk. She looked at the scene before her and beckoned for both of us to come round the desk and join her. We were already up and moving. We peered over her shoulder, to see what she was looking at. The monitor screen showed a view of the Hospice lobby, and there he was, the Sun King, standing there in his Coat of Vivid Colours, looking happily around him at everyone else while everyone else looked at him. Patients who'd only returned from the previous crisis looked him over suspiciously while security people came hurrying forward from all sides. Because they could all feel the sheer power radiating off him. But once the security people had him surrounded, they didn't know what to do. They stood there, helpless in the face of something so much bigger than them. They couldn't even find the strength to point their guns at him.

The Sun King looked around him, taking his time, taking it all in, the patients and the security people and the new place he'd come to. He shook his head slowly, frowning. And then he clapped his hands, once; and every man, woman, and child in the lobby was completely cured of whatever ailed them. Illness was banished, fading organs were repaired, injuries put right. The lame walked, and the blind could see, and each and every person had an apple in their hand. The lobby was suddenly full of whoops and cheers, tears and laughter and celebration. Patients danced with each other, and the security people lowered their guns, smiling foolishly. And the Sun King stood there, in the middle of it all, enjoying every moment of it.

Dr. Benway was already up on her feet and working her teleport bracelet. Julien and I moved in close beside her, determined not to be left behind. Immediately, we were down in the lobby with everyone else. A party had broken out, with booze and glasses appearing as if by magic. Even the reception staff were dancing and giggling and hugging people. Benway headed straight for the Sun King, and everyone else took one look at her cold, determined face and got the hell out of her way. Julien and I stayed back. This was her moment. She slammed to a halt right before the Sun King, and he looked at her politely.

"Yes? Can I help you?"

It was obvious he didn't recognise her. Hadn't a clue who she was. Benway swayed on her feet, like he'd hit her. She made herself face him squarely.

"This is my Hospice. But then, you never did care whose toes you trod on, did you, Harry?"

The Sun King recognised her voice immediately. He looked at her closely, and his eyes widened, and for a moment he clearly didn't know what to say.

"Yes," she said flatly. "I got old. That's what people do, in the real world."

"You were so beautiful," he said. "My Princess Starshine . . ."

"That was then, this is now." Benway looked at him defiantly. "So here you are, back in town after all these years, and you didn't even come to me first. I had to hear about your glorious return from someone else."

"I had my work to be about," said the Sun King.

"You always did," said the woman who used to be a princess.

They looked at each other for a long moment, and both their faces softened. The Sun King put out a hand, and Benway took it, and they held on to each other like they would never let go. Everyone else watched, silently, caught up in the moment. They were in the presence of legends, and they knew it.

"Why?" Benway said finally. "Why didn't you take me with you, into the White Tower? I tried to follow you in, but the wall closed after you . . . I called to you, pounded on the wall with my fists; but you never answered. Did your Big Cosmic Daddies order you not to let me in? Did they tell you I wasn't worthy?"

"That's not how it was," said the Sun King. "I wanted to take everyone in with me. I thought I'd only be in there for a moment, and I could walk back out and invite you all in. I wanted everyone to be living gods, like me. But that wasn't how it worked. When I did come out again, years had passed, and the world had moved on. Oh, Princess . . . all the years we've lost. The life we could have had together. You've changed, Princess."

"You haven't," said Benway.

The Sun King smiled. "Some old wrongs can be put right."

He pulled his hand out of hers. She sighed and almost fell, as though some basic strength had been taken away from her. The Sun King dropped both hands onto her thin, bony shoulders, and he shook her, once. Dr. Benway cried out, in shock rather than pain, and all the years fell away from her. The Sun King laughed, took his hands away from her, and stood back to look at what he'd done. The whole lobby looked on in silent and respectful awe, at the beautiful young woman standing where Dr. Benway had been. Long blonde hair fell down around a flawless face, and Princess Starshine held up her hands and looked at them. Young hands, without a mark on them. She brought her hands to her face, and cried out again, at the untouched skin her fingers found. Someone in the crowd stepped forward and humbly presented her with a mirror. The princess looked at her young face with something like shock, as though she was looking at someone she only vaguely remembered. Someone she hadn't seen in a long time. Her beautiful young face was full of awe and wonder. She lowered the mirror and looked at the Sun King with clear blue eyes; and he bowed to her without a hint of mockery.

"Welcome back, my Emily. My Princess Starshine, and my one true love. Welcome . . . all the way back. I am the Miracle Man, once again. Walk with me, as we did before in that far-off land, and embrace your power again. The living god and his living goddess, come to put the world to right."

"I can't," she said, in a voice rich with youth and emotion. "I have responsibilities here. My hospital, my patients . . ."

"You have no more patients," the Sun King said gently. "I cured them all. My gift to you."

"Even the ones in Ward 12A?" said Princess Starshine.

"The unfortunates and the untouchables? The abducted and distorted? Oh yes, my princess, those most of all. There but for the grace of the Entities from Beyond, go I." He paused, frowning slightly. "Well, when I say I cured everyone, obviously I didn't include the vampires. Or any of the other inhuman scum. Or any of the really ugly people. No. I killed all of those."

"What?" The princess looked at him shocked. "You killed . . . ? Who gave you the right . . . ?"

"I did!" said the Sun King. "Only the beautiful people belong in the marvellous new world we shall make."

The princess slapped his face, hard. The impact slammed his head round. The sound was flat and ugly on the still air. No-one said anything. The Sun King slowly brought his head back round, to stare at the princess. His face was completely empty of expression or emotion.

"You killed my patients!" screamed the princess. "How dare you? They came here for help! We're here for everyone who needs us. We don't make distinctions. Hospitals are for everyone! That's the point!"

The Sun King looked down on her, his face cold and disappointed. "You always did think too small, Emily."

He waved his hand tiredly, and Dr. Benway was old again. She cried out once, as the years weighed down on her again, then she turned away from the Sun King, bent and withered with the renewed burden of age. She started to raise the mirror to look into it again, but she couldn't do it. She let the mirror go, and it fell to the floor, and broke. And then she straightened up as much as her old body would allow, turned back, and glared at the Sun King defiantly.

"And you always were the selfish one, Harry. Everything always had to be done your way. Well, let me tell you this; you're not worthy of me! You never were!" She lost her voice for a moment, the angry words choking her. She clamped her mouth shut, shook her head fiercely, and quickly had control of herself again. "You won't make me cry. I shed my last tears for you long ago, when you abandoned me in San Francisco. You'll never make me cry again."

"Watch me," said the Sun King.

He started forward, and I moved quickly to stand between them, blocking his way. Julien was right there with me. The Sun King smiled on both of us.

"Here we all are again! I knew you two couldn't keep away! Not when I have such wonders to show you . . ."

"Leave her alone," Julien said harshly. "I won't let you hurt her any more."

"Ah, Julien, you always did have a soft spot for the ladies. And you always made such bad choices in women . . ."

"I remember your healing the sick in Haight-Ashbury," Julien said steadily. "You never made any distinctions, then. And to heal a whole hospital full of patients, in a moment? You've come a long way, Harry. Where did you get such power?"

"From all those years in the White Tower," said the Sun King. "Sitting at the feet of my masters, learning the truths of the universe."

"Yes," I said. "We get that. But who are these Entities from Beyond, exactly? Why can't you tell us their name?"

"You want a name?" said the Sun King. "Is it really so important to you? Oh very well, then; call them the Aquarians. Yes, call them that. Because through the power they have bestowed on me, I shall finally bring about the long delayed Age of Aquarius."

I looked at Julien. "Never heard of them. You?"

"The Age of Aquarius was another name for the Big Dream of the sixties," Julien said slowly. "He's playing with us." He met the Sun King's gaze squarely. "No more games, Harry. Not among such old friends. All those long evenings we spent talking together . . . You always believed in the truth above everything. So tell me—all this power that matters so much to you. Where does it really come from?"

The Sun King stared steadily back, smiling. "You'll find out."

I opened my mouth to say something, and the Sun King stopped me with a glance. I was so surprised, I let him get away with it. No-one had ever been able to do that to me before.

"You don't get to question me," said the Sun King. "Little man. Annoy me again, and I'll turn you into something more amusing. I will do what I will do; and no-one will stand in my way." He dismissed me with another look and concentrated on Julien. His words were suddenly playful, teasing. "You remember what we used to say, Julien. If you're not part of the solution, you're part of the problem. And I'm really not in the mood to put up with any more problems."

"So what are you going to do?" said Julien. "Kill me, like everyone else who opposes you? Like all the poor people here who weren't pretty enough for you?"

"Killing is easy," said the Sun King. "I can do better than that. I think I'll start here, with you and Taylor and the woman. All such a disappointment to me. I think I'll do something really impressive to you, to send a message. Start as you mean to go on, that's what I always say."

He moved towards Benway, and Julien immediately stepped forward to block his way. "I told you, Harry; I won't let you hurt her again."

"Oh please," said the Sun King. "Always the perfect English Gentleman. Or did you feel something for sweet little Emily, back in the day; when I was too busy to notice? I think I'll make you watch what I'm going to do to her, so I can enjoy listening to you scream . . ."

He walked forward, smiling easily, with all the confidence in the world; and I stepped forward to meet him and threw a handful of coarse-ground black pepper right into his eyes. He cried out in shock, then again in agony, as the pepper ate into his eyes. He staggered backwards, clawing at his streaming eyes with both hands, unable to think of anything but the horrible thing I'd done to him. I grinned at Julien.

"Some shit I don't put up with. And the old jokes are always the best. Living god, my arse. For all his admittedly impressive power, he's still a man. Let this be a lesson to you, Julien. Never leave home without condiments. Condiments are our friends."

"I'll kill you!" screamed the Sun King, staggering blindly back and forth. "I'll kill you all!"

"So much for peace and love," said Julien. "It's always sad, to see an old dream die."

He stepped forward and booted the Sun King square in the groin. He put all his strength and weight into it, and the force of the kick actually lifted the Sun King right off the ground for a moment. He tried to scream, but the pain blocked his throat. He fell to his knees, all the strength and all of his breath knocked right out of him. He bent forward over his pain, air rattling in his constricted throat, tears streaming down his face from puffy, squeezed-shut eyes. He didn't look like a living god any more. I looked at Julien with something very like shock. You don't expect the Great Victorian Adventurer to fight dirty. But he was looking down at the Sun King, genuinely more in sorrow than anger, and when he spoke, his voice was tired, and soul-deep weary.

"Stay down, Harry. I know a lot of tricks a lot worse than that one. You always liked to hear stories of my old days as an Adventurer, fighting the forces of evil. But you never understood what that meant. You were never a fighter."

The Sun King's head came up slowly, and he forced his eyes open so he could sneer at Julien. His face was flushed a dark and unhealthy purple with rage, and when he forced his hands away from his aching groin, they were trembling with rage, too.

"Don't you laugh at me. Don't you dare laugh at me! You wanted the power. Have it!"

The Sun King stabbed one hand at Julien, and a fierce light erupted out of his fingertips, hitting Julien in the chest like a lightning bolt. He cried out and staggered backwards, then the same terrible light blasted out of his eyes. Julien howled horribly, clutching at his face, and the light blazed right through his hands, outlining the bones within like an

X-ray. The light shone out of Julien's face, and out of his hands, and from his chest. He fell to his knees. He seemed to catch on fire from the light, blue flames bursting out all over him without burning or consuming him. His whole body shook and shuddered, as though he might explode at any moment.

Patients and security people scattered away from him, screaming and shouting. I had to fight my way through the press of bodies to get to Julien. There was no heat from the blue flames, only the terrible light blazing out of him. The Sun King laughed breathlessly. He was still holding himself as though something inside was broken, but his eyes had cleared, full of an awful laughter.

"He's too small a thing to hold the power I gave him. He can't control it, he can't even hold on to it. Any minute now, the power will break loose and destroy this whole building and everyone in it. And that's what you get, for mouthing off to a living god." He looked at me, and sniggered. "Of course, you can stop all this, John Taylor. I left you a way out; because I am a kind and considerate living god. You can stop this; save everyone in the hospital. All you have to do is kill him. Kill your friend, kill the legendary Great Victorian Adventurer, and the power will return to me. But you'd better do it quickly, while there's still time!"

He disappeared, still laughing.

I looked around, and there was Dr. Benway, staring at Julien in horror. She hadn't run, but she couldn't bring herself to move any closer.

"What do I do?" I screamed at her. "How do I stop this? How do I save him?"

But she shook her head numbly. For all her experience in Ward 12A, this was beyond her. I grabbed Julien by the shoulders, holding him still against the power within him, which was shaking him like a rag doll. The blue flames burned my hands, but I wouldn't let him go. He turned his face to me. The light blazing from his eyes was almost incandescent now. He forced words out, painfully.

"Do it, John. Kill me. You can't let all these people die."

"Julien, I can't!"

"You have to! It's all right, John. I understand. Never did think I'd die in bed. At least this way, I get to die saving lives. Doing something that matters."

"Julien . . . please . . ."

"Sorry I won't be there for your wedding. Now say good-bye, and kill me. Save the Hospice. Then track down the Sun King and stop him. And don't screw it up, or I'll come back and haunt you."

"Good-bye, Julien," I said. And then I took his head in both hands, and snapped it all the way round, breaking his neck.

All the light disappeared, and he was just a man again. He collapsed into my arms, and I held him tightly, ignoring the throbbing pain in my burned hands. I didn't cry. There was so much anger in me there wasn't room for anything else. I would find the Sun King. And I would kill him. Because he'd made me kill my good friend. The only decent man in the Nightside.

"Stop him!" Dr. Benway yelled suddenly. I looked up to see her pointing a shaking, accusing finger at me. "Someone stop that man! He killed Julien Advent!"

I lowered Julien's body carefully to the floor and got to my feet again, looking at Benway, frowning. "What are you talking about? You saw what happened!"

"You murdered him!"

"It wasn't like that! You know it wasn't like that!"

People all around were pointing at me and shouting my name, crying out to everyone that I'd killed Julien Advent. Some of the security people were pointing guns at me.

"Don't let him get away!" shrieked Benway, tears streaming down her face. "Murderer! Murderer!"

"It wasn't like that!" I cried.

But there were too many of them, shouting my name. I turned and ran, breaking through the crowds, as they fell back before me. I ran out of the Hospice lobby and into the car-park, and the crowd spilled out after me, yelling my name. People everywhere turned to look. A great cry went up behind me, that I'd murdered the Great Victorian Adventurer. People on the street began to shout and point.

I ran through the streets of the Nightside, with an angry mob behind me, my name a curse on their lips.

EIGHT

Old Friends and Enemies

And I went running, with horror at my heels.

Everywhere I went, people stopped to scream abuse at me. They threw stones and worse things. Some had guns, some had spells. I ran and dodged and ducked, trying desperately to work out where best to go, to hide from the whole damned Nightside. The word was out, to this side and that and sometimes even ahead of me. I'd been on the run before, back in my younger days, for various reasons, good and bad, but never anything like this. Julien Advent was a much loved and admired figure in the Nightside, far more than I ever was. I'd always thought it more important to be feared; and now my reputation was catching up with me, big-time.

I didn't dare use my Portable Timeslip. Far too easy to track something that powerful. So I ran.

Why the hell had Benway called me a murderer? She was

right there, she saw what was happening, she had to know why I did it. Unless . . . the Sun King was messing with her head. Making her see what he wanted her to see. I grinned savagely as I ran, a humourless snarl that had people falling back before me and hurrying to get out of my way. Things were finally starting to make sense. The Sun King was responsible for everything that was happening to me now, to keep me occupied, too busy trying to stay alive to stop him doing what he planned. That was why everyone was so ready to abuse and attack and pursue me, when normally most of them would have kept their heads down and concentrated on their own business. I laughed briefly as I ran, the sound like the bark of some dangerous animal, and people hid in doorways or hurried down side streets, rather than confront me.

I spent a lot of my early years running and hiding from people who wanted to kill me, from all the usual villains and scumbags, and from the Harrowing. Those faceless homunculi sent back through Time by my Enemies in the Future, to punish me for something I hadn't even done yet. What doesn't kill you makes you very light on your feet and very hard to find; and as I raced through the Nightside, old skills and knowledge swiftly came back to me. I raced through the busy streets, taking this turn and that, charging through the front door of a big store, slipping through the crowds, then darting out the back door. Raised voices fell away behind me, caught up in new and unexpected quarrels with people who didn't take kindly to being shoved. I scrambled over low walls, doubled back and forth, always keeping to the darkest shadows, taking all kinds of short cuts and connections that most people didn't even know existed.

And, finally, I ended up in a garbage-strewn back alley, somewhere downwind of the old theatre district; leaning heavily against a wall covered with overlapping yellowing posters, advertising old shows and faded triumphs. Breathing so hard my chest ached, and trying to persuade my racing heart to return to something like normal behaviour before it burst right out of me. My head pounded, my face was wet with sweat, and my hands were shaking so bad I couldn't even haul a handkerchief out of my pocket to mop my face. Getting far too old for this on-the-run shit.

I comforted myself with the memory of the Sun King's face as I threw black pepper in his eyes; and again, when Julien booted him in the 'nads. Thinking he could impress me with all that living-god crap. I've fought my way up and down the Street of the Gods more than once. And I looked forward to seeing his face again, when I finally tracked him down and took my own sweet time killing him. It had been a long long time since I'd felt this angry, and I hugged that cold comfort to my heart. I would see the Sun King die in agony and horror for what he'd made me do to Julien. Not that Julien would have approved or even wanted such a revenge taken, on his behalf; but then, he always was a better man than me.

Revenge is simply justice with teeth.

I slowly straightened up and looked around me. I still couldn't breathe without hurting, but my vision had cleared, and my thoughts were finally racing faster than my heart. I couldn't stay here. It was enough out of the way to give me time to consider what to do next, but with so many on my trail, someone would find me soon, if only by accident. So I raised my gift and used it to find a way into the cemetery dimension attached to the Necropolis. We bury our dead in a very separate pocket dimension, only loosely attached to the Nightside. Because when we put our dead to rest, we prefer them to stay that way and not come back and bother us. It seemed to me that the cemetery's many protections and defensive magics might well be enough to hide my presence. And, of course, most people have enough sense to stay out of the cemetery. It's not a good place; it's meant for the dead, not visitors.

I focused my gift, found one of the drifting places where the cemetery dimension occasionally overlaps with the Nightside, and concentrated hard. A door that hadn't been there before, and never would be again, appeared in the alley wall opposite me. I held the door in place with my gift and pushed it open with an effort of will. Beyond the door was only darkness. I walked gratefully forward into it, and the door closed behind me.

The cold got to me first, hitting me hard and cutting me like a knife. It rattled in my lungs like razor blades, and sucked all the warmth right out of me. I hugged myself tightly and stamped my feet hard. The graveyard stretched endlessly away before me, a whole world of the dead. The Nightside has been burying its reluctantly departed in this very private place for centuries. Row upon row, rank upon rank, graves and their headstones, for as far as the eye could see in any direction.

It was a different kind of night from the Nightside, darker, with an almost palpable gloom. A thick pearlescent ground fog curled slowly around my ankles, almost deliberately. Like some great grey cat making itself known, not necessarily affectionately. Up in the black black sky, there was no moon, only a few long smears of multi-coloured stars, gaudy as a cheap ring on a tart's finger.

Headstones everywhere, of stone and marble, steel and porcelain, according to the fashion of the day, with lengthy inscriptions or none at all. Catafalques and mausoleums, simple or ornate, decadent or utilitarian. Some with cold neon, some without. Statues of weeping angels and shifty-looking cherubs, while crouching gargoyles leered down from the tops of monuments, guarding family repositories. And everywhere you looked, all kinds of religious symbols. Ancient and modern, sacred and profane; and some from religions no-one even remembers any more.

I moved slowly forward, careful to keep to the officially designated gravel paths, laid out for those stubborn few who insisted on visiting people who wouldn't have been buried here if they'd wanted visitors. One of the main reasons for being interred in this very isolated location is to make sure your grave won't be disturbed or interfered with. So outside the gravel paths, you wander at your own peril. In our cemetery, the helpless dead are defended: by land mines, booby-traps, invisible floating curses, and other less obvious but even nastier forms of security and preservation.

The cemetery was full of shadows and a grim silence. Enforced peace and solitude hung heavily over the still scene. Even the crunching of my feet on gravel seemed strangely subdued and muffled. I stopped and sat down on a nearby headstone, so I could think. Then I thought to get up and take a look at the stone's inscription. It read NOT DEAD ONLY SLEEPING. And since this was still the Nightside, I moved along and sat down on another stone with a less worrying inscription. Because you can't be too careful.

No-one had followed me; no-one had found me. I was alone.

I got out my mobile phone and called Alex Morrisey at Strangefellows. While reflecting that it was a good thing I'd recently upgraded my service, to cover all the pocket dimensions and hidden worlds of the Nightside. Alex answered the phone immediately, as though he'd been waiting for my call. His voice came through clearly, and there didn't seem to be any noise in the background. Which was odd, for Strangefellows.

"John!" said Alex. "Where are you?"

"Think I'll keep that to myself, for the moment," I said. "Does sound rather quiet, at your end. Would I be right in thinking my stag do is over?"

"Are you kidding?" said Alex. "Most of the people who were here are now out on the streets looking for you, and not in a good way. Turned out a lot of them were great admirers of Julien Advent, on the quiet. And the reward money the Authorities have put up for you is the biggest anyone's ever heard of! They want your head, John, preferably in a box."

"I suppose I shouldn't be surprised the news is out," I said. "Nothing travels faster in the Nightside than bad news."

"Did you really murder the Great Victorian Adventurer?" said Alex. "Tell me you didn't, John; tell me this is all some terrible mistake."

"It's all some terrible mistake," I said. "Really. I did kill him, but . . ."

"John! How could you?"

"He asked me to do it! He was dying anyway; and it was the only way to save a whole hospital full of innocents."

"You killed Julien Advent!"

"It wasn't like that!"

I did my best to explain about the Sun King, and what he meant to do, and the power he put into Julien . . . but I could tell it sounded unlikely, even for the kind of cases I usually get involved in. I could tell Alex was having trouble believing it. I wanted to say *You had to be there* . . .

"The official story is that you murdered Julien Advent in cold blood," said Alex. "Though no-one seems too sure why. I know you were always jealous of him, John, but . . ."

"You really think I'm capable of something like that?" I said.

"You've done worse," said Alex. And I had no answer to that.

"It's like the whole Nightside wants you dead," said Alex. "The Authorities, or what's left of them, are really mad at you. First, you let King of Skin die, right in front of you; and now you've murdered Julien Advent? They think you've gone rogue, and possibly feral . . ."

"How big a reward have they put on my head?" I asked, honestly curious.

"Big enough to tempt anyone," said Alex. "If I didn't have a bar to run . . ."

"I can't believe I chose you as my best man," I said.

"You don't really think you're still getting married tomorrow, do you?" said Alex, incredulously. "The only church service you're likely to be attending in the near future involves a big hole in the ground and a priest trying to find something positive to say about you."

"Alex," I said. "What am I going to do?"

"You can't come here," Alex said immediately. "It's the first place they'd look. And I've only just got the place cleared up after the last fight you started. Maybe . . . you should leave the Nightside. Go hide out in London Proper, until things calm down a bit. You could always claim sanctuary at Castle Inconnu, with the London Knights. They owe you, after that business with Excalibur. And they're far enough outside the Nightside they might not be tainted by the Sun King's influence. If that really is what's behind all this . . ."

And then his voice dropped away suddenly, as someone else snatched the phone from him. A cold ghostly voice came clearly to me, more than usually animated with furious emotions.

"Julien Advent was my friend!" said Razor Eddie. "And a better man than you or I will ever be. And you killed him. I know where you are, Taylor. I'm coming for you. And I will soak my razor in your blood."

His voice cut off as Alex wrestled the phone away from him. I could hear them shouting at each other, then Alex's voice returned.

"Get the hell out of my bar, Eddie, or I will have Betty and Lucy frog-march you out, then hose you down with something seriously disinfectant! God, you stink . . . You still there, John? He's gone. Disappeared right in front of me, leaving only his stench behind. A smell so strong it feels like it wants to make friends with you and follow you home. I don't think I've ever seen him so angry before . . . It seems like a lot more people admire Julien Advent dead than were ever prepared to say so while he was still alive. John, have you talked to Suzie yet?"

"I don't want her involved," I said immediately. "She'd kill anyone to protect me."

"Yeah," said Alex. "But would she kill everyone?"

"Probably," I said.

"Suddenly, I have cold chills all over me."

"I have to find the Sun King," I said. "Stop him, kill him . . . But how the hell am I supposed to do that when it seems like all my old friends and enemies are out on the streets looking to stop and kill me?"

"I suppose you could hide out here, for a while," said Alex. "In the cellars under the bar. Given that both Merlin Satanspawn and Arthur Pendragon were both buried down there for centuries, undetected, it seems likely there's enough power left behind to hide you . . ."

"Thanks, Alex," I said, and I meant it. "But the way the Sun King's got everyone stirred up, I don't think all of Strangefellows' protections put together could keep them out if they did track me there. The whole world could turn up at your door, baying for my blood. I wouldn't want to bring that down on you."

"Does this mean I'm reinvested as best man?" said Alex.

"Don't lose the ring," I said.

I broke the connection and sat on my tombstone for a while, hefting the phone in one hand while my mind chased in all directions at once. The phone rang. It was Suzie. Her voice sounded cool and calm as always.

"I've heard," she said. "Did you really kill Julien Advent in cold blood?"

"Of course not!" I said. "How could you even think that of me?"

"It didn't sound like you," said Suzie.

"I killed him at his own request, to save a whole bunch of innocents from being killed."

"That sounds like Advent," said Suzie. "Where are you, John?"

"You'd better stay out of this, Suzie. I can handle it."

"Of course you can. Where are you, John?"

It was the second time she'd asked, and something in her voice made all the hackles rise up on the back of my neck. "Why do you want to know, Suzie?"

"Because the Authorities have hired me to track you down," said Shotgun Suzie. "My biggest bounty ever."

"And you said yes?"

"It's a really big reward," said Suzie. "Biggest I've ever been offered. And it is what I do best. It's a matter of professional pride, John. I can't let anyone else get to you first."

"And you never bring your bounties back alive," I said.

I cut her off and shut down the phone, just in case. It wasn't like I wanted to talk to anyone anyway. I simply sat there, staring at nothing, trying not to think, trying not to feel. Because it felt like someone had punched my heart out. I'd never felt so alone.

I rocked back and forth, hugging myself tightly to keep from falling apart. Tears burned my eyes, but I was damned if I'd give in to them. Instead, I clung to the rage within me, warming my heart on its heat. I had to stop the Sun King. To save the Nightside and avenge Julien Advent. I would stop him, then put him down, in the worst and messiest way I could think of. And after that, the whole damned Nightside and everyone in it could go straight to Hell, for all I cared.

I looked up sharply. There was a new presence on the air, a new power forcing its way into the cemetery dimension.

Something was coming my way, cutting its way through Space and Time to get to me, and I knew who it was, who it had to be. Light burst suddenly into the cemetery gloom, bright neon glare from the Nightside, falling through a narrow gap that split the air before me from top to bottom. The gap stretched wide, forced apart by one man's unstoppable will; and through that hole came Razor Eddie, the Punk God of the Straight Razor. His feet crunched loudly on the gravel before me, and the gap slammed shut behind him, cutting off the light. Razor Eddie, a grey presence in a filthy coat, with dark eyes and a haunted face, holding his pearl-handled straight razor out before him. The steel blade shone supernaturally bright. Eddie moved slowly towards me, cold and implacable as an avenging angel, and it seemed to me I'd never seen him look so angry, so . . . emotional, before. I never knew he had it in him.

I got up from the headstone, unhurriedly, and waited for him to come to me. I can honestly say it never even occurred to me to run, to use my gift to get away, even though that would have been the sane thing to do. He stopped at the very edge of the gravel path and stared at me as though he'd never seen me before. He hefted the shining razor; and it occurred to me that the razor's magics shouldn't work here, in the face of so many defensive magics. Instead, it glared more fiercely than I'd ever seen before. Fuelled by the rage of the god who held it. Eddie held it up, so I could get a good look at the killing thing.

"I am a god," he said, in his ghostly whispering voice. "People tend to forget that the Punk God of the Straight Razor isn't just a title. I take my power with me, wherever I go. I exist to protect the innocent and punish the guilty. I have never allowed anything to get in my way."

"You won't even give an old friend the benefit of the doubt?" I said, standing very still.

"The friend I thought I had, the man I thought I knew, would never have murdered Julien Advent in cold blood."

"I didn't!"

"Liar." Razor Eddie smiled at me slowly. "What a long, strange road it's been, John. Sometimes friends, sometimes allies, sometimes enemies. Typical enough, I suppose, for the Nightside. And now here we are, ready to go head to head, like in the prophecy . . . You should have listened, John. Dagon is never wrong about these things." His smile slowly widened into a cold and remorseless thing. "All these years we've danced the dance, circling around each other . . . You must have known it would come to this, eventually. You must have wondered, which one of us would win, in a fight to the death?"

"No," I said. "I can honestly say, the thought never crossed my mind."

"Liar," said Eddie, almost fondly.

"Eddie," I said. "You don't have to do this."

"Yes, I do," he said. "For Julien Advent. Who never once approved of me, and quite right, too."

He launched himself at me while he was still speaking, an old trick, but I was ready for that; and we went fighting up and down the gravel path, through the cold grey silence of the cemetery. And the fog swirled around us like the disturbed waters where sharks are circling with bad intent.

I knew I couldn't face his razor, so I kept falling back before it, dodging and ducking where necessary. The brightly shining blade sliced clean through the top of a headstone, when I put it between myself and Eddie; and the blade hacked off the top corner in a moment, cutting through solid stone like it was paper. I kept moving, darting this way and that, trying to stay alive long enough to come up with some kind of strategy. He wasn't even trying, yet. He was playing with me. So, when in doubt, raise the stakes. I stepped deliberately off the gravel path, into and among the graves, daring Eddie to follow. I could See the hidden dangers, but he couldn't, for all his Punk Godness. He didn't even hesitate. He stepped off the gravel path and straight onto a land mine.

The explosion was deafeningly loud on the quiet, and a great cloud of pulverised stone and earth filled the air. Bits of gravel rained down like shrapnel. And Razor Eddie came walking forward out of the dust cloud, like a wolf out of hiding. Untouched and unscathed, like the murderous force he was. I kept backing away, and he kept coming after me; and the ground between us erupted, as a rock golem, a clumsy, misshapen thing, twelve feet tall and more, with a featureless face and huge fists like mauls, rose out of the dark earth between us to confront him. It went for Razor Eddie, and he moved so quickly he was only a blur. His razor flashed like lightning, sparking on the air, everywhere at once. And when Razor Eddie stopped moving, the rock golem was gone, leaving only piles of scattered rock pieces to show where it had been. Very small, finely cut rock pieces. Razor Eddie smiled at me, and a cold hand clutched my heart.

I retreated further into the cemetery, being very careful where I put my feet, hiding among the looming mausoleums and family crypts. Razor Eddie came after me, cutting his way through a forest of tombstones and carving the sad faces off sculpted angels because they got in his way. I was still thinking furiously. I could have killed him. I'm pretty sure I could have found a way to kill him. Eddie had his razor, but I had all kinds of weapons, and a lifetime's supply of dirty tricks. But he was still my friend, in his own strange, cold way, and I didn't want to kill him. So I did what I always do, when I'm backed into a corner—improvise with extreme prejudice.

I goaded him into rushing me. "Getting old, Eddie! Getting soft and slow. Getting past it!"

He rushed forward as I finally stood my ground. And at the last moment I whipped off my white trench coat and threw it over Razor Eddie. It wrapped itself around him as he crashed to a halt, blinded and confused, fighting the coat's enveloping folds and getting nowhere. Now, my coat has enough nasty magics and awful protections built into it that it could probably have won the fight on its own; but to be on the safe side, I picked up a chunk of stone that Eddie had sliced off a tombstone, and hit him over the head with it.

Eddie slumped to his knees, but he didn't stop struggling, so I hit him again, putting all my strength and weight into it. The impact jarred my hand and arm painfully, and Eddie fell forward onto the ground between the graves and lay still. I took my coat back off him, and put it back on again.

"Don't try and kid me you're dead," I said finally. "I might have rattled your brains a bit, Mr. high-and-mighty Punk God of the knife with attachment for getting stones out of horses' hooves, but you don't get taken out of the game that easily."

I kicked his straight razor away from him, and his head came up immediately, to fix me with a cold dark glare. Blood ran thickly down the side of his face.

"Leave that alone!" he said. "Damn you, John. You only won by cheating, and you know it!"

"You always were a bad loser, Eddie," I said. "The operative word is *won*. So I suggest you take a nice little rest until you've got all your marbles together again. Don't try and follow me. Or I might have to do something more permanent to you."

"I will find you!"

"No you won't," I said. "Good-bye, Eddie."

I used my gift to find the tear he'd made in Space and Time with his razor, to let himself into the cemetery dimension. It was still there. I could See it clearly, hanging on the air over the gravel path. The wounds Razor Eddie makes in the world take time to heal. I moved quickly back between the graves and onto the path, pushed the sides of the gap apart, and squeezed up my eyes against the bright flare of light that fell through into the grey cemetery world. I looked back, just in time to see Razor Eddie stretch out one hand

and the straight razor fly through the air to slap into his palm. Definitely time to be going. I stepped through the gap and back into the Nightside, letting the tear close behind me. I used my gift to find a way to close and seal it permanently, so he couldn't come straight after me, and only then looked around to see where I'd ended up. I was pretty much where I'd expected, in the street outside the Necropolis itself. Ugly great building; a hulking brick monument to our continuing fascination with death.

I didn't hear the car coming, but long years of experience surviving in the Nightside made me look round suddenly. And there, coming straight at me at speed, was the great shining silver bullet of Dead Boy's futuristic car. I didn't hear it approach because it had no wheels, floating serenely on super-scientific energy fields, and an engine that barely murmured at the best of times. I threw myself out of its way, and the car's front bumper hit me a glancing blow as it shot past. The impact sent me sprawling, rolling over and over. I hit hard and took my time coming to a stop; afterwards I lay there, gasping for breath. My hip hurt like hell, but I didn't think it was broken. And while I lay there, trying to get my thoughts back together again, the car swung smoothly round at the end of the street, moved unhurriedly back towards me, and stopped a respectful distance away. The driver's door swung smoothly open, and Dead Boy lurched out, resplendent in his purple greatcoat with a black rose at the lapel. He sauntered down the street towards me, his face completely relaxed and utterly remorseless.

"My car has the best tracking systems in the world," he said easily. "She knew where you were going to reappear before you did. I've been parked at the end of this street for ages, waiting for you to turn up. Killer."

"It wasn't like that!" I said, forcing myself up onto one knee, and checking myself over for damages.

"Oh please," said Dead Boy. "Don't embarrass yourself.

I've heard the story of how Advent died too many times, from people I have every reason to trust. Julien Advent was a good man. He taught me about honour. He believed in me even though I was dead. He was always there for me . . . Even when you ran away from the Nightside and hid out in London Proper for all those years. He never abandoned me! He taught me how to live again!"

"I didn't murder him," I said, somehow clambering up onto my feet again. It had been a long day. I stood swaying before him, meeting his unwavering gaze with my own. "After all we've been through, after all the things we've faced together; can't you trust me?"

"You?" said Dead Boy, and tired as I was, I had to admit he had a point.

He moved suddenly forward, crossing the intervening space between us in a moment. He took two good handfuls of my coat lapels and held me easily in the air with his unnatural strength. My feet kicked helplessly a good yard above the ground. I grabbed his wrists with my hands, but it was like gripping cold steel. I wrestled against his grip, but couldn't break it. I let go, and punched him in the side of the head, with as much strength as the awkward angle would allow. I hurt my hand, but I didn't hurt him.

He laughed at me. "Come on, John; you know better than that. I don't feel pain. I don't feel anything unless I take my special pills. But I think I will feel something when I kill you. I will feel something when I avenge Julien Advent."

"He never could stand you," I said.

He threw my against the wall behind me, on the other side of the street. I hit hard; and the world went away for a while. When it came back, I was lying in the middle of the road. My face hurt like hell, and blood was dripping from my mouth and nose. Dead Boy had been busy while I was away. I looked carefully around me, without raising my head. Dead Boy was standing over me, looking down the street towards his futuristic car. I was already recovering, but he didn't know that. He didn't know about the werewolf blood. He couldn't know how quickly I could put myself back together again. Dead Boy laughed softly and looked down at me.

"You can stop playing dead, John. I know you're awake. I heard your breathing change. You always were a tough little bastard. But after the way I bounced you off that wall and slapped you around, you won't be getting up anytime soon. So I think I'll run you over with my car. Over and over and over again."

He called to his marvellous futuristic car, and the engine murmured into life. The car headed straight for me, taking its time. Dead Boy stayed right where he was, so he could see it all in close-up and savour it. His smile vanished as I sat up, spat out a mouthful of blood, and grinned at him.

"Have to do better than that, you brain-dead animated corpse."

Dead Boy leaned slowly towards me, not allowing himself to be hurried, his dead hands clenched into fists and his dark eyes fixed on me. The car was still coming, building speed, aimed right at me. I waited till Dead Boy was bending right over me, then I used my gift to find all the stitches, staples, and yards of duct tape that held his much-abused dead body together. And once I had them, it was the easiest thing in the world to find all their weak spots. The stitches broke, the duct tape ruptured, and rusting staples flew out of him like tiny shrapnel.

It was an old weakness of Dead Boy's. I'd seen someone else do it to him before. And I never forget a weakness I might need to make use of someday.

Dead Boy cried out as he fell helplessly to his knees, clutching at his opening wounds to stop his internal organs from falling out. The car was almost on top of us, slamming on its brakes as it worked out what was happening . . . too late, too late. I rolled casually to one side, and the car ran right over Dead Boy as he lay broken and helpless on the ground. When the futuristic car finally lurched to a halt, it had run over Dead Boy, its back wheels resting right on top of him, pinning him firmly to the ground. And before it could decide whether to move on or back away, I sauntered over and placed one heavy foot on the back bumper.

"Back off now, and you'll tear him apart," I said to the car. I was pretty sure it could understand me. "And if you try to go forward, I'll do something even more unpleasant to him. And you." The car didn't move, so I looked down at Dead Boy's strained face, glaring up at me. "You can treat a mule with kindness," I said. "But first you have to hit it over the head with a two-by-four, to get its attention. I am not guilty of murdering Julien Advent, you idiot. And to prove it, I'm not going to kill you."

"You can't kill me," Dead Boy said craftily. "The clue's in the name."

"All right then, I won't damage or destroy your body, or shove it in the furnace and dance around singing Hallelujah."

Dead Boy considered this for a while, looking up at me thoughtfully. "You could find a way to get rid of me, couldn't you? Typical John bloody Taylor. All right, let's talk. If we must. I got a call to go to the Hospice. Anonymous, but you get used to those, in the Nightside. It told me Julien Advent was dead. I didn't want to believe it, so of course I had to go. When I got there, he was lying there, stretched out on the floor. I didn't see any blood, so for a moment I hoped, but . . . Some doctor was weeping over him. Nurses and patients, too. I knelt and looked Julien over, but he was definitely gone. The dead know death when they see it. The doctor said you'd killed him, for no reason. I always knew you'd go rogue someday."

"I find my friends' lack of faith in me disturbing," I said.

"Go on! Kill me, if you can! Find a way to destroy my body! But you'd better make a really good job of it; because it's the only way you'll stop me from avenging Julien Advent!"

"Why is everyone so keen to avenge him?" I said. "None of you ever had much time for him when he was alive."

"I couldn't help him, then," said Dead Boy. "What could someone like me do for someone like him? But I can do this!"

"I'm not going to kill, destroy, or disassemble you," I said patiently.

"Why not?"

"Because you're my friend."

"All right," said Dead Boy, slowly. "One of us has definitely mellowed; and it sure as hell isn't me. Something is very wrong here. You never killed anyone that you weren't prepared to boast about afterwards; and you never showed mercy to anyone who threatened your life. Are you sure you didn't kill Julien Advent? Because . . . as much as I want to believe you, something is yelling in my head that you did it."

"I only ever killed people who needed killing," I said.

"Good point," said Dead Boy. "I'll think about it. But you'd better run, John, while you can. Because once I get out from under this car, if I've thought about it and made up my mind that you are guilty . . . I will come after you. Because I can't let Julien Advent's murderer get away with it."

"Of course," I said. "I wouldn't expect anything less from you."

I walked away. Behind me I could hear the futuristic car reversing very slowly off Dead Boy, while he yelled *Careful, dammit!* and *Don't worry, baby; it wasn't your fault.*

I found a short cut that took me straight to the H. P. Lovecraft Memorial Library, only to find it wasn't there. It was only then that I remembered hearing that the Library had recently vanished and been replaced by a doppelganger from some alternate dimension. The Linda Lovecraft Library of Spiritual Erotica. Takes all sorts . . . A large crowd of extremely interested observers had gathered before the front doors, at what they hoped was a safe distance, watching while men in heavy-duty protective clothing checked the place out first. Because some kinds of forbidden knowledge are more dangerous than others. Everyone there was so interested in what might be going on inside that no-one even noticed my arrival.

I stood as deep in the shadows of a side alley as I could get and frowned thoughtfully. The Linda Lovecraft Library was no use to me. I had one particular book in mind, and for that I needed the original building back again. So I raised my gift, reached out with my mind in a direction I could sense but not point at, grabbed hold of the missing Library, and brought it back again. It took up its old position quite comfortably, nudging the intruder back to its own world. No explosions, no earthquakes, not even any bright lights. It helped that I was only reversing an existing transfer; someone had taken our Library and replaced it with theirs. And later on, if I was still alive, I would have to find out why.

Loud cries of shock, outrage, and deep disappointment came from the watching crowd. They'd really been looking forward to discovering exactly what kind of informative books the new Library might contain. The men in protective clothing came stumbling out of the front door, shaking their heads. One of them was heard to state, quite loudly, that he wished *some people* would make up their minds. The crowd began to disperse.

I couldn't move. I was so tired I had to lean against the alley wall and wait for my strength to come back to me. I was using my gift too much, again. Not that I had any choice. But I'd been through a lot in a short time, and even werewolf blood and Alex's pick-me-up could only do so much. They could heal my body, but abusing my gift was doing serious damage to my mind and my soul.

Someday, I'd go too far, and not come back.

After a while, the pain in my head began to subside, and I

wiped my nose on the back of my hand. I stared at the long streak of blood I left there, then took out a handkerchief and wiped it away. I moved to the entrance of the alley and looked across at the front entrance to the Library. Most of the crowd was gone. The H. P. Lovecraft Memorial Library was strictly for those interested and discerning minds concerned with ancient knowledge and secrets preserved in forbidden books . . . the kind of thing that could only be dug out through hard work and harder research. Strictly for only the most hardened scholars. And who had time for that, in the Nightside, when so many other more immediate pleasures were to be had, on every side? Only the most dedicated students of the strange and unnatural came to this Library, men who had no time for anything else. Each to their own . . .

The scholarly boys would be heading back the moment they heard the old place had returned, so I had to get in and out quickly if I didn't want to be noticed. Fortunately, I knew of a very secret side entrance to the Library, shown to me by the last Head Librarian but one, who owed me a favour for finding a rather important book that had gone walkabout. (Apparently it was mostly bored. The Head Librarian made arrangements for it to be read continuously, in shifts, and that took care of that.) I drifted carefully and very inconspicuously down the side of the Library and used the key that I'd taken in part payment for my work. (Not only for finding the book but for keeping quiet about what it was about.)

Inside, the Library was still and quiet. I moved quickly through the deserted stacks, in pursuit of the one book I was increasingly sure I needed to take a good look at. No-one else had got in yet, not even the very dedicated and more than a little unhinged scholars of the weird and appalling who normally have to be beaten off with big sticks or hosed down with Ritalin and thrown out bodily, when they got too attached to a particular volume and wouldn't give it up to anyone else. Hell, some of them would sleep in the stacks if they were allowed. But the Library's security would keep the scholars at bay until they'd had a chance to do a full sweep of the building and make sure everything was where it should be. And that the stacks hadn't picked up any dangerous hitch-hikers from where it had recently been. I kept a careful eye out but didn't see anything unusual. Or at least, no more unusual than usual.

I finally found my way to the Really Restricted Section, where they keep the kind of books most scholars aren't even supposed to know exist. I knocked on the closed door, said the proper passwords, and the door opened before me. I walked in, and the ghost of the Head Librarian, a thin, dusty presence, with dark eyes and a disapproving look, appeared before me, blocking my way. (He had been eaten by a book, then brought back by the other books, apparently because they approved of him. Because even though he didn't have much time for people, he loved books.) I was forced to acknowledge his presence or walk right through him.

"John Taylor," said the Ghost Librarian, in a voice of spiritual accusation. "I might have known."

"Don't get snotty," I said. "I brought this place back from wherever it's been. Where did you go, anyway?"

"I don't like to think about it," said the Ghost Librarian, sounding distinctly embarrassed. "Some alternate worlds are more alternate than others. A very . . . uninhibited culture, indeed. Thank you for bringing us back. Would it have killed you to wait a few days? Anyway, what are you doing here? You don't have access to the Really Restricted Section."

I pulled a card out of thin air and showed it to him. "Oh yes I do. See? I have special clearance. Courtesy of Ebeneezer Scrivener, the last Head Librarian but one. And, no, you don't get to ask why. But I have full clearance, for everything, cannot be refused or revoked."

The Ghost Librarian sniffed dustily. "They'll let anyone in these days. Oh, very well. If you must. But treat the books properly; if I find one dog-eared page after you've gone, I'll have you indexed. And make sure you put everything back where you found it."

I left him muttering to himself in a spectral way and pressed on into the gloomy depths of the Really Restricted Section. The Library could provide perfectly good lighting, like everywhere else, if it wanted; I think they do it here for atmosphere. All the reading desks have their own lights, complete with a large red panic button. This particular section holds more ancient tomes of forbidden lore, and spiritually dangerous books, than the human mind can comfortably cope with. Not even my special-access card could keep me safe from all the threats and dangers in this Section. Some books were padlocked inside cold iron cases, to keep their extreme energies from leaking out and contaminating the area. Or rewriting the other books. Some were chained to the shelves, not to keep them from being stolen but to keep them from attacking people. And some had their very own illuminated warning signs because in the H. P. Lovecraft Memorial Library, some books read people.

There are books bound in dragon skin, black goatskin, and human skin; and I could hear them muttering and stirring on the shelves as I walked by. A few actually silently vanished away, rather than have me read them, which I felt was a bit harsh. But then, books can be terrible snobs.

I was also hoping the Library's many layers of protective spells and privacy enforcements (built up over the centuries, to protect the books and keep them under control, and prevent anyone from getting in without paying the proper fee), would be enough to conceal my presence from all those looking for me. But I still couldn't afford to waste any time. I wasn't just on the run; I had a target nailed to my back. By the Sun King. I had to wonder where he was, right now, and what he was doing; but I couldn't let myself get distracted. I hurried through the stacks, while some books whispered seductively *Read me!* and others snorted *Don't even touch my binding, unworthy one!* One book bound in very pale elf skin glowed unhealthily in the gloom, poisoning the air with its aetheric radiations. I gave it plenty of room. Elves have always been big on revenge, even when they're dead. Especially when they're dead.

It took me a while to find the particular book I wanted. I couldn't use my gift, not in a place like this. I had to do it the old-fashioned way, checking the index and working my way up and down the shelves. The book was exactly where it was supposed to be, for which I gave quiet thanks to the Ghost Librarian. He might be fond of books, but he didn't take any shit from any volume on his watch.

You're welcome.

I pretended I hadn't heard that and eased the book carefully off the shelf. The books on either side immediately shuffled closer together to take up the intervening space. The shelf was very tightly packed. I took the book over to the nearest reading desk, and the green-shielded light turned itself on. I thought I heard a faint sigh of relief from the other books, that I wasn't interested in them; but that could have been my imagination.

The book I'd wanted was a lengthy and exhaustive history of the Hawk's Wind Bar & Grille, in life and in death, so to speak. Written by Julien Advent, in 1977. I paused for a moment as I looked at his name on the title page and let my fingertips drift over the printed letters. I had my own signed copy at home. He gave it to me years ago. Hadn't looked at it in ages. So much to do . . . But this was the full, unexpurgated version. I leafed quickly through the pages, looking for . . . something. Something to jog my memory. Because something about the Hawk Wind's sudden disappearance was bugging me. I'd missed something, forgotten something, but I was damned if I could think what. But I knew it was something significant. I flicked quickly through the chapters, letting words and phrases flow past my eyes, but nothing jumped out at me. I already knew all this . . .

And then I looked up sharply. Footsteps were heading my way. Two sets, heavy but unhurried, apparently completely unconcerned that I might hear them. I closed the book, tucked it carefully into the large shoplifting pocket inside my trench coat, got up, and turned around, to meet whoever it was who'd been clever and fast enough to find me here. I could probably have got away, given that I knew the layout of this Library better than anyone who didn't actually work here, but I was curious to know who it might be. And to take care of them here and now, so they wouldn't follow me any further.

They came walking through the stacks towards me, and very dangerous books shuddered back on their shelves to get away from them. From Tommy and Larry, the Oblivion brothers. They both caught sight of me waiting for them at the same moment, and they came to a sudden halt, side by side. We stared at each other for a long moment.

"Of course," I said. "The existential private eye and the Dead Detective. I should have known. It always takes one PI to find another."

"Or in this case two PIs," Tommy said brightly.

"Shut up, Tommy," said Larry. "This is business. Serious business. It's always trouble when one of us goes bad."

Tommy nodded and gave me his best disappointed look. Larry looked at me as though this was what he'd always expected of me.

"How did you find me so quickly?" I said.

"We are detectives," said Larry.

"Good song," said Tommy.

"Shut up, Tommy!"

"Is Hadleigh with you?" I said.

"The Detective Inspectre is apparently busy," said Larry,

trying to keep the distaste out of his voice, and not even coming close.

"Oh good," I said. "I thought I might be in trouble, for a moment."

"Now you're just being nasty," said Tommy.

Larry stared coldly at me. "Put up a fight, Taylor. Go on. Give me an excuse to stamp your arrogant murderous face into the floor."

"I always wondered how a good man like Julien Advent could survive in a place like this," said Tommy. "But I never thought you'd be the one to finish him off, John."

"I can explain," I said, but they were already shaking their heads.

"Don't," said Tommy. "Please, John. Don't lower yourself."

"You'd say anything," said Larry. "And we don't care enough to listen. This is for the Great Victorian Adventurer; you bastard."

He brought up his hand, and suddenly there was an elven wand pointing right at me. Larry Oblivion stabbed the wand at me, then frowned, when nothing happened. He stabbed the wand at me again, a little less confidently, and slowly lowered the wand as I smiled at him.

"I took precautions to protect myself against that thing the moment I discovered you had it," I said. "I always knew you'd find a reason to turn on me, someday. And I always knew a lot more about elves than you ever did."

Larry said something quietly obscene and made the wand disappear again. Tommy seized the moment and stepped forward. He smiled engagingly at me.

"Come, let us reason together . . ."

"Let's not," I said, very firmly. "Because you are the existential private eye, who can persuade anyone of anything. Who could talk the hind leg off a donkey, then use it to club the poor beast's head in. I have extensive mental training, from when I was a young man learning my craft with old Carnacki; but even so, I don't feel I want to test that training against your unnatural gift. So don't try it on with me, Tommy Oblivion, or I will punch you right in the throat."

And all the time I was speaking my mind, and the Oblivion brothers were listening to me, I was edging closer to the nearest bookshelf. I couldn't hide my movements from them, but as long as I was still talking and not running, they stayed where they were. Confident that they were blocking the way to the exit. But I wasn't thinking about running. Not yet. I grabbed the nearest book, feeling it squirm in my hand, and threw it at Larry. He flinched away as the book swooped angrily about his head, flapping its leather covers like stiff wings. Tommy cried out piteously and put both hands up to protect his head. He'd always had a thing about anything getting in his hair.

Larry grabbed the book out of mid air, holding it firmly with both hands. The book fought him, struggling fiercely, strange energies sparking and spitting on the air around it; but Larry was dead, and the book couldn't hurt him. He forced the book closed with his dead strength and pushed it firmly back into its proper gap on the shelf. He then backed quickly away, while all the books on that shelf vied to make the loudest and most obscene noises of defiance. Larry smiled briefly.

"I may be dead, but I still have my reflexes. Tommy, will you please put your hands down! The danger, what there was of it, has quite definitely passed."

And while they were both distracted by all of that, I slipped behind the bookshelf, put my shoulder to the wooden frame, and threw all my strength and weight against it. The bookshelf resisted, but I insisted, and with a lurch and a groan the whole bookshelf tilted to one side, then fell onto Tommy and Larry Oblivion. They both looked round to see it coming, but not in time to do anything about it. The heavy weight of the packed bookshelves slammed down onto both of them, throwing them to the floor and pinning them there. Tommy cried out piteously again. Larry didn't. He had his pride. And besides, unlike Tommy, he was dead and therefore felt no pain.

When I was sure they were both safely pinned to the floor, I moved forward to smile down at them.

"You bastard," said Larry.

"Takes one to know one," I said. "Now, will you listen to me?"

Larry turned his head slowly to look at Tommy. "Can you move?"

"Not in the least. Haven't got any leverage to work with. You?"

"No." Larry looked up at me. "All right. What have you got to say for yourself, you murderous little shit?"

I explained the circumstances of Julien Advent's death in some detail, making sure they understood about the Sun King, and what he was planning to do while everyone was distracted running after me. When I was finished, Larry looked at Tommy.

"Do you believe him?"

"Stranger things have happened," said Tommy.

"Our enemies have always profited by turning us against each other," said Larry.

"And if the Sun King is the one responsible for Julien's death, I want his heart's blood," said Tommy.

"You always were the vicious one in the family," Larry said fondly.

I looked at them both thoughtfully. "You're both being very reasonable. Don't you feel the Sun King's power, pressing on you not to believe me?"

"No," said Larry. "I have to say . . . I don't feel as utterly convinced of your guilt as I did before. Could be the Library's defences, protecting us from the Sun King's influence. And, of course, we are more resistant than most. Tommy being existential, and me being dead."

"It affected Dead Boy," I said.

Larry sniffed loudly. "That boy's brains have been leaking out his ears for years. I'm amazed he can still put one foot in front of the other without consulting a manual. All right, say we do believe in you. That you were framed by the Sun King. How do we find the bastard?"

"My gift can't find him anywhere," I said. "He's either protected by his power or by that of the Entities."

"That leaves simple deduction," said Larry. "We are supposed to be detectives, after all. Where would he go, in the Nightside? What would he see as a weak spot? What would he most easily recognise, or be drawn to, in the Nightside?"

"The Hawk's Wind Bar & Grille!" Tommy said immediately. "The Sun King is a child of the sixties, right? And what's most representative of that period here? The Bar! And being a ghost of its former self would make it a weak spot in reality! God I'm good."

"The Hawk's Wind disappeared recently," said Larry. "I can't believe that's a coincidence. Get this thing off us, Taylor. We're going with you."

"I'm sorry," I said, and I meant it. "But no, you're not. You could fall under the Sun King's influence the moment you leave the Library and attack me again. But I think you're right about the Bar. Too many unanswered questions there. How did he make it disappear? Where has he sent it? Why is it so important to him? I thought it must be because the sixties incarnation of Julien Advent was in there at the time . . ."

"He is?" said Tommy.

"Call yourself a detective?" I said, not unkindly. "There has to be a connection, between the Sun King and Julien Advent and the Hawk's Wind; but I'm not seeing it yet. I'm afraid you two are going to have to work your own way out while I get on with the job. Once you are out, if you can fight off the Sun King's influence, it would be a help if you could intercept Razor Eddie and Dead Boy and keep them busy while I work."

I walked back through the stacks, which seemed to edge back from me a little. Behind me, I could hear Larry and Tommy arguing.

"Can you shift your end?" said Larry.

"What do you think? You're nearer the edge than I am, you must have some leverage," said Tommy.

"I'm deceased, not a contortionist. Look, one of us is going to have to use all his strength and worry about the damage afterwards."

"Good idea," said Tommy. "Doesn't matter if you take any damage, so you first."

"Just because I'm dead . . ."

"Come, let us reason together . . ."

"Don't you dare!"

NINE

Ghosts Know Everything

Getting out of the Library wasn't a problem; deciding what to do next took rather more time. I hid in the darker shadows of the Library's side alley and ran through my various options. It didn't take long. I needed to talk to someone I could trust. Normally, this would have been Suzie, but . . . I thrust my hands deep into my coat pockets and frowned so hard it hurt my forehead. Who was there left, who hadn't been poisoned against me or influenced by the Sun King? Who was there left, that I could depend on? I took a deep breath, mentally crossed my fingers, took out my mobile phone and hit speed dial for Cathy.

I used her emergency mobile number, the very private phone I gave her, in case she needed help after a particularly boisterous party. I didn't see how anyone could listen in on my phone, after all the money I'd invested in top-of-the-line security, but I wasn't feeling at all trusting any more. Cathy took her own sweet time picking up, and I was actually beginning to wonder if she was deliberately holding out so someone could track my position, when she finally answered my call.

"Boss? I've been waiting for you to call me, but I was expecting it to come through the office phone. I left this one tucked away in the bottom of my bag, for emergencies. I'm on my own here, in the office, packing up. The hen party broke up when the news about Julien Advent reached us. Suzie's out somewhere, looking for you."

"Yes," I said. "I know."

"Are you all right? Are you hurt? Every time someone rings me with the story, the details are different."

"I'm fine," I said. "I . . ."

"Where are you? I'll come and get you."

"Cathy," I said. "You don't believe I murdered Julien Advent, do you?"

"Of course not! How long have we known each other? I know bullshit when I hear it, boss. You never killed anyone without good cause. Hell, I'm more vicious than you. Particularly when I've had a few . . ."

I hadn't realised how tense I was, until Cathy said she still believed in me. I felt my whole body slowly relax as her familiar rush of words washed over me. If Cathy had turned on me, like Suzie, I think I would have given up . . .

"Meet me . . ." I said, then stopped to think again. I couldn't bring her here because I couldn't afford to hang around anywhere near the Library. A mob could catch up with me at any time, or Larry and Tommy Oblivion might be overcome by the influence again, the moment they left the Library and all its protections. So where could I go next that my enemies couldn't follow me? And then the answer hit me, and I smiled briefly.

"You remember the street where we first met?" I said. "Don't say the name! . . . But you do remember?"

"Of course," said Cathy. "How could I forget? It was where

you saved my life by rescuing me from something that only looked like a house. Is that really where you want me to meet you, boss? The area hasn't improved, you know. It's still where the really wild things live."

"No-one goes there who doesn't have to," I said. "Hardly anyone I know would think to look for us there; and the poor bastards who live on that street tend not to care about the latest gossip." *Or would care that I'd killed Julien Advent,* I thought, but didn't say.

"And anyone who did go there looking for you would be lucky to get out alive anyway," Cathy said cheerfully. "I'll meet you there in half an hour, boss. I take it you're going to need transport? Thought so. Can you get there in that time? Of course you can; you're John Taylor, what am I thinking?"

She cut off the call, and I shut my phone and put it away. How was I going to get to Blaiston Street, right on the other side of the Nightside, without being spotted along the way? I still couldn't use my Portable Timeslip. The Sun King, or his precious Entities from Beyond, might well track the energy trail and be there waiting for me when I arrived. They might even arrange for all my old friends and enemies to be there, waiting. I shuddered at the thought.

And . . . I couldn't walk down the streets, hiding out as just another face in the bustling crowds. My white trench coat made me far too easy to spot. Everyone knew my coat; it was part of my image and my rep. But I couldn't take it off and dump it. My trench coat contained a great many useful tricks, and powerful defences, that I might still need. More importantly, I couldn't give it up because . . . it was my coat. Letting it go would be like giving up a vital part of me. I was damned if I would. I'd already lost too much that mattered, to the Sun King.

I had to get to Blaiston Street, and that meant I needed transport. I couldn't trust the taxis, or any of the other usual means . . . Hell, I wouldn't trust them under normal conditions.

Usually, there were people I could call on, like Dead Boy and his futuristic car; but he'd already turned against me. There was Ms. Fate, the Nightside's very own costumed adventurer . . . but her bright pink Fatemobile was even easier to spot than my white trench coat. My enemies would already be keeping an eye on that car, just in case.

So, when in doubt, cheat. I hurried out of the side alley and down the street, till I came to the nearest underpass. People were already turning to look at me as I clattered down the stone steps and into its concealing gloom. I raised my gift and used it to find one particular underpass, on the other side of the Nightside. And then it was the easiest thing in the world to move myself from one to the other. So that when I reached the bottom of the stone steps, I was walking into a completely different underpass, not far from Blaiston Street.

The tunnel was a lot darker and dirtier than I was used to, and the smell was pretty bad. Things had died down here, quite recently; but some hadn't died nearly enough. I moved quickly through the underpass, being very careful where I put my feet. I made a point of breathing through my mouth, though it didn't help much. Half the overhead lights had been smashed, with malice aforethought, to give the things that lived down there an advantage over those of us passing through. And because some things can only be done in the dark.

The buskers were an ugly lot, with their battered, stolen, and improvised instruments, all but demanding money with menaces from those who didn't drop money into their caps quickly enough. Having heard what the buskers considered music, I couldn't help feeling that all they had to do was threaten to play another song, and we'd all dig deep into our pockets. Heavy dirt and dust stains on the curving stone walls formed into eyeless faces that turned to follow me as I hurried past. Luckily, my reputation was still potent enough to keep them from forming mouths and proclaiming my name.

I kept up a steady pace, staring straight ahead, not pausing for anyone or anything. Animals can smell fear. And weakness. So I strode right on, giving every indication of being ready to walk right over anything or anyone who didn't get out of my way fast enough. The other people in the underpass went out of their way to be polite and give me plenty of room; but a shadow of a man with no man to cast it rose suddenly up before me to block my way.

I smiled, unpleasantly. I'd been waiting for something over-confident or arrogant enough to try it on. I needed to make an example of some poor damned fool, so everyone else could see I was still dangerous, and spread the word that I should be left strictly alone. So when the dark shape rose before me, spreading out its over-long arms to fill the tunnel, I already had a salamander ball in my hand, palmed from an inside pocket when no-one was looking. I triggered the pasty white ball and threw it into the dark, featureless face; and the salamander ball exploded in a fierce vicious light that filled the underpass from end to end. Everyone cried out in pain and shock as the incandescent glare overloaded their eyes temporarily. I, of course, had my eyes squeezed tightly shut, with an arm raised over them, just in case. When the light faded enough for me to see again, the dark shape was gone, blown apart into tiny dark fragments that spiralled on the air like midnight confetti. I walked straight through them, and they swung madly on the air to get out of my way. It's nice to be respected.

I have known people to get really snotty about salamander balls, saying they're expensive, you don't get much bang for your buck, and they're a bit on the small side. But as I always point out, you only get two to a salamander.

I kept walking, not looking back or even glancing about

me, and everyone else pressed themselves against the sides of the tunnels. If there were any enemies or bounty hunters down in the underpass with me, none of them bothered me. And when I finally walked up the steps and out into the open night air again, I was only half a dozen blocks down from Blaiston Street.

I had to stop for a while and lean against a handy shop-window while I got my breath back. (The shop was called Hope, and it was shut. That's all you need to know about the Nightside, right there.) I looked at my reflection and hardly recognised the gaunt and drawn face that stared back. Blood was streaming thickly from my nose, as though it had been hit, and I could taste the bad coppery stuff in my mouth. I spat hard to clear my mouth, and the crimson stuff ran slowly down the shop-window. I was tired, bone-deep tired, and when I fumbled a handkerchief out of my pocket, I could hardly feel it. My fingertips were dangerously numb. Somehow, I managed to pinch the bridge of my nose till the bleeding stopped, and spat more blood across the window-glass till I ran out. I mopped roughly at my face and stuffed the hand-kerchief back into my pocket. A slow, hot pain pulsed behind my eyes. I had to sort this case out soon, while I still could. Overusing my gift was causing me serious physical and maybe even neurological damage. I could feel it. And God alone knew what it was doing to my soul. I'd never had to use my gift so often before.

I finally pushed myself away from the blood-streaked window, straightened my back, and raised my head through an act of sheer will-power, and headed determinedly for Blaiston Street. I was deathly tired, every muscle ached, and I still couldn't feel my fingertips. And I would have killed for a deep-crust pizza and a whole bunch of drinks to wash it down with. Not really in my best condition to face a threat that could mean the end of the Nightside, forever.

Some days, you can't get a break.

• • •

Didn't take me long to get to Blaiston Street. A nowhere street in a nowhere place, the really bad end of town. It made the area outside Green Henge wall seem like a petting zoo. I could feel the property values plummeting the closer I got, and the people looked less furtive and more feral. Though none of them did more than watch me carefully from a safe distance. Even down here, they'd heard of me.

Blaiston Street was a ragged collection of shabby buildings in a shabby setting. Where every single street-light had been smashed because the inhabitants felt more at home in the dark. Filth and garbage piled up everywhere, left to sit in festering heaps. Rats crouched here and there, not even bothering to look away as I strode past them. Every wall was covered in obscene graffiti, rough and brutal stuff, like dogs pissing to mark their territory. Kicked-in doors, boarded-up windows, dark doorways and darker alley mouths. Only two long rows of ancient, battered tenements, neglected and despised, by those within and those without.

Blaiston Street is where you go when nobody cares, not even you.

Not many people about. Normally, you'd expect a street like this to be teeming with the lost and the desperate, like maggots in an open wound. But the street stretched away before me, completely deserted, still and silent. As though they'd known I was coming and wanted to be well out of the way before the trouble started. Reasonable enough. They'd emerge afterwards, to rob the bodies or eat them. There were definitely unseen eyes following me as I strolled unhurriedly down the middle of the empty road as though I didn't have a care in the world. I could feel the watchers even if I never saw them.

Didn't take me long to find the right house. Years had gone by, but I'd never forget that house-front. It wasn't the original house, of course; I'd destroyed that nasty thing long ago, for disguising itself as a house so it could prey on people. It called to the homeless and the hopeless, with a voice they couldn't resist, lured them inside, then ate them all up. Suzie and I rescued Cathy from it. No; this . . . was a cheap copy. The previous Walker had discovered traces of damaged alien tissue left behind and had the stuff studied and cultivated, so he could make his own living house trap. I don't know why he wanted it; to feed people he disapproved of, probably.

The first copy was destroyed during the Lilith War; I don't know how many generations beyond the original this one was. It sat there, squatting in place, looking like a house and stinking the place up. No-one was ever so homeless or so desperate they'd want to venture inside this house. I sat down on the cold stone steps before the front door, put my back to the house, and waited.

It felt like sitting with my back to a giant freezer with the door left open. A cold bad enough to chill the soul as well as the body. There was a constant sense of being watched—by something that would hurt me if it could. I didn't care. Didn't even look back at it. I had too many bad memories of the original house. And of a woman named Joanna, who turned out not to be a woman, any more than the house was a house. Poor Joanna. I could have loved her if she'd been real.

Some people you shouldn't remember. If only because the Nightside can find so many ways to hurt and haunt you . . .

For a moment, there, I had to wonder if maybe the Sun King might not be right about the Nightside after all . . .

And then there was the roar of a mighty motor, and Cathy turned up, taking the far corner on two wheels, racing down Blaiston Street in an old MINI Cooper, complete with bright Union Jack colours. The "Self-preservation Society" song blasted out of the open windows. I should never have brought her that DVD. Cathy brought the MINI to a squealing halt right in front of me, and the passenger door jumped open of its own accord. I got up off the steps and hurried over, clambered into the passenger seat, and Cathy had the car off and away before the door could even shut itself again. I looked for a seat belt, and, of course, there wasn't one. You can take authenticity too far. I clung to the dash-board with both hands and braced both feet against the floor, to hold myself firmly in place in my seat. Cathy drove us out of the area at great speed and headed towards the main flow of traffic like a shark scenting blood in the water. She darted a glance at me and grinned fiercely.

"Just like old times!" she said loudly. "You were right; we owed it to ourselves to have one last adventure together, before the old firm closes down!"

"Having to come back to Blaiston Street didn't . . . bother you?" I said carefully.

"Come on, boss; that was Where we met! Best thing that ever happened to me! So where are we going now?"

"I need to see the place where the Hawk's Wind Bar & Grille used to be," I said. "I've already been there once, but I can't help feeling I missed something."

It felt good to be able to relax again. I hadn't felt safe with anyone since Julien Advent died. I hunched down in my seat, so as to present a smaller target. The music system was playing a Matt Munro song. I smiled . . . I wanted to close my eyes and sleep, and not have to wake up until the whole mess was over. But I couldn't do that. Cathy reached a main road and threw the MINI Cooper into the main flow of traffic like a knight entering a joust. I told her about the Sun King, about everything that had happened, and what might still happen if I couldn't stop it. She didn't get a lot of the sixties stuff—way before her time. So she concentrated on the bit she did understand.

"If you're going to be dealing with a ghost," she said, hitting her horn imperiously and steering her car like it was an offensive weapon, "you're going to need help and advice from someone who specialises in the differently departed. Ghosts can be really difficult characters."

"You have a specialist in mind?" I said.

"I always have someone in mind," Cathy said loftily. "I know everyone, or at the very least, everyone worth knowing. I'll take you right to the gent in question, but I'll warn you now, boss; you're really not going to like him. No-one ever does. *Get out of the bloody way!* I hate people who change lanes without signalling. Where was I? Oh yes. You probably know the guy, and not in a good way. But he knows more about talking to ghosts than anyone should who hasn't actually been nailed into a box and waved good-bye under six feet of wet turf."

"I'm really not going to like this person, am I?" I said.

"Boss, you're going to hate him on sight. Everyone does."

Cathy finally pulled up outside a really sleazy nude dancing club, specialising in ghost girls. SPIRITED DANCING, it said on the sign. It looked like the kind of place where you could contract a whole new kind of STD, have your wallet lifted, and do a dozen things that were morally bad for you, all before you sat down. Cathy parked her MINI half on the pavement, got out, and glared around her at anyone who even looked like they might object. I clambered carefully out and managed to whip the tail of my trench coat out of the way before the door slammed itself shut. Cathy slapped a display sign on the windscreen, reading EXORCIST ON CALL! THIS CAR IS PROTECTED BY SOMETHING YOU WON'T EVEN SEE COMING!

"Is it really?" I said.

"Who can say?" said Cathy, beaming brightly. "Would you risk it?"

I gave my full attention to the front of the club, which was basically an open door surrounded by photos of dancing girls wearing nothing but smiles. Not the girls we'd be seeing inside, of course. Ghosts don't photograph well; normally, all you get is a shimmering blob of ectoplasm. The barker at the door was a large, muscular type in a tweed suit who gave me his best professional smile.

"Come on in, sir! They're dead, and they dance! They're all naked and not in the least departed! Oh, hello Cathy. How's it going?"

"Not too bad, Tim," said Cathy. "Do you know my boss, John Taylor?"

"No, and I don't want to," the barker said firmly. "You go in. I'll go and hide in the toilets till the trouble's over. Give me a call when it's safe to come out again."

"It would appear my reputation proceeds me," I said, as Cathy led the way in.

"Isn't that what a reputation's for?" said Cathy.

We barged straight past the ticket-seller in her little glass cage. She took one look at me and ducked completely out of sight. Inside, the club was dark and dingy, with a side order of openly disgusting. It smelled like something really bad had happened in the toilets. Very recently. The floor was sticky under my feet, and I didn't want to think with what. There was a general air of cheap and nasty, including some of the girls and most of the customers. Sawdust had been scattered thickly on the floor around the edges of the raised circular stage, to soak up the usual spilled fluids.

Ghost girls danced on the spotlit stage, sliding up and down steel poles in defiance of gravity, leaping and soaring through the smoke-filled air, often passing in and out of each other's translucent figures. Their faces pretended delight, but their eyes were empty. Faded rainbows moved slowly across their semi-transparent forms, like the colours you see sliding across the surface of a soap bubble. The girls moved sexily, even gracefully, but with little emotion. They were only the memories of living flesh, going through the motions.

Row upon row of customers pressed close around the raised stage, jostling each other to get in close. Sweat gleamed on their fascinated faces, and they couldn't look away. None of them offered money; ghosts have no use for cash. They sucked a little life energy out of any customer who got close enough. Sucking them dry, bit by bit, and making them love it. Not too different from any other such club, really.

Cathy took it all in her stride. I looked at her suspiciously.

"You've been here before. And you knew the man outside by name. How is it you even know places like this exist?"

"Ask me no questions, and I'll tell you no lies," Cathy said calmly. "You really don't want to know about how I spend my spare times, boss. I'm all grown-up now. And you probably have enough trouble sleeping as it is. This way . . ."

She beckoned imperiously to a figure at the bar, and the owner of the place came smarming forward to join us. I knew immediately why Cathy hadn't told me his name. Because if I'd known we were going to talk with Dennis Montague, I would have hurled myself out of the car and into the on-coming traffic. Oh yes, I knew Dennis of old. This wasn't the first disreputable club he'd owned. I'd shut down several of them on moral-health grounds and because his very existence offended me.

Dennis, or Den-Den, as he preferred to be called, in the mistaken belief that it made him seem more engaging, was a minor player and major-league scumbag who always seemed to land on his feet, no matter how high a building you threw him off. He came sleazing forward to greet Cathy and me as though we were most-favoured customers, smiling and smiling as though he were genuinely pleased to meet us. A short, shiny butter-ball of a man, with slicked-down black hair, a face like a boiled ham, and large, watery eyes. He looked like he ought to leave a trail of slime behind him when he moved, like a snail. Though given the state of the floor in this club, it would probably have been an improvement. He came to an abrupt halt before us, bobbing his head repeatedly and rubbing his soft, podgy hands together.

It was a masterful performance, to make himself appear nothing more than another harmless letch; but he needn't have bothered. I remembered Den-Den. A cheat and a liar, a ponce and a pervert, given to abusing and profiting from anyone weaker than himself. But I also knew why Cathy had brought me here to see Den-Den rather than anyone else. Because once upon a time, Dennis Montague had been a rising star, a young man with a great future ahead of him, as the most talented field agent the Carnacki Institute had ever produced. The Institute exists to track down, identify and then do something about all kinds of ghosts and hauntings. And for a while, Dennis Montague was their top man. Till they found out what he was really up to and threw him out. And quite rightly, too. I looked at Cathy.

"Are you *sure* there isn't anyone else?"

"Not who can do what he can do. And you're really not too popular in the Nightside right now, boss. We have to work with what we can get. What's so bad about Den-Den, anyway? I mean, apart from the obvious. He knows his ghosts."

"Did he ever tell you why he was kicked out of the Carnacki Institute?" I said. "Tell her, Den-Den."

"For having sex with ghosts," said Dennis, quite proudly.

"Can I just say *Oh ick!* in a loud and carrying voice?" said Cathy. "How is that even possible?"

Dennis sniggered until I glared at him, and he stopped. "Best not to ask, dear," he said to Cathy, smiling happily. "Not at all the kind of thing you want to talk about in public." He looked me up and down, still rubbing his hands together, considering how best to squeeze money out of me. "Welcome to my humble establishment, Mr. Taylor, yes . . . Make yourself at home, do. See anything you like? All wery tasty, wery clean, and all at wery reasonable prices, I assure you."

"You even hint to anyone we were ever here," said Cathy, "and I will burn this place down around your ears."

"Oh, I believe you," Dennis said immediately. "Mr. Taylor's reputation isn't the only one that proceeds him, you little minx, you. You can rely on old Den-Den not to breathe a word, oh yes. I have no problems with Mr. Taylor's being here! No! Anyone capable of seeing off Julien Advent is clearly a man to be reckoned with. A man on the way up, heading for greatness. I always knew you had it in you, Mr. Taylor. If you're looking for new members of a new Authorities, once you've finished off the others, I would of course be wery honoured . . . I am a man of refined character and a wery successful business man . . ."

"No you're not," said Cathy. "You're a sleazoid with delusions of grandeur who does mucky things with ghosts. Don't you go getting ideas above your station."

"Well, if you're not here to see me in my position as a business man, then why?" said Dennis, apparently entirely unmoved by Cathy's fierce words.

"Because you were trained by the Carnacki Institute," I said.

"You did talk to ghosts, as a field agent, didn't you?" said Cathy. "When you weren't trying to touch them inappropriately."

Dennis sniggered again. "Those so-called sophisticates running the organisation never did approve of me. Even though I got results no-one else could. Bunch of prudes and Puritans, the lot of them, my dears. Some of us are a little more open to the more interesting opportunities to be found in life and death. Still, what can you expect from an organisation that takes its name from a man who cared more about the dead than he ever did about the living?"

He stopped talking abruptly as I fixed him with a cold, hard stare. "I was trained by old Carnacki himself, back when I was starting out," I said. "He was a good man. One more word from you against him, and I will rip the soul right out of you and send it screaming down into Hell."

Dennis looked at me uneasily. He wasn't sure I could actually do that; but he wasn't sure I couldn't, either. There are a lot of stories about me running round the Nightside, and I make it a point never to confirm or deny any of them. Because you never know when they might come in handy.

Dennis scowled, then forced his face back into its usual smarmy good nature. "A splendid fellow, that Mr. Carnacki! A most knowledgeable man, yes. I've always said so! Certainly he had enough integrity to walk away from the Institute that bears his name when it let him down."

"So he did," I said. "Now, Den-Den . . . I have need of your assistance."

"But of course, Mr. Taylor! You know me! Always happy to help out . . ."

"I need you to come with me, right now," I said. "To talk to a ghost, on my behalf."

"But . . . but . . . I can't simply leave the club!" said Dennis. "Not . . . just like that!"

"There must be somebody here who can run the place while you nip out for a minute," said Cathy. "Isn't there anyone here you can trust?"

"Please," said Dennis. "Remember where you are."

"It's up to you," I said. "Either you come along with us, right now, or Cathy can sing a quick chorus of *There'll be a hot time in the old town tonight* . . ."

"I'll be right with you," said Dennis. "I knew I should have signed up for fire insurance when I had the chance . . . Let me talk to somebody."

"If I even think you're running for the back door, I will make your knee-caps disappear," I said.

"Mr. Taylor! You wound me!"

"Almost certainly," I said.

Dennis sleazed away to talk with the tall, cadaverous figure behind the nasty-looking bar, while I looked thoughtfully at Cathy.

"When, exactly, did you acquire this reputation for aggressive pyromania? Did I miss something?"

"Almost certainly," said Cathy. "You know how it is, boss; you're out on the town with a few friends, drinking it up; you're young, you've got incendiaries . . . shit happens."

Perhaps fortunately, Dennis came back at that moment, giving us both his best professional smile. "All arranged, my dears! Now let us get this all over and done with. Maurice will look after things, in my hopefully short absence. He'll cheat me on the take, no doubt about it, but better to lose some than all by having to close up. No-one appreciates the trials and tribulations of the honest business man."

"Least of all you," I agreed. I held his gaze firmly with mine. "If I ever find out you're holding any of these ghost girls against their will . . ."

Dennis came as close to real laughter as he dared. "Do me a favour, Mr. Taylor! They come to me! They ask for this. Every girl working here is a volunteer. They need the lifeforce they suck out of the punters every night, to hold themselves together. To maintain their grip on this world. You couldn't make them leave here if you tried. Couldn't drive them out, with bell, book, and candle. This is their club, Mr. Taylor; I get to run things for them. Of course, I also get a bit of the old rumpy pumpy, from time to time . . ."

"Oh, *ick*!" said Cathy, firmly.

Dennis sniggered. "Every job has its perks, my dears. Can I help it if I like my ectoplasm cold?"

We all clambered into Cathy's MINI Cooper and headed off into the Nightside rather more swiftly than I was comfortable with. Dennis enjoyed the trip immensely, waving his podgy fingers out the window at people he recognised though most of them chose not to recognise him. If nothing else, he made a great distraction. I thought hard about what I was going to do when I revisited the hole in the ground that was all that was left of the Hawk's Wind Bar & Grille. I also kept a watchful eye on Cathy and Dennis. I wasn't too concerned about dear old Den-Den. You always knew where you were with him. He didn't care that I'd killed Julien Advent because he didn't care about anyone. He'd back-stab me for the reward in a moment, given half a chance, but we both knew he didn't have the balls to do it to my face. He'd do whatever I told him, in the hope of favours to call on, further down the line. But Cathy . . . worried me. Why hadn't she fallen under the influence of the Sun King? Like Suzie had? I couldn't ask Cathy. I didn't want her to think I didn't trust her.

When we finally pulled up alongside the great hole in the ground where the Bar used to be, it all looked exactly as it had before. Big and ugly and completely lacking in any supernatural energies. We all got out of the MINI Cooper, moved over to the edge of the hole, and stared down into it. No difference at all. Just a hole, where something marvellous used to be. Something about the scene bothered me, and I realised it was the quiet. I looked quickly about me. Most of the watching crowd had disappeared, gone in search of something more interesting to look at. Never any lack of that to be had, in the Nightside. And . . .

"Why aren't there any naked people here?" I said suddenly.

Cathy gave me a sideways look. "Should there be? Were you expecting naked people; or are you at a funny age, boss?"

"I mean the Tantric Troops," I said. "The Authorities' new attack dogs. They were all over the place here before."

"Oh, them," Dennis said wisely. "The Fuck Buddies. Oh yes, my dears, we've all heard about them. Talk about making a virtue out of a necessity . . . Last I heard, the remaining Authorities had scattered them across the Nightside, looking for you, Mr. Taylor. After all; it's not like there's much here for them to guard . . ."

I nodded and went back to looking into the hole. "I was here before, with Julien. Talking about the Bar's sudden disappearance. And I can't help feeling I'm missing something . . ."

I took the book out of my inside pocket, and leafed quickly through it. Cathy frowned slowly.

"Does that book, by any chance, come from where I think it does?" she said. "From, in fact, the much-respected and even-more-feared HPL?"

"I borrowed it, for a while," I said. "Unofficially. Without telling anybody. Though they've probably noticed by now."

Cathy was already shaking her head. "You're a lot braver than I am, boss. They'll send the Library Policemen after you. The big men, with hammers."

"I have more pressing things to worry about," I said, still flipping quickly through the pages. It was all very familiar. I'd read it all before. I knew everything that was in the book; so what was I missing? And then I stopped, as a very familiar phrase jumped out at me. The Bar burned down in 1970, possibly in self-immolation as a protest against the breaking up of the Beatles, then came back as a ghost of itself. The Hawk's Wind *chose* to come back! That was the answer, right there! The Bar made a conscious decision to return, which meant the building was sentient. Not just a ghost image of a missing place but a conscious entity in its own right! That's why the Bar was able to be so solid and hold aspects of the sixties within itself. And as a real, sentient, ghost personality . . . I should be able to ask it questions and get some answers.

I slammed the book shut, put it away, and quickly explained my thinking to Cathy and Dennis. They both nodded quickly—Cathy excitedly, Dennis reluctantly. I looked out over the empty hole.

"Den-Den; can you . . . ?"

"I've been trying ever since we got here, Mr. Taylor; and I

can't feel a thing. Wherever the Bar's gone, it's way out my reach."

So I had no choice but to raise my gift again. It didn't come easily. It was like lifting a dead weight, then forcing it to do tricks. But I made it work, through sheer will-power, and reached out with my gift to find the Hawk's Wind Bar & Grille and call it back.

It really was only a ghost, this time. A grey, semi-transparent shape, its colours a faded memory, with transparent walls, through which could be seen dark human figures, standing or sitting at tables, very still. All the people trapped inside when the Bar was forced out of Time and Space. It was a very tenuous, very flimsy manifestation; but it was quite definitely there, right in front of me. I could sense its presence, feel its living, conscious thoughts . . . but I couldn't understand them. The Bar might be a sentient thing, but it wasn't in any way human. How the hell was I going to get any answers out of it?"

I turned to Dennis, but he was already shaking his head. "Wery sorry, Mr. Taylor, but I only work with deceased peoples."

"Try!" I said, very coldly. "Because every damned soul in the Nightside is depending on us, right now, and if we screw this up . . ."

And then I stopped, as one of the dark figures inside the ghostly Bar rose abruptly from its table, then walked slowly through the Bar to the front door. None of the other figures moved, or even acknowledged it. The front door opened of its own accord, and the dark figure stood there, in the doorway. It looked at me. A cold hand took hold of my heart, and squeezed it tight. I knew that face. I hadn't known Julien Advent back in the sixties, but he hadn't changed at all. I wasn't even born then, but he looked exactly the same. He spoke to me; but it was the voice and words of the Hawk's

Wind, speaking through the sixties incarnation of the Great Victorian Adventurer.

I could tell.

"The Sun King didn't remove me from this reality," said the Bar, through Julien's mouth. "The Entities from Beyond did it."

"The Aquarians?" I said. My mouth was very dry.

"That's not their name. They removed me from the world because I'm the only part of the Nightside that the Sun King cares about. He went along with it because the Entities said it was important to remove the people held within me; but they lied."

"How do you know what the Entities want?" I said carefully.

"Because you can't hide the truth from the dead," said the Bar. "Many things about the world become so much clearer, once you're dead. Especially if you've chosen not to depart, just yet."

"How did you become . . . conscious?" I said.

The sixties Julien actually smiled, briefly. "You should have been here, in the sixties. It was all going on."

"Why is the Sun King so determined to bring about the end of the night, and the Nightside?" I said.

"Because he wants to bring back the great Dream of the sixties, and the Nightside is everything he disapproves of. He's always had a very limited perception of what Dreams are. You can't force them on people. He also wants everyone else to bow down to him, and admit that his Dream is better than theirs. Even if he won't admit it to himself. He's still very human."

I nodded slowly. So far, it all sounded plausible enough. Ghosts know everything because the world can't hide anything from them, any more. The trick is to get ghosts to tell you the truth. Because the dead always have their own agendas. Hopefully, the Hawk Wind's interests were the same as mine, in this case.

"The Entities are lying to the Sun King," said the Bar, in Julien Advent's voice. "They always were. And they never were what he thought they were. Everything he does, he does to serve them and their true instincts. They will destroy me, and everyone trapped inside me, eventually. They're only holding on to us now in case the Sun King should waver. We are hostages to his fortune. The Entities aren't what he thinks they are."

"Then what are they?" I said. "Really?"

"Hungry," said the Hawk's Wind.

"Boss?" Cathy said quietly. "What's it saying? I can't hear anything!"

I looked at her, then at Dennis, who shook his head quickly. "I can see the ghost but not hear it," said Dennis, sounding more than a little put-out. "A wery fascinating presence, quite unlike anything I've ever encountered before. And I've been around. In more ways than one. So I am moved to ask, How is it you can hear it, Mr. Taylor, and I can't?"

"I told you," I said. "I trained with old Carnacki. And he knew all sorts of things he never shared with the Institute that took his name." I looked back at the Julien Advent shade in the doorway. It hurt to look at him, knowing he was as dead as the Bar now. Thanks to me. "Why did the Entities allow the Sun King to return?"

"Because he's ready. Programmed and primed, to do what they want. And, because the Droods are gone. The whole family, gone in a moment. Only Eddie remains, the last Drood. Arthur Pendragon and the London Knights are also gone, off fighting the good fight in another dimension. When they try to return, they will find the Entities have closed and sealed the dimensional gates behind them. And the Carnacki Institute . . . is preoccupied with its own problems. There are still certain individuals who might hope to stand against the Entities: the Walking Man, the Regent of Shadows, the Detective Inspectre. But by the time they can come together, it will be too late. The Entities will be in control. That leaves only you, John Taylor."

"How do I stop them?" I said urgently. "How do I stop the Sun King?"

"Show him what the Entities really are," said the ghost. "Show him what they really mean to do with this world. And what they really think of his precious Dream. He's still asleep. Wake him up."

The sixties Julien Advent turned his back on me and walked into the Bar. The door closed itself. And despite everything I could do to hold on to it, the Hawk's Wind Bar & Grille slowly and silently vanished, and was gone.

"You couldn't have hung on a little longer?" I said angrily. "Not for one more question? Like, Where is the bloody Sun King? Where can I find him?"

"Boss," said Cathy. "You're shouting at empty air. And freaking us all out. I mean, I'm sure it's all very therapeutic, but . . ."

"I thought the Entities took the Bar because that was where they intended to break through," I said. "But I was wrong. I was so sure I'd find the Sun King here, but . . ."

"What did the Bar tell you?" said Cathy.

"Not what I needed to know. Think, think . . . Where is the Sun King, right now? Where would he go, to raise the sun and bring down the Nightside?"

"He needs a weak spot," said Cathy. "So where's the oldest place in the Nightside? What's been here longest, boss?"

"Of course!" I said. "St. Jude's! That was here before it was a church, before Christianity even got started!"

"Then that's where he'll be," said Cathy.

She was right, of course. The oldest and most powerful spot in the Nightside was also its weakest because it had been around so long. The church is one of the few places on Earth where the physical world can make direct contact with the spiritual world. Could the Sun King use that as a doorway, a way to break in and out? Maybe. Some days, all you can do is wing it.

I didn't want to go to St. Jude's; but I couldn't tell Cathy why. Because Suzie might still be there. I hadn't told Cathy about Suzie. How could I? But I had to go there. I had to go to St. Jude's, right now . . . and all I could do was hope that Suzie was somewhere else, hunting me down.

My back twinged briefly, where she'd shot me once, long ago.

I turned abruptly to Dennis. "All right, that's it. Turned out I didn't need you after all, Den-Den. Go on back to your club. I think I've enjoyed about as much of your company as I can stand."

"Lots of people say that," said Dennis. "Glad to have been of service. Be assured I bear no ill will at being dragged out of my wery own bar, hauled half-way across the Nightside, only to find I'm not needed. Perish the thought! I suppose a lift back's out of the question?"

"What do you think?" I said.

He gave me a look of sleazy dignity. "Your mother knits socks in Hell."

And he turned and strode away. That's Den-Den for you. Always knows exactly how far he can push it.

"Boss," said Cathy. "Your eyes are bleeding."

I put a hand to my face, and the fingers came away bloody. I could see the blood, but I couldn't feel it. Cathy handed me a handkerchief, and I mopped roughly at my face till the bleeding stopped. Crying tears of blood was not a good sign. I couldn't keep on using my gift like this. It was killing me by inches. I offered Cathy her handkerchief back; but she looked at the bloody mess and shook her head quickly. I tucked the handkerchief away in an inside pocket. Not the kind of thing you want to leave lying around, in the Nightside. There's a lot you can achieve with someone else's blood, little of it good. When I looked at Cathy again, she was looking at me as though she was already buying the wreath.

"Boss," said Cathy. "What's happening to you? You look like shit. You look like death warmed up and allowed to congeal."

"It's the gift," I said, as steadily as I could. "You go to the well too often, you get blood instead of water. I'll last. I've still got things to do."

"We need to get you back to Strangefellows," said Cathy. "Alex has all kinds of stuff there that will put you right."

"No," I said. "I think I've gone beyond anything Alex can help me with. It doesn't matter. We have to get to St Jude's. That's got to be Ground Zero. You don't have to come with me, Cathy."

"Yes I do," she said sturdily. "I'm damned if I'll let anyone interfere with the wedding preparations for tomorrow. You promised I could be maid of honour, and I'm holding you to it." She stopped, and looked at me thoughtfully. "Do you suppose . . . the Lord of Thorns will be there?"

"I'm banking on it," I said. "He's the only weapon I've got left."

TEN

Truths and Consequences

St. Jude's is still the only real church in the Nightside, tucked away in an area where nobody goes and a hell of a long way from the Street of the Gods. Because St Jude's is the real deal. It's only an old, cold, stone structure, built so long ago no-one remembers when, with featureless grey walls, unmarked by time or weather or the designs of man. No tower, no bell, no crucifix on display, a few slit windows, here and there, and one narrow doorway. St Jude's isn't meant to be easy to find or easy to enter. This is a church where you can talk directly with your god, and expect to be heard. And, more worryingly, answered. Dreams can come true, and miracles can happen. So be very careful what you ask for.

I had Cathy park the MINI Cooper some distance away from the church, and after she'd locked it up and armed the defences, we left the car where it was and made our way slowly, and carefully, and hopefully very quietly, down the long, narrow street that led to the church. St. Jude's stood grim and alone in the moonlight. There was no-one else about, and even the ever-present roar of traffic seemed faded and far-away. As though we had come to a whole new place, where everyone kept their heads down to avoid being noticed. It's one thing to pray to God when you're in trouble; it's quite another to have Him take a personal interest in you.

St. Jude's stood alone because it liked it that way. It existed in its own small and very private world, and always had.

"You really think the Sun King won't hear us coming?" said Cathy. "It's so quiet here you could hear a mouse thinking about farting."

"Why make it easy for him?" I said. "I've reached the stage where I'll take any advantage I can get my hands on."

Cathy gave me a sideways look. "You really believe all this living-god crap, boss?"

"I don't know," I said. "I've met powers and dominations in my time, and any number of gods and demons, but the Sun King . . . is something else. When he says he wants to change the world, he's not being metaphorical. Look how easily he turned the whole of the Nightside against me. Even my mother couldn't do that during the Lilith War; and she's a Biblical Myth."

Even as we drew near St. Jude's, keeping alert for any sound or sight of the Sun King, I was still keeping a careful watch on Cathy. If she was going to betray me, this would be the perfect time and place. I didn't want to believe that, didn't even want to think that; but after Suzie . . . I didn't know what to believe any more. But all the way up the narrow road, right up to the church itself, Cathy said nothing, did nothing but stick close by my side, ready for anything. I felt ashamed to have doubted her. She always was a better person than me.

We stopped a few yards short and looked the place over. St. Jude's looked solid and implacable, as always, ancient and immovable, something you could trust and believe in. Not for mercy or compassion, or even justice; St, Jude's stood for the truth. Because St. Jude's was the one true thing in an ever-changing world.

"What the hell are you suddenly smiling at?" said Cathy. "If there's anything funny here, I missed it. This whole location is creeping me out, big-time."

"St. Jude's," I said. "Patron saint of lost causes. How appropriate."

"You're weird, boss."

Strange lights blazed through the slit windows of the old church, stark, unrelenting lights that cut through the surrounding gloom like knives. More of the fierce light shone from the open door; pushing back the night like the glare from an open furnace. You only had to look at the light to know it wasn't of this world. This was light from Outside, light seen from the other side.

"The Lord of Thorns has got to be here. Hasn't he?" said Cathy, uneasily. "There's no way he'd allow anyone to misuse the church."

"I am sort of depending on his being here," I admitted. "He's one of the biggest guns I know, in the powers business. But look at the place. I can't see the Lord of Thorns putting up with this . . . But then, I can't see the Sun King being powerful enough to drive the Lord of Thorns out, either."

"So how powerful is the Sun King, boss?"

"He's as powerful as the Entities from Beyond need him to be," I said. "And they . . . are starting to worry me."

"The Lord of Thorns has always worried me," said Cathy. "He represents all the aspects of God most people don't want to think about. I've never been too sure what he really is, or what he's really for."

"I have had long conversations with him, on that very point," I said. "And I have to say I'm no wiser. I need him to be on my side, one more time. Because I'm running out of options." I looked at the light streaming out of the slit windows and shuddered briefly, as though something had pissed on my grave. "I don't want to believe the Sun King can go head to head with the Lord of Thorns. If the Entities from Beyond can slap him down, we are all in deep doo-doo."

"You can say shit, boss," said Cathy. "It's all right. I'm all grown-up."

And then the Sun King popped his head out of the open front door and smiled engagingly at us.

"You can stop muttering and sneaking about. I've known you were there for ages. Come on in! The Entities weren't sure you'd get here after all the crap I rained down on you, but no, I said, John Taylor will be here, for the finale. Because you really are a stubborn little soul, aren't you, John?"

"Oh he is," said Cathy. "Really. You have no idea."

The Sun King looked at her doubtfully. "And this is . . . ?"

"Cathy," I said. "She works with me."

The Sun King shrugged, beckoned for us to enter St. Jude's, and disappeared back inside the church. And after only a moment's hesitation, I led the way in after him. Unarmed and unprepared, but doing my best to look cocky and confident because you never let the opposition know they've got you worried. The light at the doorway was sharp, even sinister, and painfully bright. Light with all the warmth and goodness taken out of it. I screwed up my eyes and strode straight into the light, doing my best to look like I knew what I was doing.

I made a point of stopping just inside the church, to let my vision clear. I couldn't afford to seem weak or helpless. Cathy stayed close beside me, as I looked unhurriedly round the church, taking my time. The interior hadn't changed, but then it never does. Two rows of blocky wooden pews, with a narrow central aisle leading down to the great slab of ancient stone at the far end, covered in a cloth of white samite. A simple altar, for a simple church. No statues, no stained-glass windows, not even a pulpit. Nothing but the essentials.

Nothing to distract you from what you came here for. Faith and worship at their most basic and brutal. There were rows of candles to every side, none of them lit. There was only the awful light, which seemed to come from everywhere and nowhere. Light from Outside; from where the Entities from Beyond were.

The Sun King was lounging lazily against the altar; smiling happily, even arrogantly. The smile of a man who knows he's already won and is waiting for you to notice, so he can indulge in a little quiet preening and gloating. His Coat of Vivid Colours looked over-bright and even gaudy in the new light. Or perhaps it always had, and I needed to see it in its proper setting to realise. The Sun King pushed his tinted granny glasses down his nose, so he could peer at me over the top of them. His eyes were full of childish mischief and a terrible certainty.

"All the time and trouble it took you, to get here," he said. "And all of it for nothing. You even found time to pick up a girl side-kick! I am impressed. But there's nothing you can do to stop me now, or even slow me down. It's all going to happen right here, in this most ancient of places, where the Nightside had its beginnings."

"I know," I said. "I was there, when it happened."

The Sun King looked at me uncertainly, then shrugged. "You do get around, don't you, Mr. Taylor? It doesn't matter. I will raise the sun, and the dawn will come, and the longest night in the world will finally come to an end."

"Girl side-kick? You arrogant little tosser! You don't mess with my boss!"

Cathy had a very large pistol in her hand, aimed right at the Sun King's chest. I grabbed her arm and pulled it down, then wrestled with Cathy till I was sure she wasn't going to try that again. She stopped fighting me, breathing hard, and glared at me. I glared right back at her.

"Why not, boss? Give me one reason why not?"

"You really think a bullet is going to stop him? Or the Entities behind him? He could turn you inside out just by looking at you! Where did you get hold of a gun, anyway? No, don't tell me, I don't want to know."

"Suzie gave it to me."

"Of course she did. Please, Cathy, as a personal favour to me, put the gun away. Before he decides to do something amusing to it. Or you."

Cathy snarled but made the gun disappear somewhere about her person again. I had to lean on the nearest pew for a moment. Even the brief struggle with Cathy had taken a lot out of me. There wasn't a lot left in me to draw on. Cold sweat beaded my face, and my legs were trembling. I could barely feel the rough ancient wood of the pew, under my hands.

"Not looking too good there, John," the Sun King said cheerfully. "In fact, I'd have to say you were looking pretty shit. Been having a hard time, have you? Getting near the bottom of the barrel? I knew there was a reason why I had the Entities mess you up and drive you round the Nightside like a mad thing. Killing you would have been far too kind. I wanted you to catch up with me and be here for my final triumph. Because it's never enough to break your opponents; they have to admit they've been beaten."

"That'll be the day," I said. I pushed myself upright and turned away from the pew, with an effort I hoped wasn't too obvious. I met the Sun King's gaze steadily.

"You made it as difficult as you could, but I'm still here. And I will stop you."

"How did it feel, John?" said the Sun King. "Having to kill your old friend, Julien Advent?"

I heard Cathy's breath catch in her throat. "You killed him, John? You really did kill him?"

"I need you to trust me, Cathy," I said, not looking round. "I have no right to ask it of you, but . . ."

"Of course you do. You risked your life to save me. Nothing else matters. You can fill me in on the details later."

"Yes. I promise I'll tell you everything, later." I took a step towards the Sun King. "I did what I had to do. I've always been able to do the hard, necessary thing."

"Yes, but how did it feel, John? Did it break your heart? Well, now you know how I feel. The world, the future that I gave my heart and soul to, betrayed me by not becoming what it was supposed to."

"Wallow in self-pity on your own time," I said. "Where's the Lord of Thorns?"

The Sun King shrugged easily. "I had the Entities lure him away, with urgent news. Though I can't believe anyone his age still believes in angels. Only room for one living god in this church, and that's me."

"But why here?" said Cathy bluntly. "Come on; you know you want to tell us. Your sort always likes to make speeches and justify yourself."

"Girl side-kicks should be seen and not heard," said the Sun King. "If they like having their tongues attached. But she's right, John; I always have loved addressing an audience. Those were my happiest days, preaching in Haight-Ashbury. So why St. Jude's? Because this particular place was here before the Nightside was here. A holy place, where Heaven touched Earth, briefly, and made a connection. This location was sacred long before someone built a church here, and made it Christian with a saint's name. Think of St. Jude's as a conduit, where here meets the hereafter. Where reality itself can be overwritten, by a greater power.

"I will call on the Aquarians, and they will fill me with their power, in this place where miracles happen and dreams come true. I will bring the sun here, and let the sun shine in, and it will shed its natural light over this unnatural darkness and make it what it should always have been. Sunnyside! Let us all hail the Age of Aquarius, and the soul's true liberation!

All things shall be made well, all hurts healed, and good things will happen every day."

"You can't do that," I said.

He glared at me, irritated at being interrupted in midflow. "Oh, I think you'll find I can. I must. I have to save the world. From itself, if need be."

"You don't understand!" I said. "You've never understood how important the Nightside is, just as it is! We are the last-ditch defence, against things like the Aquarians, or whatever they really are. What the good guys can't do, we will. The Nightside is here to do whatever needs doing, to defend Humanity, and the world. Your Aquarian masters need you to destroy us, so they can invade our reality. You must see that! They're not Entities, they're Enemies!"

At the end I was shouting at him, but he didn't flinch. None of it touched him. He smiled coldly, condescendingly.

"You're so desperate now you'd say anything, anything at all to stop me, wouldn't you? Well, tough. Here comes the Sun."

At that moment, the shotgun blast hit him square in the chest, punching him right off his feet, and backwards over the stone altar. Blood flew on the air, and the Sun King hit the floor behind the altar. He hit it hard, and didn't move again. And while the sound of the shotgun blast was still ringing on the close air of the church, I turned to look; and there was Shotgun Suzie, my Suzie, standing behind me. Smoke still rising from both barrels of her pump-action shot-gun. She stood tall and proud in her black motorcycle leath-ers, my blonde-haired Valkyrie. She smiled at me.

"You didn't really think I'd leave you to do all this on your own, did you?"

"I thought you'd never get here," I said. Because I had to say something.

Suzie racked new shells into place and strode forward to join me, tilting the gun up and back to rest on her leather-clad shoulder. I made myself stand very still. Hope was a small and fragile thing in my heart, and I didn't want to do anything to disturb it.

"I knew someone would be listening in on my phone," she said, in her cool, calm voice. "It's what I would have done. So I said what they expected me to say. And once everyone knew I was pursuing you for the bounty on your head, most of the other would-be bounty hunters quietly dropped out of the race. Rather than go up against me. I've been trailing you at a distance for ages, taking out anyone who looked like getting too close. You've no idea how many times I've saved your life, tonight. You didn't even notice, did you? All caught up in the thrill of the chase. You always did need me to watch your back. And now here we are, at the end of the trail. Together again." She cocked her head slightly to one side. "You're being very quiet, John. You didn't really think I'd turned against you, did you?"

"Of course not," I lied.

Suzie looked at me, for a long moment. "It must have been very hard for you, out there on your own. All your friends turned against you. I'm glad you found Cathy."

"More like I found him!" Cathy said cheerfully. "So you never wanted the bounty on John's head?"

"There's only ever been one bounty, as far as I was concerned," said Suzie. "And that was on the Sun King. No-one messes with my man and gets away with it."

"You are a very frightening person," said Cathy. "Don't know what he sees in you."

But they were both smiling. They never doubted me for a moment. They were always better people than me.

We all stopped, and looked around, as we heard sounds of movement from behind the altar. And there was the Sun King, rising to his feet, brushing himself down in a fussy sort of way. He turned to face us and smiled, completely unharmed. His Coat of Vivid Colours had no bullet-holes in it, and no blood-stains. His gaze was very cold.

"I can't believe he's getting up again," said Suzie. "I must be losing my touch."

She stepped forward and shot him in the face with both barrels, at point-blank range. The sound was deafening, and smoke filled the air. But when it cleared, he was still standing there, untouched. He smiled at Suzie, showing his teeth, defying her. I'd always suspected that with the power of the Entities behind him, no mortal weapon could stop the Sun King. Suzie lowered her shotgun, not even bothering to rack fresh shells. Oddly, she didn't seem that upset. She looked at me and surprised me with a quick wink.

"Good thing I brought a few friends along," said Suzie.

Razor Eddie and Dead Boy strode into St. Jude's as though they'd been waiting at the door all along, ready for their cue. Which they probably had been, though only Suzie could have persuaded them to go along with such a plan. (Because Razor Eddie doesn't take orders, and Dead Boy always wants to be the first into any dangerous situation.) Razor Eddie looked uneasily about him. As far as I knew, he'd never seen the inside of St. Jude's before. He might be the Punk God of the Straight Razor, but he was in the presence of a greater power now, and he knew it. He nodded brusquely to me.

"I would have beaten you in the cemetery if something hadn't been messing with my head. Not my fault if my heart wasn't really in it." He smiled at me for a moment, then turned to glare at the Sun King. "As for you, when I decide to kill John Taylor, it will be my idea and no-one else's."

"Can't take you anywhere," said Dead Boy. He pushed in beside Eddie and smiled ruefully at me. "We would have been here sooner, but it took me a while to put myself back together again. Did you have to take me apart quite so thoroughly? You know I've never been any good at sewing. Still, I'm sure you'll be relieved to know that you didn't damage my car in the least."

"Are you both clear in your minds towards me now?" I said, smiling despite myself. "Are we all friends again?"

"Move on," said Razor Eddie. "I wasn't myself." It was as close to an apology as he could get.

"Being dead means never having to say you're sorry," Dead Boy said solemnly. "It was Suzie here that did it. Having her around was enough to break the influence. She is a very . . . single-minded person, and very attached to you, in her own endearing and really quite scary way."

Razor Eddie nodded. "She intimidated the influence right out of me. Nothing like having a shotgun shoved up your nose to concentrate the mind wonderfully."

"You have such friends, John," said the Sun King. "You should be very proud of them."

Larry and Tommy Oblivion came strutting in, to join the party. Tommy was grinning broadly, and Larry looked as pleasant as his dead face and dour personality would permit.

"Once the Library broke the Sun King's influence over us, it never got a proper grip again," said Tommy happily. "And then we joined up with Suzie and these two bad boys, and came here." He glared at the Sun King and stuck out his tongue at him.

"And it did help," said Larry, "When we were presented with proof that Julien Advent wasn't dead after all."

Footsteps approached the church from outside, and I spun round to face the door; a sudden wild pleading hope filling my heart to bursting. And through the door came Dr. Benway and Julien Advent. I staggered and almost fell as the strength went out of my legs, and I had to grab onto a nearby pew to hold myself up. Julien smiled at me; and in that smile was all the understanding and forgiveness in the world. I ran to him, and hugged him, and held on to him like a drowning man who's finally been offered an outstretched hand. He patted me on the back as I held him to me, and I didn't need to see his face to know he was looking extremely embarrassed. Neither of us has ever been the touchy-feely kind. But right then I didn't care. I finally let him go and stepped back to look him over. He looked fine.

"No," he said, smiling. "I'm not dead. I never was." He looked at the Sun King, and his smile was strangely understanding. "You could have let me die, but you didn't. Because you couldn't bring yourself to kill me. Despite everything, despite your masters' orders, you couldn't do something you knew was wrong."

"No," said the Sun King. "How could I kill my oldest friend? But I needed John Taylor distracted, and the whole Nightside outraged enough to want him dead, so I went with the thing that would have upset me most." He looked at me. "All an illusion, John. You only thought you killed him. I put him in a coma and tucked him away in Ward 12A. Seemed appropriate. And then I convinced everyone else to see things my way. You keep thinking of me as the villain, John, but I'm really not. I only do what I have to do, for the greater good." He looked at Julien. "You were quite definitely in a coma. How . . . ?"

"Shouldn't have put me in Ward 12A," said Julien. "You and your sense of humour . . . Dr. Benway spotted me the moment she made her next rounds. She woke me up, and we went out into the Nightside together and joined up with these good people."

"Suzie broke the influence, but it kept creeping back," said Dead Boy. "Until they came along. Hard to believe someone is dead when they're standing right in front of you insisting that they're not. I mean, I know dead; and he isn't."

"Suzie brought us here," said Razor Eddie. "So we could make amends for being . . . mistaken."

"And so we could kick the Sun King's arse," said Larry Oblivion. "The Nightside may be a spiritual cesspit, but it's our spiritual cesspit."

"You old romantic, you," said Tommy.

The Sun King wasn't paying any attention to us. He only had eyes for Dr. Benway. He studied the old woman, with her grey hair and lined face, still wearing her white doctor's coat, and his smile was a very gentle thing indeed.

"So, after all these years . . . Princess Starshine has returned to join her Sun King," he said. "You always were my touchstone, Emily. You were the one I wanted to make a better world for. When I finally came out of the White Tower, and you weren't there . . . When I found out I'd lost you, and the life we should have had together . . . It was like I'd lost everything that mattered. All I had left, was the Dream. It's all I've got left now. I will bring about a better world. Because I am the good guy here, and I will not be stopped."

"I keep telling you," I said. "In the Nightside, it's not enough just to be the good guy. To fight the real bad guys, like your Aquarian masters, you need fighters, monsters, outcasts, like us."

"No!" said the Sun King. "I have given my life to this! I saw the Dream, in the Summer of Love, and it was a real thing! It should have happened; it would have happened if I'd still been here! Well, I'm here now, and I will make up for my absence; and all of you together aren't enough to stop me! I will do this! I will! You aren't enough!"

"Just as well I'm here, then," said the Lord of Thorns.

We all looked round again. The Lord of Thorns didn't walk through the doorway; he was suddenly there, with us, a cold, forbidding presence in his long, grey robes, long, grey hair and beard, leaning on a heavy wooden staff. Looking like one of those Old Testament prophets who never did believe in sugar-coating God's words. He smiled upon the Sun King, and it was not a good smile.

"Did you really think you could lure me from this sacred place with your petty stratagems?" he said, his voice as unyielding as the ancient, grey, stone walls of St. Jude's. "I have been here all along, watching and waiting. For this moment."

"You can't stop me!" shouted the Sun King. His face was flushed red, his eyes puffy as though he wanted to cry tears of sheer frustration, and there was something of the thwarted, petulant child in his voice. "Even all of you together don't have the power to stand against me! All those long years I spent in the White Tower, learning terrible wisdoms at my masters' feet, all to gain the power I needed, to do this thing! To do this one, necessary, thing!"

"It's not your power," I said. "It never was. You have nothing except for what the Entities let you have. To do their work. If you could only see who and what they really are, you'd throw that power back in their faces."

"What?" said the Sun King. "I don't understand. What are you talking about? Why would I do such a thing?"

"Because you're the good guy," I said. "And they're not."

And I raised my gift one last time and reached out with my mind, to find the Entities from Beyond, the Aquarians, or whatever the hell they really were. It took everything I had left, every last bit of hoarded strength. Blood coursed down my face, from my eyes and my nose. It ran from my ears, and spilled from my slack lips. I could feel things bleeding and breaking inside me, important things. I'd pushed myself and my gift further than I ever had before. Too far. No coming back from this. But after everything I'd done, after my lack of faith in those who'd loved me most, how could I not? It needed doing, so I did it. That's always been my job. My legs started to buckle, and Cathy and Suzie moved quickly in on either side to hold me up. They were both speaking to me, saying urgent things, but I couldn't hear them. I pushed past all the pain, refusing to be beaten by my own weakness, and concentrated on my gift. And I found my way to the Entities from Beyond and the world where they lived.

And once I'd done that, the greater power in St. Jude's rose and bound all of us, everyone in the church, together; and used us as a focus to open a door between the Nightside and the other place. I couldn't have done it on my own, but I wasn't alone. My good friends were with me. In St. Jude's, where prayers are answered, and miracles can happen.

The gateway lay before us, a great circle cut in the air itself, through which the other reality could be seen. Don't ask me where it was. Outside; that's all I can tell you. Not simply another world but another reality. A harsh light blasted into the church through the gateway, thick and foul and somehow spoiled. Far worse than the few drops of light that had spilled through before, pulled through by the Sun King's presence. This was an alien light, from an alien place, never meant for human eyes. And through that light, that gateway, I could see the other place, so alien as to be almost beyond human comprehension. Think of a whole world, a whole universe, made up of insects crawling over a ball of dung, forever and ever. That's as close as I can some to describing what I saw there.

The Sun King cried out, in horror and disgust, as the Entities took him over and spoke through him.

"Yes. This is what we are. This is what we do. We use up worlds, consuming them entirely. And then we move on, to the next. Because we're always hungry. This world, this reality, is all used up. We need . . . a new ball of dung. Your world. Your reality. So we made this man into a weapon, to open the door for us. To let our light shine over the Nightside and make it our feeding ground. And after we are done here . . . your world is such a fine, rich, fecund place. Who knows how long we can make it last? A population like yours will feed us for generations. We are not the Entities from Beyond. We are not Aquarians. If you must have a name for us . . . call us Shiva Rising."

The Sun King took off his tinted glasses with a trembling hand and let them drop to the floor, so he could look at us clearly. I'd never seen such misery in a man's eyes.

"Send them away," I said, through numb, unfeeling lips. "You brought them in; only you can send them back."

"But then . . . I wouldn't be the Sun King any more," he said, in his own voice. "Only ordinary, everyday Harry Webb."

Dr. Benway moved forward to stand with me, holding the Sun King's gaze with her own. "That was enough for both of us, once."

"Harry Webb was my friend," said Julien Advent, moving forward on my other side. "I've missed him. I could always depend on him, to do the right thing."

"I was a drug addict, before I met you," said the Sun King. "I thought . . . I'd found something better. But it was just another kind of addiction. Still, I know how to fight that."

Shiva Rising's voice filled the whole church, too huge a thing to be channelled through one man.

You cannot stop us! You cannot reject us, Sun King! We made you! We own you!

"Is that true, Harry?" said Dr. Benway.

The Sun King slowly turned his head to look at me. "I was wrong. I only saw what I wanted to see. But I . . . am still the good guy. So kill me, John Taylor. Do the hard but necessary thing. Break the link, and drive the Entities out of here. Save the world; because I can't."

"Haven't you learned anything yet?" I said. "It's easy to make amends by dying for a cause. Do the hard thing; live for what you believe in. Defy the Entities by deciding who you are for yourself. You invited them in; you can kick them out."

"But I'm not strong enough!" said the Sun King.

"Good thing you're not alone then," said the Lord of Thorns. "And that this . . . is St. Jude's."

The Sun King smiled slowly. "I am the last one who

remembers the Dream. The Summer of Love. The beautiful people. The love generation." He turned and looked back into the gateway, at the Entities who had never been what he thought they were. He looked right into the terrible light, and he didn't flinch. "I am the Sun King; and I am not what you made me, or intended me to be. In that wonderful summer of '67, I was the most wonderful thing in it. And I still hold within me the love from that time, and the light. Take it."

The power rose in St. Jude's again, older than the church, older than Christianity, older than we could hope to comprehend. But still, something kind, something that cares for us. It bound us all together, and together we called up the love and the light from that distant summer, and threw it at Shiva Rising like a weapon. *And the sun shone down.* For the first time in centuries, sunlight came to the Nightside, and filled the Church of St. Jude's, a pure white light, stamping out the sour and awful light that had spilled in from the Other side. It poured through the gateway, into the other place, and the Entities couldn't stand it. They screamed. They pulled back from the Sun King, from the light and the love of the Summer of Love, and slammed the door shut forever, to protect themselves.

Sealed up in that dark and terrible place, to feed on each other, until there were none of them left.

The Light snapped off and was gone. But all the candles in St. Jude's were lit, glowing cheerfully away. Where the Sun King had been, now stood an ordinary-looking young man in a T-shirt and jeans. Harry Webb. And walking slowly towards him, a beautiful young woman in a doctor's white coat, who had once been called Princess Starshine. Because the power in St. Jude's might be harsh and sometimes even brutal in its demand for the truth, but it also knew mercy and compassion. I knew that, because I felt really good. Totally relaxed, all my hurts gone, complete and ready for anything. I stretched slowly and laughed easily. And then

Cathy and Suzie went to clean the blood off my face with handkerchiefs and spit; and I hugged them both to me.

Julien Advent nodded easily to Harry Webb, as though this was something that happened to him every day. "Good to have you back, my old friend. You did the right thing in the end; as I always knew you would. What will you do now?"

"I still believe in the Dream," said Harry. "So I suppose it's up to me to convince everyone else. One day, one step, at a time. Try to shed a little light in the Nightside. With a little help from my friends . . . Hello, Emily. It's been a while."

"You should never have left me behind," said the young Dr. Benway. "See what trouble you get into, without me?"

"I think we could all use a nice little sit-down and a chat, and a beverage of something pleasant," said Julien. "I suggest we adjourn to the Hawk's Wind Bar & Grille. It's bound to be back by now. There are all kinds of useful contacts you can make there, Harry, including some old friends you might recognise."

"All right!" I said. "That's it! Everybody out! I have a wedding to prepare for."

"Damn right," said Suzie Shooter.

ELEVEN

All the Best Stories End in a Wedding

The wedding turned out to be a very happy and peaceful event. Everything went exactly as it should, with the Lord of Thorns presiding over the ceremony in St. Jude's. Not a particularly traditional service, but the Lord of Thorns made a very thorough job of it. Made you feel that no-one would ever dare put asunder what he had put together. Suzie wore her black leathers, though I did manage to talk her out of the bandoliers of bullets. Because she was Suzie Shooter, Shotgun Suzie, now and forever. And I wouldn't have it any other way. She looked wonderful—tall and proud and finally at peace with herself.

I wore the best-tailored formal suit the Nightside could produce, instead of my usual trench coat; because if Suzie wasn't going to wear white, neither was I.

Alex was there as best man, and Cathy as maid of honour. Alex wore a more dignified version of his usual all-black outfit, dispensing with the shades, just for me. I'm not entirely sure what Cathy was wearing, but it was very colourful, and I'm sure deeply fashionable. Suzie and I decided early on to keep the guests to a minimum. Dead Boy was there in his purple greatcoat, and Razor Eddie in a whole new raincoat and a cloud of anti-perspirant. Larry Oblivion in his smart suit, and Tommy in his finest and most flouncy New Romantic silks. Julien Advent, in his finest Victorian garb, complete with scarlet-lined opera cloak, representing the Authorities. (The other members sent their best wishes, and a very nice automatic tea-maker. Least they could do, under the circumstances.) The London Knights sent their representative, Sir Gareth. And Bruin Bear and the Sea Goat turned up, claiming to represent Shadows Fall. I think they just like weddings. Certainly the Bear beamed happily throughout the ceremony, while the Sea Goat drank vodka straight from the bottle and cried big happy tears all through the responses. And the front door from my old office building, propped up at the back and humming happily to itself. Because I'd promised.

Suzie and I remembered all the words, in all the right places; Alex remembered the ring; and everything went perfectly. Made a nice change.

Afterwards, while we were saying good-bye to our guests, before they all went off to the reception at the Adventurers Club, I spotted a familiar face right at the back of the church, keeping to the shadows. No-one else seemed to notice. I excused myself, and went back to speak with him. He nodded politely.

"Hello, John. Hope you don't mind me dropping in like this, without an official invite."

"Hello, Walker," I said. "Good of you to make it to my wedding, after all."

He tipped his bowler hat to me. "Wouldn't have missed it for the world, dear boy. Congratulations to you both."

"So," I said. "You're not dead after all, then? I should have known . . ."

"Ah," said Walker. "I'm afraid I wouldn't know. I'm here from the Past, you see, time-travelling through the Portable Timeslip. I learned of your wedding through a friendly oracle; and I wanted to be sure I wouldn't miss it. Even though I probably won't remember most of this when I get back. Price you pay for these sudden, short-term hops."

"You knew the exact date of my wedding, in advance?"

"I'm Walker," he said, smiling. "It's my job to know everything that matters."

"My job, now," I said.

"I always meant you should succeed me," said Walker. "The Nightside doesn't need me any more; it needs a new kind of Walker. Like you. I've been quietly training you for some time."

"I'm not sure whether I should say thank you, or not," I said.

He nodded easily. "It's been that kind of relationship, hasn't it?"

"That sort of friendship," I said.

"Most of the time. You watch out for yourself, now. I won't be there to look after you."

"Is that what you called it?" I said, and we both smiled.

"You'll still have Julien Advent," said Walker. "He has a good heart, and a good head on his shoulders."

"Yes," I said. "I'll still have Julien Advent."

Walker looked at me thoughtfully. "The oracle told me I didn't have a lot of time left. Tell me, John. Did I die well?"

"You died . . . in character," I said. "Right to the very end."

"Then that's all that matters. Well, time to be going. Lovely ceremony. Best of luck. You're probably going to need it."

"It was you, who sent the message about the immortals,

wasn't it?" I said. "To get me to the Ball of Forever, in time for King of Skin's murder."

"I have made certain advance arrangements, yes," said Walker. "My wedding present to you. I thought you deserved a decent last case to go out on, as a private investigator. Good-bye, John."

"Good-bye, Henry."

He smiled, and disappeared. Gone, just like that. His real wedding present, even if he didn't know it; a chance to say good-bye properly.

I went back to Suzie. Everyone else was leaving, heading for the buffet and free champagne at the Adventurers Club, talking happily with each other while the Sea Goat sang something loud and cheerful and completely inappropriate. Suzie came up to me and leaned against me.

"I thought that went well," she said, after a time. "Who were you talking to, in the shadows?"

"An old friend of the family," I said. "Are you happy, Suzie?"

"Yes. It's not a feeling I'm familiar with; but I think I could grow to like it. As long as you're with me, John."

"Forever and ever and ever," I said. "But right now, I need you to go and take care of the reception. There's something I have to do first."

I felt the need to walk the streets of the Nightside, for a while. Wearing a suit, and not my white trench coat. Because I was Walker now. And while some things never change . . . some do.

Meet the Ghost Finders

The Carnacki Institute's operatives are the best of the best. JC Chance: sharp, brave, charming, and almost unbearably arrogant; Melody Chambers: science-geek techno-wizard extraordinaire who keeps the anti-supernatural equipment running smoothly; and Happy Jack Palmer: the telepath with the gloomy disposition, the last person anyone would want navigating through his head.

Read on for an excerpt from

GHOST OF A CHANCE

by Simon R. Green
Now available from Ace Books!

Everybody knows there are bad places in the world.

Houses that make you walk by on the other side of the street. Bedrooms that no-one in their right mind would try to sleep in. The television screen that isn't empty enough, the mirror with too many faces reflected in it, the voice in the night, and the dark at the top of the stairs. There are bad places everywhere, in crowded towns and empty fields. Places where there are no safety barriers, where the walls of the world have worn thin, places . . . where we know we're not safe. It's in these bad places that we see things we don't want to see.

As I was walking up the stair,
I met a man who wasn't there.
He wasn't there again today.
I wish that man would go away.

Ghosts. They've been around as long as we have, in one form or another. Strange sights and sounds, visitations and wonders, spirits of cold earth and empty graves come back to trouble the living. Things that won't lie down; and none of them bound by the laws of the living. The dead; and things that aren't dead enough.

There are bad places in the world, but it isn't ghosts that make these places bad; it's the bad places that make ghosts.

As the world changes, so do the ways in which we see ghosts. From dark shapes in the night and ancestral revenants to lovers separated too soon and thwarted enemies; from stone tape recordings and electromagnetic phenomena to men and women caught in repeating loops of Time, like insects trapped in amber. Ghosts have always been with us, like guests reluctant to leave the party, like bad memories that won't go away . . . Ghosts are nightmares of the Past, refusing to give way to the Present. Mankind's dark side, Humanity's unconscious.

England's dreaming . . .

And so, in this brave new twenty-first century, don't expect ghosts to be limited to old manor houses or abandoned rectories. The modern idea of the bad place, the *genius loci*, the setting that disturbs and troubles us, has moved on. These days you're more likely to see ghosts in empty car parks, in shut-down factories, or in an underpass with a bad reputation. Places where it can get very dark and very dangerous, and no-one with any sense goes there alone.

There *are* such things as ghosts whether you believe in them or not. Tapping on your window late at night, waiting patiently to be noticed at the foot of your bed, stubbornly refusing to lie down. And that's where the Carnacki Institute comes in. The Institute exists to investigate, interpret, and hopefully Do Something About all the many mysteries and strange supernatural events that flare up every year. All the things that shouldn't happen but unfortunately do. The Institute's field agents are trained to deal with spooks and spirits, poltergeists and demons, Timeslips and other-dimensional incursions. They are ghost finders, and when they find them . . . they step on them. Hard.

Of course, not all ghosts are dark forces, intent on Humanity's ruin. Some are poor lost souls, trying to find their way home. And they . . . can be the most dangerous of all.

Now available in the Ghost Finders series

GHOST OF A CHANCE

GHOST OF A SMILE

GHOST OF A DREAM

And coming in September 2013

SPIRITS FROM BEYOND